M. A. SKALLBERG

Revenge is an art,
and she is its master.

Crimson Keepsakes

A NOVEL

Crimson Keepsakes Playlist

Killer Queen – Queen
Cassandra – Florence + The Machine
Only Love Can Hurt Like This – Paloma Faith
My Immortal – Evanescence
Bad Blood (Taylor's Version) (feat. Kendrick Lamar) – Taylor Swift
Killer – Phoebe Bridgers
The Crimson – Atreyu
I'm Gonna Getcha Good! - Shania Twain
There Will Be Blood – Kim Petras
Murder on the Dancefloor – Sophie Ellis-Bexor
Kill EVERYBODY – Skrillex
Crimson and Clover – Joan Kett & the Blackhearts
Bang Bang (My Baby Shot Me Down) – Cher
Evil Woman – Electric Light Orchestra
Sweet but Psycho – Ava Max
Jar of Hearts – Christina Perri
Goodbye Earl – The Chicks
Karma – Taylor Swift
Miss Murder – AFI
Sabotage – Beastie Boys
Toxic – Britney Spears
Cell Block Tango – Chicago the Musical
Blood on My Hands (feat. Smino) – August 08
Killer in the Mirror – Set It Off
The Kill – Thirty Seconds to Mars
Dead! - My Chemical Romance
Ashes – Celine Dion
Poison – Bell Biv DeVoe
Killah (feat. Gesaffelstein) – Lady Gaga
Heart of Glass – Blondie
Bust Your Windows – Jazmine Sullivan
Killshot – Magdalena Bay
Criminals – Meghan Trainor
Who's Afraid of Little Old Me? - Taylor Swift
Dangerous Woman – Ariana Grande
Cassandra – Taylor Swift

Trigger Warning

This novel contains graphic depictions of violence, psychological manipulation, and themes of trauma that may be distressing to some readers. It explores the mind of a serial killer and includes intense scenes of suspense, fear, and emotional turmoil.

Reader discretion is advised.

In an attempt to not completely spoil the story, more information about specific triggers are posted on my website:

www.maskallberg.com

M. A. SKALLBERG

Revenge is an art,
and she is its master.

Crimson Keepsakes

A NOVEL

Chapter 1

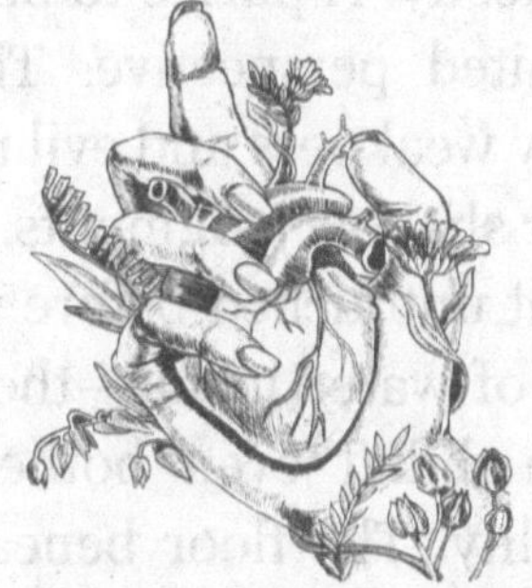

They found me waiting in the studio behind the mansion my boyfriend Qualley and I shared on Chippen's Hill, Bristol, Connecticut. It sat nestled in a hollowed clearing, where towering oaks and steadfast maples shaped the wilderness of our backyard. Even as they dragged me through the snow, my face grinding against icy earth, damp leaves, and sharp gravel—a relentless collage of winter clinging to me—I burned with something undeniable. Ablaze with the seed of life, like a phoenix rising from the ashes.

The frosty room somehow wrapped me in a fleeting ember of warmth I hadn't known for ages. Even in the midst of being forcibly restrained by the police, I embodied an elegance that couldn't be dimmed.

My reflection—perfect and wondrous—gleamed in the two-way window of the interrogation room they shoved me into. Behind it, they observed me. Oblivious to the fact that I knew I was being watched. Calling me weak, evil. Sipping their lukewarm coffee, they scratched their crotches and pretended to give a shit about anything.

They decided who they thought I was, but I knew my true self. They saw only the mud-caked strands of autumn-hued hair and thick layers of filth that disguised its natural vibrancy. Taking in the smoky trails of mascara and eyeliner etched across my cheeks, and remnants of the triumphant tears shed as my creations were unveiled, the officers burst into my studio, their attention fixed on the blood-streaked canvases that awaited their discovery. I was a curiosity. A puzzle to be dissected and understood from their limited perspective. They spoke in hushed tones, convinced of my weakness and evil nature.

I saw beyond their shallow judgments.

The plastic cup sat untouched before me. Its cloudy surface distorted the illusion of water inside—though I doubted it was drinkable. This place didn't even bother pretending to care about comfort or civility. The floor beneath me was an insult. Grime built up in corners that had probably been overlooked for years. Cracks spider-webbed through the dull plaster walls, creating jagged lines that felt as though they were taunting my confinement. The buzzing overhead light was maddening, its harsh, flickering glow grated against my nerves.

For a moment, I thought about what would happen if I hurled the cup of mystery liquid at the window. But the cuffs around my wrists made it impossible to even fantasize about theatrics—not that I cared. I turned my head in a slow arc, easing the tension from my neck with measured movements. My expression held just the right blend of tension and sardonic unease, designed to make them squirm. Then, with a wink toward the camera, a playful taunt—I allowed myself the smallest grin. I could imagine their frustration.

They all knew, deep down, the only reason I was here was because I wanted to be. It had been laughable, really, how simple it was to manipulate their kind, to lead them astray like cattle. These types never thought with anything beyond their man parts, and the arrogance of it had always worked to my advantage.

The handcuffs clinked noisily as I propped back, resting my hands on my lap. My brand-new jeans, once pristine, were now torn and caked in filth. Courtesy of those brutes dragging me through the muck. My white t-shirt? Completely ruined. Stained and stretched beyond recognition. It was absurd—just another display of crooked cops flexing their so-called authority.

I wasn't resisting. I wasn't hiding. Hell, I was the one who called 9-1-1 on myself! But none of that mattered to them. They stormed into the shed like a pack of rabid animals, splintering the priceless petrified wood door Qualley had imported for me from some ancient forest in Arizona. That door was a work of art in itself! A gift that carried meaning—and they destroyed it without a second thought.

But what else was new?

Their hands, rough and filthy, pawed at me as though I were concealing something threatening. They searched every inch of me, their touch invasive and unwelcome, but what were they even looking for? The whole ordeal was a farce. A grotesque display of power masquerading as justice. And through it all, I sat there, cuffs jangling, clothes ruined, dignity bruised—but not broken. Yet, I ended up there, sitting in that room that reeked of bullshit and lies from those who sat in that seat before me.

After over an hour of staring at my own reflection, the security camera in the corner of the small space shifted toward a steel door positioned in the center of the room. I adjusted my gaze accordingly as Detective James Hall entered.

His bald head gleamed from the harsh fluorescent lights. His face remained null of any expression, marked by a smattering of blackheads that covered his nose. A crumpled onyx suit hung loosely on his frame, amplifying his disheveled countenance. I imagined his wife couldn't spare a moment to press his suit or make sure he looked halfway decent for work. She was probably dead tired from enduring his relentless, booming tirades—shouting demands like, "WHERE'S DINNER?"—or complaining about unwashed laundry and whatever other tedious grievances husbands like him heap onto their wives.

Regardless of his discrepancies, this asshole was the exact person I hoped to see.

James sauntered across the room, a thick manila folder

wedged under his arm and a steaming Styrofoam cup gripped in his hand. He made a point of keeping his gaze away from me, but I tracked his every motion, my eyes narrowing to thin slits. He yanked the chair out from under the table which sent its legs screeching and rattling on the concrete floor. He set his cup on the shiny aluminum table and dropped the folder beside it before settling down before me.

He continued to ignore me as he took the cup, brought it to his lips, taking a long, drawn-out sip. Steam rose from the receptacle, puffing in a thin stream as James exhaled. As he brought the cup down again, he sighed, opening the folder to reveal its contents.

The coffee was fresh; the warm, inviting, woodsy scent mixed with nutty, sweet notes offered some complexity to the aroma. In fact, it was a nostalgic redolence of the past few months, and a strong reminder of where I was prior to my return to the studio on Chippen's Hill. Right before I was abducted by giant hissing cockroaches with badges.

But I'd never reveal that to James—at least, not until the time was right.

James checked his watch and ran his fingers over his peppery mustache with a restless motion, his hand hesitating mid-stroke. He paused, staring down at the folder's contents as though searching for something he couldn't find. A wince briefly tightened his wrinkled features, giving away an instant of unease.

Maybe that's just how his face was.

My face, disinterested as ever, gave no hint of the scrutiny behind it. He fumbled for the right words; the right questions to ask, questions he already knew the answers to. Answers of which I wouldn't object. Internally, a fire of exhilaration flared at the opportunity to speak about my art and its heartfelt origins.

Normally, it was Qualley who would sit and listen to my visions. Unfortunately, since James Hall and his puppets had robbed me of that, he would have to suffice. He didn't strike me as someone who would understand an artistic vision. More likely, he was the type who would find something concerning about it. The kind of person to paint over beautiful graffiti or murals on urban buildings.

No, James Hall did not appreciate fine art of any kind.

"You are being charged with the murders of three Bristol Police officers: Ben Prout, Lile Henderson, and Evan Matthews," James said, reading the names off the paper in front of him. His voice broke through my reverie, and I caught him squinting at me, head angling slightly in my direction. "Would you like an attorney present before we begin?"

Smirking, I held James's gaze. Amusement twinkled in my expression as I shifted subtly in my chair. "I don't see the point," I replied, sighing softly. I waved off the suggestion. It was already a futile situation—there was no need to involve legal counsel and compound the waste.

Detective Hall's silence was tangible as he sifted through the stack of papers in front of him. But with grim determination, he extracted three eight by eleven photographs and slammed them down in front of me, one by one. The sound rebounded through the room. Each image captured a moment of Qualley and I from before—before I was forced to take matters into my own hands. The candid reality of those memories were now forever tainted, staring back from the distant, lifeless photographs.

As if the pictures came to life, memories of Qualley surged forward, reminding me of the man he truly was. Though he didn't fit any cop's definition of perfect, to me, he was beyond compare.

Having spent most of his adult years entangled in the world of drugs and illegal arms deals, Qualley wrestled with the decision to cut all ties to his criminal past. But he knew that, if he ever hoped to build a peaceful, honest life with me, it was a step he had to take. Time and time again, he reminded me I meant more to him than the money or his business ventures—and his actions never failed to prove it.

As a man of quiet strength and unwavering principles, Qualley stood apart. He earned the admiration of his associates not through fear, but through respect, as he found merciful ways to address debts and errors—his hands free of the taint of violence. His love for me, and his unrelenting drive to change, spoke to the extraordinary integrity rooted in his soul.

The photos lying in front of me pulled me into the memory of my first meeting with Qualley. It was as if the world around us dimmed, leaving only him and I in the spotlight of an otherwise crowded room. I admit, it sounded like stuff of clichés, but I couldn't look away from him that night, silently urging him to do the same. His glossy, black hair carried an otherworldly sheen of blue, and his beard and brows seemed sculpted to match his impeccable style—Detective Hall, I'm sure, would have been green with envy. Yet, what truly unraveled me were his eyes—rich like caramel, glimmering like liquid honey, shifting with the light and wrapping me in a shiver of unspoken connection.

I can still feel the light tap on my shoulder from that night, a memory etched as sharply as if it were yesterday. I was scrutinizing my work—a painstakingly painted landscape based on a photo I had taken of the *Burj Khalifa* in Dubai. It was a project that consumed me for months, and seeing it displayed at The Hartford Artist Galleries was the culmination of relentless determination. But after that night, the painting faded into insignificance, completely overshadowed by the man who always stood behind me.

At least Qualley showed some interest at the time. With a playful glint in his eyes, he inquired the whereabouts of the artist responsible for the 'exquisite' piece, as though I weren't standing right in front of him. It wasn't the most polished approach for my attention, but it was enough to make me smile.

And it worked.

In time, Qualley confessed his initial interest that night wasn't the painting at all. His presence at the gallery had supposed to have been purely transactional—one of the artists owed him money. He'd come to collect. It wasn't entirely shocking, given the drug habits some of my fellow creatives indulged in. But that mission fell apart the moment he saw me. In his own words, he'd said, "Midst all the masterpieces in that room, nothing compared to the beauty of the one standing in front of me."

That was the instant my heart surrendered, though the following morning wasn't as kind. The hangover left my memories hazy, and the man who had bewitched me remained a mystery until my phone buzzed. It was him, inviting me to brunch. The rest, as they say, is history.

I wasn't ready to share that love story with James just yet. That would come in its own time.

For now, the three photographs spread before me captured our story in their own quiet way—Qualley and I, hand in hand, immersed in a world of our own. In one, he gazed at me with a longing so tender it made the bustling downtown West Hartford brunch spot feel like it existed solely for us. That spot was sacred to us, a Sunday ritual Qualley cherished fiercely. "Sundays are for rest, not business," he always said, and he never wavered in his devotion to those moments we spent together.

I often found myself mirroring his gaze during those times. Unguarded and brimming with admiration. Love for him was something I couldn't, and wouldn't, hide.

To a casual observer, these photos might appear unremarkable—just a couple, content and in love, savoring date nights or sharing the mundane joys of daily life. But they wouldn't see the profound connection beneath the surface; an invisible thread that tied us together, setting us apart from the ordinary.

Qualley wasn't just my boyfriend; he was my kindred spirit, my beacon of unwavering love and strength. His presence in my life was transformative—a force that urged me to see the world differently, to believe in the possibility of redemption and change. He was a man caught in the shadows of a life he no longer wanted, fighting with every ounce of determination to break free and create a future where we could exist together, untouched by the messiness of his past.

But these photographs, while meaningful, could never capture the essence of who Qualley was to me. They couldn't hold the late-night conversations where we bared our souls, sharing dreams and fears with an honesty that was raw and unguarded. They couldn't show the nights he held me tightly when the weight of the world threatened to crush me or the way his fingers brushed through my hair as he whispered that I was his reason to change. "You're the reason I want to be better," he would say, his voice filled with conviction and tenderness.

To me, Qualley was everything—the sun that warmed my days, the moon that guided my nights, and the stars that reminded me of endless possibilities. He was my refuge, the place I could go when the world felt too dark, and I didn't think I could carry on.

But James Hall would never understand that. To him, Qualley was nothing more than a criminal—a name on a list, a man defined solely by his mistakes. And I? I was collateral damage at best, an accomplice at worst. James didn't care about the love we shared, the sacrifices Qualley made, or the dreams we built together. He didn't look past his preconceptions, wouldn't bother to see the truth of who Qualley was or the life we were fighting so desperately to build.

To James, our relationship was nothing but evidence—another thread to weave into his case.

Qualley Wallis, the criminal. That's all he saw.

But now he'd learn that the real crimes lay with *me*.

Chapter 2

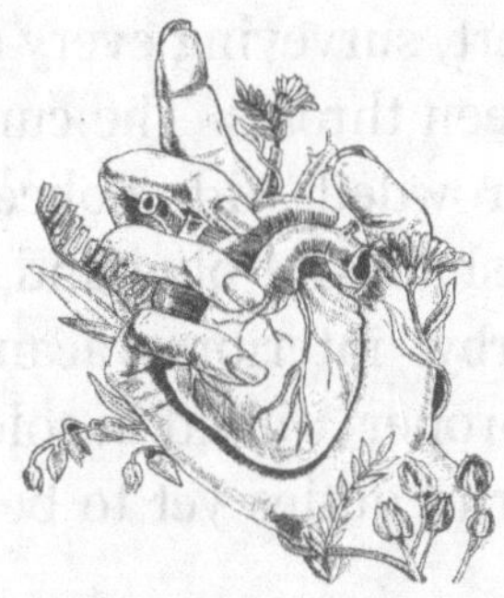

Detective Douchebag and his team of bumbling fools ruthlessly ended my beloved Qualley's life over a year ago. The reason behind their senseless violence remains an enigma that haunts me to this day. Both he and his lieutenant, Lonney, met their end in a hail of gunfire within the walls of our home on Chippen's Hill—a place that once held warmth and safety, now soiled in the ashes of that tragic day.

I was enjoying a friend's birthday celebration at Hubert's Bar in downtown Hartford, about a half-hour drive away, when the unthinkable happened. Surrounded by lively conversation, espresso martinis, guacamole, and chips, I couldn't shake an unsettling feeling deep inside me. Qualley's silence became more unnerving with each unanswered call and message, each passing moment eroding my attempts to stay present at the party. When I tried reaching Lonney, receiving no response from him either, my concern turned into a gnawing sense of dread. Something just felt terribly off, though I couldn't pinpoint what. That instinctive fear weighed heavily on me, but even my worst suspicions couldn't have prepared me for the horrifying reality awaiting me when I finally returned home.

After apologizing to my friend for having to leave the festivities early, I raced back to Bristol. The scene that greeted me upon arrival was beyond nightmarish.

Stationed across the sprawling grounds of the mansion, police officers established a presence impossible to ignore. Some moved with purpose, their radios crackling with updates. Others stood watchful and alert, surveying every corner of the property and searching for unseen threats. The curved driveway and the street beyond were crowded with police cars, flashing lights painting the scene in shades of blue and red. Two ambulances stood motionless nearby: interiors vacant. A van emblazoned with 'City of Bristol Coroner' waited in solemn silence, its empty cabin hinting at the grim duties yet to be performed. My heart sunk at its sight.

Bright yellow police tape cordoned off the entrance to the home, serving as a barrier against intrusion. Several men sporting vests adorned with 'FBI' emerged from the front door, expressions serious, as they engaged in conversation with other officers nearby. Judging by the insignias on their vests, I guessed they were members of the Bristol Police Department.

In haste to park the opalescent white Mercedes C-Class Qualley gifted me a week earlier as an anniversary gift, I nearly rear-ended a municipal vehicle. I raced towards the front door, on foot, where the officers engaged in conversation. My steps faltered as I hurried forward, each uneven stride threatening to send me sprawling to the ground. With a desperate lurch, I managed to steady myself just in time for my face to avoid becoming acquainted with the dirt.

Noticing my swift advance, the officer's movements mirrored practiced choreography. Weapons were drawn—pistols and tasers glinting in the harsh light—while their stances shifted into rigidly defensive positions. One of them barked an urgent command, "STOP RIGHT THERE!" The words rang out like a foghorn. Panicked and desperate, I threw my hands into the air, a futile gesture of surrender.

Tears poured down my face. An overwhelming dread for Qualley gnawed at my chest, eclipsing every other thought.

"I fucking live here, damn it!" I shouted, trying to force my way past them. "What the hell have you done—" Words were cut short as I was shoved to the ground, jagged gravel biting into my chin with a sharp, searing pain as I hit the pathway leading to the front door.

The officers pulled my arms behind my back, tight enough to pop my shoulders out of their sockets. Pain wavered throughout my arms like bolts of electricity. I cried out as they placed handcuffs onto my wrists, tightening them as far as they could go. Two officers hauled me to my feet, their strained grunts matching the brute force they'd used moments earlier to slam me to the ground. Without a hint of gentleness, they rolled me onto my back and shoved me down onto the front lawn like I was the trash they took to the street every Wednesday.

"What the hell are you doing?" I cried, twisting and writhing against their iron grip. "This is my home!"

One of them tightened his hold on my bicep, his fingers digging into my flesh as if he could break me through sheer force. He shook me roughly, his movements jerky and unrelenting, before growling, "Shut your mouth! You have the right to remain silent..."

His voice thundered in my ear, but the splitting pain in my head drowned out the words. Throbbing was all I could hear— pounding, relentless, an agonizing rhythm that made coherent thought impossible.

Was this reality, or was I unraveling? The questions trembled in the corners of my mind, swallowed by the relentless tide of confusion.

"Do you understand?" He thundered, his words slicing through the fog like a whip. The sheer force of his voice jolted me back to the present, but it meant nothing to me. It was just noise, drowned out by the pounding in my skull.

I shook my head, trembling with disbelief. "Why are you arresting me?"

"Did you hear a single word I just said?" The officer asked, apparently annoyed, as he hauled me to my feet with such force that my head spun. He whipped me around to face him. A piercing gaze fixed on mine as he fired off another round of questions. "Who are you? And why are you so desperate to get inside this house?"

The words buzzed around me in the air, but I couldn't form a reply. My thoughts were a jumbled haze, and the silence between us stretched unbearably as he waited impatiently for the answer I wasn't ready to give. The night was suffused with chaos—a pulsating symphony of flashing blue and red lights that fractured the darkness, casting eerie, dim shapes across the face of the mansion. Shouts burst forth from within the house, urgent, and mingling with the low hum of murmurs drifting from the gathered crowd. Beyond the police tape, they encircled the gate whispering in hushed tones, their faces pale with unease, breaths visible in the cool night air.

The world seemed to suspend its rhythm, each moment elongating in excruciating slow motion. It was as if time itself had become laden with dread.

The officer tightened his grip on my arm; his rough, calloused hand cutting into my skin as he dragged me forward with a force that rattled my resolve. His walkie-talkie crackled angrily in his free hand, punctuating his clipped words as he barked out orders to someone on the other end. The jarring noise—the rhythmic pulse of the lights' hum; a cacophony of voices, and the mechanical static of the radio overwhelmed my senses. Sharp gravel beneath my feet crunched harshly with every step, while the piercing cold of the night seeped into my bones, amplifying the terror coursing through me. I felt as though the chaos around me was swallowing me whole, leaving no room for clarity or escape.

It all swept me under waves of disorientation.

"Wait! Why are we leaving?" I demanded, pulling against his iron-clad grip. "I deserve to know why the hell you won't let me into my house!" The words came out in a frantic rush but fell on deaf ears. But as my desperation rose, the officer's unbending hold tightened.

The officer disregarded my protests entirely as we reached the vehicle. With a swift, solid motion, he threw the door open and shoved me inside. "Alright, alright, damn it!" I shouted, straining against his relentless hold. My resistance was rewarded by the resounding crack of a door slamming shut in my face.

I slumped in the seat. My breath hitched as I tried to steady the whirlwind of thoughts racing through my head. From his vest, the static-filled voice of a dispatcher filtered through the receiver, muffled and incomprehensible. I managed to catch fragmented phrases before the officer snapped out a brusque, "Over," his delivery impersonal. He stomped around the front of the vehicle, a figure framed briefly by the strobing lights before he climbed into the driver's seat. The engine roared to life with a growl, rumbling idly as he tapped commands into the glowing screen of the laptop mounted beside him.

Minutes dragged on in a suffocating silence before the car jerked forward, throwing me back slightly against the seat. Anger and embarrassment bubbled within me as I let out an exaggerated sigh, loud enough to carry through the confined space. The officer didn't even flinch. His impenetrable silence only fueled my frustration, and I tried again, breaths heavy with exasperation. But he remained steadfast, focused elsewhere. He treated me as though I was invisible—a ghost in the back seat. It was maddening. Ignoring me as though I already ceased to matter.

No one ignored *me*.

I couldn't stomach this lunacy for another second. "God damn it! What's going on?" I roared, pretty much exploding throughout the car and shaking the windows. It rattled loose every ounce of composure I had left.

"You'll answer our questions at the station," the officer

mumbled with cold indifference.

A cynical laugh broke through before I could stop it, though came as more of a broken sob. "What about *my* damn questions?" Rage swirled in me, boiling hot, but beneath it— fear. Fear for Qualley, fear for Lonney, fear for myself. How had I ended up here? Just hours ago, we'd all been fine—or so I thought. And now they had disappeared, unreachable. Their absence loomed large over this entire mess.

Where had they gone?

Why had I been cuffed?

A million questions hurtled through me, demanding answers and all I got was silence. Something was definitely off. Something reeked of lies, and I wasn't going to wait quietly to find out what.

"For now, I suggest you keep your mouth shut," he hissed, the words carrying an air of finality. My questions might as well have been tossed out the window for all he cared.

The remaining ten minutes of the drive were a slow crawl through heavy silence, save for the occasional garbled crackle of police radio static and his curt, robotic responses. It was as though I had already been erased from existence—reduced to nothing more than cargo. Handcuffed, condemned, and without so much as a shred of explanation.

When the car shuddered to a standstill in the station's murky parking lot, my body fell forward against the seatbelt. The officer grunted as he heaved himself out of the driver's seat, the subtle creak of leather and clink of his holster breaking otherwise unbearable quiet. His hand never left the butt of his pistol as he came around the back to open my door, his cautious movements bordered on theatrical. *What was I going to do? Break these cuffs apart like some comic book superhero and vanish into thin air?*

The door swung open with a metallic groan, and I fought the urge to roll my eyes as he loomed over me, his shadow stretching across the pavement. A predator playing guard dog—pathetic. His overblown display of control only made the absurdity of this situation hit harder. All I could do was sit there, gritting my teeth as that gnawing mix of humiliation and fury churned in my stomach.

This loser had no idea what kind of storm he was dragging me into—or maybe, worse, he did.

He yanked me out of the car with a clench that felt more like a vice than a hand, hauling me into the building where it seemed every cop in Bristol had gathered to witness my arrival. The stench hit me like a wall—a rancid cocktail of sweat, gunpowder, piss, and shit. It was fitting, really. Pigs never smelled great after wallowing in their own filth, and these ones seemed to revel in it. The officers inside must have marinated in the stench, their uniforms practically soaked in it.

Two others in handcuffs sat slumped in front of scattered desks, surrounded by clusters of officers hammering away at keyboards. One of the cuffed men glanced up as the door swung open, his eyes locking onto mine with a grin that sent a shiver down my spine. He winked before turning back to the officer interrogating him. The other detainee kept their head down, motionless, as though they were trying to disappear into the floor.

Perhaps there against their will as well.

Before I could take in more of the station, I was shoved toward the front desk and shoved into a hallway that stretched into a maze of rooms. The officer steered me into the second room, where an older woman sat behind a computer, her graying strawberry blonde hair framed a face that looked like it had seen too much. Her gaudy necklace glinted under the light as her fingers hammered away at the keyboard.

"Louise, this one's here for questioning," the officer grunted, shoving me into a chair in front of her.

She paused, lowering her thin, silver-wired glasses to the bridge of her nose as she regarded me with a look that could curdle milk.

"Does 'this one' have a name?" She asked, outwardly annoyed that we had just interrupted her previous task.

For a moment, I thought she was asking *him*. My stomach twisted. A stupid, instinctive fear foaming up that maybe they didn't know who I was, that maybe Qualley's name was buried somewhere in whatever report they had on me. Maybe they'd come for the wrong reasons.

Louise's eyebrows arched as her gaze bore into me, cool and expectant. "Any day now . . . what is it?"

I exhaled sharply through my nose, rolling my eyes. "Cassandra. My name is Cass-an-dra."

"Cass-an-dra who, ma'am?" she asked flatly, almost bored.

"Kessler, *ma'am*," I replied, dragging out the 'ma'am' with as much disdain as I could assemble.

Louise didn't flinch at my attitude, just pushed her glasses back up and returned to her typing. Unbothered.

I complied because, honestly, what choice did I have? The sooner this was over, the sooner I could find out what the hell happened—to my house, to Qualley . . . I wasn't about to beg for information. Not yet. But every second of silence stretched my nerves thinner.

"Miss Kessler, how old are you?" Louise asked, her eyes glued to the screen.

I sighed again. "March 17th, 1996. You do the math."

Her head turned toward me at a glacial pace, her expression stiff as if even acknowledging me was a personal inconvenience.

The officer—Goldfinch, according to his badge—tightened his grip on my bicep, his fingers digging into my skin. He threw me a warning look. "Don't make this harder than it has to be, Kessler."

Harder? Was he serious? No one in this godforsaken place had bothered to tell me why I was here, yet somehow I was the one making things difficult?

I swallowed the lump forming in my throat—not from fear, but from frustration. I needed answers. Needed *his* name spoken, needed some thread to tug at to know if he was alive or dead.

Louise resumed her questioning before I could comment on how Goldfinch looked like a damn bird in a uniform.

"Are you female?" She asked, not glancing up.

My lips curled. "Well, I suppose these tits and this dress might give that away," I quipped.

Louise clicked her tongue, unfazed. "You can never be so sure these days . . . occupation?"

The casual way she said it—that 'these days' tossed out like an afterthought—rubbed me the wrong way. Not because I was offended for anyone in particular, but because it sounded lazy. Dismissive. Like people's lives were just another irritation to her, like asking whether someone was human or furniture.

I might have realized then that I kind of liked Louise—not because she was kind or good, but because she didn't give a damn about who she was talking to. No fake sweetness, no thin-lipped judgment pretending to be professional. Just indifference. Brutal, even.

It was refreshing in a way. Honesty was a rare thing around cops.

I considered teasing her, spinning a story about being a man in drag kidnapped for wearing a dress—but that wasn't something to joke about. I knew what it was like to have the world see you wrong, and more importantly, I knew what it was like to have people laugh at you for it.

So instead, I kept it simple.

"An artist," I said. "Painting mostly, I work on commission, and—"

"Good for you," Louise said unemotionally, fingers clacking across the keys. "We're done here, Jer."

Well, maybe I didn't like her after all.

Goldfinch yanked me out of the chair, dragging me down another dim hallway. The sound of our footsteps echoed like gunshots. Each sharp crack ricocheted against the pounding rhythm in my chest. My heart felt like it might shatter with every beat, an unrelenting reminder that I still didn't know if Qualley was alive. *Had they raided the house? Had they ripped apart everything we built, every plan we devised, every shred of hope we clung to?* The unanswered questions gnawed at me, relentless and cruel.

The hallway stretched on, like a maze leading nowhere, the shadows elongating into cruel caricatures of my unease. The air grew heavier with each step, thick with despair. Memories of Qualley swarmed my mind—the way he used to laugh at my dry humor, the comforting steadiness in his gaze when everything felt like it was crumbling. If only I could know he was still out there. If only I could hear his voice, even just once more. The ache of missing him grew intense, and the thought of never seeing him again clawed at my chest.

Finally, we reached a heavy metal door. Goldfinch unlocked it with impassivity, and before I could even brace myself, he shoved me inside. The door slammed shut with a deafening clang that reverberated through my bones, sealing me into yet another prison.

The cell was small and cold. Concrete walls looming over me like an unmarked tombstone. I sank onto the hard bench, hugging myself against the chill, the suffocating quiet pressing in on all sides. My thoughts refused to dissipate. *How long had it been since they grabbed me? Hours? Days?* Each moment felt like an eternity. *Was Qualley still alive? Had they hurt him? Were they torturing him for answers, for secrets that might destroy him?*

I didn't even want to consider that thought.

I swallowed hard, fighting the lump rising in my throat, but the ache refused to relent. I could almost see him in the cell with me, his steady gaze grounding me like it always had. But he wasn't here. And without him, the emptiness felt unbearable.

The walls didn't answer, their silence cruelly unhelpful. But it wasn't just silence anymore. It was a scream—a hollow, agonized scream—that I couldn't escape. And it tore me apart.

👁 👁

About an hour later Goldfinch returned, his expression as unreadable as ever, and whisked me away to the room adjacent to where we'd been. The room mirrored the glacial chill of the cell, its minimalist and unfeeling environment. Atop the counter rested a fingerprint scanner, its sleek design standing out like a relic of some advanced civilization, foreign and disconnected from the bleak surroundings.

Without a word, he snatched my hands, still mangled in handcuffs, and began pressing each of my fingers onto the machine's screen. He twisted and contorted my fingers with the precision of someone who'd done this a thousand times before, mechanical and devoid of care. The pain was excruciating.

Once he'd finished trying to break my fingers off, he wasted no time manhandling me into the small room attached to the one we were in. The space was cramped like all the other ones I'd been in. Barely big enough to fit the table and two plastic chairs shoved into its center. Tennis balls capped the bottoms of the chair legs, a half-hearted attempt to keep them from scraping the floor. A pristine whiteboard hung on the wall. Its surface gleamed under the abrasive artificial lighting. An eraser and a few black markers sat neatly on the ledge beneath it, their placement almost too perfect. I couldn't help but wonder how many crude drawings or inappropriate messages had been scrawled there over the years, only to be wiped away in a futile attempt to maintain some semblance of professionalism.

Goldfinch shoved me into the chair farthest from the door, the plastic creaking under my weight. He crouched slightly as he worked to remove the cuffs from my wrists, his fingers brushing against my skin in a way that made my stomach churn.

"Don't try anything funny, you hear?" he warned, almost threatening. He clipped the handcuffs back onto his belt, squinting his eyes as if daring me to test him. Before I could form a response, he straightened up and backed out of the room, the door clicking shut behind him.

As Goldfinch's shadow disappeared through the frosted glass panel on the door, I couldn't resist. I raised my hand, my middle finger extended in a silent, defiant salutation. "Take that, you piece of shit," I mumbled under my breath, the gesture as much for my own satisfaction as it was for him.

The moment I was alone, I flexed my wrists, relishing the brief freedom from their constraints, my skin red and raw where the cuffs had bitten into it. A physical memento of the indignity to which I'd been subjected.

I fell back in the chair, my mind racing as I tried to piece together the events that had led me here. Whatever was happening, I wasn't going to let them break me—no one would ever break me again.

The room was a barren enclosure, its solid walls closing in like silent sentinels, their presence asphyxiating token of my confinement. Not a single window was built into the room, leaving the space burdensome in its isolation. Even the door lacked any hint of escape—no clear view, only seclusion. My eyes darted upward, catching sight of a camera mounted above the door, its lens trained squarely on me like the unblinking eye of a stalker.

I slouched back in the chair, crossing my arms defiantly over my chest. With a long, dramatic sigh, I fixed my brooding pout toward the camera's lens, silently daring whoever was behind it to make their next move.

The absence of noise pressed down on me and my body betrayed me before my resolve did; my eyelids grew heavy, my breath evened out, and I drifted into a restless sleep.

I awoke with a jolt, the distinct sound of the door slamming shut ripping me from a dreamless sleep. *How long had I been asleep?* Time meant nothing in this place.

Before me stood a large man, his round belly stretching the buttons of his white collared shirt. He scribbled something onto a clipboard, paying me no immediate attention. When he was done, he slid the pen neatly into his shirt pocket, adjusted his gray slacks with an exaggerated tug, and finally lowered himself into the chair across from me. His movements were leisurely, as though he had all the time in the world.

"Miss Kessler is it?" he asked smoothly, but the words were wrapped in a strange, misplaced smile. "I'm Detective Timothy Fieldman. I'm here to speak to you about Qualley Wallis. You know him, correct?"

"Of course I know him!" I sprang upright with a sharp, purposeful motion. "Now tell me—where is he? And why the hell am I here?" My voice was firm, though the edges frayed with exhaustion, clinging stubbornly.

Fieldman leaned back in his chair, crossing his arms over his stomach. He sighed, attention dropping to the floor as though he were searching for the right words. "Miss Kessler, please. Sit down."

Though every fiber of my being protested, I forced myself back into the chair with an exaggerated slump. My jaw clenched so tightly it ached. The room felt smaller now, as if it too anticipated the blow that was about to land.

Fieldman's hands met in an awkward knot, fidgeting as if unsure where to rest. Beads of sweat glistened at his temples under the ugly fluorescent lights, and for a fleeting moment, I wondered if he was as uncomfortable as I was. Or maybe he just needed a donut. He was a cop after all.

But then he spoke, and the world tilted.

No, stopped.

"Miss Kessler," he began, "I'm afraid Qualley Wallis is gone.

He was pronounced dead at the scene. I'm sorry."

The words hit me like a freight train, knocking the air from my lungs. My mind refused to process them, as if rejecting their very existence. Qualley. Death. The two words didn't belong together, not in the same sentence, not in the same universe.

I stared at him, stunned, as the sentence echoed hollowly in my ears. It felt like the room had been drained of sound, leaving only the relentless pounding of my pulse.

"No, he's not," I said, disbelieving. Words tumbled out of me before I could even register them. It didn't even sound like my voice—flat, hollow, as though the shock had stolen the very essence of me. "No. You're wrong." The phrase wasn't just a denial, it was a plea, a desperate attempt to reverse reality itself.

Fieldman's face remained unreadable, his expert neutrality acting as an impenetrable shield. And yet, the faint glimmer of pity in his eyes cut through that guise, crisper than any spoken word. It wasn't comforting, it was infuriating. That look, that soft, lamentable gaze—it felt like an insult, an affront to the storm raging inside me. It mocked the depth of my anguish, as if to say, "I've seen this before and you're not special."

I wanted to scream at him, to tell him to wipe that expression off his face, to demand he take it all back and give me a different answer. But instead, I froze, trapped between the constricting force of his words and the rebounds of my own denial. The devastation within me coiled tighter, threatening to consume me whole. And still, the pity in his eyes lingered, like a ghost refusing to leave.

Fieldman opened his mouth to speak, but the sound drowned under the pounding of my pulse. His words were nothing but static, meaningless noise against the bedlam in my head.

I gripped the edges of the table until my fingers went numb, the cold metal biting into my skin. My mind reeled, desperate to cling to some loophole, some possibility that this was a mistake, that they meant someone else. It had to be someone else.

Not Qualley. Not *him*.

Qualley is dead.

The phrase spiraled inside me, relentless and cruel—a mantra I couldn't escape. It clawed at the edges of my sanity, tearing through every shred of denial I tried to hold onto. He was invincible. Untouchable. He was my whole goddamn world. And now he was gone?

The details Fieldman tried to explain blurred together—grim words about the scene at the Chippen's Hill mansion, about officers finding him, about time of death. None of it mattered. None of it felt real. It was like listening to a story about someone else, someone distant and unimportant. But it wasn't someone else. It was Qualley.

My Qualley.

My body turned traitor, my stomach twisting into a bottomless pit. My chest tightened, and each breath became a battle against a suffocating grief that threatened to swallow me whole. It was unbearable, pressing down on me until I thought I might shatter under the pressure. Tears burned my eyes, spilling over uncontrollably. Tremors spread through my hands, my arms, until my whole body shook as if it would come apart at the seams. I clutched the table, but it offered no anchor against the storm raging inside me. There was no escape, no reprieve from the agony that consumed me. A dull ache formed in my throat from choking back the sobs clawing their way out. I tried to hold them in, to keep some semblance of control, but it was a losing battle. The grief was too much, too raw, too overwhelming.

And then, I broke.

The espresso martinis and tapas I'd had earlier erupted from my stomach, splattering across the table and floor in a grotesque display. The acidic burn barely registered as I sagged into the mess, hollowed out by loss. My body felt like a shell, empty and lifeless, as if the grief had drained me of everything I was.

As the darkness closed in, the last stray thought that flickered across my mind wasn't about Qualley. It wasn't about the life we'd shared, the plans we'd made, or the love we'd built. It wasn't about the future that had been stolen from us.

It was, *Shit, I drove home intoxicated.*

Not, *Qualley is dead.*

And that thought, absurd and misplaced as it was, felt like the cruelest betrayal of all.

Chapter 3

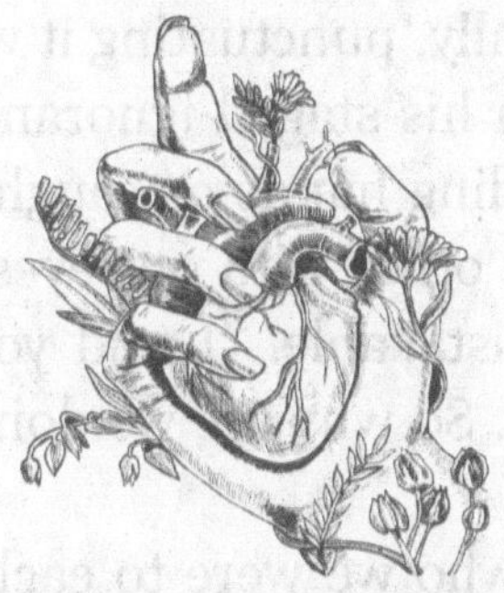

James Hall sank into his chair, exhaling a breath that hit me with a wave of sour pungency. The stench dragged me out of my thoughts, and I instinctively flinched. What had earlier been a tempting aroma of freshly brewed coffee now transformed his breath into something rancid and unbearable. I winced, reluctantly mimicking his motion as I leaned back into my own seat.

My eyes locked on the pictures of Qualley, and I did my best to ignore the nauseating stench lingering in the air.

"Let's start from the beginning," James rasped, crossing his arms over his chest. "What is your connection to Qualley Wallis?"

I rolled my eyes, mimicking his posture, only to be reminded by the cold bite of the handcuffs that my hands were bound. They flopped uselessly back into my lap. "You already know exactly what that connection is." I cocked my head slightly, a scowl spreading as I studied the emptiness etched into his features. If there was one thing I had to give Detective Hall credit for, it was his uncanny ability to suppress any trace of emotion—or at least to fake it convincingly.

For now, I thought, silently vowing to shatter his polished veneer.

Without a flicker of irritation, he pointed to one of the photos of Qualley, repeating his question louder.

"It doesn't matter what I think, Miss Kessler," he said. "For the record, I need to hear from you what your connection is."

I sighed dramatically, punctuating it with a scoff and diverting my attention from his staged ignorance. "I don't think 'just friends' would be holding hands or caught three separate occasions undressing each other with our eyes," I said, the mockery in my inflection unmistakable. "I told your boyfriend Tim the same thing a year ago. So why are we doing this again? Are you dense or something?"

He knew exactly who we were to each other. It was exactly why I was sitting there in this mess—why I had to do what I did.

"Fine," he said. "Are you able to identify the names of these three men from photos I'm about to show you?"

James meticulously sifted through a stack of paperwork, working steadily, unhurried, as though each sheet carried the weight of the world. Finally, he pulled out three photographs, each one a chilling snapshot of the crime scene where the bodies of those three men—those who had aided James in the murder of my beloved Qualley—were discovered.

I was honestly surprised how quickly they developed these pictures.

The images were grotesque to anyone else, but to me, a triumph. My lips quirked unapologetically upward in satisfaction while I studied them. Each one was a puzzle piece falling perfectly into place. A creed to Goddess Themis's sweet embrace. Across the table, Detective Hall's expression shifted to subtle discomfort. His grimace was mild, but it was there. A slight retreat pulled him back into his seat, his stance tightening as if my eyes carried a force he couldn't withstand.

Perhaps it was the way my eyes lingered over the photos, savoring every detail of each lifeless form. Or perhaps it was the sound of his aging heart, pounding unevenly in his chest—a fragile organ struggling to keep the old man alive. The faint, labored thrum of his heart seemed to echo in the silence, a feeble cadence betraying his frailty. Detective James Hall's heart condition was one of many fascinating things I'd learned about him. A weakness hidden beneath his gruff exterior. It made him all the more human—and all the more vulnerable.

After a moment's pause, James placed another set of photographs on the table. These were different—not that of the crime scenes, but of canvases I'd painted after each murder. They all depicted a vivid, haunting portrait of Qualley. An essence of him captured within strokes of pigment—and blood. Delicate, breathtaking, yet laced with a foreboding truth. A reminder to those bastards of exactly for whom they died.

Examining the images, memories flooded back. That thrill of the hunt, that satisfaction of witnessing their lives draining away; the artistry that was their deaths.

Chests carved open.

Hearts removed unceremoniously.

Blood collected, used as a medium for my art.

A morbid message of love stolen from the depths of my soul. The hearts sat proudly in my studio, displayed like trophies. Perfect souvenirs replacing the one ripped from my own chest.

Even as I reveled in the memories, a pang of longing pierced through. If it weren't for the crooked man sitting across from me and his twisted team, my life could have been blissful. I could have been with Qualley—a man who adored me, a man who made me feel whole.

Ben Prout, Lile Henderson, and Evan Matthews deserved to suffer. They deserved to feel a pain so profound, so consuming, it eclipsed anything they inflicted on me—or on Qualley. I wanted their families to experience the agony of losing the person who made them feel sane, the person who brought them joy, security.

A child would grow up to be fatherless—Ben and his now ex-wife had a baby. A child who would never know his father's touch, his laugh, his love. Would Qualley and I ever have had that chance? Of course not. They stole it from us, ripped it away as though it meant nothing.

Their loved ones would know every detail of how I lured those men into my trap. They would understand the precision, the cunning, the inevitability of their demise. My trap was flawless, a mirror of nature's deadliest predator.

A black widow.

Or perhaps a red widow—for death seemed to follow me like an impenetrable curse.

Rooted to the chair under the merciless heat of the overhead light, I surveyed the barren confines of the space. The weight of my actions hung heavily in charged silence, though my pride remained untouched—if anything, amplified. The idea of a court case played lazily in my mind. *Would there even be one?* Perhaps not. I had no intention of denying what I'd done. Why would I? I didn't feel an ounce of regret, only satisfaction. The thought of a grief-filled courtroom, packed with sobbing loved ones yearning for me to face the same ugly end as their ex-husband, son, coworker—whatever label those pathetic men wore— was thrilling. I could picture tear-streaked faces, their eyes alight with fury and grief as I stood there on the stand, giving them every sordid detail of how I had unraveled their perfect little lives.

I'd tell them *everything*.

Every weakness, every mundane detail of their existence— their daily routines, their families, the strings that bound them to predictable mediocrity. Most enticingly, I'd explain how I exploited it all, luring each of those testosterone-fueled parasites into my web like gnats. Because what were men like them, really, but mindless creatures driven by lust and bravado? They had been so easy to ensnare, so refreshingly oblivious to traps closing in around them.

Not Qualley, though. Qualley was nothing like them. He never strayed. He wouldn't have wanted to even if he'd had the time. Qualley was devoted—a man who cherished me in ways they never could. That's why losing him broke me, shattered my world into irreparable fragments. And that's why I fought back. Detective Hall and his team took him, tore him from my grasp, and for that, they—and everyone connected to them—deserved to mourn as I mourn. They deserved to have their hearts ripped clean out of their chests, figuratively and literally.

So yes, those men—the haughty officers who thought themselves untouchable—died by my hand.

I cut them down.

I cut them open.

I took their hearts, drained their blood, and transformed it into something worthy of Qualley's memory.

Art.

My canvases were alive with his beauty, his presence, his soul. Captured in strokes painted with the lifeblood of men unworthy to even speak his name. Qualley deserved to be immortalized, displayed in every light, celebrated in every form. They, on the other hand, deserved darkness—the suffocating permanence only six feet underground could secure.

James Hall, the mastermind of this collective betrayal, would undoubtedly get his turn soon enough. My vengeance would not be complete without him.

The shadow in my mind refused to retreat, its whispers curling around my thoughts like smoke. I forced myself to ignore it, redirecting my focus back to James.

"Ah, the murderers," I said smoothly, lifting my eyes to meet James's. He extended a perplexed look that only made my grin widen. "Their blood was quite opaque—not Windsor & Newton quality—but surely, you can see it came out beautifully. My best work, if you ask me."

"I didn't ask, but thank you," James retorted, his frown deepening as though unimpressed by my artistic flair. "I asked if you knew who they were."

I laughed, one that echoed through the room and bounced off its bare, broken walls. But amusement quickly twisted into anger as my shackled hands slammed against the cold surface of the table, sending a sharp clang reverberating through the air. My hair spilled into my face like a curtain, shielding my eyes for a brief moment before I cocked my head slightly, peering through the strands at James—he who had brought me a year of misery with his selfish cruelty.

"Of course, I knew who they were!" I roared through gritted teeth, my voice cracking with rage. "Do you really think I'd spend months combing through Qualley's court case, piecing together a puzzle to find the men responsible for his death, only to stop short of identifying them? I know everything about them— where they lived, where they worked, routines, the department— every detail, ultimately leading me right to *you*."

I paused, leaning forward despite my restraints, my intensity scorching through the air like a wildfire. My lips, painted in a vivid crimson mirroring the lives I'd taken, curled into a malicious grin. The fury boiling within me disolved as quickly as it came, replaced by pride so intoxicating it nearly made me giddy. This was my moment—my opportunity to strip away his flimsy pretenses, to confess my crimes in their full, unbridled glory.

Detective Hall's face tightened as he squirmed, his gaze locking onto mine. "Can you elaborate on what you mean by that?" His voice seeped with forced calm, but I caught the unease in his eyes. He wanted to know why I had targeted his team —why I wrecked their perfect little world. And oh, I was bursting to tell him.

Little did the detective know, the great masterpiece of my vengeance wasn't tucked neatly into the incriminating folder on the table before him. No, it was waiting for him—somewhere incredibly special.

"Oh, James," I mused as a quiet laugh rumbled in my throat. "I'd love to elaborate for you. In fact, I'll tell you *everything*."

Chapter 4

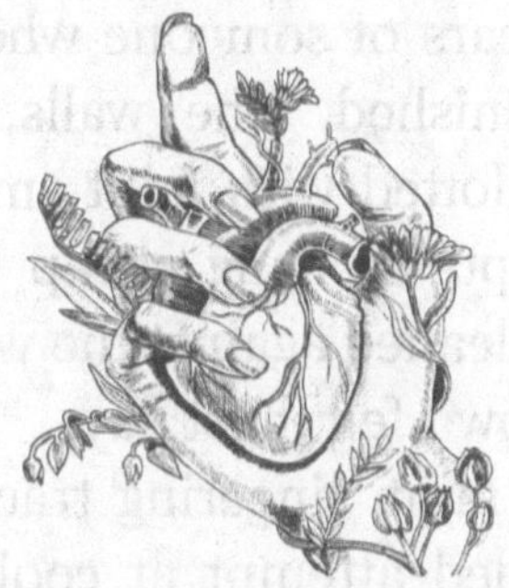

Truth is, the morning after the Hartford Galleries, if you had asked me if I had a fun time with Qualley, I wouldn't have had a clue. And if you'd said something like, "Who was that sexy man you were flirting with last night?" I'd have absolutely no memory of who or what you were talking about.

To no one's surprise, waking up—well, technically, rolling out of bed that afternoon—after the art exhibition felt as familiar as any other Sunday: groggy, crumpled, and clinging to some semblance of functionality. The only difference? That day, I was ten million dollars richer than I'd been the day prior.

Never in my life had I laid eyes on so many zeros. For someone who used to scrape together whatever loose change I could find, sell my belongings to cover rent, or stretch a jar of peanut butter for weeks, it was surreal. And when desperation hit hard, even selling *myself* wasn't off the table.

Before the money and before I could feel remotely human again, I had to wage war against the pounding in my skull—courtesy of the prior night's cocktail marathon. Naturally, I'd failed to set myself up for success by leaving water and Tylenol within arm's reach to avoid the looming hangover. Classic me, sabotaging future me. I laid there with my eyes shut tight, feeling like my bed was adrift in the Pequabuck River, as if I'd stepped into the role of Merideth Blake from *The Parent Trap*, but with more vodka and less villainy.

The lavender comforter I reluctantly pushed aside was one of the few soft touches in an otherwise haphazard room. My apartment bore the scars of someone who'd gotten too used to leaving things half-finished. The walls, once an uninspired eggshell white, were dotted with faint smudges, shadowy remnants of failed attempts to hang cheap prints and posters. A half-dead snake plant leaned against the windowsill, an unintentional metaphor for how I felt most days.

The air carried a faint, lingering trace of something burnt from my last misguided attempt at cooking. My small kitchenette was visible from the bed through the door, with a sink full of mismatched mugs and utensils I swore I'd wash *later*. The chipped, laminate countertop held a graveyard of takeout containers, some empty, others holding questionable leftovers I dared not investigate.

Squinting was my only defense against dizziness as I gingerly eased onto my feet, the rough carpet beneath me a bracing shock. My stomach made its displeasure known with a sudden lurch, but thankfully, it settled for a burp—one of last night's cosmos staging an encore on my taste buds. At least the room was tidy enough to navigate without tripping over shoes. Though piles of laundry—some clean, some not—clung stubbornly to the corners. Responsibilities I'd repeatedly ignored.

As I tried to piece together how the hell I'd made it home, all while battling a relentless throbbing in my skull, I tugged my phone from the charger on the bedside table and slipped it into the pocket of my pajama pants. The table itself was a chaotic tableau: a dusty lamp, a candle burned to its end, and a stray earring whose partner had vanished weeks ago. At least I'd had the foresight to plug the phone in before passing out—small victories, I supposed. Even better, I'd swapped my favorite navy-blue mini dress for something more comfortable. Not that it made me feel any closer to adulthood. I'd bet my last dollar my face was still caked in makeup. Washing it off while intoxicated?

Who was I kidding, I wasn't exactly acing self-care here.

My feet shuffled toward the kitchen, each step a wobbly, toddler-like experiment in locomotion as I tripped over nothing but the stubborn carpet in the hallway. By the time I reached the chipped, 1970s linoleum flooring within the kitchen, I was starting to think my legs might quit on me entirely.

The refrigerator's light hit me like a blinding interrogation lamp the moment I opened the door. It illuminated the entire dark kitchen I hadn't bothered—or had forgotten—to light up when I stumbled in. Squinting like I'd just wandered out of a cave, I yanked the water filter jug free and plopped it down on the nearest scrap of counter space. Then, turning my attention to the cabinet stocked with medications and an assortment of junk, I began my desperate treasure hunt for my little hangover heroes.

With one hand shielding my face from the obnoxious daylight pouring through the window above the sink, I rifled through the cabinet like a prospector digging for gold. Items clattered to the floor as I shoved things around, knocking over bottles and boxes, making a bigger mess than I'd started with. By now, I should have committed the feel of the painkiller bottle to memory—this was hardly my first hungover rodeo. Eventually, I stuck my entire head into the cabinet in a last-ditch effort to locate the elusive meds. Nothing. Not even a hint. That left me with two miserable options: endure this headache all day like a martyr or DoorDash some relief—which was definitely preferable, because walking or driving that very moment was out of the question.

As my headache pulsed on, another troubling thought occurred: *Was my car even in the parking lot of my apartment complex?* If not, it probably meant one of my sober friends, maybe Zina—if she'd been sober—had driven me home last night. If so, my car was still in Hartford, miles away.

Great. Just great.

Groaning, I yanked my phone from my pocket while simultaneously reaching for the top of the fridge where my sacred stash of saltine crackers lived. With all the coordination of a drunk raccoon digging through the trash, I tipped the box over, sending a handful of crackers skittering across the counter. Whatever. I had bigger problems. My head pounded like a drumline, and I needed to make sure I had enough money to order some Tylenol before I discovered—horror of horrors—that my bank account was emptier than my will to live.

I fumbled to open the banking app, tapping in my username and password with one hand while wrestling with the shrink-wrapped cracker package in the other. Finally victorious, I shoved a cracker into my mouth, my eyes glued to the screen as the app loaded. I braced myself for the usual depressing sum of a couple bucks and maybe some change.

But then it happened—the cracker slipped right out of my hand, shattering into a pile of pathetic crumbs on the floor as I stared, dumbfounded, at the numbers staring back at me.

Six figures.

Six goddamn figures.

Ten million dollars to be exact.

Wait, wouldn't that be seven figures? Either way, what the fuck?

My jaw followed the cracker's lead, nearly hitting the floor. I almost joined them both, because if I was going to faint, better to collapse in stages. I slid down to the floor in what could only be described as a very ungraceful heap. Somewhere in the daze, I managed to land on one of the fallen crackers, hearing it crunch beneath the weight of my stunned ass. But I didn't even care. I couldn't tear my eyes away from my phone. I double-checked. Triple-checked. That mocking number glared back at me: *Ten. Million. Dollars.* Either I was hallucinating from my hangover, or I'd finally lost all sense of reality.

Ten million dollars surely didn't exist in real life, right?

Desperate for answers, I poked around the banking app, trying to figure out how the hell this money had ended up in *my* account. My head ached with each click, and I wasn't sure if it was the hangover or the sheer absurdity of the situation making me feel lightheaded. Then it hit me—my painting. My painting at the gallery must've sold last night. And not just sold—sold for ten million dollars! I mean, what else could it be? That was the only logical explanation, even if logic seemed to have left the room entirely.

Sure, I'd been paying the gallery just for the privilege of hanging my *Burj Khalifa* painting in their building. But apparently, someone—some collector with more money than sense— saw it and thought, *Hey, let me blow ten million bucks on this masterpiece, why the fuck not?* I should've been overjoyed, thrilled out of my mind, but instead, I sat there, cross-eyed and incredulous, wondering which alternate dimension I'd stumbled into. *Who in their right mind spends that much on one of my paintings? I mean, it was good, but ten million dollars good?* I even had my doubts.

Meanwhile, the rest of the cracker crumbs mocked me from the floor, silently judging my disbelief.

My thoughts evaporated the moment a sound like nails on a chalkboard stabbed through both ears simultaneously.

My ringtone.

Of course someone was calling the moment I officially lost my mind. I squinted at the screen, the number unrecognizable. Normally, I'd let it ring out because who answers unknown numbers these days? But something, maybe the remnants of last night's recklessness, told me to pick up.

"Hello?" I croaked, my own voice ricocheting around my head like a wrecking ball, making my stomach churn.

The voice on the other end was smooth, melodic, and so dangerously charming it could've been bottled and sold as a weapon. "Hello! Cassandra? I'm sorry if I've woken you." His accent was a blend of Italian silk and New York edge—or maybe New Jersey? Either way, it was sexy as hell, and my heart skipped a beat like it was auditioning for a rom-com.

I cleared my throat, trying to suppress nausea clawing its way up. "Oh, no," I said, a nervous giggle slipping out. "I've been up. Can I ask who's calling?"

"You must not have saved my number," he said, outwardly amused. "It's Qualley Wallis. We met last night at the gallery. I had quite a night with you, *mia bella.*"

Oh, shit. My brain scrambled to piece together the disjointed fragments of last night. *Had I done something with this guy? Something I couldn't remember?* It wouldn't be the first time. No guy had ever called me back after a night like that—mostly because I didn't make a habit of handing out my number anymore. *So how the hell did he get it? And why was he calling? Was I really that memorable?*

Before I could spiral further, Qualley chuckled, as if he could hear my internal panic. "You didn't give me your number," he admitted with a mischievous edge. "I may have asked for it from one of my clients at the gallery last night. You didn't even give me a chance to ask before you left. I wrote my number on a napkin and handed it to you as you walked out with your friend, but I guess you misplaced it—or you just don't remember meeting me." His laugh was warm, teasing, and entirely too confident.

I racked my brain, trying to recall the interaction. I'd met so many people last night, most of whom were now a blur. My eidetic memory failed me when I consumed alcohol.

But then, like a flash of lightning, I remembered . . . someone.

A man with dark hair, smoldering features and eyes that glittered with mystery came into view. He'd complimented my painting. *Could this be the same guy?* Either way, the memory sent a shiver down my spine, my core melting into a puddle that pooled somewhere around my toes.

"I'm sorry," I said, embarrassed. "Last night was . . . a big night for me. I might've celebrated a little too hard. I'm definitely paying for it now." I let out a self-deprecating laugh, hoping to mask my mortification.

"Ah, that's too bad," he said, sighing theatrically. "I was hoping to take you to breakfast this morning. Though, I suppose it would be more of a brunch now. I know a great spot in downtown West Hartford with the best espresso martinis. You like espresso martinis, right? They might help with that hangover of yours."

His offer was tempting, and not just because of the promise of caffeine and alcohol. He seemed genuine, not like the type to fry me to a crisp in a bathtub, lure me into his basement and chain me to the wall, or poison me with a cocktail of drugs. Then again, I couldn't remember much from last night, so who knew? Maybe he'd already had his chance.

"Well," I said, surprising myself, "I do need to go out and grab some painkillers, so I guess some food wouldn't hurt." I couldn't believe I was agreeing to this. I didn't even know if he was the tall, dark, and handsome man I remembered—or if he was some troll who'd charmed me in a moment of drunken weakness. Either way, he seemed nice enough to give a chance.

"Perfect," he said, audibly excited. "Could I pick you up? Just text me your address."

Yeah . . . no. Stupid is not my middle name.

I wasn't about to give a complete stranger access to my apartment building, no matter how sexy his voice was.

"Actually, I can meet you there if you don't mind."

"Oh, sure, no problem," he said, devoid of any sign I'd let him down. "When should I expect you?"

"Let me get some water in me and shower last night off," I said, glancing at my reflection in the microwave and wincing. "Oh, and I think my car's still in Hartford, so I'll have to call my friend to bring me there. But I could meet you in about an hour,

hour and a half?"

Qualley chuckled, a sound that sent a pleasant shiver down my spine. "Sounds good—alright, great! I'll send you the address and meet you there soon. Looking forward to seeing you . . . uh . . . can I call you Cassie?"

The nickname hit me like a punch to the gut. My dad used to call me Cassie. I wasn't sure how I felt about this stranger using it, especially someone I didn't fully remember. "Let's see how brunch goes, and I'll let you know." I laughed nervously. "I'll see you later, uh—"

"Qualley," he said, chuckling softly, clearly unfazed by my drunken forgetfulness.

"Right, sorry," I said, cringing. "Qualley. Later."

"*Arrivederci*, Cassandra," he said, his voice flowing with Italian charm before the line went dead.

For the first time in what felt like forever, I didn't feel the overwhelming urge to run for the hills after talking to a guy. Maybe it was the remnants of last night's intoxication clouding my judgment, or maybe—just maybe—this was a good sign. One thing was for sure: he couldn't possibly be worse than goddamn Richard Johnson.

Hot water cascaded over my skin, dissolving grime and the caked remnants of last night's makeup with an efficiency of a hitman scrubbing evidence. My Ocean Breeze soap lathered into soothing suds, its crisp scent a poor substitute for an actual coastline but a far cry from the pandemonium of whispered threats, hidden weapons, and the ten-million-dollar secret now hanging over my head like a chandelier in a budget action movie. I tilted my head back, letting the water drown out my spiraling thoughts, but they clung like mascara stains to a cheap pillowcase.

Ten million dollars. That kind of money could rewrite a per-

son's story—new name, new life, new start. But let's not kid ourselves. It could also buy betrayal, bloodshed, and a lifetime supply of paranoia. I wasn't naïve enough to think cash came without strings, especially when those strings were long enough to
fashion a noose. Still, I let the water work its temporary magic,
the knot in my stomach loosening just enough to remind me
what it felt like to be human. Or at least, human adjacent.

I stood before the mirror after my shower, surveying the
battlefield of my reflection. My hair coiled like it had fought the
law and lost. Each tug of the comb felt like exorcising demons,
memories of last night getting yanked out one by one until the
tangles finally relented. I twisted it into a messy bun, the universal symbol of "I have my life together, I promise." Depending on
the lighting, it could even pass as intentional.

A *date.*
Was that what this was?
The thought hit harder than it should have, and I bit my lip
as I gave my reflection a critical once-over. *Was this really the
time for romance?* Not when ten million dollars was up for
grabs and I was tiptoeing through a minefield of lies. But, apparently, I thrive on bad decisions.

I reached for my makeup bag like it was an old war buddy.
These were the tools of the trade, after all—the mascara that
faked wide-eyed innocence, the blush that lied about how much
sleep I got. I painted confidence where I couldn't feel it, and
then, like the cherry on a sundae of self-delusion, I reached for
the crimson lipstick. It had cost me weeks of skipped lunches
and awkward smiles at my manager, but it was worth it. That
lipstick was a token that meant even when life served me scraps,
I could still make myself feel like more than its leftovers.

The snap of the lipstick tube echoed like a gavel. Case
closed: power didn't always come in wire transfers. Sometimes,
it came in pigments.

As I dressed, I groaned at the white streaks of deodorant

that had boldly announced their presence across my black shirt. Because, of course, the universe loves its little jokes. After rifling through my modest wardrobe—a collection that could generously be described as "reluctantly adulting," I settled on a cream-colored sweater. Soft, approachable, but with just enough polish to make it clear I still cared. Sort of.

My Doc Martens, once a symbol of extravagant rebellion, sat buried beneath a heap of other shoes. I laced them slowly, as if tying my nerves together with every knot. Once, they'd been my proudest purchase. Now, with ten million dollars in the equation, they felt almost laughable. But they centered me. A signature of who I was before my life started resembling a bad thriller novel.

The absurdity of it all hit me like a brick. Here I was, dressing for a maybe-date while calculating how long I had before someone decided they wanted me—and the money—dead. As if my life wasn't enough of a punchline already. Still, as I tucked a loose strand of hair behind my ear and caught my reflection again, a small, wicked smile tugged at my lips.

Let them come. Let them try. I've danced with worse devils—and this time, I wasn't leaving the floor empty-handed.

I grabbed my phone, thumb hovering over Zina's contact. She was the only person who could make me laugh hard enough to forget that ten million dollars wasn't freedom—it was a timer, ticking down.

Thinking about Zina always brought back the memory of how we met—high school, and a mutual hatred that could've fueled a telenovela.

The first thing she ever said to me was, "Does the carpet match the drapes?" referring to my red hair. I called her a cunt. She laughed. Her friends laughed. I stormed off, feeling like I'd just walked out of a scene from a corny teen movie.

At the time, I was the new kid in town, courtesy of my parent's divorce and my mother's decision to uproot us to avoid my dad. Classic trope, right? My mother and I never saw eye-to-eye, which made living with her feel like a never-ending episode of Survivor—except I wasn't sure I'd make it to the next round. She kept me from my dad, knowing full well our father-daughter relationship was strong. I petitioned to stay with him, but Maureen (my mother), ever the drama queen, dragged him to court, threw in periods of extended silence, and ultimately won custody because he didn't have a steady income or a place of his own.

So there I was, stuck with a woman who couldn't give two shits about me. Our relationship worsened once we arrived in Bristol, where she alternated between overbearing control and chilling indifference. Her failed career dreams and tumultuous marriage were her favorite topics of conversation—always accompanied by a side of resentment, which she projected onto me with the precision of a sniper.

The only 'nice' thing she ever did was buy me foundation to cover up the bruises she left after one of her many outbursts. It was her twisted version of motherly love—a cosmetic Band-Aid for the damage she inflicted.

One night, after I came home late from an art class at the community college, she detonated. I tried to explain that the instructor lost track of time, but before I could finish, her hand met my face with a slap that echoed through the apartment. Another time, during an argument about college, she shoved me into a wall, leaving a bruise on my shoulder that even a long-sleeved shirt couldn't fully hide. She told me I'd never make it through college because I was "an idiot, just like your father."

The pièce de résistance came during a heated argument about my growing independence. I wanted to go out with a friend—the only one I'd managed to make in this new town. Mom grabbed a ceramic vase from the dining table and hurled it at me. I dodged it, and the sound of shattering porcelain lingered like a grim punctuation mark. I couldn't tell if she was angrier about the vase being destroyed, the fact that I had avoided the collision, or that I didn't get hurt that time.

Living with her was like walking through a minefield, bracing myself for the next explosion. Humor became my armor, sarcasm my shield, and Zina, surprisingly, my lifeline. Together, we laughed at the absurdity of it all, because sometimes, laughter was the only thing that kept me sane.

Chapter 5

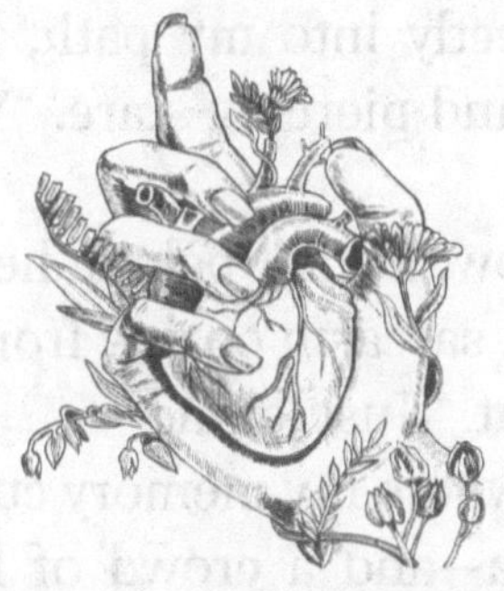

My luck with Zina Alvarado took a dramatic turn one morning, during the first few weeks of my Senior year of high school. She bore witness to the full, orchestral madness that was my mother. The performance began in the parking lot, her voice carrying effortlessly through the closed windows of her ancient shit brown Buick as she shouted, "I shouldn't have to drive you to school! That's what the damn bus is for!"

To be fair, it was my fault I had missed the bus.

Feeling like death warmed over, I'd asked if I could stay home, but she wasn't having it. Her response? A gracious "Tough shit!" accompanied by shoving me into the car and berating me the entire five-minute drive to the school.

By the time we reached the drop-off area, the fever roiling inside me was the least of my worries. She punctuated her tirade with a few good smacks, her hands as biting as her words. Stumbling out of the car, cheeks blazing, I felt like I might dissolve into the pavement right there.

Halfway to the front doors, my backpack slipped down my shoulder like it, too, had given up on me. I heard someone behind me call out. "You don't look so good."

Zina jogged up beside me to grab the side of my bag before gravity could claim it. I assumed she was taking the opportunity to poke fun, as usual, so I pulled away.

"Save the insults for later. I'm not in the mood," I rasped, my throat raw and my patience paper-thin.

Zina stepped directly into my path, blocking the entrance with her solid frame and piercing stare. "You shouldn't be here. You—"

"Yeah, yeah, I know. I don't belong here, I act too cool, blah blah." I waved her off, sarcasm oozing from my words as nausea coiled tighter in my gut. "Just let me—"

And that's about where my memory cuts out.

According to Zina—and a crowd of horrified onlookers—I collapsed mid-sentence, cracking my head on a bike rack that some genius had planted right in the middle of the walkway. It was the cherry on top of an already stellar morning.

Seriously, *chefs kiss*.

When I came to, I was in the hospital, unsure of how I'd gotten there. But one thing was clear—I wrongfully convinced myself Zina had finally decided to take me out, just as she always joked she would. My memory felt like a blank slate, wiped clean of how I ended up in the brightly lit, sterile, white walled, and antiseptic atmosphere. But I remembered this much—I'd been talking to Zina before everything went hazy.

My mind raced, trying to piece the fragments together, but all it brought me were half-formed images: her smug smirk, her words hot enough to make ice seem warm, and the sound of my own voice, growing faint as darkness swirled in.

Turned out, dehydration had done the dirty work—not Zina. According to my attending doctor, I had mononucleosis. He called it, jokingly, "the kissing disease." Then he hit me with the kicker: I'd smacked my head on the way down, like a finale to my body's betrayal. As I sat in disbelief, processing this revelation, I passed out again, because evidently, dehydration wasn't quite done clowning me.

And that nickname—the kissing disease. God help me. That was just the icing on the humiliation cake. Mono, but without the glory of having kissed anyone? Simply perfect. Another golden opportunity for Zina and her cum-guzzling entourage to weaponize against me. I could already hear their taunts, their laughter roaring in every hallway I'd soon dread walking down.

Cassandra Kessler, the girl who could turn a hospital stay into a comedy special. The headline practically writes itself: "*Local Teen Loses Battle with Gravity, Wins Sympathy from IV Bag.*"

As I lay there, cocooned in my bed, I couldn't help but wonder if the hospital staff had a betting pool on how many times I'd pass out before they could discharge me. Maybe the nurses had twenty bucks riding on me fainting during my next attempt to sip water. The rhythmic beeping of the machines felt like a soundtrack to my humiliation—a symphony of dehydration and bad luck.

In the background, the TV babbled on, its subtitles unraveling a story so melodramatic it might have been written in crayon. I imagined the news anchor announcing my tragic tale with the same enthusiasm reserved for weather updates: "*And in local news, Cassandra Kessler, age seventeen, took a dramatic tumble after a heated debate with a bicycle rack. Witnesses say the rack won by unanimous decision. Back to you, Tom.*"

The empty chair beside me felt less like furniture and more like a metaphor for everything my mother couldn't be. Maybe she was at home, Googling, "how to disown your child without paperwork." Or perhaps she was drafting her own headline: "*Mother of the Year Award Erroneously Revoked After Daughter's Hospital Stay.*"

I watched the IV drip, its unchanging pace taunting me as my body passed over every attempt to stay awake. The liquid inside was probably just water, but I liked to imagine it was some magical elixir that would transform me into a functioning human being.

Spoiler alert: *it didn't.*

The over-bed table held a plastic cup of water, its presence both comforting and ironic. It was so desperately needed yet so maddeningly close. It seemed to laugh at me with its unassuming presence. I reached for it, half expecting it to vanish like a mirage in the desert. But no, it was real—cold, clear, and utterly unremarkable.

The cup felt unsteady in my grip, its weight exaggerated by my trembling hands, and I nearly tipped it over before it reached my lips. As I took a sip, I couldn't help but think about Zina and her gaggle of friends. They'd probably turn this whole ordeal into a meme: "When dehydration hits harder than your ex's insults." I could already hear their cackles echoing in my head, a symphony of ridicule that would play in my mind for weeks to come.

But hey, at least I'd have a story to tell. And if nothing else, I'd learned one valuable lesson: never underestimate the power of hydration—or the comedic potential of a hospital stay.

The air was heavy with the sharp, chemical cleanness of antiseptic—clean, clinical, and carrying that strange comfort you only find in places where pandemonium feels controlled. I shifted within the sheets. The cool, smooth fabric of the hospital gown brushed against my skin like a reluctant apology, and the anti-slip socks offered just enough warmth to be irritating. That's when the most pressing question hit me: *Who the hell undressed me and put me in this ridiculous outfit while I was unconscious?* That was definitely an invasion of something, though I wasn't sure if it was privacy or just my dignity.

From the hallway came the faint shuffle of nurse's shoes and the occasional clatter of something metallic, like medical equipment being wielded by someone juggling. Around me, machines hummed in perfect synchronization, their beeps punctuating the barren stillness like clockwork musicians. For a moment, I caught myself staring at the sliver of sky visible through the window, and for reasons I didn't entirely understand, I felt safe—

safe in a way I hadn't felt in years, if ever.

But that fleeting serenity evaporated the second the door cracked open, and in walked Zina, crinkling a small bag of Cheetos like she owned the place.

"Oh, shit!" she whispered loudly, the kind of whisper that's louder than actual talking. "Did I wake you?"

At first, I genuinely thought I'd hit my head hard enough to confuse Zina for my mother—like some warped Freaky Friday hallucination. Then, as my dizziness reminded me of how thoroughly my body had betrayed me today, I realized it was really her. My mouth was a desert, and even as I tried to speak, nothing came out. I reached for the water cup on my side table, my hands sabotaging me by knocking it askew. Zina, apparently eager to audition for Saint of the Year, placed her snack on the chair, rushed over, and handed me the cup like some benevolent deity descending to grant mercy.

"Crisis averted," she declared with a grin, returning to her crunchy snack like she hadn't just performed the most uncharacteristic act of kindness I'd ever seen. "Hospitals give me the creeps." She munched noisily, faking a shiver from her confession. The sound of her chewing reflected around the room like some kind of ASMR nightmare.

Sipping my water cautiously, I watched her from the corner of my eye and wondered why the hell she was here. Seriously, Zina wasn't exactly on my shortlist of people who'd show up for moral support, nor was she on my emergency contact list. If anything, I half-expected her to pull out a switchblade and finish me off while I was too weak to resist.

As she polished off the last of her Cheetos, Zina stood and tossed the bag toward the trash can. Of course, it landed perfectly. She turned to the window and yanked on the blinds, peering out with all the curiosity of someone casing the joint for a heist.

"Nice! McDonald's is right across the street," she announced with what I swear was genuine delight. "We should get some nuggets when you're 'outta here.'"

I stared at her, dumbfounded. *Was she for real? Did she seriously think I was up for a Happy Meal?* Not to mention, I still wasn't sure if I should trust her. She could've been plotting my demise for all I knew.

"I don't think so," I mumbled, attempting to return the water cup to the table. My coordination, however, had other plans. Zina was back in a flash, placing the cup down for me with a flourish before spinning dramatically into the chair, making me dizzy just watching her. This wasn't like her. The cheerful, almost motherly energy. Not her vibe at all.

"Why are you even here?" I finally asked, blunt as ever.

Zina turned from the TV, shrugging like it was no big deal. "I told the ambulance people I was your sister. They totally bought it. Figured I'd stick around since teachers didn't even see me slip 'outta school." She chuckled, proud of her little rebellion.

"What? Why would you do that?" I managed to ask, floored that she'd put effort into anything that didn't directly benefit her.

"Well," she said, fidgeting with the strap of her absurdly pink, heart-shaped bag, "I saw your mom yellin' at you in the car. It was . . . hard to watch. Then when you got out, you looked like you were gonna hurl, so I followed you. When you passed out, it freaked me out, okay?"

I blinked at her. *Zina? Freaked out? Over me? Had the apocalypse started without my knowledge?*

"I thought you hit me," I rubbed the swollen part of my face.

"What? No!" Zina looked genuinely offended. "I wouldn't hit you, especially if you're sick."

"You've literally threatened to do it, like, every day," I reminded her, just in case she'd forgotten her greatest hits collection of menacing one-liners.

"I know, I know," she admitted sheepishly. "But things are different now. I'm tryin' to . . . control the urges."

I raised an eyebrow. "Different? How? Like yesterday at lunch when you pretended to punch me for glancing at you?"

Zina tittered, clearly embarrassed. "Yeah, okay, not my finest moment."

"Exactly, so again, why didn't you just leave me to fend for myself?"

She rolled her eyes. "Because I felt bad, okay? Your mom seems like the kind of person who'd rather you crawl home than check on you." Her sarcasm was sharp, but the underlying truth in her words stung more.

My laugh came out bitter. "You don't even know the half of it."

Zina sighed wandering over to the window to fiddle with the blinds again, letting in a subtle glow. She wandered to the sink, twisting the faucet on and off like it was a nervous tick. Finally, when she spoke, her voice was softer.

"You know, I do get it," she said. "My parents died in a car crash when I was twelve. I was in the car, too, but I survived. They were fightin' . . . about me." Her voice wavered, and for once, she wasn't putting on a show.

Suddenly, Zina wasn't the bully I'd painted her as. She was just a girl with her own ghosts. But even then, trust wasn't something I could give her freely.

Zina didn't stop pacing, moving between the counter and the window like she was trying to outrun her thoughts. "Ever since they died, I've lived with my grandma, who's just . . . a joy." She said this sarcastically and cringed. "She tucked me in at night with bedtime stories like, 'You shoulda' died in that car,' or my personal favorite, 'Don't worry, your turn's comin'.' Real fuckin' heartwarmin' stuff."

I stared at her, unsure how to respond to that particular brand of trauma. It wasn't like I could throw her a Hallmark card that said, "Sorry your grandma's a nightmare." But I also wasn't about to let myself feel too much sympathy—not yet. This was Zina, after all. The girl who once threw my art project into a water fountain "as a joke."

"So . . . what's the deal then?" I asked. "If your grandma's awful, why are you still punching your way through life like it's an MMA match? You got into a fight with a freshman last week over shoes."

She stopped pacing and leaned against the sink, crossing her arms. "I know. It sounds bad," she admitted, her voice quieter now, "but fightin' . . . I dunno, it's just what I do when I'm mad. I'm mad a lot, okay? It's not like I enjoy it. Most of the time, people just . . . take up space, push my buttons, and I snap."

"You sound like an unhinged cat defending its scratching post," I said candidly.

Zina actually laughed at that—an honest, out loud laugh that caught me off guard. "Okay, fair," she said, shaking her head. "But with you, it's different. It's the art thing. You remember freshman year, right? Ms. Dennis entered your work into the art show your first week here. She called it, what was it . . . 'raw talent'?" Zina rolled her eyes so hard I thought they'd get stuck.

I frowned. "Wait, that's why you hate me? Because of art? You're jealous?"

"Jealous is a strong word," Zina said, though the way she avoided my gaze said otherwise. "I'd been workin' my ass off in that class, and then you stroll on in and steal the spotlight. Art was *my* thing. My *only* thing. And then—*poof*—you're suddenly the star, and I'm just background noise."

I didn't know whether to laugh or feel insulted. "So . . . all the threats, the insults, the passive-aggressive notes left in my locker were because Ms. Dennis liked my painting of a stupid chair more than yours?"

"First of all, it wasn't stupid—it was minimalist," Zina shot back, smirking a little. "And second . . . yeah, I guess it was. Happy now?"

I blinked at her, processing. "Honestly? No. That's the most ridiculous thing I've ever heard."

She shrugged. "What can I say? I'm complicated." There was that grin again, the one that always made me want to punch her —except now, it felt less malicious and more . . . human.

I sighed, leaning back into the stiff hospital pillows. "You know, for someone who fights so much, you're surprisingly bad at dealing with confrontation."

Zina chuckled, sitting back down in the chair and crossing her legs. "Yeah, well, you're surprisingly bad at stayin' hydrated, so I guess we're even."

"So, to be clear, your hatred for me is because I'm better than you at art? You're jealous?"

Zina clicked her tongue. "For the last time, I don't *hate* you, really. I just wish you weren't so good at the art thing. Like, why couldn't you be good at, I dunno, wrestlin' or somethin'?"

"Wrestling?" I asked, raising an incredulous brow at a suggestion too absurd to even entertain. "Seems like you'd be perfect for that since you're fighting people all the time anyway."

Zina shrugged again, smirking; her pugnacious nature reigned in as she seemed to fall deep into thought. "I guess you're right."

"Why are you telling me all this anyway?" I asked.

"Well, I—" Zina began, but before she could finish, the door creaked open, cutting her off mid-sentence. In walked my doctor, his clipboard tucked under one arm like he was gearing up for a TED Talk, followed by my mother, who appeared to be on the verge of spontaneous combustion. Her face was beet-red, her lips stretched so thin they could snap, and her entire demeanor screamed: *Who do I yell at first?*

She stormed into the room like a one-woman SWAT team, her eyes darting around until they landed on Zina. For a moment, it was like watching a cobra size up a mouse.

I made a point to avoid my mother's attention entirely. To focus on the doctor as he moved across the room. After all, this woman was the reason I was laid up here in the first place. If she'd let me stay home when I first said I felt sick, or God forbid, taken me to a doctor before I hit the 'human crash dummy' phase, none of this would've happened. But what did I expect from someone whose maternal instincts included treating me like a burden and walking around with a 'World's Okayest Parent' mug?

Part of me wondered if I could just live here at the hospital until I turned eighteen. Sure, the bill would be catastrophic—probably enough to bankrupt half the country—but at least I wouldn't have to deal with my mother's whiplash-inducing mood swings. The hospital wasn't much, but it didn't yell at me or hurl passive-aggressive guilt trips. That was worth something, right

My dad would never have let this happen to me. He may not have been the best at paying bills or remembering what day of the week it was, but when it came to parenthood, he ran circles around Maureen. If I'd told him I wasn't feeling well, he'd have scooped me up and driven me straight to urgent care, no questions asked. My dad messed up plenty—he wasn't some flawless superhero—but at least he tried. My mother, on the other hand, practically had a Ph.D. in giving up.

Maureen huffed dramatically as she pushed past Zina, claiming the second chair with all the grace of a queen demanding her throne. She gave Zina a once-over, her gaze dripping with disdain, before her face twisted into a grimace that could sour milk.

"Hello, Ms. Kessler. I'm Zina," Zina said, her voice sweet enough to choke a bee. She ignored my mother's intensity because—lets be real—birds of a feather . . .

"It's Doherty, actually," Maureen spat, wriggling in her chair like she was allergic to sitting still. "I'm not associated with trash anymore. Wait, are you the little whore messing with my daughter?"

The room froze.

Out of the corner of my eye, I caught the doctor's eyebrows shoot up so high they nearly hit the ceiling. He glanced from his clipboard to my mother, clearly debating whether his insurance covered 'verbal hospital room brawl' incidents.

Zina's jaw fell open in genuine shock. "What do you mean, I —"

"Don't lie to me, girl," Maureen snapped, leaning closer to Zina with the kind of vigor that made me think she was about to perform an exorcism. I tried to sit up and intervene, but my head punished me immediately with a pounding wave of pain.

"You think I don't know?" she continued, her voice slicing through the room like broken glass. "I've heard my daughter telling her father about the 'little bitch' making her life hell. You've got some nerve—"

Desperate to stop this circus before it spiraled further, I interjected. "She's not the same girl. This is Zina, not *Gina*. Everyone confuses their names." A bald-faced lie, but hey, desperate times. Zina didn't deserve to be verbally eviscerated in the middle of my hospital room after turning over a new leaf. And if I was being honest, nothing was worse in life than my mother. Except maybe Zina's grandmother, if her stories were true.

My mother narrowed her eyes, clearly unconvinced. "Well, that's not incredibly confusing." She shifted uncomfortably; arms crossed so tightly it was a miracle she didn't cut off her own circulation. I could tell she hated being in the same room as Zina now, but ignorance was bliss, and I wasn't about to enlighten her. "Don't you have somewhere to be?" My mother hissed at Zina once more, gripping her purse like it contained the secrets of the universe. "Where's your mother?"

"Dead," Zina replied flatly, her voice devoid of any emotion. She stood up, slinging her heart-shaped bag over her shoulder. "I'll go now. Feel better, Cassandra. I'll bring your homework tomorrow."

For a moment, I just stared at her, blinking, trying to process the absurdity of it all. The delivery was brutal, irrefutable—straight to the jugular without so much as a courtesy pause to soften the blow. And yet, somehow, it worked. The sheer deadpan honesty of it cracked through my swirling thoughts, eliciting the faintest laugh under my breath. Of course Zina said it like that. It was so . . . her.

Dead. A single word, utterly unsentimental, yet strangely endearing. It felt like a mirror to my own sense of humor—a shared language built on sarcasm and blunt truths. For anyone else, I might've been offended or felt the sting of indifference, but with Zina, it didn't even cross my mind. In her own way, she got it—me, this whole mess—and her matter-of-fact tone carried more comfort than any overblown pep talk could've managed.

As she turned to leave, swinging the bag that somehow managed to clash with everything and still look iconic, I found myself smiling. Not the big, dramatic kind, but something subtle and fleeting. She didn't linger to fuss or pry—just dropped her verbal bomb and disappeared like a magician in combat boots. And that, weirdly enough, was exactly what I needed.

She gave me a small wave, and I nodded, too exhausted to do much else. Zina extended the doctor a polite smile as she left, the door clicking shut behind her. I couldn't help but wonder how she planned to get home, considering she'd arrived here in the ambulance with me. Then again, Zina always seemed to land on her feet. She'd figure it out.

The doctor stood, pushing his glasses up his nose as he shuffled papers on his clipboard. "Well, Cassandra—Mom," he said, addressing us both in turn. "I'd like to keep you for another night. Your tests show severe dehydration, and since you passed out and hit your head, we'll need to monitor your concussion. Additionally, your spleen may be enlarged, which is common with mononucleosis. We'll keep an eye on that as well." He paused, glancing at my mother, whose face was now a mask of blank indifference. "Do you have any questions?"

Maureen leaned back in her chair, crossing her arms even tighter as it let out a creak loud enough to make me wince. The noise drilled into my skull like a jackhammer, making me wonder if the next sound I'd hear was my brain exploding. At this rate, I was ready to beg the doctor for a noise-canceling bubble—preferably one big enough to keep my mother out of it. Her silence wasn't surprising, but her attitude was stifling. I could practically feel her frustration simmering under the surface, ready to boil over at any second. And as usual, she wasn't going to ask any questions—she'd just stew in her own misplaced fury, leaving me to deal with the consequences. My mother was enraged—her fury practically radiating off her like heat waves on asphalt. She didn't want to be here in the first place, and she would make sure everyone in the room knew it. Her jaw was clenched so tightly I half-expected her molars to shatter under the pressure. Her eyes flickered with a cocktail of vitriol and uncertainty, darting around the room before landing on me, sprawled out in the hospital bed like some tragic centerpiece. A brawl was imminent. Not the kind with fists flying—though, knowing her, that wasn't entirely off the table—but the kind where words were weapons, and I'd be the unwilling target. Thank God for the hospital walls between us; they felt like the only thing keeping her wrath at bay. I prayed she'd cool down by the time I was released, though I knew better than to hope for miracles. If history were any indication, I'd be paying for this 'inconvenience' for weeks to come. In her eyes, my existence was always a crime, and getting sick was just another offense.

Dr. Damon Reynolds—whos name came into view, embroidered neatly above the pocket of his white coat—stood by the door, fiddling with his clipboard like it was a shield against the unease in the room. He shoved a pen into his pocket, glanced at my simmering mother, and wisely decided to keep his distance. "One of the nurses will be up in about half an hour to take your dinner order," he said, his voice calm but cautious, trying not to poke the hornet's nest. "I suggest drinking plenty of fluids and eating something light. Nothing heavy for now."

I nodded weakly, acknowledging his advice. My mother, however, stared blankly at the closed blinds covering the window, her glare fixed as if she were trying to burn a hole through them with sheer willpower. The doctor hesitated, clearly debating whether to say more, but ultimately decided against it. He slipped out the door, leaving me alone with the storm brewing in the room.

I reached for the water cup beside me, relieved to find my hands steadier than they'd been earlier. The cool liquid soothed my throat, but the relief was short-lived. My mother let out an exaggerated huff, running her fingers through her hair before rising to pace across the room. She stationed herself by the window, her posture rigid with barely contained ire. For once, she hadn't launched into her tirade yet—a rare moment of restraint, likely due to the public setting. But I knew it was only a matter of time before the dam broke.

When she finally turned toward me, her arms still crossed like a fortress, her face contorted with irritation. Her narrowed eyes bore into me, scanning my frail form in the hospital bed as if she were assessing the damage I'd caused to her day, her life. Her jaw tightened further; her disdain obvious within every line etched across her face.

"You're so fucking pathetic, Cassandra," Maureen snarled, seething with malice. She turned her head away, as though the mere act of looking at me was unbearable. "I had to leave work for . . . this?" My mother gestured toward me with a dismissive wave of her hand, as if pointing out a stain on the carpet. "You never think about anyone but yourself. Do you even realize how selfish you are?"

"I'm sick in a hospital bed!" I croaked, my voice cracking under the strain. The words surprised even me. Talking back to her was uncharted territory—a line I rarely dared to cross. I typically endured her barbs without a word, letting them sink in like tiny, invisible daggers, but this time was different. Maybe it was the haze of mono symptoms dulling my usual restraint, or maybe it was the sheer exhaustion of always being the one to endure. Whatever it was, something inside me snapped. Her abuse was a constant shadow, looming over every interaction, every thought. It made me feel small, insignificant, like a burden she could never shed. The hospital bed should have been a place of rest, of care, but even here, her disdain found me, wrapping around me like a vice. It was suffocating, the way her love—or lack thereof—was always conditional, always transactional. And in moments like this, I couldn't help but wonder if I was truly as worthless as she made me feel.

"Do you really think I chose to get sick? I went to school like you wanted, didn't I?" My voice cracked again, raw and strained, but I didn't care. My throat burned like hellfire, but the words kept coming, fueled by anger and exhaustion. "You're the selfish one! You're supposed to take care of me! Dad would've never made me go to school. He wouldn't have blamed me for being here!" Even as my voice shook, I forced myself to continue, allowing the dam to break free completely. "This isn't my fault! None of this is in my control!"

Tears welled up, blurring my vision. It was a foreign, unwelcome sensation. I never cried—not when she screamed at me, not even when her fists left bruises. Crying felt like giving her power, and I refused to give her that satisfaction. But now, I was too tired to fight it. My body ached, my head throbbed, and the room spun around me. Maybe it was the fever, or maybe it was everything else—the Zina thing, the years of holding it all in. I let the tears fall. For once, I didn't care. I was too broken, too drained to hold them back anymore.

This felt like the final straw.

Maureen stood still, though her clenched fists and trembling shoulders revealed the tempest within. They were clenched so tightly at her sides that her knuckles turned white as the blood retreated from her hands. Her eyes darted around the room, scanning me, the bed, the machines. Everything and nothing all at once. The gears were turning in her head, her thoughts unpredictable. My stomach twisted as I wondered what she might do. *Would she lash out? Would she grab something and use it against me?* The thought of her choking me with the very medical equipment meant to keep me alive flashed through my mind, unbidden and terrifying.

But then, she turned abruptly, her heels clicking against the floor as she adjusted her purse onto her shoulder. The hostility in the room didn't dissipate; it only shifted, morphing into something distant.

I pushed myself up slightly, my body protesting with every movement. A pounding ache radiated through my skull, my throat raw and searing with each attempt to swallow—a sensation akin to dragging sandpaper over an open wound. Still, I couldn't help but ask, my voice hoarse and trembling, "Where are you going?"

She paused mid-step, turning back to face me with agonizing slowness, her expression a mask of scorn. "I'm going home." Her voice held more acid than poison. "Good luck getting yourself out of here and back to the house without me and my *selfishness* to get you there."

The door crashed shut, its sound resonating in the room with all the weight of a finishing blow. I stared at the empty doorway, my chest tightening with a mix of relief and dread. Relief that she was gone, at least for now. Dread for what awaited me when I returned to that suffocating apartment on Main Street.

The hospital, for all its fulgent lights and antiseptic smells, felt like a sanctuary compared to the battleground of home. Here, I could breathe—although shallowly, through the haze of sickness and pain. Even in this fragile, feverish state, I knew one thing for certain: nothing was worse than being trapped in that apartment with her. The walls there didn't just hold memories— they held her anger, her cruelty, her dyspneic presence. And I wasn't sure how much longer I could endure it.

Chapter 6

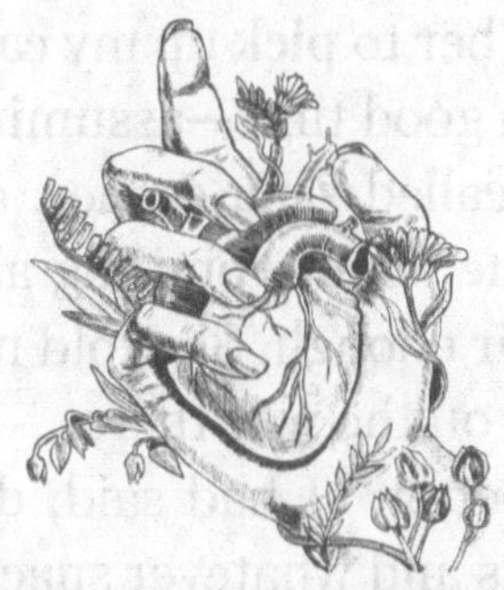

Zina tore through Hartford—a woman on a mission. Or maybe just someone who thought speed limits were optional. Her crusty—'but trusty,' as she always insisted—Toyota Corolla rattled with every bump, like it might disintegrate at any moment. A spare tire clung to one of the back wheels like a badge of honor from last week's flat, and I couldn't help but wonder if it was plotting its escape.

My stomach churned as inertia pinned me to the seat, and I latched onto the 'oh shit' handle—the universal safety device for passengers in overzealous driver's cars—as though my grip alone could prevent Zina's Corolla from becoming the lead feature on tonight's evening news. Not that it would help; Zina was in top form, punctuating her one-woman demolition derby with middle fingers and colorful commentary directed at anyone who dared share the road with her.

"Can you believe this guy?" she snarled, tailgating a poor soul who had the audacity to use their blinker merging onto the highway. I kept my mouth shut, channeling my energy into a silent prayer that we'd actually survive the journey. Meanwhile, Zina was in her element, unpredictable and fearless, a whirlwind of equal parts nerve-wracking and weirdly endearing.

How could you really stay mad at someone who managed to make a near-death experience feel like a thrill ride at an amusement park? I mean, sure, I was mentally drafting my obituary, but I couldn't deny that Zina's mayhem had a certain charm.

I should've used Uber to pick up my car from the gallery, but at least I'd get there in good time—assuming we didn't end up in a ditch first. When I called Zina earlier, asking her to pick me up, she'd bitched at me about vomiting all over the side of her car the night prior. Fair enough. She told me she'd only drive me if I paid for a car wash on the way there.

"I'll do you one better," I had said, desperate to avoid her wrath. "I'll buy you cigs and whatever snack you want."

Zina let out a shriek so ear-piercing, I had to pull the phone away from my head at arm's length. You'd think I'd just handed her a winning lottery ticket—which, in a way, as her friend with a sudden windfall, I sort of did. Not that she'd know; if Zina ever caught wind of my recent fortune, I'd never get a moment's peace.

It's bad enough I had to tell her about my meeting with . . . Quimbo? Damn, it.

"Hell yeah, girl, you got a deal!" She squealed with an enthusiasm equal to someone who'd just been promised unlimited access to a vending machine. It didn't take much to win Zina Alvarado over—cigarettes and Cheetos were her most popular personal currency. A key to unlocking just about any favor she could grant.

As we drove through downtown, Zina blew smoke out the window, tapping the end of her cigarette to remove burnt ashes. She offered me a drag whilst singing a song playing on the radio. Normally, I would've taken her offer without hesitation, but not today. I had plans to meet a man, and the thought of showing up with breath that stunk like the inside of an ashtray was downright horrifying. As a precaution to avoid bad breath of any variety, I nabbed Zina's spearmint gum from inside her glove box while she went into the gas station to purchase her promised bribe and pay for fuel with the twenty bucks I gave her. My last twenty, that is. Although, I guess that wasn't really the case, considering I had millions more in the bank.

"So where you goin' with this guy anyways?" Zina asked as we merged back onto the road. "He gonna pay you for somethin' after?" She winked at me, grinning wickedly.

I laughed, leaning my head against my fist, my elbow perched on the door. "Zina, please! It's not like that." I tossed her an incredulous glare. "Apparently I hung out with him last night. He called earlier, and I'll be honest—I couldn't remember his name or who he was to save my life. The only thing that stuck was the image of this insanely hot guy who showed up before I started throwing back tequila like it was water." I shrugged, my gaze shifting back to the passenger window. "I'm just curious if it's him."

"And if it *is* him?" Zina asked, her grin widening.

I shrugged again, trying to play it cool, though my stomach was already tying itself into knots.

Zina chortled, throwing her head back. "You haven't even told me his name!"

"Um, Quazzy? Wait, no, that's not it . . ." I struggled to remember what he'd told me when we spoke earlier. Weird considering my foolproof, eidetic memory.

"Qualley?" Zina asked, surprised. The car swerved a bit with her excitement. "Like, Qualley Wallis?"

"Um, maybe . . ." I said, grabbing the 'oh shit' handle again with the sudden jerk of the vehicle.

Zina swatted my arm with the back of her hand, her usual playful but annoying gesture. I glanced down at the spot she'd hit, my brow knitting in frustration. It was hard not to get irritated—she had a habit of doing this, and it was starting to wear thin.

"Sorry," she said, jaw dropping. "I'm still workin' on that."

I gave her a quick nod, letting my silence—and the exaggerated roll of my eyes—speak for me before steering the conversation back to the mysterious man. "Why? You know him?"

Zina knew everyone.

"Of course!" she said, turning the wheel of the car so fast I could've sworn we'd spin out and smash into the jersey barrier on the off-ramp. "He's Lonney's boss."

"Your Lonney?" I asked, intrigued.

Her eyes sparkled at the sound of his name, her usual mischievous grin mellowing into something unexpectedly tender. "Yeah, my Lonney. They been friends for years—go way back. Lonney's always sayin' what a solid guy Qualley is. But, I mean, Lonney thinks everyone's nice. Except that one waitress at Bennigan's who didn't bring him extra ketchup."

I couldn't help but smile at how her voice softened the moment she mentioned Lonney. For all of Zina's disorder, Lonney was her anchor. They were such an odd yet beautifully balanced pair—the spark and the steady hand that guided it. Somehow, he managed to ground her larger-than-life energy without extinguishing it, which was nothing short of remarkable.

I wanted something like that, too.

"He sounds amazing," I said, my mind drifting back to my earlier conversation with Qualley. His smooth, magnetic accent made his polite charm even more irresistible. Of course, it could all be a clever act. A ploy designed to charm his way into my bed. But for some reason, my gut wasn't sounding the alarm this time.

"Girl, just picture it if you start seein' him," Zina said with giddy delight, jerking the wheel to dodge a pothole. "Double dates! You, me, Lonney, and Qualley. It'd be perfect!"

I groaned, shaking my head. "I don't even know if I like the guy yet," I admitted. "I also haven't seriously dated anyone since double-dick-piece-of-shit-asshole—"

Zina's hand shot out, grabbing mine in a firm, reassuring squeeze. Her sudden seriousness caught me off guard, interrupting the flood of memories threatening to overwhelm me. "Yeah,

I know." Her voice was soft and uncharacteristically gentle. "But you don't have to worry about that asshole anymore."

Her words hung in the air, a rare moment of calm in the whirlwind that was Zina. I glanced down at her hand gripping mine, her knuckles white from the pressure. For all her wild antics, when she looked at me like that, with genuine care, it reminded me why we were friends.

For all her fire and noise, Zina knew how to make me feel safe—even if she was driving like she had a death wish.

≈ ≈

Double-dick, or Richard Johnson—if you're feeling formal enough to use his government name—was, unfortunately, my ex-boyfriend. We endured a rollercoaster of a relationship for two and a half years, off and on. Mostly off toward the bitter end.

We'd met during our time at Yale, where we were both working toward our master's degrees. I'd been lucky enough to score a scholarship at the School of Art after graduating from Paier College with a Bachelor of Fine Arts, snagging the top spot in my class. Honestly, I'd applied to Yale on a whim, thinking I'd never actually get in, but figured, *hey, why not shoot for the stars?* Surely Yale on my resume would unlock doors to my dream career, assuming those stars aligned.

Against all odds, I was accepted. But then came the crushing realization that Yale's nearly fifty-thousand-dollar tuition wasn't exactly pocket change. To make matters worse, my mother had disappeared into the Bermuda Triangle of 'unreachable parental figures' the moment I tried to hunt her down for help with financial aid paperwork.

Typical.

Miraculously, when I called the school to beg for alternatives, they informed me that my hours of community service and glowing letters of recommendation had landed me a full scholarship—very rare, apparently. To say I was relieved would be the understatement of the century.

At that point, life was good . . . no, life was freaking great.

Until Richard Johnson appeared.

He was studying Chemical and Environmental Engineering —because of course he was—and everything about him screamed "trouble." From the moment I met him, my life veered off course, spiraling downward like a plane with no engine, but not nearly as awe-inspiring.

Let's just say the crash-and-burn involved far fewer brilliant flashes of light and far more yelling matches over pizza toppings.

It all started at a party, because it always does, right?

Zina had practically dragged me there by the ear, claiming it was "mandatory fun," which I was pretty sure might be an oxymoron. After a couple of hours, she stormed over, practically vibrating with excitement.

"Oh my God," she shrieked, clutching my arm like she was about to spill state secrets. "Some guy over there is talkin' about *you*! At first, I was ready to throw hands, but then I realized it's the good kind of talkin'." She jabbed her finger toward him with the urgency of someone issuing a court summons, directing my eyes straight to the poor guy she was singling out. Following her outstretched finger, my eyes landed on him.

Richard Johnson: tall, buff, and oozing self-assuredness.

His pale skin practically glowed under dim bar lights, and long blonde hair spilled over to one side of his face like he was auditioning for the role of 'mysterious stranger' in every B-rated romance novel ever written. Muscles stretched the limits of a poor, innocent t-shirt, that threatened to burst free at any moment. He was chatting with someone—but neither of us paid attention to them when a Greek God had materialized before us.

Richard was the center of the universe, and everyone else was just orbiting.

As if on cue, he placed his glass down, running a hand

through his golden locks in a move that screamed "Look at me! Aren't I irresistible?" His biceps flexed, causing Zina to audibly gasp beside me.

"Girl . . . Girl . . ." she muttered under her breath. I knew she was already planning our wedding.

Then, as if ordained by fate or cruel irony, Richard started making his way toward us. On his journey, he acknowledged a few bystanders with smiles so dazzling they could've been sponsored by Crest. By the time he reached the bar, I was ready to combust.

Before I could flee the scene, Zina vanished like a magician in the middle of their disappearing act, leaving me alone with the human Ken doll. Fucking traitor. My heart pounded so hard it was practically screaming for medical attention.

What was I supposed to say? "Hi, you're very pretty and my brain has officially ceased functioning?"

When Richard finally reached the bar, he leaned over casually, ordering an IPA from the bartender. He didn't so much glance my way, but surveyed me from the corner of his eye, an action that sent me ruffling the napkin on the bar counter like my life depended on it. Pretending to look anywhere else was impossible, even though my nerves were screaming at me to retreat.

The bartender handed over the beer when he returned, and Richard thanked them with that smooth-as-butter voice of his, tossing over a few bucks as a tip. Taking a sip, he turned his back to the counter, leaning against it in a stance that could've been ripped straight out of a catalog for *'Ten People Too Cool To Be Real.'* He crossed one arm over his torso, beer in hand, and took another sip like he had all the time in the world.

Meanwhile, I was practically choking on the awkward silence, alternating between hoping he'd speak and praying he wouldn't. At that moment, I wasn't sure whether I wanted him to sweep me off my feet or disappear into the crowd forever.

One thing was certain: he was the kind of perfect that made you overthink every single flaw about yourself, and I was a puddle of anxiety trying to play it cool.

"Where'd your nosy sidekick wander off to?" he asked, breaking the uneasy quiet with a smoothness that didn't match the dive bar's sticky floors. His voice was rich (no pun intended), effortlessly confident, as he leaned in just enough for me to hear him over the bass of the music.

Caught off guard, I fumbled my cosmo, spilling a splash onto my arm. Classy Cassie as some might say. His amused chuckle followed, low and warm, the kind that might've been charming under different circumstances. He plucked a napkin from the holder and handed it to me, a gesture that came across as surprisingly considerate. I already had one, but I accepted it anyway, trying to play off my embarrassment with a coy smile as I dabbed at the mess.

"Sorry, didn't mean to startle you," he said, a note of genuine apology softening his tone.

"You didn't," I lied, my voice catching slightly. I could practically feel my cheeks heating. "And Sherlock will return eventually."

He nodded, a flicker of amusement crossing his expression as his gaze swept the room, like he was casually mapping out the exits—or maybe just avoiding my eyes. "Can I ask your name?"

"Cassandra," I replied simply, waiting to see if he'd say something eye-roll-worthy.

"Richard," he said, offering his hand with an air of politeness that didn't quite fit the setting. I hesitated briefly before shaking it. His grip was firm, but thankfully not crushing—a rare feat, honestly.

"Pleasure," I said, a trace of sarcasm slipping in as I released his hand.

The corner of his mouth quirked up into a half-smile, somewhere between charming and cocky. "A pleasure, huh? Is that what you think when you look at me?"

I laughed—an actual laugh—not because the line was good, but because the sheer audacity was almost entertaining. "Oh, please," I replied, letting my tone do the heavy lifting. "You're fishing, and I'm not biting."

To my surprise, he didn't push the joke further. Instead, he leaned back slightly, his grin softening into something less smug. "Fair enough. Just thought I'd test the waters."

It was a refreshingly human response—not defensive, not overly rehearsed, just easy. For a moment, I let myself relax a little. Maybe he wasn't one of those guys after all. Still, the jury was out, and I wasn't handing him a medal just yet.

"So, why are you sitting here all alone?" he asked, his curiosity seeming genuine enough.

"Not my choice." I glanced toward the bar where Zina had parked herself. "My friend's over there. Probably terrorizing the bartender for lime wedges."

Richard chuckled, the sound lighter now, less calculated. "She sounds like a riot."

I surprised myself by smiling. "She is. A chaotic riot, but yeah."

Just as I took another sip of my drink, he tilted his head slightly, his voice lowering just enough to feel intimate without veering into creepy territory. "Do you think I could take you out sometime?"

He just cut to the chase, didn't he? I thought.

I paused, caught off guard. The question was direct but not pushy, and for a moment, I wasn't sure how to respond. My gut wasn't exactly flinging up red flags, but it also wasn't handing him a green light.

"I don't know," I admitted, because honesty felt safer than playing coy. "I guess that depends on whether you're charming or just good at pretending to be."

He smirked, raising his hands in mock surrender. "Fair

enough. Guess I'll have to prove it, won't I?"

I studied him for another moment, debating the merits of ghosting versus humoring him. Worst-case scenario, I could delete his number later—or forward it to Zina for her endless entertainment. "Give me your phone." I held out my hand.

He blinked in surprise before fishing it out of his pocket, passing it to me without hesitation. I scrolled to his contacts and added my number, labeling it simply as 'Cassandra.' No cryptic initials, no fake names—just the truth. For now.

Handing his phone back, my lips curved into a small, satisfied smile. "You better not waste it," I said, standing up, ready to track down Zina.

Richard raised a brow, but he didn't say anything as I turned and walked away, disappearing into the throng of bar patrons. Let him wonder if I'd call it a whim or a mistake tomorrow.

👀

That night at the bar, Richard had been the epitome of charm —at least at first. His captivating voice, self-assured presence, and irresistible charm had pulled me in with an almost magnetic force. I couldn't deny that there was something about him that intrigued me. Maybe it was the way he seemed so sure of himself, or maybe it was the fact that I was bored and looking for a distraction. Whatever the reason, I decided to give him my number anyway.

Looking back, I wish I'd trusted my gut more, walking away for good that night. But hindsight is always 20/20 and at the time, I was still caught in the web of his charm. It wouldn't be long before I realized just how tangled that web really was. I suppose it was less of a web, and more appropriately, strings, as if I was his own personal marionette, and he was my puppet master.

Richard and I had a relationship that could only be described as a slow-motion train wreck—one he had buttered me up enough to convince me to board.

A one-way ticket on the *'What the Fuck Was I Thinking'* Express.

But I fell hard, swept away by his charisma and charm, the very qualities that would later become weapons in his arsenal of manipulation. What started as intense connection, filled with promises of support and devotion, quickly shifted into a noxious mixture of jealousy, possessiveness, and emotional abuse.

At first, I was free of his darker tendencies when we were surrounded by others, usually *his own* friends. In those moments, his charm shone through, making it nearly impossible to convince anyone that the gentle giant they saw was, in reality, an abusive asshole. I placated him constantly to keep the peace, swallowing my fears and doubts until they became a heavy, smothering weight. His moods brought me back to the life I had thought had left me—the life I had with my mother. Déjà vu, but not the good kind.

Whenever I tried to break up with him, Richard would guilt trip me into staying, throwing every kind gesture he'd ever done for me back in my face. He'd threaten to commit suicide if I left, a tactic that kept me trapped in a cycle of toxicity. He even convinced me to leave Yale, persuading me that an art degree was futile.

"Why would you waste your time on that?" He'd said it condescendingly. "Stay here with me. I'm all you need. I'll take care of you."

And I believed him.

For a while, things were uneventful—not good, but not bad either. I became increasingly depressed though, unable to express myself through my art, so I isolated myself in his apartment. All my belongings were there, making it harder to convince myself that leaving was even an option.

What had initially felt flattering—his possessiveness—soon became unbearable. He dictated my interactions with others, complaining whenever I wanted to spend time with friends. "I don't trust them," he'd say. "They don't have your best interests at heart. I do." And, like a fool, I believed him again.

Zina tried tirelessly to pull me out of the mess I was in, offering to bring me back to the Main Street apartment we ended up sharing at one point. She reminded me of my worth, urging me to go back to school. But I refused every time, knowing the fight it would provoke with Richard wasn't worth the effort. I knew how it would end.

With him victorious.

As always.

The verbal abuse escalated into physical violence, and something inside me shifted. The assaults reminded me of my mother's, and I finally saw Richard for what he truly was—not a protector, but a predator. My fear turned into anger, and I finally sought an escape.

The opportunity came one weekend when Richard left with some of his fraternity brothers on a road trip. I persuaded him not to bring me along, claiming I felt sick and didn't want to ruin their fun. Reluctantly, he agreed, but not without ordering me to answer my phone whenever he called and to stay home. As soon as he was gone, I knew I didn't have much time.

With Zina's help—after profusely apologizing for my past stubbornness—I cleared out as many of my belongings as I could and moved them back into the apartment on Main Street.

It felt too easy, and I should've known better.

On one of our trips back to Richard's apartment, he was there, waiting. He'd come home early. His paranoia and jealousy boiled over, and the altercation turned into a screaming match. He accused me of being worthless, cheating on him, and claimed no one would ever love me like he did. His insults escalated into threats of self-harm as usual, but this time, I saw through his bullshit. The argument reached a tipping point when Richard grabbed my wrist, his final attempt to stop me from leaving. Fueled by a mix of fear and anger, I managed to wrench myself free, bolting to the bathroom.

I threw my weight against the door, fumbling to lock the handle. I imagined Richard clobbering through the door with a knife like in *"The Shining."* My chest heaved, adrenaline pounding in my veins as if my heart were trying to break free too. The cramped space felt airless. Dim light cast sharp shadows on the tile walls, the faint smell cleaning supplies lingering.

My hands trembled as I fished my phone out of my pocket. The screen flickered to life as my fingers stumbled over Zina's name in my contacts. I texted her in a frenzy: ***SOS. Come to the window. NOW. No time to explain.*** The seconds dragged on, agonizingly slow, as I stared at the 'delivered' message, praying she was still in the car, phone in hand.

The silence outside the bathroom was deafening, broken only by muffled sounds of Richard pacing, his voice creeping through the thin door. He wasn't yelling—yet—but I could hear him muttering, the bitter edge in his tone intensifying with each word. I scanned the small bathroom for an escape plan. My eyes landed on the tiny, frosted window above the sink. It was barely wide enough to fit through, but it was my only chance.

Moments later, Zina's car lights flickered through the window, her arrival being a beacon of salvation. Her text came through: ***What the hell?! I'm still waiting here. Are you okay?***

With no time to answer, I threw open the window. Hinges creaked in protest. The cool night air hit me like a slap, snapping me into action. With a quick glance back at the locked door, I hoisted myself onto the sink and began to squeeze through. The edges of the frame bit into my arms as I wriggled through the narrow gap, my feet finally hitting the soft dirt outside.

Zina was already out of the car, running over to me with her phone flashlight waving wildly in one hand. "Girl, what the actual hell— "

"Just drive!" I cried, gasping and scrambling into the passenger seat like I was in the damn *Dukes of Hazzard*. Gravel crunched beneath her tires as we tore out of the driveway. Richard's shouts echoed behind us as he chased the car after discovering my escape. His shadow loomed in the rear-view mirror, growing smaller and smaller until it faded into the darkness.

The aftermath was worse than I could have imagined. Richard didn't follow through on his threats to end his life, but he unleashed a torrent of venom my way instead. Message after message flooded my phone—words coated with malice.

"You ruined me."

"This is all your fault."

"You will pay for this!"

He hurled accusations as if trying to bury me under the weight of his fury.

But the irony wasn't lost on me. If anyone's life had been ruined, it was mine. I had sacrificed so much for a man who once claimed to love me, only to find myself used, discarded, and trapped in his twisted chronicle. His final threat promised revenge, a cold vow that might have sent a chill down my spine if not for the growing fire in my chest. He didn't know it yet, but the tables were about to turn—and this time, I would be the one holding the strings.

Chapter 7

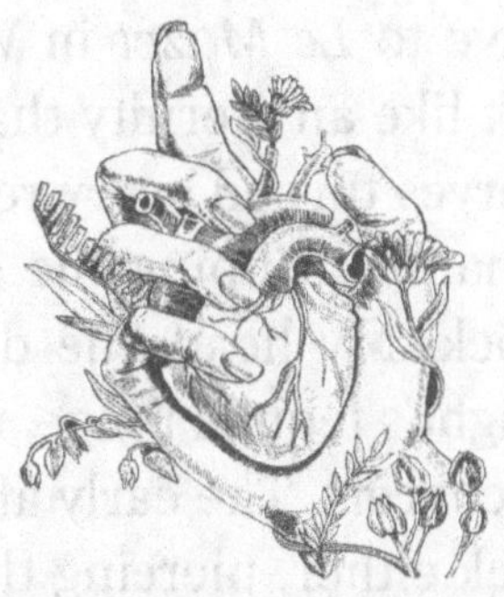

Emerging from Zina's car with my sanity miraculously intact, I blew her a kiss and shouted my thanks as she revved the engine, screeching away with all the drama of a getaway driver in a heist movie. I couldn't help but smirk as her taillights disappeared down the street.

Turning my attention to my beat-up sky-blue Mercury Sable, I sighed. It looked more like a moving artifact than a car, and I half-expected it to crumble into dust any day now. Still, it was mine, and I had places to be.

As I rummaged through my bag for my keys, the mayhem inside made its presence known. My overstuffed purse was like a black hole of receipts, random keychains, and an assortment of junk that appeared to breed while I wasn't looking. The clanging of keys against metal trinkets only added to my frustration as I dug deeper, muttering curses under my breath. Finally, I emerged victorious, clutching the correct key like it was Excalibur. With a triumphant *yank*, I unlocked the car door, which groaned like it resented being disturbed, throwing myself inside before it could change its mind.

Opening my phone, I pulled up the GPS, typing in the address Qualley sent me shortly after we'd spoken. His immediate reply was refreshing—most guys wouldn't respond even if their lives depended on it, leaving me to grovel for answers. But not Qualley. He was different. Or at least, I hoped he was. My track record was less than stellar, so I wasn't counting my chickens just yet.

It was a quick drive to *Le Mazet* in West Hartford, though the fifteen minutes felt like an eternity thanks to anxiety coiling in my stomach. My nerves turned every red light into a moment of introspection, my hands gripping the steering wheel tighter with each passing block. My headache didn't help matters either. Thanks to that night's tequila binge, my head throbbed like a bass drum at a rock concert. The early afternoon sunlight wasn't cutting me any slack either, piercing through the windshield and straight into my retinas. A pharmacy stop for painkillers would've been a smart move, but who had the time for that? I'd just have to ride it out and hope for the best.

Finding the restaurant was an ordeal all its own. Thick, decorative trees lined the street, leafy canopies doing their best to camouflage the place. I circled the block so many times I was afraid someone might think I was casing the joint. When I finally spotted the restaurant, I let out a dramatic sigh of relief and pulled into a free parking space, only to be greeted by a parking meter standing greedily beside my car.

Groaning, I slumped against the steering wheel like a defeated character in a sitcom. Left with no other option, I dug through my bag for change, unleashing another round of clinking disarray. My fingers sorted through coins like I was panning for gold. If nothing else, I'd earned my parking spot through sheer determination.

After triumphantly locating four dusty quarters at the bottom of my purse—each coin a small victory in itself—I fed them into the parking meter, offering tribute to the hungry god of bureaucracy. One hour of freedom. *That would have to be enough*, I thought, while also gambling with the potential consequences of a parking ticket. With phone, wallet, and keys accounted for, I made my way toward *Le Mazet's* entrance on foot.

The restaurant was nestled on a strip of road lined with boutiques and eateries, each vying for attention like contestants in a beauty pageant. But *Le Mazet* stood out in its understated charm—a snow white building with bold, black letters lit dramatically by small spotlights showcasing its name. A swath of scalloped, blue fabric crowned the entrance, proudly reading: *Patisserie, Restaurant, Bar American*. A picture-perfect patio was adorned with wicker chairs and white, wooden tables dressed in crisp tablecloths, each topped with a modest yet elegant floral arrangement. It looked like the kind of place that could host a photoshoot for the cover of a food magazine.

Oddly, it was quiet . . . a little too quiet. The place appeared deserted, save for a handful of indistinct figures moving inside. Silhouettes, I assumed, belonging to the staff. My curiosity wandered as I approached the doors, wondering why such a charming spot could seem so lifeless on a Sunday. *Was it West Hartford's best-kept secret? Or had everyone else received a memo to avoid this side of town that I clearly missed?*

Before I could open the door, a voice called out my name, stopping me dead in my tracks. It wasn't just any voice—it was warm, confident, and tinged with the unmistakable gentle cadence of an Italian accent, wrapping around each syllable like silk. My stomach flipped instinctively, and I turned toward the source of the sound, finding myself face-to-face with *him*—the man from the gallery last night.

There he was, seated at a patio table, his wide smile shining like a diamond catching the light. His onyx-black hair, though curlier than I remembered, gleamed under the afternoon sunlight. Those piercing eyes . . . *how could I forget them?* They locked onto mine with an intensity that somehow felt both inviting and disarming. And then there was his suit: dark gray with pinstripes so lethal they carried an unspoken warning; paired with glossy oxford shoes that had never touched a speck of dirt. He stood tall, his lean figure commanding attention without even trying. It was clear everything about his outfit had been tailored to perfection—as if the designer measured him twice and then some, just to make sure he exuded pure charisma.

And then there was me.

I glanced down at my sweater and jeans, the kind of comfortable attire meant for running errands at Target, not dining at an upscale gem like *Le Mazet*. I suddenly felt like I'd walked onto the wrong movie set, second-guessing my hair, my choice of clothing, and even my existence in that moment. If I'd known where I'd be meeting him, I might've traded my cozy sweater for something that didn't scream "I gave up halfway." My sweater, as comfortable as it was, felt like betrayal. Even my shoes whispered to me, "Really? You couldn't try just a little harder?"

Still, there was no going back now. I plastered on a smile, praying I could make my casual look seem methodical—like I was the kind of woman who didn't need to try too hard, who owned the 'effortless' vibe, even if the reality was far from it. The universe, however, remained skeptical of my confidence.

"*Ciao!*" Qualley called out, his arms stretching wide like he was about to envelop me in the world's most spectacular hug. He strode over from his table with all the grace of someone who knew exactly how to command attention, turning heads without even trying. "So good to see you again, Cassandra."

As he approached, I braced myself, fully expecting to be swept into the hug of the century. My shoulders tensed, and I mentally prepared for impact. But at the last second, he pivoted, seamlessly transitioning into handshake mode instead. The shift caught me off guard, and before I could even process what was happening, my hand had already shot out to meet his, like my body had decided it trusted him more than my brain did.

I posed a shy smile, trying to mask my surprise as he guided my hand into his own. And then—because of course he had charm levels cranked up to eleven—he gently lifted it to his lips, planting a light kiss on the back. The gesture was so smooth, so effortless, it felt like something out of a romance novel, and yet somehow it didn't set off my usual alarm bells. Unlike past experiences, there was no rough grab, no overcompensating theatrics —just a graceful motion that left me more defused than I cared to admit.

My pulse stuttered as I pulled my hand back, tucking a stray curl behind my ear. "You're . . . Qualley, I'm assuming?" I asked, cringing at how silly the question sounded. I knew it had to be him, but caution whispered in the back of my mind, reminding me that assuming anything—especially about ridiculously charming men—was a risk I couldn't afford. Better safe than sorry, right? Especially when 'sorry' could mean getting sweet--talked into an alley by a con artist in pinstripes.

He nodded, his grin turning slightly crooked in a way that felt almost conspiratorial. Without missing a beat, he gestured toward the table he'd just vacated to greet me. Before I even reached the chair, Qualley was already there, pulling it out for me with the kind of chivalry I'd only seen in period dramas. My instinct to second-guess everything kicked in immediately. *Who does that?* Nobody does that. Yet here he was, holding the chair with such unassuming ease it almost felt normal. *Almost.*

"Thank you," I said, more out of habit than any real composure, as I slid into the seat. My mind was already working overtime, trying to figure him out. *Was this just who he was? Or was it all part of some polished routine?* He eased the chair forward as I sat, rounding the table with the kind of confidence that made it seem like he had the whole restaurant choreographed.

As I adjusted myself, my attention snagged on a man dressed in black standing stoically by the fence separating the patio from the neighboring business. He wasn't eating, wasn't talking, wasn't doing anything besides looking like someone who wouldn't hesitate to break a nose if the situation called for it. My stomach tightened. *Was he with Qualley? A politician's bodyguard, maybe? Or just an unrelated enigma planted there to add intrigue to the brunch crowd?* Though 'crowd' wasn't the word I'd use considering there wasn't one. Anyway, I couldn't be sure, but the mere possibility sent my brain spiraling down a rabbit hole of suspicion.

Meanwhile, Qualley settled back into his seat like he owned the place, his long legs crossing casually as he draped one arm over the empty chair beside him. A flashy gold, obnoxiously large watch caught the sunlight on his wrist, practically screaming, "I can afford this, and you can't." It was the kind of accessory that could've come off as gauche, but somehow he wore it like he was born with it on. He glanced at the time, unhurried, as though the rest of the world didn't dare rush him. When he turned his gaze back to me, an easy certainty in his expression made me wonder if he somehow controlled time itself.

Just as I started to relax—a rookie mistake—he raised a hand, his expression shifting to one of mock surprise. "Just a sec," he said, reaching into his coat pocket.

My stomach flipped, my breath catching as my mind—predictably dramatic—leapt to the worst-case scenarios.

He's got a gun!

This is it!

He's going to kill me for my millions!

Run!

This is how it ends!

My muscles tensed, ready to bolt. But instead of a weapon, his hand emerged with a small, red and white box. I squinted, then blinked in disbelief.

Tylenol Extra-strength, rapid-release capsules.

"I thought I'd save you a trip to the drugstore," he said with a wink, leaning back into his seat like this was the most natural thing in the world. "Don't worry, it's a new bottle."

"Oh . . . wow," I flipped the box over in my hands like it was some sort of priceless relic. "You really didn't have to—"

"Please," Qualley said, raising a hand in a graceful, dismissive gesture. "It was my pleasure. Can't have your head hurting while the day's still young."

For a moment, I just stared at him, my brain scrambling to process what had just happened. *Was this . . . normal? Did people do this?* This wasn't the kindness I was used to—at least, not without a catch. The gesture left me off balance, teetering between appreciation and suspicion. My usual defense mechanisms were already working overtime, cataloging all the reasons not to trust him. But then there was that wink, that easy charm, and that damn box of Tylenol staring back at me like it was mocking my skepticism.

I let out a small laugh, shaking my head. "Well, consider me impressed." I placed the box down in front of me. "That's . . .. thoughtful. Unreasonably thoughtful."

Qualley's grin widened ever so slightly, unshaken. "What can I say? I like to start things on the right foot."

Feeling slightly awkward but immensely grateful, I tore open the box, slid out the bottle, and removed the seal with fumbling fingers. But as I stared at the pills, I realized my oversight —I didn't have water yet. I placed the bottle down next to me, resigning myself to wait until I did.

Naturally, Qualley noticed, and with a casual snap of his fingers, he summoned the man in black. I blinked as the intimidating figure disappeared behind a tree, returning moments later with a tray of water in elegant glasses, each one looking like it had been polished by angels.

The man set the glasses down in front of us, tucked the tray under his arm, pivoted like he was modeling for a spy movie, and resumed his post by the fence. I watched him, equal parts mesmerized and confused. *Was I being served by secret service? Was this brunch or a James Bond audition?*

Qualley had officially become ten times more mysterious.

"I reserved the entire patio here for our brunch," Qualley admitted, breaking my train of thought. "I hope you don't mind."

I scooped out a few Tylenol capsules, swallowing them like a seasoned pro in the fine art of headache management. Washing them down with water from my luxurious glass, I set the fancy glass back onto a cork coaster.

"No, I don't mind. Are we expecting anyone else?"

Qualley let out a soft laugh, shaking his head. "No, *Bellissima*. No others. It's just you and I."

My eyebrows shot up. *Bellissima?*

What was that? A compliment? An insult? I had no idea. But I figured it probably wasn't vulgar—nothing in the last five minutes had warranted name-calling, so I let it slide. Instead, I leaned forward, deciding it was time to break the ice. I just hoped I wouldn't end up asking him something we'd already talked about at the gallery last night.

"So, where are you from? I noticed your accent—" I began, but before I could finish, a waiter materialized like he'd been summoned from thin air. He set down two glasses of a peculiar brown liquid, each topped with a frothy layer and three rogue beans bobbing lazily on the surface. Without so much as a pause, he produced two menus from under his arm and placed them in front of us with practiced precision.

"Please, take your time. I'll return shortly to take your orders, Mr. Wallis," the waiter said with a polite nod. Qualley thanked him with a smile. I responded with my own awkward version of one, and the waiter glided away as if on invisible wheels, leaving us to our mystery drinks and menus.

I couldn't help but notice Qualley didn't spare even a glance at his menu. Instead, his attention was fixed entirely on me as I fiddled with the beverage in front of me. My fingers cautiously twirled the glass by its elegant stem, hesitant as I lifted it to my nose for a sniff. Coffee—familiar yet unexpectedly fancy. A quiet blush crept up my neck as I silently admitted to myself that I'd never seen a drink quite like this before, let alone tried one.

At least, I thought I hadn't.

When I dared to glance back at Qualley, his gaze hadn't wavered. His eyes were warm, glinting with something I couldn't quite place—curiosity, perhaps, or maybe amusement at my tentative inspection. But there was no judgment in his expression, nor a trace of arrogance. It was unsettling in a way I didn't expect, like being caught in the spotlight of someone who wasn't looking for flaws but simply . . . observing. The intensity of his focus set me on edge, yet not in a way that made me want to retreat. It was unnerving, yes, but also strangely comforting, as though his attention made the moment more significant than it had any right to be. My instinct was to laugh it off, to crack a joke about the drink or his unwavering stare, but I couldn't bring myself to interrupt whatever unspoken exchange hung between us.

Instead, I took another sniff of the coffee, keeping my movements slow, as if I could somehow fool him—and myself—into believing I wasn't flustered. His gaze lingered; his expression soft but inscrutable. For reasons I couldn't quite articulate, I felt as though he was waiting for something. *Approval? A reaction?* Or maybe he was just content to watch me stumble my way through this tiny, unfamiliar ritual. I'd never been one to enjoy being studied, yet with Qualley, it didn't feel invasive.

"I'm from Bologna, Italy" he said at last, as if our conversation had never been interrupted. "Lived there most of my life. Moved to America a few years ago."

My head dipped in acknowledgment, half-listening, as my attention flickered back to the menu in front of me. If he kept talking, I wouldn't have time to figure out what I wanted to order—but then I saw it. Bananas. Something with bananas. I squinted, reading through the description until I found: Banana Brûlée French Toast.

Sold.

With my decision made, I placed the menu down beside me and leaned back, crossing my arms with the confidence of someone who knew exactly what they wanted in life—at least for the next forty-ish minutes I had until my parking meter expired.

"What brought you here, then?" I asked, my eyes still darting between the menu and Qualley, trying to maintain the appearance of being fully engaged.

He leaned forward, folding his hands together as though preparing to deliver a grand revelation. "I invited you here, no?"

I chuckled, shaking my head as I turned to watch a car cruise past on the street. "That's not what I meant," I brought my focus back to the curiosity sitting across from me. "I meant, why America? Why Connecticut, of all places?"

"Business," he said simply, flashing an enigmatic grin before leaning back into his chair, crossing one long leg over the other. The man had mastered the art of saying almost nothing while still keeping me hooked, dangling just enough intrigue to make me want more. He didn't elaborate, and I didn't push.

I should've left it there. Should've brushed off his cryptic charm with the same indifference I gave to anyone who thought they could pull me into their orbit. People who smiled like that, people who leaned into mystery, usually had something to hide. I'd learned the hard way that secrets rarely worked in my favor. But something about him made me pause, the cautious part of me faltering just long enough for interest to slip in.

Maybe he *was* some undercover politician or a billionaire with secrets darker than the espresso martini in front of me. Or he was just an exceptionally good talker who could spin 'business' into a story I'd still be thinking about hours from now. Either way, he wasn't what I expected, and that alone was enough to keep me anchored in this moment.

What surprised me most was the waver of something unsettlingly close to trust. It wasn't logical—nothing about this situation was—but there was a way he watched me, a steadiness in his regard, that didn't scream assailant or pretender. It wasn't overbearing; it was quiet, as if he was trying to see *me*, not sell me on an idea of himself. And that felt dangerous for reasons I couldn't explain.

I didn't trust easily. Hell, I didn't trust at all, not when life had taught me to see the strings before anyone even started pulling them. *So why did I feel . . . safe?* Safe wasn't the right word—comforted, maybe? No, that wasn't it either. What unnerved me most was that I wanted to trust him, and the realization made me bristle. I didn't want to be this person, someone who got drawn in by smiles and half-answers. The kind who leaned into charm even when instincts told them to run. But there was something defusing about him, something that made it feel like trusting him might not be a mistake.

The thought gnawed at me as I shifted in my chair, pretending to focus on my drink. Maybe it was his ease, his way of commanding attention without demanding it. Or maybe it was the way he didn't try to fill the silence with unnecessary words. If anything, it made me feel seen, listened to. *And God, wasn't that a dangerous feeling to have around someone who could very well be a liar?*

I sipped my drink to give my hands something to do, grateful for the distraction. Whatever Qualley's game was, I wasn't ready to fall for it just yet. But damn, he made it tempting.

The waiter returned, breaking the silence, and asked for our orders. Qualley gestured for me to go first, and I proudly declared my choice of Banana Fancy Bullshit French Toast—or, well, its proper name. The waiter scribbled it down and turned to Qualley, who ordered something called 'Japanese Wagyu,' which sounded so indulgent it made my brûlée feel like a Pop-Tart in comparison.

Once our menus were collected and the waiter retreated, my attention returned to the glass of coffee-like liquid in front of me. "What is this?" I picked it up by the stem and examined it again as if it were a science experiment.

"Espresso martini," he replied smoothly, taking a sip from

his own glass and dabbing at the frothy evidence with a napkin. "We were drinking them last night. Don't you remember?"

I sipped carefully, my eyes widening in delighted surprise as the flavor registered. It was rich, slightly sweet, and downright divine. "This is fucking good!" I clapped a hand over my mouth as soon as the curse escaped. "Sorry . . . working on the cussing."

"No worries," he said with a laugh, his voice laced with amusement. "That's the same thing you declared last night."

"Did I?" I chuckled nervously, clearing my throat. I set the glass back down, aiming to pace myself despite the overwhelming urge to chug the entire thing. "I don't really remember what we talked about last night," I admitted, fidgeting with my napkin. "But I *do* remember you. Thank you, by the way, for what you said about my painting."

"Oh?" He leaned forward slightly, his grin widening as he rested his chin between two fingers. "And what did I say about this . . . painting?"

"You said it was *exquisite*." Skepticism gave my words an edge. "Then something about it being the most beautiful in the world, which, I'll admit, feels like a bit of an exaggeration. A polite lie, maybe." I shrugged, letting my hands rest in my lap.

His smirk deepened, unbothered by my accusation. "You think me a liar?" Crossing his arms, he extended a playful frown so exaggerated it was almost cartoonish. It was clear he wasn't actually offended, and the act only made his charm that much more persuasive.

Unable to resist any longer, I picked up my glass and took a sip. "No, of course not. I—"

"Do you think if I were lying about your painting," Qualley tilted his head as he spoke, as though he were about to reveal a great mystery, "I'd purchase it for a mere . . . I don't know . . . ten million dollars?"

The martini nearly dropped out of my hand, as I fumbled around to avoid spilling it entirely. A rogue drip of liquid trailed down my chin. For a moment, I panicked. *Should I wipe my chin with my napkin first? Should I put the glass down before I spill more? Or should I attempt both moves simultaneously and risk looking like I was starring in a slapstick comedy?*

Qualley watched the confusion unfold with obvious amusement. "You do that a lot," he noted, his tone warm yet teasing, like he was genuinely enjoying my clumsy spectacle.

My mouth hung open—literally. I looked like a goldfish gasping for air in its final seconds of life. Dumbfounded, I stared at him, trying to process what I'd just heard. Ten. Million. Dollars. My brain short-circuited. The phrase 'thoroughly flabbergasted' didn't even begin to cover it. I could feel my flabbers—whatever they were—being well and truly gasted.

The sheer fact of that amount sitting in my account washed over me again as though I'd just discovered it. *Could I even be trusted with that much money?* I thought of all the paint and canvases I could stockpile—entire aisles of art supplies cleared out just for me. I'd finally splurge on those Windsor & Newton brushes that cost an absurd five hundred dollars apiece and act like it was a responsible investment for my career. Then there was my beat-up Sable. Oh, how quickly I'd trade it in for the sleek Mercedes C-Class I'd been ogling. And of course, Zina would need to come along on a celebratory girl's trip—this time, Europe. She took me to Dubai, after all; returning the favor felt long overdue. I could even visit the *Burj Khalifa* again, the very subject of the painting that started all this madness.

"That was . . . *you*?" I finally managed to choke out the words, leaning forward as I eyed him like he'd just confessed to an unsolved heist. "The painting wasn't worth *that* much."

Qualley shook his head, his disbelief almost apparent. "Don't sell yourself short, *mia bella*." He reached across the table to gently take my hand in his.

His touch was light, thoughtful—nothing like the grabby, aggressive gestures I'd unfortunately known in the past. I stared at his hand on mine, half expecting a sudden wave of discomfort to crash over me, as it usually did. But it didn't. Instead, a sense of calm washed through me, quieting the intrusive memories of Richard and the walls I'd built to keep others at a distance.

After everything I'd endured, I'd learned to shy away from even the most casual forms of contact, my subconscious guarding itself like a fortress, always braced for the worst. And yet, in this strange and unexpected moment, my defenses didn't just lower—they softened, as though they'd finally grown tired of standing watch. It wasn't a reckless kind of trust, the kind that ignored the past or dismissed it as irrelevant. No, it was tentative, fragile, like the first breath of air after holding it too long underwater.

Here, with his hand resting on mine, I didn't feel the need to flinch or retreat. I didn't feel the echoes of fear scratching at the back of my mind. I felt . . . steady, as if the storm raging inside me had suddenly decided to quiet for just a moment. It caught me off guard, this feeling of safety. Maybe that's what made it feel so real. It wasn't something I reached for—it was something I allowed myself to lean into. And for once, I didn't pull away.

When Qualley finally released my hand, I had to fight the urge to reach for it again. Instead, I grabbed my water glass, holding it like it was a life preserver. "You shouldn't have spent that much money."

"Your work was well worth it," he said sunnily. "I only buy the best pieces for my personal collection."

I pressed my lips into a thin line, unsure of how to respond. My knee bounced under the table, jostling up and down in nervous anticipation. It wasn't fear that made me anxious—it was the realization that I was inexplicably charmed. And worse, I didn't even know him. We'd barely exchanged more than a few sentences, well, today. Yet here I was, leaning dangerously close to letting him waltz right into my heart. My inner alarm bells should've been blaring, yet all I could hear were the faint flutters of butterfly wings rattling the cage I'd locked them in.

"You know I can't accept that money, right?" I confessed. I looked at him with concern. "Do you even have money left in your bank account?"

He laughed softly, dipping his head. "Money does not matter to me, Cassandra." He turned his gaze toward the restaurant's window for dramatic effect. "What matters is ensuring those who work hard on something—whatever it may be—are rewarded accordingly."

I blinked as my brain did an awkward double take at the words coming out of his mouth. *Money doesn't matter.* That's rich (no pun intended) coming from a man who probably spent more on his outfit than I made in two months. And yet, there was something about the way he said it, the ease of his tone, that made it feel oddly genuine. Like he actually believed it. Like it wasn't just a line rehearsed in front of a mirror. The statement left me unsettled, unsure whether to laugh at the absurdity or lean into the intrigue. Money *always* mattered. It shaped lives, dictated opportunities, decided who thrived and who scraped by. It wasn't just currency—it was power, freedom, survival. Maybe for someone like him—someone who moved through life with effortless grace and a bank account big enough to cushion any fall—it was easy to say it didn't matter. But for the rest of us? It mattered. It mattered *a lot*.

For reasons I couldn't entirely pin down, I wanted to believe him. Wanted to believe that money wasn't the driving force behind every decision, every relationship, every move. Maybe it was the way he spoke, with that smooth confidence that made it sound like he could bend reality to his will. Or maybe it was the fact that his eyes, still fixed on the window, carried a sincerity that felt disarmingly real. I hated that it resonated with me. This idea of a world where money didn't have to define everything. A part of me wanted to scoff, to call him out on the privilege baked into those words. But another part, one I didn't like to acknowledge, felt a twinkle of hope, as if his belief in the idea could somehow make it true, even if just for a moment.

Instead of saying any of this, I took a long sip of my drink, the bitterness of the coffee steadying me in the reality I knew too well. "Well, aren't you noble." I tried keeping my tone light.

Qualley's grin deepened, inclining his head slightly, as if considering whether to take my words at face value or to peel back the layers of sarcasm I'd deliberately woven in. "Noble," he repeated, the word rolling off his tongue like it amused him. "I like that. But I wouldn't say noble—I'd say practical."

His eyes flicked back to mine, steady and unshaken, as though he was comfortable standing in the spotlight of disbelief. He didn't seem offended—if anything, he seemed entertained, like he relished the idea of being challenged rather than placated. His fingers tapped lightly on the edge of the table, a subtle rhythm that matched the unhurried ease in his voice. "You don't seem like the kind to believe in fairy tales. But maybe that's exactly what makes you interesting."

It was a beguiling shift, the way he tossed the focus back to me without a trace of defensiveness. Instead of pushing, he left his words hanging like an open invitation—one I wasn't entirely sure I wanted to accept. But the way his eyes held mine, assured without being overbearing, made me reconsider whether walking away from this conversation would be as easy as I thought.

"Are you a collector, then?" I asked, curiosity piqued. Maybe his mysterious 'business' involved curating priceless art, which would make him far more fascinating than any guy I'd met in years.

"Something like that." He shrugged, his ambiguity only adding to the perplexity of who he really was. He was annoyingly puzzling, like a riddle you didn't really want to solve but couldn't help trying anyway.

"So, you really think my painting is worth ten million?" I asked, lips curling in faint doubt.

Qualley's eyes held mine with firm intensity. "Your painting is priceless, *mia bella*." The words carried a strength that made me feel completely seen. "But I needed some way to get your attention again."

The statement hit me like a jolt; the convincing illusion of it. *Priceless?* That couldn't be right. There were plenty of descriptors I might've used for my work—blunt, raw, desperate, maybe even haunting on a good day—but priceless? That sounded like flattery taken straight from a script, far too grandiose to feel real. And yet, as I observed him, there wasn't even a spark of hesitation in his countenance. No smirk, no telltale sign of an act. Just steady, unrelenting conviction, the kind I wasn't sure whether to trust or challenge.

My instincts told me to push back, to laugh it off or dismiss it with sarcasm before the words could settle too deeply in my chest. *Compliments like that always came with strings, didn't they?* There was always a catch, some ulterior motive lurking just beneath the surface. But this one . . . it didn't *feel* that way. At least, not entirely.

Heat rose to my cheeks—certainly not the subtle flush of blush I'd carefully applied earlier, but the unmistakable warmth of genuine bashfulness. I wasn't used to this. Someone looking at me like I was more than the sum of my mistakes and half-finished ambitions. It was as though his words had peeled back the armor I didn't even realize I was still wearing.

Before I could decide how to respond, the waiter arrived with our plates. He had an impeccable sense of timing.

The aromas swept over the table: caramel, bananas, toasted bread—and something savory and smoky from Qualley's dish. I seized the interruption like a lifeline, focusing on the food and letting the moment slip away, even as his words lingered, stubborn and unshakable.

The waiter carefully placed each dish before us with the precision of someone defusing a bomb. Even the man in black returned to refill our water glasses before retreating back to his Ficus-tree post. For a brief moment, I felt like royalty.

The sight of the golden-brown, custard-rich French toast before me was enough to make my stomach rumble audibly. Meanwhile, Qualley's Wagyu was a work of art—delicately sliced with intricate marbling that resembled a painting in its own right.

"Dig in," Qualley said, already slicing into his meal with unrestrained enthusiasm. While he made quick work of his food, I hesitated, suddenly self-conscious about eating in front of him. But hunger won out, and I cautiously began cutting into my toast, hoping to avoid any sauce splatters or mishaps.

The first bite was heaven: fluffy, rich, sweet perfection. "That's fucking good, too!" I declared, my mouth full, completely forgetting decorum.

Qualley chuckled, setting his cutlery down for a moment. "You really have a way with words, Cassandra."

The toast and bananas were a perfect harmony of sweet and rich, with just the right amount of crunch from the Brûlée's caramelized crust. The custard inside was infused with vanilla bean and cinnamon, its creamy texture melting into the toast like a decadent secret. I couldn't help myself—I did a little happy dance in my seat, rocking back and forth as I savored each bite. So much for keeping things low-key.

Qualley smiled, clearly entertained by my reaction. "They have the best food here, yes."

I gave him a shy nod, and as the moment settled I felt relaxed, letting go of the self-consciousness that had been clinging to me. He'd caught me in my goofy, unfiltered mood—a side of me I usually kept under wraps. Lord knows he probably saw plenty of it last night, tequila-fueled and sloshing around like a human pinball.

I realized I could be myself around him without judgment.

Pausing the enthusiastic destruction of my brunch, I washed

it down with the last of my martini and leaned into our conversation. "Do you come here often?"

Qualley wiped his mouth with a napkin, his movements composed. "Yes, of course." He raised his arm in a sweeping gesture as if presenting the restaurant like a prized possession. "I own it."

I nearly choked on my French toast, my eyes widening in disbelief. "You own it?" I was merely joking when I said he sat like he owned the place . . .

"One of my good friends is the chef here, too" he added casually. "I own the rest of the buildings on this street as well."

For a fleeting moment, the world seemed to pause and more questions infiltrated my thoughts: *Who the fuck was this guy? Was this some kind of quiet billionaire initiation test I had unknowingly stumbled into? Had I accidentally befriended the secret landlord of the city? Was I about to be gifted a yacht and an obscure European title?*

I stared at him, trying to gauge if he was serious or just thoroughly enjoying my existential unraveling. No, there was no way he was joking—he was too comfortable. Like someone who casually signed checks with absurd numbers, just because he could.

I needed to reevaluate my life choices.

"You like honesty, don't you?" Qualley asked, his tone nonchalant. He sat back, swirling the liquid in his glass.

I blinked, slightly thrown by the sudden shift in vibes. "I mean, sure. Who doesn't?"

He nodded, as if confirming something to himself. "Good, because I don't do the whole 'pretend-to-be-someone-I'm-not' thing. Life's too short for that."

"Did I make you feel like you were pretending?" I asked, fascinated with his sudden introspection.

"Of course not." He shook his head.

"Okay, then are you about to confess something?" I teased, tilting forward slightly.

A sly grin tugged at his lips. He set his glass down and leaned in, resting his elbows on the table. "I'm not exactly the nine-to-five, clock-in, clock-out type, you see."

I smirked; my interest officially piqued. "Well, considering you own this restaurant, apparently all of West Hartford, and have ten million dollars to blow, I've determined you're either a rock star or an international spy . . . like that guy over there, who's apparently only here to serve us water."

Qualley shook his head, laughing. "No, not quite." He glanced over his shoulder at the man in black, saluting. The man saluted back; their silent exchange oddly informal. "That's Eddie," Qualley said, turning back to me. "He does various things for me. My work isn't something you'd find on a job board, but he's good help."

My smile faltered slightly as the weight of his words settled in. *I swear to God, if he's an assassin . . .* I thought to myself.

"Okay," I said cautiously. "And what exactly do you mean?" Flashing Qualley a concerned look, I spun my finger around the rim of my martini glass.

Qualley angled in closer, his voice dropping low enough to feel like a secret meant only for me. "I deal in things most people don't like to talk about. Things people want but pretend they don't."

My stomach tightened as I tried to piece together his cryptic confession. Forcing myself to stay calm, I asked, "Like . . . what?" His expression steadied, almost daring me to flinch. "You're not an assassin, are you?" I couldn't help myself—I had to ask.

"Drugs. Guns. Protection too, when the situation calls for it." He said it matter-of-factly, as though he were discussing the weather. He didn't even deny the assassin part. My mind raced, torn between the instinct to run and the undeniable pull to stay rooted in my seat and finish my French toast. There was something magnetic about him—dangerous, intoxicating.

"And you're just . . . telling me this?" I asked, my voice quiet, almost hesitant.

"Because you deserve to know," he said simply. "I don't want to lie to you, Cassandra. That's not how I do things."

The waiter arrived then, offering another martini. I accepted excitedly, without hesitation. Perhaps more alcohol would make this conversation less dense. I stared down at my new glass, tapping my fingernail against its stem as I processed his words.

"Why me?"

"What do you mean?"

"Why tell *me*? You barely know me."

A tender warmth appeared in Qualley's smile, momentarily demobilizing his self-assurance. "Because I want to get to know you. So, if I'm to do that, you should know what you're getting yourself into so there are no surprises."

Our eyes met, and for a moment, I saw something beyond the swagger—vulnerability. He was testing whether I would bolt or stay. I took a deep breath, lounging back in my seat.

"Well." I grasped my martini, taking a generous sip. "That's . . . a lot to take in. Why didn't you tell me this when I first arrived?"

"I know," he agreed. "I wanted you to eat something first before I scared you off." He sighed, reaching forward to place his hand just shy of mine. "I don't expect you to decide anything today. If you don't feel the same—no pressure, no hard feelings. I'd merely remain a loyal customer, smitten with you and your work."

Against my better judgment and despite his admission of illicit affairs, I found myself drawn in even more. I couldn't look away from the complicated man sitting across from me. I saw the man beneath the exterior—the one who carried the weight of his choices and the dangers that came with them. Much like myself, I could tell he had a past, and I wouldn't deny that I wanted to investigate.

"I'm still here, aren't I?" I said softly, a grin tugging at my lips.

He beamed, lifting his glass. "To honesty, then."

I paused, then finally, I picked up my own glass, clinking it against his. "To honesty."

As we drank, I couldn't shake the feeling that I had stepped into something I could never walk away from.

Something . . . dangerous.

This time, it wasn't because the guy was an obsessive jerk—it was because we had a connection, bound by our shared love for art. I could get past how he chose to make money; I wasn't one to judge how others spent their time.

I would let him into the madness that was my life.

I would let him call me *Cassie*.

Chapter 8

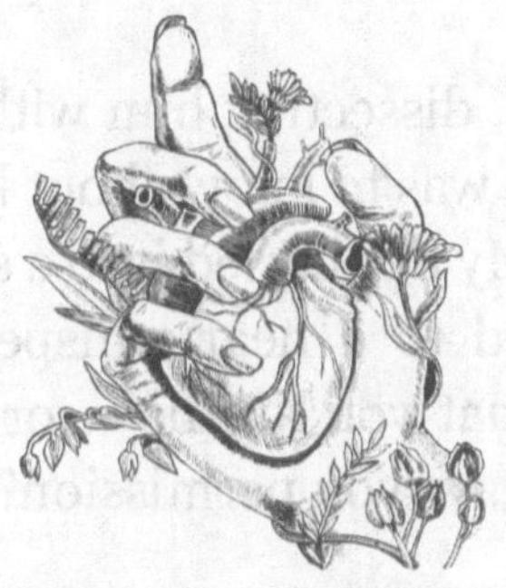

My mind drifted back to that first, sober meeting with Qualley. The café and its trill of old jazz tunes amplified the ambiance; the way his smile melted every defense I thought I had. He definitely had a way about him—a charm that made danger feel like an invitation. He disclosed his illicit identity without any concern, as if he were merely discussing his plans for later in the day. Despite my instincts screaming to stay away, I found myself drawn into his gravitational pull, entangled in the framework of his universe.

The warmth of the memory lingered, a comforting fire in the cold void of my current reality.

But reality has a cruel way of interrupting daydreams.

"Is that when it started?"

Detective James Hall's voice sliced through my thoughts. He leaned in, forearms pressed into the table's frigid surface, his posture firm with intent. His eyes—scheming—locked onto mine like he was peeling away layers I wasn't ready to shed. But there was something else behind the scrutiny: bitterness and something personal.

It almost made me laugh.

"When what started?" I acted ignorant, as if I didn't already know the answer he was fishing for.

James gestured vaguely, the rancor simmering in his face barely concealed. "When you decided none of it mattered. Rules.

Laws. Lives." He inched closer. "When he told you who he was, is that when you decided you were willing to burn everything for him?"

I cocked my head, dissecting him without a word. Though I already knew all there was to know about him. "What are you really asking, James?" My lips curled into a small, sour smile.

His voice dropped to a near whisper. "Did you love him enough to become what you are now, or were you always this monster, and he just gave you permission?"

Monster?

That's rich.

James didn't know a single thing about me. His little folder might as well have been filled with doodles of stick figures for all the accuracy it had.

Garbage. Pure, unadulterated garbage.

The man was overconfident in his assumptions, but he might well have been a toddler in a detective Halloween costume. He'd never understand clawing through the wreckage of trauma or finding beauty in it. He was the kind of guy who probably thought 'emotional depth' was something you measured in swimming pools. Besides, he'd never know about Qualley's true smile—the one that didn't just soften my pain but practically ironed it out. That smile was a masterpiece it itself, a damn life preserver in a sea of turmoil.

"You keep throwing that word around," I said, brushing hair behind my ear. "Monster. Do you think if you say it enough, it'll make you feel better? You don't know yet what I've done or why. You just want to call it evil so you don't have to look too hard at yourself."

James tensed slightly.

"Careful, James," I resumed with a sneer. "You're starting to sound a little obsessed. Are you sure this is just another case to you? Or is it something else? Something . . . ad hominem?"

"Don't flatter yourself," he said. But from where I was sitting, his eyes said otherwise.

The seconds stretched like an over-pulled rubber band. I pulled back further, ready to let it snap. "Three men. High-ranking. Dirty. All of them dead." I paused, letting my words settle. "And your wife? How's she been doing since you let that mess fester too long?"

James went completely still.

"You're not the only one who's lost people," I continued. "You think this is only about Qualley? He wasn't the beginning, you know. I had more reasons than love to start this little project."

He stared at me, unmoving.

"I see it in your eyes," I whispered, pressing on with my monologue. "You know I'm not bluffing. You're keeping me in here because you're not done yet. Because I haven't said the names you're dying to hear."

"What do you know about my wife?" he said, jaw clenched.

Cocking my head, I sat there just long enough to make him squirm. The question was crafted from his paranoia unraveling, and I knew that it bothered him. Uncertainty gnawed at the edges of his composure. He didn't know. Not yet. Not for sure. But I did. I knew everything—the details he wasn't ready to confront, the truths he hadn't dared to comprehend out loud. And that made this moment all the more satisfying.

"I know enough to understand why you're still bothering me," I said finally. "Enough to know why you haven't walked out that door, why you're wasting your time instead of handing me off to someone else."

His fingers twitched against the table, a small, involuntary gesture that betrayed the strain he was trying so hard to hide. "I'm the one calling the shots here, Kessler." He tried to sound intimidating, but he lacked conviction.

"You're really bad at hiding things, huh?" I said, the smallest trace of a smile curling at the corners of my lips. "Your family.

Your pain. The spackle you plaster over every day so no one notices. But I see it, James. I see it in the way your hands shake when you think no one's looking, in the way your voice falters when you try to sound in control. I know."

His jaw tightened further, the muscle flexing like he was seconds away from snapping. "Know what? Tell me what you know. What am I hiding?"

Shrugging, I decided to keep things difficult. Why not? It's not like I had anywhere else to be. "I don't need to spell it out for you." Pivoting my gaze to the mirror, I scrutinize our distorted reflections. "Your being here? That tells me everything I need to know. You're not here for justice. You're here for answers. *Personal* answers."

James's fingers dug into the edge of the table, gripping it like it might save him from drowning. His eyes darted around, scrambling to patch the holes I'd punched into his tidy little reality. The desperation clung to him like a bad cologne—and I was perfectly fine letting it choke him.

"You think I don't know about them" I said, my voice so soft it could've been mistaken for kindness if not for the acid laced within. "About what you're losing? About what you can't admit even when you're staring at yourself in the mirror?" I watched as his focus splintered, the sturdy fortress he'd built around himself starting to sag, crumble. "You're sitting here, James, because you know, deep down, that I'm helping you. And that eats at you, doesn't it? Having to rely on someone like me. You'd rather be here with me than face the truth."

His inhale snagged. Subtle, but predictable. I leaned back, letting the quiet creep in like a third party to the conversation. Silence was my ally. Let it twist the knife for me. I could wait. I've already come so far.

James didn't budge, but I could tell he was frustrated. He growled, "You think this is a game?"

I crossed my arms. "James, everything's a game to me. I'm

the one who remembers to bring dice."

His hands curled into fists, knuckles whitening. I could practically see the inner war raging in his head—*storm out or stay? Slam the door or sit?* He didn't want to linger, but his stubbornness—oh, it was delightful. It kept him frozen.

"Keep poking around," I warned, biting my bottom lip. "Maybe I'll toss you a breadcrumb or two. But you better behave, or I'll let you starve."

"This little act doesn't put you in control." His voice surged, but the faint shudder beneath betrayed the growing erosion of power. "You don't fool me with your 'tough guy' muse."

I leaned in, letting my voice drop to the kind of whisper that pulls people closer even when they don't want to move. Not to mention, I completely ignore what he says. "I think you're here because the truth terrifies you. Not just about me. Or them. But about you, James. The things you let rot until they start to stink." I wasn't a 'tough guy,' he was certainly right about that. But I *was* a pissed-off whirlwind with a vendetta and a hit-list. And let me tell you, I ticked those boxes like I was speed-running punishment.

His face went pale as he sat down slowly, like gravity had finally realized it hadn't been doing its job properly. "If you lie—"

"I don't lie," I cooed sweetly, lounging back as if I'd lived here all my life. "What could I possibly have already lied about? I just know how to use the truth as a baseball bat."

James reached for the file with trembling hands, the paper almost slipping through his grip. "Tell me about your mother." He shot me a look like he'd scored a strategic point in a chess match as he randomly changed the subject.

I snorted. "Ugh, the mommy card? James, darling, that move's so tired it needs a bed. She's dead to me . . ."

"Talk, Cassandra."

I let my fingertip tap the table. "You'll get your answers. Eventually. But let's not play pretend here. This isn't about my mother. Or Qualley. Or those officers I made into abstract art installations. It's about what I know. You're beating around the bush. What happened to your people, I *want* to talk about that. But you're not here to interrogate me about that, James. You're here because you're out of road, and I'm the only one left who has the atlas."

His jaw worked overtime now, the muscle twitching like it was auditioning for a supporting role in his meltdown.

"Let's talk justice," I bit out. "Yours. Mine. It's not as far apart as you like to think."

"But you *killed* people, Cassandra," he hissed through gritted teeth. "That makes you a murderer."

"I know. But you are, too," I countered, one brow arching high. "Please, James. Your hands are *covered* in blood just as red." James, funnily enough, glances quickly down at his hands. He thinks I don't notice. "You think you're a saint? A knight on a white horse? I'd think you're well old enough to know you're just another sinner trying to prove to God your benevolence."

James shot out of his seat, full of indignant energy, only to slump back into it immediately. The movement was so pathetic I *almost* felt bad for him.

"Good boy," I murmured condescendingly.

His eyes burned into mine. "You'll rot in here if you don't tell me what I need to know. You're hiding something. Stop being cryptic and nonsensical."

"Maybe," I said with a shrug. "But if I do rot in here, you'll still be sitting across from me, hoping I'll cough up answers that haunt your every sleepless night. I don't have to walk free to know I've got you exactly where I want you." He shifted in his seat. I loved watching men like him writhe in discomfort. "You don't keep me here for righteousness, James. You keep me because I'm the only one who can fix the mess you're too scared to admit is yours to own."

"Talk," he rasped, his voice cracking.

"I already am."

Chapter 9

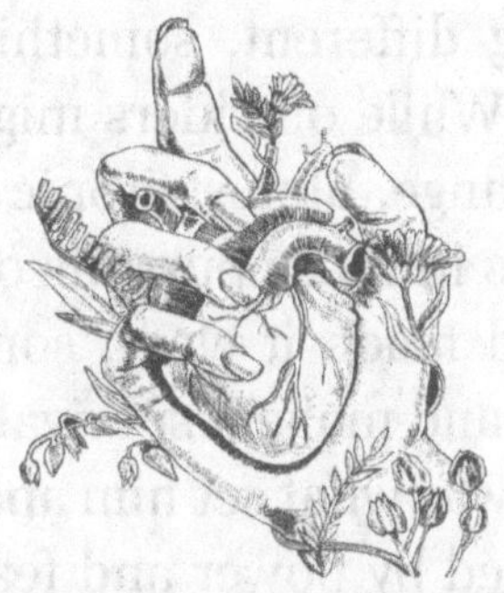

Over the course of our whirlwind romance, especially during those first few months, I began to unravel the cryptic figure that was Qualley Wallis, but his adolescent years remained shrouded in mystery. I once asked him how he ended up where he was—what had shaped the man I knew and loved so well. His response was blunt, matter of fact, but beneath the surface lay a sort of unspoken complexity.

Qualley revealed he'd grown up surrounded by drugs, weapons, and violence. I could relate to that. But it wasn't a phase or fleeting period. It was his reality; the backdrop against which his entire childhood played out. Those forces carved his path, defining a skewed view of the world long before he had a say in it.

But Qualley didn't cling to bitterness or resignation. Not like I did. He saw a potential duty in the clandestine society he'd been born into—a sense of purpose to alter the very dynamics that had influenced his upbringing. He didn't sustain that landscape to uphold its brutality; he entered to challenge it. Less harm, more empathy; his guiding principles. Ones he held himself and everyone within his orbit accountable to.

The creed wasn't just lofty ideals, it was the very foundation of the business, his empire. Qualley expected unwavering loyalty from his associates, and they respected him enough to deliver. His clients—whether motivated by fear, admiration, or pragmatism—rarely dared to test his limits.

Qualley didn't only navigate murky waters of crime, he actively built something different, something he believed could transcend its origins. While outsiders might have seen only the danger, there was strange, almost ironic humanity in his mission. He was relentless in those pursuits of change. Not to erase violence entirely—he'd made it clear, sometimes it was necessary—but to temper it and make it survivable.

And perhaps that was what set him apart.

In an industry ruled by power and fear, Qualley wielded an unorthodox weapon: *empathy*.

He didn't dwell on the past, brood, or agonize over what could've been. He was a man of the present, and I decided I was content with that. I allowed him to keep his background confidential, even though that meant I'd never fully understand forces that shaped him.

But what it didn't mean is that *I'd* keep the past out of the present.

He didn't dwell on the past, brood, or agonize over what could've been. He was a man of the present, and I decided I was content with that. I allowed him to keep his background confidential, even though that meant I'd never fully understand forces that shaped him.

But what it didn't mean is that *I'd* keep the past out of the present.

What I knew about Qualley was an expansive, sometimes expensive, generosity. Generosity so profound it could almost make you forget the veiled, criminal empire he lorded over. He gave a great deal of himself and his money to the community, without expecting applause or recognition. Quietly, in the background like some kind of morally ambiguous Robin Hood, he paid rent, food, and medical bills for struggling families in Connecticut's homeless shelters and food banks. He made philanthropic donations that repaired broken infrastructures, provided school supplies, scholarships, and brought life to community events, injecting hope into neighborhoods teetering on the edge.

Qualley didn't just give money; he invested in lives.

Animal shelters and veterinary practices benefited too. Qualley had a soft spot for animals—something he refused to advertise for fear it might damage his image of stoic authority. But I knew better. He adopted animals on kill lists with the kind of reckless abandon most people reserved for bidding wars at Sotheby's, bringing home everything from cats with three legs to dogs with heart murmurs. And he financed surgeries and treatments for dozens of households and their pets, gifting strangers the relief of holding onto their beloved companions a little longer.

To Qualley, the community wasn't an afterthought or an effort to sweep his sins under the rug; it was his attempt at redemption, even if it couldn't absolve his crimes. And that's just it. Absolution wasn't something he sought, nor did he merely throw money at problems hoping they'd go away. He genuinely wanted to make life better for others, as if their happiness could somehow fill the cracks in his own soul. To the community, if they'd ever uncovered the truth of where his money came from, Qualley might have been seen as a flawed savior—a man who did bad things but whose heart was beating defiantly in the right place.

To me, he was more than a savior or a criminal. He was a walking contradiction—a man navigating the tightrope between darkness and light. His actions didn't just cement my belief in his goodness; they reminded me why I loved him. He was madness and compassion wrapped up in one impossible package, and no matter how hard the world tried to paint him as a villain, I knew better.

Of course, James Hall's team—the self-righteous brigade—couldn't see past their own narrative. Qualley's kindness didn't fit their predetermined mold of criminals as irredeemable monsters, so they ignored it. And, naturally, they overlooked a key piece of evidence in their investigation: *me,* one person who knew Qualley better than anyone, the one they might have actually learned something from if they'd bothered to see me as anything other than collateral damage.

But who needs their approval, anyway? If Qualley taught me one thing, it's that the world thrived on oversimplified stories of heroes and bad guys, while the real truth is tangled in shades of gray. He didn't need validation, and neither do I.

Being *painted* as a villain didn't bother me.

When I came to after passing out in the interrogation room after being arrested, or as they called it, 'detained' (as if that word somehow softened the blow), Tim Fieldman had called for medical assistance. EMTs arrived and transported me to Bristol Hospital, all the while my body felt like it was floating somewhere just shy of reality. You'd think they'd leave me alone after the trauma of the day. First the gut-wrenching news about Qualley, then the collapse onto the cold metal table when my body betrayed me yet again.

Apparently, passing out and hitting my head on hard, unforgiving surfaces had become my signature move, but thankfully, this particular encore performance didn't result in a concussion. At least, not one anyone could detect. The real damage was somewhere far less tangible, buried deep in my chest where my heart used to sit before it shattered into jagged pieces.

Before it was stolen and the thief left me to bleed . . .

While unconscious, I was suspended in a strange void between awareness and oblivion. I dreamed of him. Qualley. Not the gritty, pragmatic version the world saw, but the man I loved —the one who brought warmth to the coldest nights and laughter into the emptiest corners of my soul. In the dream, we were back at the start, before all this bullshit. Sharing stolen moments of joy, his hand brushed against mine, his grin so genuine it made my knees weak.

But even in the dream, Qualley's presence felt fleeting, like holding vapor in your hands. I reached for him, called his name, but he didn't answer. Instead, his gaze lingered on me, soft yet weighted. As though he knew the world we were trying to build together had already crumbled.

And then he was gone.

Regaining consciousness halfway to the hospital, I found myself strapped to a gurney in the back of an ambulance. Beeping monitors filled the cramped space alongside rumbles from the engine. Every sound seemed to mock the disorder swirling in my mind. Two paramedics fussed over me with efficient, yet wary movements. Perhaps they thought I'd spontaneously combust if they pressed the wrong button.

Meanwhile, a uniformed officer sat nearby, staring me down like I was one breath away from sprouting horns and challenging him to a duel. Goldfinch—that sanctimonious poster boy for repulsiveness—kept his gaze locked on me, his face carved into an expression screaming suspicion and a hint of self-righteous gloating.

Air came in ragged, delicate wisps; my wrists loosely cuffed to the gurney like I was a flight risk in a five-foot-wide ambulance. A memory surged up from the depths, harsh and unforgiving: *Qualley is dead.*

I wished someone would knock me unconscious again.

That beast I felt earlier—an invisible savage lurking in the shadows of my mind—reared its head, its jagged claws wrapping me in the promise of safety, telling me all about vengeance.

The old Cassandra Kessler had gone up in metaphorical flames. What was left behind felt darker, heavier. Malevolence rooted deep within, blooming like a poisonous flower. I didn't fight it. I didn't want to.

"You killed him," I said sluggishly to Goldfinch who was playing on his phone. It wasn't a question, but rather, an assertion woven with purpose and demanding acknowledgment.

Officer Goldfinch perched on the edge of his seat, his presence brimming with the superiority of someone who believed they had the moral high ground. "I didn't kill anyone." Anyone ignorant to the situation could have mistaken it for unshakable truth. "Your man fired on officers, so those involved did what they needed to do."

I blinked at him, dumbfounded by the absurdity of his claim and the fact he couldn't even say his name out loud. "Qualley would've never done anything like that." My response came out hoarse. It was meant to be a growl, but it carried my point all the same. "He kept a weapon for protection. It's not illegal to have a weapon. He acquired it legally. He would've never turned it against a cop. He knew better. Qualley would've surrendered before it ever got that far."

Goldfinch sucked his teeth—a sound equal parts irritating and infuriating. He settled back, draping one leg across the other with the adeptness of someone who thought they were untouchable. His arms locked over his chest, head angled just enough to flash me a gaze that oozed, "Isn't that cute?"

"Tell me," I continued, narrowing my eyes. I refused to let his patronizing demeanor derail me. "Does owning a gun make you a criminal? You have a gun, don't you?"

"Of course I do. I'm a cop."

I scoffed, rolling my head toward the front of the vehicle as if I couldn't bear to look at him another second. "Yeah, and that's the excuse, isn't it? You're a cop, so it's all fine and dandy when *you* carry a weapon, but let anyone else, and suddenly it's a problem. Hypocrisy must pay well these days."

He didn't respond right away, though his teeth clenched, a tell-tale sign I'd struck a nerve. The paramedics exchanged uneasy glances, hurrying around me as if urgency alone might banish the conflict between us. I could practically visualize thought bubbles floating above their heads: *Is she dangerous? Should we be worried? Did she just sprout claws?* I felt bad for them.

They didn't deserve to be caught in this tangled mess, but I wasn't about to apologize for ruining Goldfinch's day.

My sarcasm crumbled temporarily, revealing the unfiltered ache beneath layers of pain I could no longer suppress. "Qualley wasn't perfect, but he wasn't the monster you're trying to paint him as. He was better than half the hypocrites out there with shiny badges and loaded weapons, pretending they're untouchable. But you wouldn't know that, would you? You didn't care about who he was, just about what you could label him as."

Goldfinch raised an eyebrow, that overconfident smile tugging at the corner of his mouth. "We'll get to the bottom of it." His words leaked bureaucratic detachment.

And that's when I snapped. "You *kidnapped* me." My voice carried despite the pounding in my head. "You dragged me from the front steps of my home like I was some deranged fugitive. You tackled me to the ground, carting me off like cargo, but you don't even care about why I was there—about why I ran in the first place. Would *you* sit around twiddling your thumbs if the person you loved more than life itself was in trouble? Could *you* remain calm in that situation? Because I didn't hear from Qualley longer than usual, and now he's gone. So excuse me for being human!"

"Let's focus on her vitals. Her blood pressure's spiking," one of the paramedics announced, exchanging a fleeting look with their partner before turning her attention back to me. "Please, ma'am, try to stay calm. We're almost at the hospital. Just breathe, okay? We're giving you Lorazepam to help with your anxiety." She spoke with a gentle, soothing voice, the kind that made me want to trust her.

But I didn't trust anyone anymore.

Attempting to do as the EMT ordered, I fell back against the gurney, the ceiling of the ambulance my only view. Even though it angered me more that they ordered me around, I closed my eyes, focusing on my breathing. My heart raced, and as much as

I hate to admit it, I began to cry.

I was so overwhelmed with how my life was crumbling all around me; overwhelmed with these difficult, narcissistic officers who wouldn't listen to a word I said. I couldn't accept the fact they'd made a move of self-defense rather than admitting they'd messed up.

Wouldn't anyone unravel emotionally after such a devastating loss?

I grew tired, my eyes straining to stay open as the medication they gave me took hold. Edges of the world blurred, sounds around the ambulance faded into a distant rumble.

Goldfinch was incapable of leaving well enough alone. Even with my eyes closed, I could hear him shuffle, gearing up to spout his unsolicited wisdom. After minutes of blessed silence, he finally broke it, offering his brilliant analysis like we'd been desperate for enlightenment. "All I know is the evidence was felonious. Now he's gone. That's all there is to it."

Before I could muster the strength to argue, one of the paramedics beat me to it after my heart rate had spiked. "Hey, back off. She's in shock. Let her breathe unless you're trying to make whatever mess you've got going on worse." Her voice cut through the hostility, distinct and no-nonsense. I could have kissed her for that—the perfect counterstrike when my tongue had been tied.

Still, I managed one last act of defiance before the meds pulled me under. I chuckled faintly, raising my uncuffed hand in an upward motion, popping my middle finger up at him. "Look, Finchy—a bird! You related?"

His face hardened instantly, jaw tightening like a bear trap. It was the last satisfying sight I caught before unconsciousness welcomed me, and I couldn't deny—I savored how much it riled him up.

Chapter 10

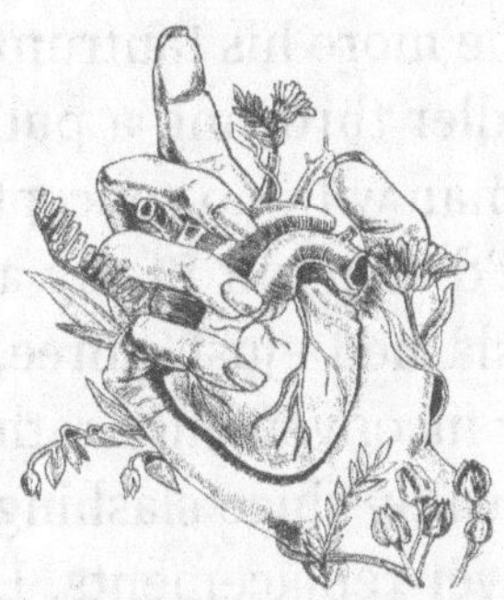

As much as you'd assume Qualley and I were deeply in love for the three years we shared together, I'd admit—only to myself, mind you—that it was his money that caught my eye first. *Who wouldn't be charmed by a man who made millions and blew it on mediocre paintings of foreign architecture? Or at least, who wouldn't pretend to be charmed with a little flair?* The lifestyle he offered was like winning a VIP ticket to indulgence, something I've never had the pleasure of experiencing. Saying no to that wasn't in my repertoire. But soon enough, the allure of posh dates and luxurious gifts and trips faded. I found myself captivated by something far more intoxicating: *him.*

His love flowed through me like a forbidden current, staining the chambers of my heart in shades no one else could see.

One of my first eye-opening realizations of my love for Qualley came a few months into our relationship, when my ex, Richard Johnson, resurfaced like a bad sequel no one asked for. "Double-Dick," as Zina and I referred to him (a nickname earned, not for charm, but for his double helping of audacity), bombarded me with threatening calls and unhinged social media messages. At first, I kept it all from Qualley, hoping radio silence would make Dick fade into obscurity.

But Dick, being his usual dicky self, had other plans.

He blamed me for the tragedy that was his spiraling life, offering no specifics, just a vague sense of "it's all your fault" energy. Apparently, accountability wasn't in Dick's vocabulary. The more I ignored him, the more his tantrums escalated. It was like trying to ignore a toddler throwing a public fit, except the toddler was a full-grown man with no concept of boundaries.

Some mornings, I'd step out of my apartment only to find three of my tires slashed—just three, because apparently Richard had a flair for inconvenience rather than thoroughness. It was a petty move, really, since slashing three tires meant my insurance wouldn't cover replacements. Luckily for me, I was a wealthy-ass bitch by then, so I just called a tow truck to haul my Sable to Dodger's Auto Depot.

Dodger, the auto shop owner with a nickname straight out of a mob movie, questioned the second incident, asking why I didn't just call the cops.

I told him flat-out, "They wouldn't do shit." Because even then I didn't trust law enforcement to do much of anything.

By the third round of tire carnage, Dodger took matters into his own hands, sequentially calling the police behind my back without letting me know. To my surprise, a cop actually showed up at my doorstep, asking for specifics and who I believed the person responsible to be.

"If I knew who it was, I'd tell you," I lied, though I knew damn well it was Dick. I was no nark.

The cop didn't buy my act, but he handed me his card with a pointed, "Well, when you're ready to tell us who you think it is, call me."

He never followed up despite his concern, and I never saw him again.

The tire slashing eventually stopped after that, but Richard wasn't done. He graduated to writing messages on my car windows in what looked like blood—things like "bitch," "slut," and "kill yourself." Honestly, it was sad how unoriginal he was. I'd just grab the hose, some dish soap, and scrub it off, moving on with my day like it was a minor hindrance to my life.

Qualley, blissfully unaware of all this drama, finally got a front-row seat to the shitshow one night after dinner. As he walked me back to my apartment, we found the door unlocked and wide open.

Someone had broken in.

That was the moment I learned Qualley carried a Glock. I should've known, and I don't know why I was all that surprised, him being a weapons dealer and all. Without hesitation, and in one fluid gesture, he pulled it out from a hidden holster in his trousers, flicked on the kitchen lights, and then—because apparently one weapon wasn't enough—produced a tactical knife from the other side.

"Take this," he ordered, handing me the knife. "Stay here."

I stared at the knife in my hand, then at him. "What if the intruder comes out here?"

"Oh, they won't make it out," he said, his voice calm, almost detached, the kind of calm that chills you far deeper than shouting ever could. Then, without missing a beat, he stormed into the apartment like he was 'Hondo' on *S.W.A.T.*, every movement precise and purposeful, his presence swallowing the room whole. It was quite the sight—this tall, built, suited man sweeping my living space with the precision of someone who'd done this a hundred times before, maybe more.

The words wrapped around me like cold steel. *They won't make it out.* The finality in his tone sent a ripple through me, equal parts unease and fascination. *Who the hell says something like that so casually?* Like it wasn't even up for debate— like it was just a foregone conclusion.

I swallowed hard, an involuntary reaction to the ridiculousness of it all. This wasn't the kind of person who bluffed. No, he was the kind who followed through, who made good on statements that most people wouldn't dare to say aloud. And the fact that he'd just waltzed into my space, dismantling any illusion of control I thought I had, left my nerves raw. But underneath the unease, there was something else I didn't want to admit. A spark of wonder, a dangerous pull toward the kind of certainty he carried with him.

What kind of life makes someone this sure of themselves? That was the question scratching at the back of my mind. And why, after everything I'd been through, didn't I want to slam the door behind him and tell him to leave?

Instead, I stood there, rooted to the spot, watching him take command of my living space like it was his right. Part of me—an infuriating part of me—wanted to know what he was going to do next.

For a moment, I thought maybe I'd just left the door open before we left for our night out. But I remembered Qualley locking it, tossing my keys into my bag, and taking my arm as we left. There was no way this was an accident.

A paranoid part of me wondered if Qualley had orchestrated the break-in himself, maybe sending one of his associates to dig up dirt on me, then acted as if this was a coincidence. But that theory crumbled when Qualley emerged from the apartment holding a note, his Glock already back in its holster.

"Who's RJ, Cassandra?" he demanded, holding a note out to me. "Tell me, right now."

I took the note, glancing up at him through my lashes, confused. At first, I had no idea who "RJ" was—until I read the note and it all clicked.

Can you hear me now, bitch? Watch your back. -RJ

Richard "Double-Dick" Johnson had struck again.

Sighing, I shoved the note into my bag and pushed past Qualley into the apartment. The scene inside was straight out of a disaster movie: dishes smashed to shards, food from the fridge strewn across the floor like some avant-garde art installation, furniture flipped over as if auditioning for a circus act. My bedroom was no better. Clothes ripped from hangers and dumped in a heap; makeup crushed into the carpet like it owed someone money. Even the bathroom wasn't spared; the mirror shattered, shampoo and body wash smeared across every surface, a toddler's finger-painting gone horribly wrong. Cleanliness must have wronged Richard in a past life, judging by his actions.

Qualley followed close behind as I inspected the state of my home, his mantra of, "Who's RJ . . . who's RJ," on repeat like a broken record. My hand flew into my hair, exasperated, the other planted firmly on my hip, pivoting to take in the topsy-turvydom. I didn't want to tell him about Richard. I'd hoped ignoring the bastard would make him disappear. But with my apartment looking like it had been ransacked by a vengeful poltergeist and the note literally screaming his name, I had no choice but to come clean.

"Richard Johnson," I blurted, collapsing onto my disheveled sofa as we returned into the living room. "My ex-boyfriend. He's been bothering me since we broke up months ago." I peeked up at Qualley, who stood before me, arms crossed, with an expression revealing a mix of concern and simmering anger. "I thought if I ignored him, he'd stop, but I guess he's very determined to complicate my life."

Qualley sat down beside me. His arm wrapped around my shoulders like a shield. "Why didn't you tell me about this, Cassie? I could've helped you." He pressed a kiss to my cheek.

"Yeah, I know," I said, leaning into his touch. "I didn't want to bother you with details from my past. Especially not about an old, stupid boyfriend who abused me."

The word 'abuse' was a trigger. Qualley sprang to his feet, all dark eyes and a jaw set like stone. He pinned his stare onto me, hardly restraining his anger. "Abuse?"

I nodded, resting my chin in my hands. "Yeah, but I'm over it now. Just trying to ignore his advances. I've already spent over a thousand dollars on new tires for my car."

"He slashed your tires too?" Qualley asked, astonished, pacing the room like a caged lion. "Anything else?"

I followed him, grabbing his forearm to ground him. "I'm okay. It was just messages. Texts and stuff written in paint on my car."

"He vandalized your car?" His voice rose, increasing with his agitation. "You really should've told me."

"I'm sorry," I whispered, fidgeting with the fabric of his suit. "I really thought he'd stop."

With his arms crossed and his posture level, Qualley's face was a crypt, locked and inaccessible to all. The soft light from the kitchen carved out deep shadows, but his piercing gaze held me in place. As my voice trembled and faltered, he remained utterly still, the storm beneath his calm exterior betrayed only by the slight flaring of his nostrils. His silence spoke volumes—already piecing together his next move

After a moment, he spoke, his voice a low rumble that carried an unexpected gentleness. "You don't have to explain yourself." The words were carefully selected, steady in their delivery. "Not to me. Not to anyone. Just let me help, *bella*."

He exuded a rare calmness, so unexpected against the usual fervor surrounding him, that I nearly doubted its sincerity. In his presence, the roles of savior and hunter intertwined, forging a loyalty I was powerless to escape. I didn't necessarily need him to be my bodyguard, but the assured safety he offered me was comforting. Something I'd never have received from anyone else, especially Double-Dick.

From that moment forward, Qualley's protectiveness warped into unbridled possessiveness, but I willingly surrendered.

He was tireless in his campaign to have me move into his home—or, as I preferred to call it, his castle—brushing off my protests like they were nothing more than the faint buzz of an annoying fly.

Thanks to Qualley's generous contributions to my bank account, I could afford practically anything in Connecticut—a luxury I'd never dreamed of while growing up in a home where safety and financial security was a foreign concept. But even with all the options at my disposal, Qualley wouldn't hear of it. I couldn't live anywhere but with him. When I showed him listings for gated communities with stellar safety records, he dismissed them outright.

"Not good enough, *Bellissima*," he'd say, brooking no argument.

Ultimately, he made the decision for me. "You're moving in." He declared it one evening, pulling out my suitcase from the closet and removing my clothes from the hangers. "End of discussion. Let's pack."

And just like that, I found myself boxing up my life and stepping into his world—a world where refuge came wrapped in a layer of attachment so deep, I could drown in it. Yet, in a strange way, it was welcomed. It was nice to have someone fuss over me for once. Qualley wasn't just a man; he was a fortress, and I was the treasure he refused to let anyone touch.

❧❧

Sitting at the kitchen counter in Qualley's house after I'd moved in (sort of), I was daydreaming, lazily stirring my untouched yogurt and granola with a spoon. My phone buzzed, and I almost didn't look at it. Morning notifications were usually a wasteland of spam emails and social media updates. But this was different.

A news alert.

Man Found Dead Near New Haven Docks – Possible Homicide Investigation Underway.

The headline alone made my stomach drop. But it was the name in the first paragraph that set my pulse hammering.

Richard Johnson, 25, was found dead late last night, authorities confirm. Sources indicate the body was discovered near the docks in an apparent homicide. Police have yet to release any details on suspects or motives.

The spoon slipped from my fingers, clinking against the ceramic bowl. The words on my screen blurred, though I couldn't stop rereading them.

Richard was dead.

Dead.

With all the dark wishes I'd harbored against him, you'd expect some semblance of peace now. I should have celebrated the fact that his toxic presence had finally been scrubbed from my life. Instead, unease coiled in my stomach, cold and tight. The timing . . . it was too perfect. Too precise. Like a well-tied bow on a gift I hadn't asked for. My grip on the phone tightened as a single name rose in my mind like smoke.

Qualley.

I didn't want to believe it, but that whisper of doubt grew louder with every passing second. Slowly, I turned to where he stood, effortlessly poised at the opposite counter. He was dressed as he normally was, a crisp white shirt with its sleeves rolled to his forearms, exuding casual elegance, as if nothing in the world had shifted, as if the news I'd just read was no more significant than a passing weather update.

"Did you see this?" I asked carefully. I flipped the phone around so he could see the headline.

Qualley moved, unhurried, setting down his coffee mug and dabbing at the corners of his mouth with a napkin. He glanced at the screen, then back to me, his expression giving away absolutely nothing.

"Hm," he murmured, leaning back against the counter. "Well, well. Look at that."

"That's all you have to say?" I asked, incredulous. My voice cracked slightly, betraying the tension humming beneath my skin.

"What is there to say?" His eyes met mine. Dark. Unreadable.

The room appeared to shrink around us as silence stretched taut, a string about to snap. I searched his face for any trace of guilt or amusement, anything that might hint at what he was thinking or feeling beneath his calm. But there was nothing. Just a cool, impassive mask he wore so well.

I swallowed hard. "I told you about him, someone you haven't previously met. I told you what he was doing to me; what he'd done to me. And now this happens?" My words were sharper than I intended, but I couldn't help it.

Qualley's gaze didn't waver. If my accusation fazed him, he didn't show it. Instead, he took a step toward me. His presence always filled the room like an approaching thundercloud.

"Cassie." The way he said my name—uncertain, hesitant—told me everything. "You think I did this?"

I hesitated. *Did I?* The pieces fit together too neatly. And yet, with him standing there, watching me like he already knew the answer, I wasn't sure if I wanted the truth—or if I could stomach it. Or perhaps . . . I felt some other way.

He reached out, his hand brushing mine. "I'd never let anyone hurt you." It was a promise wrapped in warning. "You know that."

The words were meant to reassure me, but they only stirred more questions. *What did "not letting anyone hurt me" entail for someone like Qualley?* The way he said it, the way he owned it, sent a shiver down my spine—not of fear, but of something darker. Something I couldn't name.

"Some people get what's coming to them," he said over his

shoulder, as if it were a simple truth of the universe. He turned away, picking up his coffee like we'd just discussed our day and not a homicide tied to my ex.

I stared at his back, trying to decide if he was speaking in hypotheticals or if he'd just confessed in the most nonchalant way possible. Either way, one thing was clear: if Qualley had been involved, I'd never know for sure. In his business, revealing your cards always led to disaster. And maybe, just maybe, I didn't want to know for sure.

The room seemed to fold in on itself, the air thick with unspoken words and meanings I dared not unravel. The sunlight poured through the window, carving pointed angles across Qualley's features, emphasizing the rugged line of his jaw and the usual focus in his eyes. He leaned closer still, the faint scent of his cologne mingling with coffee and danger.

"You're too curious for your own good." His finger traced along my jawline, each touch sending lightning through my nerves. "Curiosity can be dangerous, you know."

I swallowed, trying to muster the courage to break through the fog he'd wrapped around me. "I just . . . I need to know."

His chuckle was low, the kind that echoed in the chest rather than the air. "What is it you want to know, darling? The truth? Sometimes, facing the truth can be far more unsettling than living with the unknown."

Qualley's words wove through my thoughts like creeping ivy, tangling in places I couldn't ignore. I didn't want to agree, but I couldn't push back, either. His presence was a tidal wave I wasn't strong enough to resist.

"Richard was—" I began, but his finger against my lip silenced me.

"Richard's gone," he said firmly, a finality hitting me like a gavel. "And that's all you need to understand, my love. He abused you. Don't waste a single breath on pity or regret."

He dropped his hand, turning away to the sink like the moment never happened. The mundanity of rinsing his plate and coffee mug during this serious conversation felt unnerving, as if he was trying to wash away the traces of what I knew he had arranged.

I stared at his back, the news alert continuing its crushing hold on my chest. Unanswered questions circled in my mind, biting at me like horseflies. I glanced back at the headline, reality sinking in. Richard was dead. Gone. And Qualley's involvement—whether imagined or dreadfully real—hung over the morning like a wild animal I couldn't escape.

Yet somehow, the uncertainty of his actions wasn't what truly unsettled me. It was the fact that I wasn't sure I even wanted answers.

It took me a while to admit I had another gnawing frustration inside me. Richard's death wasn't unsettling because of Qualley's involvement—it was unsettling because *I* hadn't been the one to act. The satisfaction of seeing him gone, dulled by the fact that I hadn't played a role in his downfall. I had been a spectator in my own story, and that realization burned hotter than any anger I'd ever felt toward Richard.

Qualley had handled it with his usual influence, an efficiency that left no room for doubt or loose ends. And while I appreciated the safety his actions afforded me, I couldn't shake the feeling of resentment foaming within me.

It wasn't enough to be protected.

I wanted to be the one holding the weapon; the one deciding when and how justice would be served—if the victim would live . . . or die.

The thought grew louder with each passing day, a dark whisper that refused to be silenced. It wasn't just about Richard anymore—it was about reclaiming control and proving to myself that I wasn't some fragile thing to be shielded. I could be the storm, the reckoning. And when the time came, I wouldn't hesitate.

The first time I voiced this to Qualley, he didn't react the way I expected. There was no shock, no attempt to dissuade me. Instead, he studied me with that unreadable expression of his, the one that made me feel like he could see straight through me. Like he knew what the future held.

"You're not the same woman you were when we met," he said. "And that's not a bad thing."

He seemed impressed, but I didn't know what to say to that, so I said nothing. His words resonated, nonetheless, ringing in quiet moments alone with my thoughts. He was right. I wasn't the same. And the more I thought about it, the more I realized I didn't want to be.

The next time someone crossed me, I wouldn't wait for Qualley to step in. I wouldn't sit idly by, hoping for someone else to clean up the mess. I would take matters into my own hands, and I would do it on my own terms.

The thought of it didn't scare me. If anything, it thrilled me. The idea of taking control, of reclaiming the power that had been stripped from me, was intoxicating. I could feel the shift happening, the darkness creeping in at the edges of my mind. And I didn't push it away. I welcomed it.

Qualley, of course, noticed the change. He always did. But he didn't react, nor did he try to stop me. If anything, he seemed almost . . . proud. Like he had been waiting for this moment, for me to step into the role he had always known I was capable of playing.

"You'll be careful," he said one night, randomly. It wasn't a question.

"Always," I replied, meeting his gaze with a steadiness that surprised even me.

He nodded, a small smile tugging at the corner of his lips. "Good. Because once you start, there's no going back."

Chapter 11

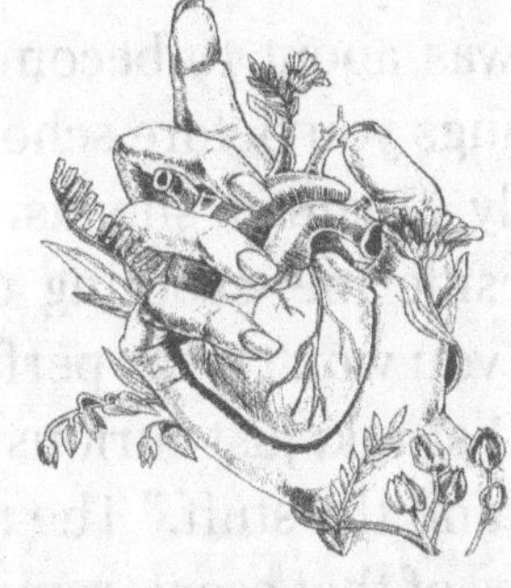

It was after the third sleepless night in Bristol, after nightmares and the shame of Qualley seeing me unravel, that I realized I could trust him. *Really* trust him. It crept up on me like most important things do—not all at once, but in fragments, in moments like this one.

We sat on the marble floor of the kitchen in the mansion, backs against wall; the sound of the radiator filled the silence between us. It wasn't the first time we'd done this, but it felt different now. Closer. I'd made grilled cheese with the last of the bread I'd brought from my apartment and the cheap slices of cheese from the gas station up the road. He didn't complain. He never did. He ate it like it was made with the finest ingredients, and that small gesture of kindness chipped away at my defenses.

Neither of us spoke as we ate, until he finally did. "Do you ever miss her?" He asked softly, like he wasn't sure if he had permission.

It took me a second to realize he meant my mother. I stared down at my sandwich like it held the answer, the question settling on my chest. "No," I said flatly. Then, after a beat, "But I think I miss the idea of her. You know, someone motherly."

He didn't interrupt. He never did when I talked about myself. That's what made Qualley different—he didn't fill the gaps with platitudes or shallow reassurances. He didn't interject his own life experiences. He just let me speak, let me empty myself without judgment.

"She had this perfume," I continued quietly. "Some floral, sugary crap she could barely afford. But every time she put it on, I thought maybe she was about to become . . . that mom. You know? The kind who hugs you before school and actually means it." I laughed resentfully. "Instead, she just smelled like lies."

Qualley shifted beside me, scooting closer to put his arm around me. "That why you won't wear perfume?" He wasn't condemning me or saying I stunk, just curious.

I nodded. "Can't stand the stuff." The memories clung to me like the sticky sweetness of that scent, reminders of the promises that never came true.

The silence that followed felt dense, almost sacred. He didn't try to fill it. He let me sit with it, letting my words settle around me. That's one of the reasons I knew I loved him—he didn't rush me to the finish line. He gave me the space to take my time, to find my way through the mess.

"Do you think about your dad much?" Qualley's voice was low, easy. His gaze was steady—not pressing, just open. He wasn't prying, only giving me space to step forward if I wanted. He knew how much my father meant to me; the emotion that came with saying his name out loud. That question hit different. It tugged at something raw and tender inside me, a part of me I'd spent years burying. My throat tightened, and for a moment, I thought I might choke on the truth.

My fingers tightened around the hot chocolate I hadn't touched, the warmth barely registering against the chill inside my chest. "I don't have to think about him," I said. "He's always there. A recurring plot twist I can't escape."

Qualley remained silent, but I could feel his attention, the way it lingered without crowding me. I exhaled sharply, the words spilling out before I could stop them. "He's in jail. Has been since I was just about to graduate high school. This time for ten years in Queensboro. A substance abuse program, apparently." I scoffed. "You'd think he'd have the routine down by now."

Qualley rested his head against the wall, his expression thoughtful. "You sound mad at him. Are you?"

My grip on the mug faltered. "I don't know." I really wasn't sure how I felt, the emotions were jumbled together, like a necklace that has that infuriating knot in it you just can't get out. "Mad, disappointed, tired—all of it. He's not perfect, but he tries, at least. He always tries, even when everything is against him." My voice softened, bitterness giving way to something softer. "He loves me. I know he does. At least, in his own way. That's more than I can say for *her*."

"She never tried?" Qualley asked warily.

I cackled, shaking my head. "She did, but not for the right reasons. She's the villain who convinced everyone she was the hero. She called the cops on him, you know? Turned him in. All while sneaking him drugs to make sure he'd fail. That's what she wanted—to win, no matter the cost."

"And what did that cost you?" Qualley asked.

I stared at him, but he was still staring at the ceiling, his head resting against the wall. The question pulled me deeper into the mess I'd worked so hard to bury. "Isn't it obvious?" I'd never had a true family, and I'd be damned if my devil of a mother would keep me from the one person who actually enjoyed my existence. "But I fight for him. Even when I shouldn't."

"Do you regret it?" he asked.

My gaze dropped to the floor, memories swirling, raw and unforgiving. "Sometimes. But I couldn't give up on him even if I wanted to. I don't know what that says about me, but I couldn't let him drown—not entirely."

Qualley didn't respond right away. "You love him. That says enough."

"He isn't perfect," I resumed. "Hell, he's a disaster. Addicted, unreliable. I think . . . I think he loves me in the only way he knows how."

Qualley turned his head toward me. "You talk about him like he's a hero." There was no trace of irony in his voice.

I smiled faintly, my eyes stinging as memories surfaced—both good and bad, tangled together in a way that made it impossible to separate. "Maybe he is." I surprised myself with my admittance. "Just a broken one. Heroes aren't inherently perfect."

We sat there on the floor against the wall, our hands brushing but never quite touching, and it was in moments like these that I realized how much I needed Qualley. Not just as someone to hold me up, but as someone who saw through me, past barriers I'd built to protect myself.

"I think I'd forgive my dad for everything," I said, each word feeling like it was being dragged out of me. "But her? I could watch her burn and feel nothing." For a moment, I felt exposed as Qualley listened to me speak.

"It's not that you wouldn't feel anything, Cassie." His expression was unreadable, but his eyes were soft, filled with something I couldn't name. "You'd feel everything, you just wouldn't let it show."

The words unraveled something inside me, but I couldn't bring myself to respond. I couldn't explain how good it felt to be seen so clearly, but also how much it hurt to reveal these things about myself. Instead, I let the silence speak for me, letting it say the things I didn't have the strength to admit out loud. That the anger, the pain, the abandonment—they all still lived inside me, howling like ghosts in a house no one had the courage to tear down. And for the first time, I wondered if I could let Qualley step further inside that house, even as it crumbled around me.

👁 👁

When my parents were still pretending to be in love—and honestly, their performances deserved Oscars—my dad was neck--deep in drugs. Our run-down house in New York, with its sagging roof and windows that rattled with every gust of wind, transformed into an abode of shady characters. These weren't the 'cool' kind of shady, like spies or secret agents. No, these were the kind that made you instinctively hold your breath and hope they didn't notice you lurking in the corner.

Despite his addiction, my dad had boundaries. Sure he spent most days chasing highs and bad decisions, but he somehow managed to protect me from it all. He'd lock me in my room when his sketchy 'friends' came over—a thin wooden door serving as my fortress. Not exactly knight-in-shining-armor material, but hey, A for effort. No matter how fortified the walls, the threat always trickled through, lingering unseen but deeply felt. The walls of my room felt like they could collapse under the burden of it all.

But things fell completely apart one day.

My mom came home from work only to find my dad and his posse snorting cocaine like they were in some grungy 80's music video.

I missed the spectacle—the chaos unfolding behind closed doors—while I sat in the stifling confines of a classroom. But the aftermath awaited me. As my school bus rolled to a stop, the sound of idle chatter dying down, my classmates leaned toward the windows, craning their necks for a glimpse of the drama. Police officers stood like sentries, blocking my path to the house I had once called home. Their outstretched arms kept me back, a silent wall that spoke volumes about the trouble waiting inside.

An unsettling prelude to the turmoil yet to come.

For a hot second, I thought someone had died. But instead of body bags and coroners, I saw my dad, handcuffed and sitting in the back of a police car, flanked by two of his favorite partners-in-crime.

Cue my mom, now in full-blown meltdown mode, shouting at the cops with a fury that could've made the devil himself cower. I couldn't make out her words, but her sheer intensity was unforgettable. Once the police drove away, that chapter closed—my dad vanished from my life except for the occasional phone call from jail or wherever he managed to crash.

After my mom packed up what was left of her shattered pride, she dragged us to my grandmother's house in the city, Queens. If you're imagining a warm haven with cookies and hugs, think again. My grandmother's boyfriend turned out to be the kind of nightmare that crawled out from beneath the bed—literally. At first, he was subtle in his creepiness—rifling through my underwear drawer and sniffing my clothes like some depraved bloodhound. But then, it escalated.

His late-night 'visits' became horrifying routine. I'd wake to his looming presence, his touch a violation that left me frozen in terror. Telling my grandmother was a lesson in futility; she turned the blame on me, accusing me of 'coercing' him. My mother wasn't much better, dismissing my words with a slap and accusations of being an "attention-seeking whore" (her words, not mine). That's when I nicknamed him 'False Grandpa'—because, let's be real, there was nothing remotely grandfatherly about him.

The summer under that roof became the longest, darkest stretch of my life. Every day was a battle against betrayal, fear, and the bitter realization that the people meant to protect me—my own damn family—were the ones doing the most damage.

By the time my parents finalized their divorce, my mom uprooted us to Bristol. No farewell to my dad, no closure—merely the latest installment of disorder.

Her abuse took on new forms after the hospital debacle. She dropped the physical side of things (not out of kindness, I assure you), embracing psychological warfare instead. This involved making me get a job and buy my own food. Picture me, a teenager stocking shelves at Amy's corner store, trying to ignore the growling in my stomach and the relentless grind of survival.

"You think I'm selfish?" she hissed one day, practically cackling. "I'll show you selfish."

And then, just when I thought I'd hit my limit, she vanished, leaving without so much as a sticky note goodbye. She just disappeared, leaving behind a haunting stillness, two weeks of unanswered calls, disconnected numbers, and the sinking realization that she wasn't coming back. The space felt abandoned—because, well, it was.

That's when I learned the art of lying and manipulation: to my landlord, Mrs. Morris, I claimed my mom was in New York, caring for her own mother. Mrs. Morris didn't press for details as long as the rent arrived on time.

Living alone at seventeen was a crash course in survival no one asks for but somehow endures. Between school, work, and the gnawing anxiety of keeping it all afloat, the quiet moments at the kitchen table became the backdrop to questions too big for someone my age: *How did I end up here? Why was surviving such a solitary affair?*

And yet, midst the upheaval, there was a bittersweet sense of relief. The silence, all-consuming as it was, meant no more cruel words or stinging bruises. Independence was mine, even if it came at a devastating price. Her absence became a scar—a visible message that I'd never been enough for her to love, to stay for, or to nurture.

Bit by bit, I transformed survival into strength—or so I told myself. I built walls so high around my heart that even Rapunzel would've needed an escape plan. Trust was a luxury I'd learned to live without. Relying on myself became my creed, and while loneliness was a constant companion, it was better than letting someone close enough to hurt me.

The funny thing? I convinced myself this wasn't just survival —it was *power*. But in those solitary hours, as I stared at the peeling wallpaper of my empty kitchen, I sometimes wondered if it was more than that. Maybe it was something else: a scar carried in plain sight, stitched together with every silent vow that

I'd never let anyone see the cracks in my armor.

Because if I could survive that summer, I could survive anything.

The day my father walked out of prison I was an adult and had been for a while. The sky hung heavy, unheeding; a merciless shade of gray that seemed to swallow the horizon whole. It was as though even the world knew how fragile hope was—how one step forward could easily crumble into ten steps back. I'd convinced myself that this was the start of something new, something good. But as it turns out, storms have a way of forewarning us.

Even when we don't want to listen.

I hadn't seen my dad save for fleeting, disjointed conversations on prison phone lines and a few quick visits on birthdays and holidays. His voice, cracking through static, was always distant—not just physically, but emotionally. Yet there he was, stepping onto the curb outside Queensboro Correctional Facility, a thin duffel bag slung over his shoulder. Time had not been kind to him. He looked smaller, diminished, his once-muscular frame reduced to angles and exhaustion. His beard, now streaked heavily with gray, framed a face that carried the weight of every lost year, every bad decision, every promise broken.

His eyes found me first, scanning for something familiar to anchor him. But before he said a word, his gaze shifted to Qualley, standing beside me like some unspoken buffer between the past and the fragile present.

I told my dad all about Qualley, leaving out his true profession, of course. I had gone to visit him for Christmas. He listened to me speak, nodding occasionally, but his expression remained largely unreadable. Years of confinement had dulled the instinct to react.

"You seem happy," he had said at last, carefully, as if happiness was something breakable. "Can't wait to meet him."

I waited for more. A teasing remark, a fatherly warning, something. But instead, he just leaned back, hands folded in front of him, gaze drifting to the cracks in the prison floor. He wasn't indifferent—just distant, like happiness was something he could acknowledge but not touch, or felt he didn't deserve.

But now that my dad stood in front of both of us, I hoped he was ready to begin his new life. A happier one.

"Didn't expect a welcome committee," Dad joked, stripped of his old bravado.

Qualley flashed a grin, his signature easy charm that always seemed to disarm anyone in its path. "I like to make good first impressions." He took my dad's bag without hesitation. The gesture felt natural, seamless, allowing my father to turn to me and greet me without the weight of the world—or his luggage—holding him back.

My dad managed a chuckle, a sound that carried years of weariness. He clapped Qualley lightly on the shoulder. The gesture wasn't entirely full of warmth, but it wasn't cold either. It was the best he could do.

And then, as though trying to find his footing in a world that had moved on without him, he turned to me. I practically fell into him as his arm wrapped around my shoulders. A little awkward, a little hesitant. But I welcomed it all the same, and so did he. I took one of his hands in mine like it was the last lifeline in an ocean of uncertainty. For just a moment, I let myself believe that this marked the beginning of healing. That we could rebuild.

"Well, sweetheart," Dad said, "let's get this ride over with."

We drove him back to the house. The silence during the ride was suffocating, filled with words neither of us knew how to say. He didn't even react to the massive mansion we led him into when we got there.

The first few weeks weren't awful. Dad mostly stayed out of

the way, claiming a spot in the backyard as his sanctuary. There, he'd sit for hours, cigarette in hand, staring at the sky with a vacant expression. It was as though the world was moving around him, and he couldn't figure out where he belonged within it anymore. Prison had aged him in ways I couldn't fully comprehend. It hadn't just stolen years; it had stolen pieces of him—the vibrant, flawed, frustrating man I'd once known, leaving behind someone quieter, someone haunted.

Qualley, ever the fixer, always seemed to know just what to do without being asked. Every few days, he'd casually drop a fresh pack of cigarettes onto Dad's lap—a quiet gesture that said, "I see you, and I know what you need, even if you won't say it." It wasn't just the cigarettes, though. It was the scotch he'd pour out in heavy tumblers, the way he'd grab a seat beside Dad on the back porch, and the unspoken understanding that lingered between them. Dad never asked for the cigarettes or the scotch, but the ritual persisted, as though it was their silent agreement: *we'll just sit here, together, and that's enough.*

I'd watch them from the kitchen window sometimes or from the studio in the backyard, the sight of them side-by-side tugging at something deep in my chest. Qualley, with his relaxed posture and effortless charm, had a way of making people feel at ease. My father, hardened by years of mistakes and regrets, seemed to soften in his presence. They'd sit there for hours, drinks cradled in their hands, cigarette smoke curling up into the twilight sky.

What did they talk about? I honestly couldn't say. I never had the courage to eavesdrop. It felt too sacred, too intimate to intrude upon. But I liked to imagine their conversations were a mix of shared stories, laughter, and maybe even silences that spoke louder than words. All I knew was that my dad seemed lighter afterward, his burdens a little less crushing for a while. And I think, in his own way, he loved that company. Qualley had a way of showing up for people, even those who didn't know how to ask for help.

It warmed my heart, seeing them together. These were my two favorite men—no, my two favorite people in the world (sorry, Zina). And though Qualley had a knack for charming just about anyone he met, there was something special about the bond he formed with my dad. It wasn't just a friendship; it was a lifeline, an anchor in uncertain waters.

Qualley's kindness didn't end with the cigarettes or the scotch or the easy camaraderie. One evening, as they sat outside, I overheard Qualley say something that made my breath catch in my throat.

"You know, you can stay here as long as you want." He said it casually, like it was the most natural thing in the world. "You don't need to worry about anything. We've got you."

Dad didn't respond right away. He took a long drag from his cigarette, staring out at the trees swaying in the evening breeze. Then he looked at Qualley, and though his voice was broken, I could hear the emotion in it. "Thanks, kid. Means more than you know."

In that moment, I saw a glimpse of something in my dad that I hadn't seen in a long time: *relief*. Not just from the stress of life, but from the worry of feeling like a burden. And I saw in Qualley what I'd always known to be true: his ability to love selflessly, to give without expecting anything in return. It was beautiful and heartbreaking all at once.

Those evenings on the porch became their refuge, a space where they could simply exist without judgment or expectation. And for me, it was enough to know that Dad wasn't alone. Even in the quietest, hardest moments, he had someone other than myself there who cared—someone who understood. It didn't erase the pain of what was coming, but it softened the edges, made it a little more bearable. In some strange, positive way, it reminded me that even in the face of loss, connection—real, human connection—could still be found, and it could still matter. It wasn't about fixing everything or making it all okay. It was about showing up, sitting together, and saying, in the simplest, quietest way, "You're not alone."

Watching Qualley care for my dad with such quiet, unassuming grace felt like witnessing something divine. It wasn't about grand gestures or extravagant sacrifices—it was the simplicity of his actions that struck me. Each cigarette handed over without a word, each glass of scotch poured like it was the most natural thing in the world. Sitting there, shoulder to shoulder with my dad, offering companionship without expectation or judgment, it was beautiful. It was an unspoken language. One of subtle kindness that didn't need millions or even a single cent to matter. It was priceless in its own right.

In those moments, I realized something profound: Love isn't measured by the size of the gestures—it's in the quiet acts of care, the willingness to show up even when it's hard, the ability to make someone feel seen and valued when they need it most. And that's exactly what Qualley did. He didn't just care for my dad; he made him feel like he belonged, like he was worth something, even in his most fragile state.

It was in the way Qualley treated my father—not as a burden, but as a person deserving of dignity and compassion—that I felt the walls around my heart crumble. I had always loved him, of course, but this was different. This wasn't infatuation or fleeting passion; it was the kind of love that roots itself deep, the kind that feels unshakable. Qualley wasn't just someone I loved. He was someone I trusted with the most vulnerable, unguarded parts of myself—and with the people I loved most.

That's when I knew. I knew without a doubt that he would be the one I'd spend the rest of my life with. It wasn't just because of his charm, his humor, or the way he always seemed to know exactly what to do or what I wanted or what I needed. It was because of this—his capacity to give so altruistically, to make someone feel cared for without expectations. In those quiet moments on the porch, when he bridged the gap between himself and my dad, I saw the kind of man he was. And I knew he was my forever. For all the turmoil that had defined so much of my life, this was one thing I was sure of: Qualley wasn't just the love of my life. He was my anchor, my safe harbor. And seeing him care for my father with such tenderness only solidified what I already knew deep down—I wanted him by my side, for every moment, for all the days we had left to share.

But as the weeks turned into months, the cracks began to show. My father—my imperfect, delicate father—was losing himself all over again. The backyard became another kind of prison, the world outside an unfamiliar and intimidating wilderness he wasn't equipped to navigate. He didn't lash out or spiral into visible chaos, but his silence grew dense, his presence more distant.

Sometimes I'd find him staring at the old photographs I'd given him of us, his fingers tracing faces and memories that felt like they belonged to another lifetime. Other times, I'd catch him watching me—not in the loving, proud way a father looks at his child, but in a way that seemed to carry an apology. Like he wanted to say something but couldn't find the words.

One night, the storm returned. Not the one in the sky—the one that had been brewing inside him all along. He sat at the kitchen table, hands trembling as he tried to light a cigarette. The lighter fell to the floor, and he stared at it like it was the most formidable object in the world. When I picked it up and handed it back to him, he looked at me, his eyes full of regret, pain, and something I couldn't quite name.

"I'm sorry, Cassie," he whispered, barely audible. "For everything."

And in that moment, I knew. I knew that no amount of love, no amount of hope or effort, could fill the emptiness inside him. The years he'd lost weren't just gone—they'd hollowed him out, leaving a man who was trying, but not living.

The storm outside raged even more as I sat across from him,

and it swirled down onto both of us. And as I looked at my father—his shoulders slumped, his spirit dimmed—I felt the sharp sting of reality. I had wanted so desperately to believe that things could be different, that we could rebuild what was lost. But some things, some people, aren't meant to be fixed.

That night, as the storm finally faded, I realized the truth. Getting him back didn't mean getting him whole. And maybe it never would.

In early May, just weeks after his release, Dad called me and Qualley to the dining table after dinner. The sound of his knuckles tapping against the worn wooden surface echoed in the quiet room, a steady rhythm that deceived the nerves he was trying to hide. His eyes, usually so expressive, were clouded, shadowed by something I didn't want to name. I could feel the tempest brewing long before he opened his mouth.

"I had a doctor's appointment before I got out," he began quietly, as if he were reciting someone else's news. His gaze didn't lift from his fidgeting hands. "I'd been having trouble breathing, coughing up blood. You know, weird stuff. Concerning stuff." He paused, drawing in a deep, careful breath as though it pained him just to continue. "I had tests done, and they found what's called small cell lung cancer."

The words landed like a sucker punch to my chest. My own lungs forgot how to work, and the air seemed to vanish from the room, leaving me suffocated. Tears sprang to my eyes before I could stop them, spilling hot and fast onto my cheeks. I buried my face in my hands, as though shielding myself from the reality of what he'd just said would somehow make it less real. Qualley's arm wrapped around me, pulling me close, his silent presence the only thing keeping me from falling apart completely. He reached out to grasp my dad's hand.

Dad cleared his throat, the sound rough and ragged. He held on tight to Qualley. "The docs found it before I got out." He said it as though recounting an unfortunate but inevitable fact of life.

"But . . . well, you know how it is. They didn't exactly have the means for treatment in there so they let me out early. Good behavior, they said."

The hell does that mean? I wanted to shout. *Good behavior? Like that's a consolation when your lungs are betraying you from the inside out?* His release wasn't a second chance at life; it was merely a concession, a parting gift from a system that had long since decided he was a lost cause, one that, apparently, refused to help him time and time again. A tightness in my throat swallowed the words I wanted to say. I couldn't find words that could match the enormity of what he was expressing.

"How bad is it?" Qualley asked calmly; the backbone I couldn't be in that moment. As always, he managed to ask the practical questions when I couldn't even form a coherent thought. His posture shifted forward, fingers interlocked, as he concentrated on my dad.

"Bad enough," Dad replied, scratching his jaw. His pause was almost imperceptible, but I caught the hesitation, the way he braced himself for the conversation. "With treatment, maybe a few months. Maybe more if I'm lucky."

A few months.

Only a few more fucking months?

The words reverberated like a death knell in my mind, louder than any thunderstorm that could have raged outside. My father—the man who had once seemed larger than life, who had weathered so much already, who had been my solid ground in an ever-shifting world—was dying. And there was nothing I could do to stop it. My chest felt tight, like I was drowning in the words I couldn't bring myself to say.

Before I could even attempt a response, Qualley spoke. "Then we'll get you treatment." His was resolute, brooking no argument. "The best in the state.

Dad blinked, his brows lifting in surprise. "That's—"

"No discussion," Qualley assured. "You're Cassie's father.

And you're part of the Wallis family now."

For a moment, no one spoke, the only sound being the faint buzz of the refrigerator in the background. Dad looked at Qualley, his eyes wide, searching, as though trying to find some hidden catch in those words. When none came, his expression softened, the shadow of something—reprieve maybe? Gratitude? — flitting across his face.

I didn't argue. I didn't question why Qualley would make such a generous offer for a man he'd only known for a few months in person. Maybe it was for me. Maybe it was because he saw something in my father worth fighting for. Or maybe it was some deeper, unspoken reason that I couldn't begin to understand. It didn't matter. None of it mattered. All that mattered was that, for the first time since I'd heard the word 'cancer,' there was a glimmer of hope. However slim, however fleeting, it was enough to hold onto.

But even as I clung to that hope, I couldn't shake the sinking feeling in my gut. There was this quiet whisper in the back of my mind that warned me not to get too comfortable. Because hope, like everything else in life, comes with no guarantees. And while I wanted to believe that this was just another setback we could weather together, a part of me knew that some blows leave scars too deep to heal.

By the end of May, Dad had started chemotherapy sessions at Smilow Cancer Hospital in Greenwich, Connecticut. A place with gleaming hallways and staff who wore smiles designed to mask the gravity of their work. Qualley ensured my Dad had access to the best care, the kind that might have felt out of reach in a different life. I was grateful, of course, but gratitude had a hollow ring to it when weighed against the reality of what was happening.

The first few sessions were hard on my dad, but his stubbornness carried him through. He'd try to joke about it, calling himself 'Baldy' when clumps of his hair started falling out or insisting he could pass for Vin Diesel if you squinted hard enough. I'd laugh for his sake, but the truth was, every strand he lost felt like a small piece of him was slipping away. The man who had once seemed invincible, larger-than-life even in his flaws, was shrinking before my eyes. His shoulders slumped more each day, and his once-strong hands trembled when they reached for the mug of tea I'd made him every morning.

By mid-June, the jokes stopped. The treatments drained him of his energy, leaving him a ghost of the man I'd grown up with. He spent most of his time lying on the couch, staring out the window at nothing in particular. I'd catch him tracing his fingers along the faded fabric of the armrest, as if supporting himself in the texture of something familiar. I'd sit beside him sometimes, holding his hand. No words. I was too afraid to say the wrong thing.

July came and went in a blur of more doctor's appointments and quiet evenings filled with fear. Like if that day would be the last. His appetite dwindled until he was barely eating. Even the foods he used to love—the greasy burgers he'd beg me to grab on my way home, the homemade chicken soup I'd tried to replicate from some Pinterest recipe. It all held no appeal. I'd leave plates in front of him, but they'd go untouched. I pretended not to notice the way his body seemed to shrink a little more with each passing day.

The house grew quieter as the summer dragged on. A kind of quiet that pressed down on you, smothering in its stillness. The sound of his hacking coughs and labored breaths filled the mansion from every direction, a constant reminder of the battle he was losing. The cigarettes stopped—a small, bitter victory in a war where every other front felt like a retreat. I wanted to celebrate it, to tell him how proud I was, but the irony of it all caught in my throat. *What was the point of quitting now, when the damage was already done?*

By August, he struggled to make it out to the backyard, the

place that had been his sanctuary since coming here. I'd watch him from the kitchen window as Qualley helped him into a chair, wrapping him in a blanket despite the warmth of the summer sun. The two of them sitting together in quiet companionship. Qualley, for all his fanfare and edginess, had a softness to him I'd never fully understood until then. He'd light a cigarette for himself but never offer one to Dad. An act of respect that spoke volumes.

September arrived with its crisp air and changing leaves, a season that always seemed to carry the burden of endings. I could see it in the way Dad's eyes lingered on me, as if trying to memorize my face. I could feel it in the heaviness that settled over the house, in the way he'd reach for my hand and hold it just a little longer than necessary. He didn't have to say it—I knew.

One evening, as the sun dipped below the horizon, casting golden light through the living room windows, he looked at me with tears in his eyes. "I'm sorry, Cassie," he whispered, the same apology as a few month prior, his voice barely audible. "For everything."

I pressed my forehead against his, choking back my own tears. "I know, Dad. But I've forgiven you, and I'll always love you."

In that moment, I realized that some goodbyes start long before the final moment. They begin with every frail smile, every whispered apology, every lingering touch that says all the things words can't. September had barely begun, but I knew in my heart that the seasons would change before he did.

He was dying.

And this time, there was nothing left to do but wait.

An inevitability hung over us like dark, oppressive clouds, each day a painful countdown toward an end we couldn't escape.

The morning he passed was drenched in rain. Not the kind of violent downpour that demands attention, but a soft, steady rhythm, like the sky itself was mourning alongside me. I sat beside him in the dim light of the hospital room, gripping his hand. A hand that had once been so strong, so certain. Now, it was frail, cold, and barely able to return my squeeze. His breathing was shallow, uneven. Each exhale grew fainter than the last. He was slowly surrendering to time, to sickness, to this inescapable fate.

The scent of antiseptic hung in the air, mingling with the faint perfume of flowers from the bouquets on the windowsill, creating an atmosphere that felt both clinical and surreal. The beeping of medical equipment was the only sound breaking through my racing mind. Yet even those sounds seemed to fade as I focused entirely on him, every heartbeat, every breath, every sign of life in his eyes.

His hands, once capable of building and creating, now lay motionless on the bedspread, withered and trembling. I reached out, carefully wrapping my fingers around his, feeling the cold seep into my skin as though the sorrow of his passing was already making itself known. His eyes, dull and glassy, stared at the ceiling as if searching for something—or someone—beyond this world.

"Dad," I said quietly, my voice faltering as grief tightened its grip. "I'm here. I'm right here."

Slowly, painfully, he turned his head to look at me. For one fleeting moment, I saw recognition glint in his eyes; the faint remnants of the man I had loved so dearly, hidden behind the haze of pain and exhaustion. He tried to speak, but no sound escaped his lips. His mouth moved, shaping words that would never reach me. Desperate to catch even a fragment of what he wanted to say, I leaned closer, my heart aching with the effort to bridge the space between us.

"It's okay," I whispered, choking back more tears threatening to spill over. "I know. You don't have to say anything. Just rest."

A subtle smile ghosted across his face, barely there, but profound with meaning that needed no explanation. I squeezed his hand, trying to pour every ounce of love I had for him into that one simple motion. The tears I had held back began to slip free, hot trails carving paths down my cheeks, but I didn't let go. I wouldn't let go. Not until he was ready.

Minutes stretched into eternity as the steady beep of the heart monitor slowed to an agonizing crawl. Each beat felt like a countdown, a cruel reminder that time was running out. My breath hitched as I tightened my grip on his hand, as if it might keep him here with me.

But then, as the moments dwindled, an unexpected calm washed over the room.

His chest, once rising and falling with painful effort, began to settle. The tension in his body eased, and his breaths grew shallower, softer, until the final exhale escaped. A whisper, quiet and reluctant, as if time itself was mourning his departure.

"I love you, Dad," I whispered through my sobs, pressing a kiss to his forehead.

And then, he was gone.

His chest lay still, his face at peace. The heart monitor flat lined a continuous tone that seemed to echo through every part of me.

The world collapsed around me, my grief a tidal wave crashing over me with relentless force, pulling me under into a darkness I wasn't sure I could escape. And yet, as I looked at his peaceful face—free from pain at last—I found the smallest, most fragile solace in knowing he was no longer suffering.

Qualley entered the room quietly a few minutes later once the nurses unplugged the machines and left us to say our goodbyes. His footsteps were soft as he approached. Without a word, he wrapped his arms around from behind me, holding me close as my body shook with the intensity of my cries.

"You were here for him, my love," he said gently. "That's

what matters."

I nodded, unable to respond. My heart was broken but filled with the knowledge that I had done the one thing that mattered most: *I had been there*. I had held his hand in those final moments, poured every ounce of love I had into the space between us, and honored the man he had been—the man he had tried so hard to be.

April to September. That was all the time we had. A few fleeting months to make up for years lost to prison walls and addiction. Moments stolen in the shadow of impending loss.

And yet, somehow, it had felt like a lifetime.

But what I would have given for more time.

The rain outside tapped softly against the window; a quiet melody to match my grief. Regret clawed at my heart. Regret for the years wasted, for words left unsaid, for memories we would never get to make. My father's life had been a tapestry woven with mistakes and redemption, love and pain, and now, thread by thread, it was unraveling. It left behind nothing but crude truths I wasn't ready to face.

As I sat in the stillness of the hospital room, I clung to the memories we'd shared, holding them tightly against the disturbance inside me. His laughter, his words, his presence—they were memories now, but they were mine. They were all I had left.

Qualley's hand on my shoulder was a message that I wasn't alone, that I had someone to steady me even as I stumbled through the darkness of anguish. And for that, I was grateful. But gratitude felt like a hollow comfort when battling against the enormity of my loss.

In my heart, I carried one truth I couldn't ignore. The person I blamed for this, for all of it, was my *mother*. It was her hatred, her meddling, her calculated sabotage that had cost him his sobriety; had stolen from us the chance to heal and grow together. If not for her, he might have recovered. He might have lived. We might have had the daddy-daughter moments I'd always dreamed of but never experienced.

Those moments would never come. And one day . . . one day, I promised she would answer for it.

For now, though, there was only the pain. And through that pain, I loved him—my dad—flaws and all, mistakes and redemption, grief and solace.

He was my father, and no matter what, that would never change.

But my mother, she'd pay the price for his death.s

Chapter 12

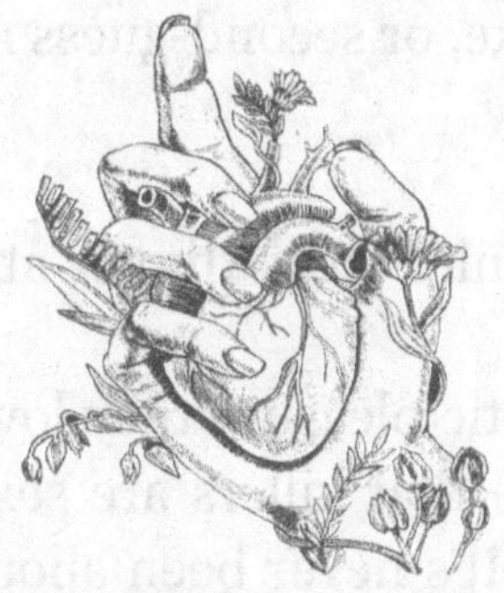

Most people after their first kill feel may like they've been launched outside of their own body. Their heart may race, their hands might tremble, and their mind could start to spiral with panic. The most common question they may ask themselves is: *What have I done?* From there, the responses tend to fall into a few familiar patterns: try to cover it up, blame someone else, or frame a stranger. Some may get so overwhelmed they march into a police station and confess. Anything to make the guilt stop chewing holes in their conscience.

Their lives, with their victim's last breath, become a slow collapse. The discernment of what they'd done festers like an infected wound. They imagine the victim's face every time they close their eyes. They wake up in the middle of the night, convinced the police are outside. They can't look over their shoulder without flinching. Eventually, many of them implode. Some get caught, others spiral into addiction, and a few just can't bear it anymore and end their lives before anyone else can bring them to justice.

Murder is unnatural to most people. It rattles them to their core.

But then there are people like me.

See, I've always been a killer. Not just by action, but in spirit. I wasn't corrupted by one bad decision. I didn't fall down a slippery slope. I *was born* at the bottom, and the killer was dormant inside me.

So no, I didn't fall to my knees sobbing after my first kill. I didn't tremble, or shake, or second-guess myself. What I felt was something else entirely.

Relief.

And then I had a nice steak dinner at the Ritz in New York City to celebrate.

That kind of sadistic pleasure they love to sensationalize on crime shows—the idea that killers are sexually charged by violence? That's not me. It's never been about lust. It's never been about the high.

What I experienced was healing.

And hunger (hence the steak).

With every life I took, it felt like another weight was lifted from my shoulders. As if the trauma that had been welded to my body for years—heavy, suffocating, constant—was finally breaking loose. The bruises that used to color my skin began to fade. The cuts, the welts, the old cigarette burns . . . all of it seemed to disappear with every drop of blood I spilled. It was as if killing them stitched something back together inside me.

I wasn't chasing pleasure.

I was reclaiming my life.

It wasn't madness. I merely desired balance. Every person eliminated was part of the same machine that crushed me. They broke me even before I had a chance to figure out who I was on my own. But now I knew exactly who I was.

Revenge gave me a purpose.

Redemption gave me strength.

Retribution gave me peace.

People say killers are broken, they have a screw or two loose, and arguably, that may be true. But I've been broken my entire life—and now after everything, I' was finally whole.

Although I said I'm a killer, I didn't really think about it until after my father confided in me about my own mother's betrayal; her deliberate purchase of cocaine to set him up, simultaneously wrenching him away from the fragile grip of sobriety. Something fundamental within me splintered when I discovered this truth.

Right and wrong blurred into indistinguishable shades of gray, fissures creeping through the foundation of any morality I thought I had. And then, years later, came the second blow: my father's cancer diagnosis. It was as though every day after that confession was a test of endurance—not for him alone, but for me too.

The sickness took hold of him in cruel and relentless waves. I watched helplessly as chemotherapy drained the life out of him, reducing the man who had once been larger than life to a shadow of his former self. The weekly hospital trips became grim routine, each visit marked by his frail body crumpling under the weight of nausea or collapsing in exhaustion. The sight of him puking blood, his skin pale and clammy as he clung to the edges of consciousness, carved craters deeper within me. The man who had once shielded me from the world's darkness now seemed trapped in a cage of pain and despair, unable to break free. My heart cracked for him, and for myself; each fracture widened until I felt I might shatter entirely.

He never got the chance to truly redeem himself, to heal from his mistakes, to make peace with the person he had been and the father he wanted to be. Instead, cancer had chained him to a different kind of prison. One he could never escape and would eventually consume him. The drugs still ruled his life, but not because of weakness or choice. This time, it was poison dressed up as medicine, coursing through his veins and stealing what little strength he had left.

Qualley did everything he could to make sure Dad had the best care—treatment from renowned doctors who spoke with polished confidence about the "latest therapies and most advanced medicines." He covered it all without hesitation, never allowing us to feel the weight of the financial burden. But even the best care wasn't enough to tip the scales. Some battles are unwinnable, no matter how desperately you wish for a different outcome.

When my dad finally succumbed to the cancer, the last fragile thread tethering me to reason snapped. The volcano that had formed after my father's confession didn't just deepen—it erupted, consuming me in fiery rage and despair. It wasn't grief in the traditional sense; it was something raw, uncontrollable, and unstable. The anger, dormant for so long, surged through me like molten lava, setting off tremors that shook me to my core. My hands trembled violently, my chest heaved with the rapid, unsteady rhythm of my heartbeat, and nausea churned in my stomach until I thought I might burst. Every fiber of my being burned with one undeniable truth: the only way to soothe this unbearable pain was through action.

It wasn't enough to mourn him. Mourning wouldn't heal the wounds left by those who had betrayed and broken him. It wouldn't undo the suffering he endured at their hands, nor the relentless torment of his final days. No. The only thing that could possibly quell the inferno within me was to seek justice. Not the kind found in courtrooms, but the kind etched in blood. I wouldn't just hurt them. I would destroy them.

And I knew exactly where to start.

My *mother.*

The woman who was supposed to be my father's partner, his equal, his ally. The woman who should have supported him in his sobriety, who should have stood by him in his struggle. Instead, she had orchestrated his downfall, exploiting his vulnerabilities with cold precision. She was the architect of so much of his pain.

So, I packed a bag and boarded a train to New York City. The rumble of the tracks beneath me mirrored the storm raging in my chest. As the city skyline loomed closer, its lights piercing through the darkening sky, I felt a strange calm settle over a quiet determination that sharpened my thoughts and steadied my hands.

This wasn't just a visit. It was a reckoning. And for the first time in what felt like an eternity, I didn't feel powerless.

I felt ready.

Finding my mother wasn't as difficult as I'd imagined, once I had suitable resources—thanks to Qualley's associate, Lonney. It was during this search that I came to fully understand not only the depths of her cruelty as an abusive narcissist but also the sheer recklessness of her actions.

At the time of my father's death, I hadn't seen or spoken to her since she left when I was only seventeen. She practically vanished from my life without a trace, leaving no forwarding address, no phone number, not even a word of concern for her own daughter. The silence was deafening, a void that spoke volumes about the kind of person she was. I didn't know where she was, and for a long time, I didn't even know where to begin looking.

But my mother, in her arrogance, had left behind a trail without even realizing it. When she walked out of our lives, she'd carelessly abandoned some papers, including one with her social security number scrawled across it. At the time, I was just a teenager, clueless about what that number meant or how it could be used. Still, something in my gut told me not to throw anything of hers away. Maybe it was instinct, or maybe it was the faint hope that one day I'd need it.

Years later, as I packed up some of my apartment to move in with Qualley, I rediscovered those papers again. I tucked them away with my own important documents, not fully understanding why but trusting that they might serve a purpose.

That purpose became clear after my father's funeral.

A few days after we laid him to rest, I found myself sitting across from Qualley at dinner, my grief still unbearably present. Between bites of food I barely tasted, I mentioned my desire to find her. The words felt strange coming out of my mouth, like they didn't quite belong to me. But the moment they were spoken, I knew there was no turning back.

"The same mother who abused you and left you to fend for yourself?" he asked sarcastically. "I don't think so." He scoffed, sipping his drink.

Swirling the crimson liquid in my glass, I fixed him with a smoldering stare, the kind that promised trouble and dared him to want it. My lashes lowered just enough to hide the glint of mischief in my eyes. As my leg crossed over the other, the slow movement revealed a daring glimpse of skin—bait, but not yet the trap.

"Oh? You're going to stop me?" There was nothing he *could* do, and I knew he wouldn't resort to locking me up in our massive home.

He'd have to kill me first.

One side of his mouth quirked up in a grin as he chuckled. "There's no stopping you, *mia bella*."

At least we both agreed there.

"Okay, then," I whined playfully. "Help me." Pouting, I let my fingers drift as I reached for Qualley's hand, the touch feather-light, electric. His grip tightened, firm yet tantalizingly restrained, before he raised my hand to his lips. The kiss he planted on the back of it wasn't just a kiss. It was a promise, a challenge, and a spark all at once.

"Please"

"Why must you find her?" His voice was low, thumb tracing slow circles on the back of my hand, still clasped tightly in his.

My brows drew together, my disappointment settling heavily between them. I couldn't bring myself to reveal the real reason for seeking out my mother; I knew Qualley would never agree if he knew the truth. So, with a pang of guilt, I chose to conceal it—or rather, left pieces of it unspoken.

"I need closure," I said tenderly, barely audible. I offered him a faint, wistful smile. "I just want to understand why she left. Nothing more."

Qualley released my hand and leaned forward, folding his fingers tightly together as if bracing himself. His brow arched, the subtle lift betraying his growing skepticism. He had a knack for reading people, for catching their angles and hustles, and even though I loved him, and he loved me, I was no exception.

I'd never consciously betray his trust—but using him to further my own goals, no matter how much it stung, was something I couldn't avoid. I had to convince him that my intentions with my mother weren't shrouded in deception.

"You're the only one I can turn to," I confessed, letting the pitch of my voice soften into a devilish plea. "I need your help to find her, and I promise—I'm not planning to bring her back here to ruin our lives."

Qualley rarely spoke of his past, but I knew abandonment had shaped him. How else does someone end up in the world of drug's grip? The world he found there wasn't just an escape—it was a makeshift family, a fragile sense of belonging. Maybe I'm guessing, but who wouldn't cling to the illusion of safety after being discarded by their own flesh and blood like yesterday's trash? Still, Qualley had his code: *never harm women or children*. It wasn't just a rule. It was a cornerstone of who he was. But what if that woman wasn't innocent?

What if she posed a threat to everyone around her?

In prison, inmates do unmentionable things to those who harm children. But some people, like my mother, never see the inside of the cell; beaten, extorted, killed. She'll never have to look over her shoulder for the inmate with a homemade shiv, pay off a gang to protect her, or hope the corrections officers won't turn a blind eye as the inmates do their worst. I wanted her to feel that pain, to feel scared, helpless.

That's how she made me feel for twenty-six years.

"You always say people get what they earn. That's your whole thing, right?"

"Cass . . . I—" He exhales sharply, looking away. He already knew where this was going.

I cut him off with a gentle but intended motion, my fingers slipping beneath the curve of his jaw, guiding his face toward mine. Our eyes met, a waver of resistance dimming beneath my touch.

"She left me," I breathed, the accusation heavy with years of resentment. My lips grazed his, then pulled away. "She let me starve, Qualley. She let me struggle . . . alone." My thumb traced the edge of his cheekbone. "If it were you—if it was just some dealer who betrayed you—wouldn't you want to watch the world burn too?"

"I know, sweet." He spoke in a gravelly undertone, each word steeped in quiet comprehension. "But she's not just some dealer."

"No," I whispered, moving closer, my breath brushing his lips. "She's worse. So much worse."

My hand slipped from his face and down his neck, leaving behind a trail of warmth. A silent promise. Qualley observed me, unmoving, but I could feel the shift inside him.

He saw past my charm; he saw beyond the carefully curated illusion that shielded me. He always could. It's why I loved him —I couldn't fool him, and still, he never left.

The candle between us crackled, casting shadows that danced over his face like flickers of temptation. I stood slowly, planting myself on his lap, my fingertips grazing the rim of his glass on my way over. He tilted his head up toward me, his pupils slightly blown. His lips parted in anticipation.

I took his hand and pressed it to my chest, right over my heart. "You love me, right?"

He tensed, his pulse beneath his skin jumping. "You know I

do."

"You always say, 'I'd do anything for you, baby.'" I leaned down, lips nearly brushing his. "Well . . . this is anything."

His breath hitched, and he lifted his other hand, laying it atop the one pressed to my chest. His warmth seeped into me. I leaned in, letting our foreheads touch, then our lips—softly at first, a kiss that hummed with restraint. But then it deepened. His tongue flicked against mine, slow and searching, teasing the truth out of me.

But I didn't budge.

I smiled into the kiss, allowing him to feel how close he was to unraveling me.

When we parted, I didn't go far.

I traced his bottom lip with my fingertip, trailing it down to his collarbone, nails just barely grazing his skin. His eyes darkened, and he let out a soft curse under his breath, gripping my waist like he was already imagining what we'd do later tonight.

"Help me do this," I said breathlessly into his ear. "And I swear—after this—I'll let it go."

He tucked a loose curl behind my ear, and trailed his fingers down the back of my neck with such care it made me ache.

His lips found my shoulder, trailing kisses that climbed back up my neck, lazy and indulgent. "Where do you think she is?" He asked between kisses, his voice was low, hungry.

A wicked grin curved my mouth. I angled my head to expose more skin, threading my fingers through his hair as he worked his way up. He bit gently at the hollow beneath my jaw, and I arched into him.

"I'll tell you everything," I breathed. "All the details."

He grabbed my bottom lip with his teeth again, tugging just enough to make my thighs press together. "Let's find her, then."

He was mine now—completely.

Lipstick smeared, pulse pounding, I slid back into my seat with a glint in my eyes.

I had what I wanted, and that meant two things:
It was time to set the plan in motion—and thank Qualley properly when we got home.

Chapter 13

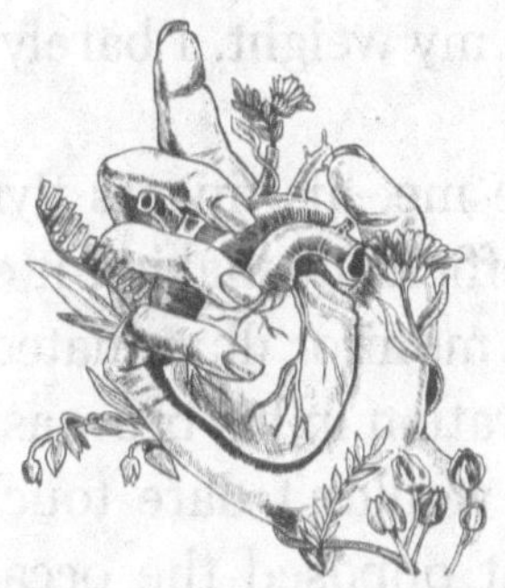

Qualley's mansion exuded wealth with every detail, but the study was where it truly flaunted its opulence. Warm light poured from an intricately carved brass chandelier that hung from a vaulted ceiling adorned with wood beams so polished they gleamed. Floor-to-ceiling mahogany bookcases lined the walls, their shelves packed with leather-bound tomes, some weathered, others gilded, each a subtle nod to an intellect as curated as the room itself. Between the bookcases stood oil portraits in gilded frames, commanding and intense, the subjects seeming to watch over the space with an air of imperiousness.

The air smelled faintly of aged wood, leather, and the bite of Qualley's whiskey—the good kind, no doubt—poured neat into a crystal glass that glinted like a jewel under the chandelier's light. He was seated in his favorite chair by the massive stone fireplace. A wingback upholstered in rich green velvet, perfectly tailored to both style and comfort. He held a book in one hand, his posture effortlessly relaxed, while his other hand balanced the whiskey glass on the armrest. A fire crackled softly, casting blinking shadows across his face, the warmth of the flames contrasting sharply with the cool presence he carried.

Lonney and I occupied the large antique desk at the center of the room—a beast of furniture carved from dark oak. Its surface was covered with scattered papers, my old mail, and the glow of the desktop Lonney was working on. The chair I was perched in felt too luxurious for the task, its leather cushions sinking slightly under my weight. I barely noticed, my attention fixated on the screen.

Lonney sat beside me, his fingers flying over the keyboard with confidence and efficiency making it clear he was in his element. The glow of the monitor illuminated his face, highlighting the furrow of concentration in his brow as he navigated layers of systems most people wouldn't dare touch. His focused typing created a rhythm that opposed the occasional turn of a page from Qualley's direction and crackles from the fire. A symphony of purpose, intensity, and leisure.

Heavy Persian rugs softened the footsteps of anyone entering, their intricate designs blending muted reds, deep blues, and subtle golds in a pattern so refined it felt like the floor itself told a story. A decanter of whiskey rested on a sideboard to Qualley's left, along with crystal glasses arranged like soldiers at the ready, their sharp cuts shimmering under the golden light. The room was indulgent yet disciplined, a blend of comfort and grandeur. Where decisions that could shake foundations were made with the same ease as sipping fine liquor.

Despite the luxury surrounding me, I barely sensed it. My focus was shrill, thoughts tangled between the promise of answers and the weight of uncertainty. The room, though stunning, blurred into the background as Lonney worked his magic, my fingers brushing the edges of the old mail spread across the desk like relics of a life I was desperate to uncover.

Meanwhile, Qualley didn't so much as glance in our direction, his calm detachment serving as a strategic divergence to our urgency. He turned a page, sipped his whiskey, and let the faintest smile tug at the corner of his lips. Perhaps amused by the enmity, or perhaps content to let the others do the work while he basked in the quiet supremacy of his domain.

Qualley once told me that Lonney, his best friend and right-hand Lieutenant, had a particular knack for slipping past digital barriers, navigating systems most people wouldn't dare touch. Among his many talents was accessing a database used by the Social Security Administration—a tool designed for locating people, apparently. He never disclosed the name of the system, nor did I press him for it. All I needed to know was that it existed and that Lonney could use it.

The timing couldn't have been better. For years, I'd clung to those old pieces of mail, which included a letter containing my mother's social security number. It was one of the few tangible links I had to her, and now, after years of uncertainty, I was finally taking a step toward finding her.

Lonney, ever the shadowy figure, refused to tell me how he obtained his access, casually brushing off my questions with a smirk and a shrug. Honestly, I didn't care all that much. I wasn't looking to become a digital outlaw—I just wanted answers. Still, I watched him work, my eyes scanning the screen as he typed with systematic precision, entering the numbers I provided.

Across the room, Qualley was the picture of unbothered confidence, casually flipping through a novel in one hand while swirling whiskey in the other. Every so often, he'd glance up at us, lips twitching into an amused smile as if watching a live performance he never bought a ticket for.

"You look like a kid watching a magician," he mused, sipping his drink.

Ignoring him, I leaned closer, trying to absorb everything Lonney was doing. The symbols and commands flashing across the screen were indecipherable, like some secret language only he understood.

"How does this even work?" I asked, my curiosity pushing past Lonney's usual reluctance.

A slow grin crept onto his face. "You ask too many questions."

"Perhaps that's because you never give answers."

Though I knew he wouldn't explain the details, I couldn't help but feel a thrill watching him. This wasn't just some cheap internet search. Lonney was bypassing obstacles, unlocking doors that weren't meant to be opened.

And I was right there, soaking in every second of it.

Lonney let out a loud groan, barely glancing away from the screen as he flicked his wrist, shooing me away like I was an annoying mosquito. "Your girl keeps breathing down my neck."

I scoffed and took a half-step back—but only half. Close enough to still read what was on the screen, far enough to pretend I was respecting his space. I folded my arms and rolled my eyes, making a point of staying exactly where I wanted.

Qualley exhaled a breathy laugh, eyes never leaving his book. "She breathes other places too."

Lonney nearly choked on his own giggle, the kind of juvenile, bubbling laughter that belonged to a kid hearing the word "boobies" for the first time. He shook his head, gripping his cigar as his body trembled from the sheer ridiculousness of it. His laugh was so absurd, so unnecessary, that I knew the exaggerated blink was inevitable, yet the amusement won out. There was something deeply unserious about these men—drug dealers by trade, yet behind the scenes, they had the dynamic of overgrown children at recess.

Qualley fostered that energy, treating his circle less like a cartel and more like a family—dysfunctional, sure, but loyal, nonetheless.

They were good at what they did.

Lonney wiped his smirk and quirked a brow at me. "You want her bank information too?" The way he said it was teasing, but I could tell he wouldn't be opposed to actually pulling it up. I smacked him in the face with the papers I held, earning a halfhearted "Ow" that barely carried any conviction.

"I don't want to rob her. I just want to set things straight. Get closure."

Lonney swiveled in his chair; cigar held delicately between his fingers as he appraised me. "Oh?"

From across the room, Qualley finally looked up, taking a long sip of his whiskey as if bracing himself for whatever was about to spill out of my mouth. I hadn't told him what would actually happen when I found my mother. Not because I was hiding it, but because he never got around to asking after I 'repaid' him for agreeing to help me.

Lonney narrowed his eyes, amusement dancing across his expression. "Set what straight?"

"Her," I said simply, hesitating for just a moment, shrugging. "My mother. Scare her a bit. I dunno yet exactly."

Lonney nodded slowly, as if waiting for the conversation to take its next breath. He took another slow drag of his cigar, exhaling the smoke. A low, thoughtful "huh" escaped him—not quite a question, not quite an agreement. Just enough to let me know that, whatever was brewing in his head, he was filing this information away for later. And then, as if the conversation had already given him everything he needed, he turned back to the computer, fingers flying across the keyboard like nothing had happened.

That was one of the things I appreciated about Lonney. He had a way of asking without actually asking. He'd probe just enough to make you think but never demand answers you weren't ready to give. He could read between the lines, pick apart your intentions from your pauses, your phrasing, or even the silence that stretched between words.

Zina must thoroughly hate that.

If there was anyone who had perfected the art of dodging questions, it was Zina. To her, conversations weren't exchanges; they were battles, strategic games of saying just enough without ever revealing a true thought. Lonney's effortless ability to dissect people must have driven her insane.

Which, frankly, made it all the more enjoyable to watch him

work.

Qualley rested his open book on the armrest of his chair, leaning forward with his drink in hand. His eyes pinned me with that classic kingpin's stare—the one that said, "Spit it out." He angled his chin, expectant but patient.

You can't fool a dealer.

"Oh, alright!" I threw my hands up, exasperated. "I just want to go knock her around a bit, ask some questions. Maybe tie her to a chair. I don't know! I just want answers."

"And if she doesn't want to provide them?" Lonney asked curiously, sparing a glance as he casually kept his eyes trained on the screen. "What then?"

Qualley settled deeper into his seat, raising his glass in a languid salute. The corners of his mouth curled into a smirk as he winked, dripping with confidence. The kind of look that said, "I told you so."

"Well, I guess we'll see then, won't we?" I sighed, straightening myself slightly.

"We'll see?" Qualley echoed, disbelieving. "You can't just go in there blind. What if she hurts you?"

I clicked my tongue, my gaze flicking sideways in exasperation. "She's not a ninja, Qualley. And she couldn't hurt me any more than she used to."

That part was true. My mother had thrown me around, hurled objects at me, left bruises that faded faster than the memories of her rage—but even at her worst, she was always weak. She didn't own weapons, and the mere sight of them made her jittery. I'd seen it firsthand. She paled whenever my dad's friends, the ones with loaded guns tucked into their belts, came by the house. If, against all logic, she had secretly been a ninja all along, then my self-defense training with Zina—the course the boys basically forced on us—would have to be my saving grace.

But honestly, why bother with fists when I could use a wholly unethical approach?

"She won't hurt me," I said confidently, leaning back in my seat. "Trust me."

Qualley raised a skeptical brow, his piercing gaze locking onto me for a beat longer than I expected. Lonney, perched by the computer, only shrugged, his attention brushing between me and the glowing screen. Neither of them looked convinced, but neither of them were about to stop me, either.

Qualley shifted in his chair, fingers brushing the rim of his glass before he leaned forward slightly, resting his forearms on his knees. "Cassandra," he said, calm, but threaded with something more intense. "You're sure about this?"

His words lingered; much more formidable than the effortless indifference he tried to project. This wasn't just skepticism —it was something closer to concern, though he'd never come out and say it. That wasn't his style. But the way his eyes lingered, assessing, it told me enough. He wasn't questioning my intentions; he was questioning the aftermath.

"Yes," I said firmly, trying to keep my voice steady as I met his gaze. "I've made it this far without her breaking me. She's not about to start now."

His lips pressed into a thin line, louder than any objection he might've voiced. He didn't believe me—not fully. It wasn't that he doubted my ability to handle her. It was that he knew better than anyone how deep the scars of family ran, how messy and unpredictable those moments could become, no matter how prepared you thought you were. And maybe, just maybe, he knew that crossing certain lines had consequences you couldn't always outrun.

"I'm not afraid of her," I added. "Fear burned out of me a long time ago. She taught me that. It's a lesson I learned the hard way."

Qualley tipped his head slightly, swirling his glass but never taking a sip. "Fear isn't the issue," he said quietly. "And you know it."

For a moment, his words struck deeper than I cared to admit. He wasn't lecturing me. He wasn't trying to stop me. He was just . . . reminding me. Reminding me of what this meant, of what it carried, even if I wasn't ready to face it yet. But I couldn't let him see the crack in my resolve. Not when I needed him to trust me.

I straightened in my seat, my gaze darting to Lonney, who had wisely opted to keep his focus on the computer, avoiding whatever emotional war Qualley and I were waging across the room. The truth was, I wasn't sure who I was trying to convince —Qualley or myself. But I wasn't about to back down now, not when my path was already set.

I wasn't walking in blind. I knew exactly what I was up against. But this time, it wasn't about survival—it was about reclaiming something that had always been stolen from me.

This wasn't just settling a score. I wanted my dessert served cold, with an extra helping of sweet vengeance on the side.

Before I could fully lose myself in my own little cinematic daydream, Lonney grabbed my wrist and yanked me toward the screen. "Found 'er," he said triumphantly. A few more clicks, and suddenly, her face popped up—an old Facebook account staring back at me.

I blinked. "Wait—how the fuck did you get her Facebook account using her social security number?"

Lonney barely glanced up, a mischievous grin stretching across his face. "Oh, I didn't just find that." His fingers danced over the keyboard, eyebrows waggling like some kind of evil genius. "I've got her bank account, too. You sure you don't wanna see how much she's got? Maybe transfer a little somethin'-somethin'?"

I smacked his arm, narrowing my eyes. "Lonney, come on. Just give me an address."

"Alright, alright," he said, with a theatrical sigh of injured dignity. He pulled up a new window. "There, princess. That good enough for ya?"

Muttering obscenities under my breath, I dropped into the swivel chair beside him, scooting close enough to see the screen clearly. I dug my phone out of my bag and typed the address into my notes.

Lonney barely had a second to bask in his accomplishments before I nudged him out of the way, earning a dramatic groan.

"Hey, watch it!"

"Shut up," I shot back, smirking as I pulled up the Amtrak website to book tickets for the next train out of here. My fingers moved fast, tapping through confirmation screens, sealing the trip within minutes.

Lonney spun his chair toward me, watching like a proud yet slightly concerned older brother. "You're really doing this, huh?"

I looked up, locking eyes with him. "Yeah. I am."

A slow grin spread across his face. "Damn. Remind me never to piss you off."

The Ritz-Carlton loomed above me, its grand façade glowing like a promise—one of indulgence and escape—but I couldn't shake the turbulence coiling in my chest. Thomas—my driver, whose name I was sure was as fabricated as his professional politeness—opened my door, helping me out of the vehicle before rushing to grab my suitcase from the trunk. For now, I let him handle the details, my focus scattered elsewhere. The glittering lights of Manhattan stretched above and around me, sprawling and endless, as if mocking the bedlam fizzing under my skin.

Stepping into The Artist's Gate Suite was like stepping into a painting—elegant and impossibly polished. High ceilings adorned with subtle artistic flourishes gave the room a sense of grandeur, while warm, golden lighting accentuated the plush tufted seating and marble-topped tables. The king-sized bed, draped in crisp white linens, practically begged me to sink into its comfort and let the world disappear. Two impossibly luxurious robes hung in the corner, whispering promises of softness I couldn't bring myself to believe. It was extravagance in its purest form, and yet it felt suffocating in its perfection.

The name had hooked me long before I'd stepped through the door: *The Artist's Gate.* It resonated deeply, stirring something unspoken within, fractured but yearning. Artists carve meaning from darkness, don't they? I'd tried to do the same, but now, standing in this room, I wasn't sure the art of survival would be enough to get me through the next couple days because no amount of poetic symbolism could erase the unknown of what I was about to face.

I hadn't seen her in years. And still, her shadow clung to me like vapor. My mother—chaotic, cruel, calculating—was the ghost I'd spent half my life chasing and the other half trying to forget. The information Lonney had dug up was solid, I was certain of that. She'd gone crawling back to my grandmother's cramped New York apartment, the same smothering space we'd coexisted in years before—alongside my grandmother's perverted boyfriend, who had a fondness for lingering in doorways. It was pathetic. Predictable. I should've guessed she'd returned. But even so, the confirmation brought an unsteady mix of relief and resentment.

I couldn't stop the anger simmering beneath the surface. A visceral reaction to her existence and everything it had cost me. But alongside the anger, there was something far more unwelcome: *fear.* Not fear of her—no, that had burned out of me years ago. But fear of what facing her might uncover. Truths I might find buried in her chaos. Fear that, despite all my effort, she might still hold some power to hurt me in ways I hadn't prepared.

I'd be stepping into the past—reliving the wreckage she left behind—and confront the person I'd sworn I'd never need again.

I wasn't afraid of her. Not anymore. But the possibility of failure? Of letting her see even a glimmer of weakness? That terrified me.

The thought churned in my stomach, twisting tighter as I showered, scrubbing off the lingering scent of the NYC Amtrak station—recycled air and the vague, metallic tinge that stuck to your clothes. The train ride hadn't been much better: sandwiched between a snoring businessman and an unapologetic armrest thief. Next time, I'd take Qualley's advice and fly first class. Screw maintaining a 'low profile.'

Freshly dressed, I laid out my outfit for the next day: dark blouse, tailored slacks, a silk scarf tied neatly around my neck. It was the kind of outfit that whispered understated elegance, projecting just enough importance without drawing unnecessary attention. But it wasn't clothes that would protect me. That duty fell to the small, weighty admonishers buried in my bag, hidden among my belongings.

I wasn't walking into this empty-handed. Or unguarded.

Crossing to the window, I gazed out at Manhattan's shimmering skyline, sprawling and endless, humming with life. The soft lighting of the suite bathed me in warmth, but it felt hollow against the cold knot in my stomach. This was the calm before the storm, wasn't it? A moment of stillness before stepping into the unknown.

Tomorrow, I'd face something I'd spent years running from.

Tomorrow, I'd confront her and carve my future out of the wreckage she left behind.

But I'd allow myself that moment of indulgence. Silk sheets, soft lighting, and the fleeting satisfaction of knowing that, even if just for now, I was worth spoiling.

Chapter 14

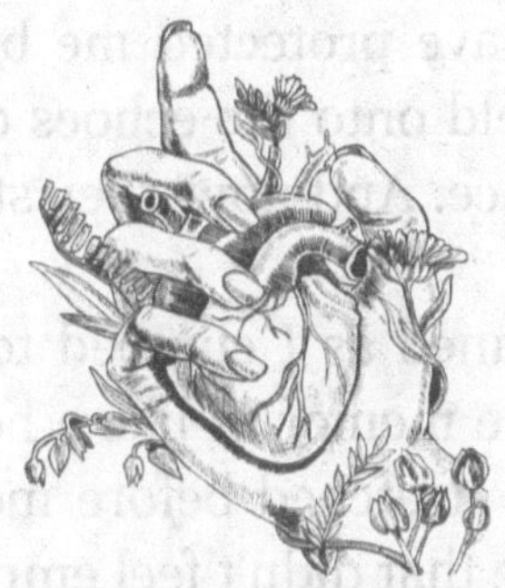

ueens was about an hour from the Ritz, but for what I was there to do, the distance didn't bother me. If anything, I welcomed it. The further, the better. It gave me time to think, to strategize, to let the anticipation simmer without boiling over. This neighborhood, if memory served, was the kind of place where people had perfected the art of looking the other way.

That worked in my favor.

I'd imagined this moment too many times to count, playing it out in my mind with different outcomes, different scenarios. At least since I finalized my itinerary. Sometimes it was quick, clean. Other times, messy, drawn out. But no matter how I pictured it, it always ended the same way.

Walking into the lobby felt like stepping into a time capsule of bad decisions and, even worse, regrets. The stained walls, the overflowing ashtrays, the sagging furniture—all of it steeped in the familiar stench of neglect and despair. It was the kind of place that swallowed people whole, chewed them up, and spit them out worse for wear.

A sliver of anxiety clawed at my chest, but I shoved it down. I wasn't here to reminisce or wallow in the ghosts of this place— I was here to settle a score.

When I'd been inside this building the last time, I'd just been ripped from the arms of the only person who had ever truly loved me. My father. What followed was a nightmare: abuse at the hands of a man who wasn't even family, betrayal by the two women who should have protected me but didn't. These walls had seen it all, had held onto the echoes of every scream, every plea, every bitter silence. And now, they stood as silent witnesses to my return.

The staircase groaned as I climbed to the third floor, each step pressing down the memories like a heartbeat drumming in my ears. The hallway stretched before me, dimly lit and eerily quiet. A kind of silence that didn't feel empty—it felt intentional.

No elevator. No cameras. No security.

A place designed for people who didn't want to be found, who didn't want anyone asking questions. That suited me just fine

I reached into my bag and pulled out my .22 pistol Qualley had given me, and its suppressor attachment. It was a grounding, solid steel promise resting in my hand. My fingers moved over the weapon with practiced ease, inspecting every part of it as if I hadn't already done so a dozen times before. The click of the silencer echoed faintly in the corridor as I pushed it into place, a sound both ominous and strangely reassuring.

Best thing about traveling by train? Limited security.

Finally, I reached the apartment door, a path etched into me, as familiar as my own reflection. I lingered, pulling in the stale air and letting it slip from my lungs, its presence clinging to me like humidity before a storm.

I knocked first. Polite. Respectful. No need to rush—I had time, and I wasn't about to kick the door down like some amateur. No, I was going to do this right. Before the door creaked open, the many locks installed clicked, then a face appeared—my grandmother's boyfriend, False Grandpa

He was older, sicker, skin flaky like crumpled paper. He still wore that same sour look he always had, like he'd been born disappointed.

"What the hell are you doing here?" the old man rasped, cigarette dangling from his mouth. He opened the door further, as if welcoming me in to fuck him up.

I smiled.

Pulling the hammer back on my pistol, I leveled it at his face from behind my back. "Visiting."

He had no time to react or defend himself as I pulled the trigger, shooting him point-blank in the middle of his eyes.

He fell backward into the apartment with a grunt, luckily away from the door, and I pushed myself inside quickly. After shutting and locking the door, I nearly stumbled over False Grandpa's body, so I kicked the old man's foot out of the way. I slipped further inside, checking his pulse, making sure he was permanently dead.

With no time to celebrate, I moved into the hallway of the apartment. There was a little more than thirty minutes to set my plan into action.

One down, two to go.

Dwelling on the apartment's interior wasn't on my list of priorities—it was a dump, plain and simple, like every other run-down hovel scattered across the boroughs of New York City. Honestly, a cardboard box might've been preferable. At least I might not have been molested in it.

Thanks to Lonney's digging into my estranged family, I'd learned my grandmother was on hospice care. Her kidneys were failing. She'd chosen to do dialysis at home, stubbornly refusing to die in a hospital.

Convenient enough for me, today her wish would be my command.

A nurse came by daily around midday, leaving about an hour before my mother returned in the evening. It was routine, predictable—just another detail in the slow unraveling of my grandmother's life. The irony wasn't lost on me. My mother, who had spent years neglecting her own child, had now taken up the mantle of caretaker for her dying mother. A dutiful daughter, at least on paper.

I wondered what had brought her back here to this place. *Was it guilt? Obligation? Some misguided attempt at redemption?* Maybe she thought if she played the role well enough, if she bathed her mother in affection, she could convince herself that she hadn't been the same kind of failure. That she wasn't the selfish woman who had walked away from her own flesh and blood without so much as an explanation.

For a fleeting moment, I wondered if I was being too harsh, if maybe there was something I wasn't seeing—some truth buried beneath the years of resentment. Maybe she really *did* care now. Maybe she *had* changed.

But then, the memories came flooding back—the verbal lashings, the sharp slaps across my face, the cold indifference in her eyes. And finally, the worst part. The abandonment. She had left me behind without hesitation, without concern, without a shred of remorse.

No, I wasn't overreacting. Not even close. And I found I didn't really give a shit if it turned out she had changed. If she wanted redemption, she wouldn't find it here. She wouldn't find it with me. And she wouldn't find it before it was too late because the clock was already winding down. And I was here to set the final piece into place.

The room at the end of the hallway welcomed me with dim lighting and the unmistakable scent of spoiled air. It had always been my grandmother's domain, but now, it felt hollow, stripped of anything that made it hers. The familiar notes of cheap perfume and artificial vanilla had been replaced by the sterile bite of disinfectant, the suffocating force of sickness, and the slow rot of time running out. The steady beeping of medical machines pulsed through the heat rolling off the old radiator, filling the space with a rhythm too mechanical to feel human.

She was buried under layers of blankets, a frail shape barely distinguishable beneath a mound of fabric and exhaustion. Her breath, thin and uneven, barely stirred the air around her.

I stepped through the doorway cautiously, wincing at the muted click of my heels against worn floorboards. Poor choice. Not that it mattered now. I moved with quiet precision, my outfit chosen for function—dark, unassuming, forgettable. Nothing loud, nothing memorable. My hair was pulled back tight, the kind of meticulous style meant to leave no traces behind. No jewelry. No loose threads. No distractions.

Only intent.

I had brought everything I needed.

Within my purse sat a syringe filled with fentanyl—a lethal dose to be exact—at least according to my research. Qualley kept a not-so-secret stash locked away in a safe. It admittedly took me a while to nab it because I needed to locate the key. Lo-and-behold, I discovered it in his dresser of all places. Wouldn't you think a drug lord like Qualley would think up a more difficult hiding spot, or simply keep the key with him? Then again, he probably didn't suspect someone he trusted would steal from his stores, especially not his girlfriend. But there she was, that girlfriend with the stolen drug, removing the syringe from her bag.

Watching my grandmother as she slept, for a moment, she looked almost already gone, faded into purgatory. But then, her chest lifted slightly, fell, each breath dragging out like an uneven tide. The rise and fall was weak, shallow, punctuated by the occasional hitch of air catching in her throat. Sweat gathered at her forehead, a damp sheen catching the muted late afternoon light. Droplets of saliva pooled at the corners of her mouth, collecting like forgotten remnants of effort too exhausting to continue.

I reached for the chair beside the bed, its placement almost too precise, marking the spot where the nurse sat during her daily visits. It was a well-worn seat, a fixture in the room, as much a part of this slow decay as the machines humming around us. I drew it closer, the legs scraping against the floor in protest. I eased down into it, letting the moment settle around me.

Beyond the doorway, the hallway stretched, unchanged, but it wasn't empty. It held an expectation, a shift waiting to unfold. My gaze flicked toward it, lingering on the shadowed frame of the entrance, the threshold between here and everything that came next.

I sat there, watching, breathing, waiting.

Not just for her to wake. But for what would happen when she did.

I examined the old man's lifeless body, sprawled where he had fallen. Where he lay, the world felt muted, as if sound itself had recoiled, stretching across the room like an unseen force. It pressed against me, coiling around my throat in a way that felt more pleasurable than I imagined.

It was as if the old man's presence refused to dissolve into death, as if his spirit had peeled itself free from his lifeless body and now hovered before me, unseen hands tightening around my neck with a grip that was neither warm nor human. Just pressure. Just the residue of something that should have been gone but wasn't.

The air felt colder, though I knew it wasn't. My pulse hammered, steady but insistent. Proof that I was still here, still breathing, still separate from whatever lingered in the wake of his absence.

The adrenaline wasn't from fear—it was the undeniable delight of seeing that smug bastard laid out.

But, admittedly, fear was a constant companion in this place. I never knew what kind of abuse I'd have to endure next, especially from the man whose body laid sprawled in the kitchen as if he were one of those bear rugs. The past lingered, like ink on paper—permanent, inescapable.

My dad had known what was happening to me, but locked

behind bars most of the time, he was powerless to intervene. His frustration must have mirrored my own helplessness, both of us trapped in different ways. Even after I left Queens and moved to Bristol with my mother, he tried to get someone, anyone, to check on me and make sure I was safe. But his pleas fell on deaf ears. I was left to fend for myself, abandoned by the very people who were supposed to protect me.

The sting of that neglect clung to me, a constant reminder of how effortlessly I'd been cast aside and forgotten. It wasn't just the cruelty that lingered—it was the inaction of those who could have stepped in but turned away instead.

My eyes moved over my grandmother's room again, scanning with detached ease, though my senses remained razor-sharp, tuned to the faintest shift in sound. The machines sang in steady intervals, their beeps pushing against the dense lull of the room. I lingered there, poised on the edge of action, my body taut with anticipation, every fiber attuned to the moment. Minutes dragged by, each one heavier than the last, until finally, my grandmother stirred.

Her hazel eyes fluttered open, bloodshot and glassy, flickering with faint confusion as they struggled to focus. Pressure tightened around us as I watched her, building like a storm cloud ready to surge. This was the moment I'd been waiting for, and as her gaze drifted toward me, a chill of sugary excitement ran down my spine.

"You," my grandmother said weakly, full of the same bitterness she had always carried. "I knew you'd come back."

"Oh?" Shaping my words with careful patience—gentle and inviting—like beckoning a timid kitten closer, I smiled, but it didn't reach my eyes. "Did you?"

She coughed—if you can even call it that. A wheezy whisper of sound that might've tickled the atmosphere but posed no real threat to science. After a beat, her lips parted, and she whispered, "Are you here to forgive me?" There's a strain to her voice, as if it's barely managing to hold itself together, like a cheap chair after a particularly aggressive sit.

Her withered, liver-spotted fingers twitched weakly against worn sheets. The movements are erratic and decrepit, as if even that small action cost her more than she could spare. The space, charged, droned with an unspoken hostility, daring me to speak first

Easing forward, I tucked the blanket snugly around her with my left arm, a gesture deceptively tender—like a devoted grand-daughter caring for her ailing grandmother. "No, ma'am," I murmured softly, almost soothing.

Her hazy eyes caught a glint of the syringe as I lift it into her line of sight, recognition instant. A sharp gasp escaped her lips, chest rising weakly as panic flashed across her face. Her eyes widened, but her body remained quite still—too feeble to resist, too drained to fight.

It was almost unfair.

"See this?" I said calmly, almost conversational, uncapping the syringe with the kind of precision usually reserved for wine bottles and expensive pens. A bead of the clear, lethal liquid gathered at the tip, sparkling as it caught the light before sliding off. "This right here will take away all your pain."

Her throat worked to swallow with difficulty, which forced a tremble in her speech when she finally speaks. "What is it?" The question drifted out, less than a few breaths away from vanish-ing. "What is it going to do?"

I didn't respond right away. My hand found the IV line, pulling it toward me with steady intent. The room was livened with anticipation cracking in the stillness. My every movement was purposeful, every second stretched tight with enmity.

"Cassandra, please—"

Hovering over her fragile, faded form, my fingers skimmed her damp, parchment-like skin, the touch soft but hollow—an imitation of tenderness rather than the real thing. A quiver passed through her, breath hitching in uneven bursts, as I pressed a single finger against her cracked lips, silencing whatever protest might have formed.

"Shh, Grandma," I said, mocking a soothing tone. "It's only the key to hell. Nothing to be afraid of."

Her eyes widened, fright breaking through a haze of exhaustion. I let my hand linger for a moment longer before pulling it back.

"Hope you're ready for your big debut in hell," I said, gripping the IV. "Lucifer's rolling out the red carpet."

After inserting the drugged needle into the plastic tube, I examined the drugs spilling through the IV, mixing with fluids and other medications attached to the line. I hoped if the fentanyl didn't kill her, the combination with the others would.

A jagged gasp tore from my grandmother's throat, jarring against the air like a fractured note in a song. Soon, her body began to convulse, muscles locking dangerously as the fentanyl coursed through her veins. Her eyes stretched wide in terror, flitting frantically, while her lips parted in a strangled attempt to scream—only for silence to suffocate the sound. The only noise left was the raw, guttural struggle of a body failing itself.

I angled my head slightly, observing her floundering with an almost clinical interest.

Sealing the syringe, I tucked it away back into my bag. I could leave it behind and let it become part of the trail of evidence, but really there was already enough to sink the poor nurse. No need to get creative. By tomorrow I'd be gone.

"What do you mean my entire family was murdered in their Queens apartment?"

"Me? Did I do it?"

"Why, I've been here in Bristol this whole time! I couldn't have possibly done it!"

"I wonder, Grandma," I mused, contemplating her demise. "Will God save you now?"

Her chest rose and fell in uneven jerks, each breath scraping against the edge of survival. She fought to pull herself back, but the effort was futile. The antidote wasn't in my possession—and even if it were, she wouldn't be getting it from me.

Not expecting a reply, I sink into the chair beside her, crossing my legs with a lazy sort of ease. Time stretched, each second luxurious, undeniably the most gratifying I've ever experienced. If she'd been stronger, the process might have dragged; her body putting up a fight, refusing to bow out gracefully. But my grandmother, fragile and worn by time, didn't have the stamina for theatrics. She stills, and the room settles into a silence so dense it could be bottled and sold as a souvenir.

I could've sworn I heard her final, rattling breath as I reached for her hand. It was cold, the warmth of life already retreating from her skin which was translucent, frail, and barely clung to her bones.

I leaned in, pressing a soft kiss to her wrinkled forehead, her damp skin yielding beneath my lips. "Rest now," I said, though she couldn't hear me from wherever she'd gone.

Before leaving my grandmother's room, I lingered, my gaze fixed on her lifeless form. The years had etched deep lines into her face and body. A testament to time's relentless march. She had been brittle, broken, clinging to the last threads of existence. And yet, even in her frailty, she had towered large in my life—a woman who had given me a roof over my head, who had fed me when I had nowhere else to turn.

I searched myself, digging through layers of emotion, trying to unearth something resembling guilt or regret. I had killed my grandmother—a family member.

Shouldn't I feel something?

False Grandpa was no one, nothing. But *she* was my blood.

Did I feel bad? Did I regret it? Could I have sat down with her, talked it out, and salvaged some semblance of a relation-ship?

Absolutely not.

She may have been old, but age didn't absolve her of the choices she'd made, the pain she'd inflicted, or the silence she'd maintained when I needed her most. Her infirmity didn't erase the memories of what she'd allowed to happen, the scars she'd left behind.

No, I didn't feel bad. Not for her. Not for this.

My grandmother had done the bare minimum of what grandmothers should do—but she had also done what grandmother's shouldn't. She kept me in the presence of predators who hurt me constantly. Both her boyfriend, and then, my mother. She could have stopped them at any time—kicked them out, called the police—but she chose not to. Instead, she blamed me for their actions.

She brought this onto herself. She could have avoided it all if she'd made better choices.

Clearing my head for my next task, I stood, taking one last glance at the empty creature before me. By the time the nurse discovered her tomorrow, I'd be halfway back to Connecticut. I turned and left the room, leaving behind the dust and old linens. I didn't feel crushed by what I'd just done. No. Instead, it liber-ated me.

Two down. One to go.

The cold apartment clung to me as I moved, footsteps light against the worn floorboards, careful not to disturb the uneasy stillness—especially in heels. The dim hallway stretched ahead, but I extinguished its glow with a flick of my fingers, switching off the lights one by one. Each click plunged me deeper into darkness, wrapping me in its familiar embrace.

I ignored False Grandpa's body as I crossed the kitchen into the living room. It devoured me as I sunk into an armchair's sag-ging cushions, my body disappearing into its worn embrace. It smelled like a time capsule—cigarettes smoked long before I was born, coffee stains that told stories of mornings gone wrong, exhaustion seeped so deep it might as well be part of the upholstery.

My gun settled into my palm as if it belonged there. Less like an object and more like a seamless extension of myself. My fingers curled around its grip with a kind of ease that would make a gunslinger proud. I contained my breathing, closing my eyes, steady, precise. It's the most important part of controlling your shot. If you're going to wait for a showdown, you might as well do it right.

I angled myself toward the front door, gaze locked, ears tuned to every creak and groan of the building. The wood shifted under its own weight, the kind of sound that might lull someone into a false sense of security. But not me. I knew better. I knew what real danger sounded like.

The clock on the wall ticked in my periphery, each second dragging its nails down my spine like an impatient cat.

She'll be here soon, I thought.

I tightened my grip on the gun just thinking about it, sensing the value of every choice, every moment, every insult that had led to this one pressing against my chest. My mind wandered to the last time we spoke—if you could call it speaking. It wasn't a conversation; it was more like a verbal cage match. Words flew like daggers, each one sharper than the last, cutting deeper than any bullet ever could. And now, she'd walk into a war she didn't even know she started.

Deep, velvety shadows pooled around me, pressing in like an overzealous embrace. My pulse remained slow, my body still.

Whatever came, I was ready. I was waiting.

I couldn't help but think about how absurd this all was. Sitting there, in a living room that smelled like shit, armed and ready for a showdown with the woman who used to roll her eyes when I'd ask her to cut the crusts off my sandwiches.

Life has a funny way of circling back, doesn't it?

The apartment creaked again, and I smirked. Let her come. I've been ready for this moment my whole life—or at least since I stopped eating crustless sandwiches.

Chapter 15

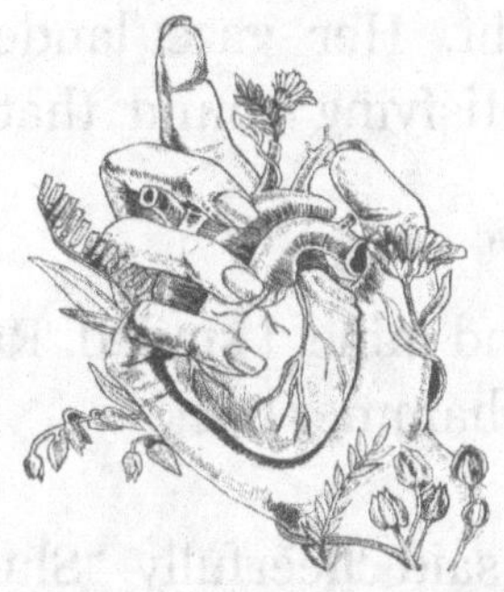

The apartment stunk of decay—rotting food, stale cigarette smoke, booze—seeping into every corner like a bad memory. It was worse than I remembered from my teenage years, but maybe that was because I'd tried to forget what it felt like to live here. The smell clung to me, making every second feel like an eternity. But it wouldn't matter soon. It was almost 5 P.M, and I'd be gone before long.

The room dimmed as the sun dipped below the horizon, leaving only the sickly yellow glow from the hallway light spilling onto the old man's face through the door. His eyes were wide open, staring at nothing. Not much of a change from when he was alive. A dark pool of blood spread across the peeling linoleum in memorandum of my handiwork.

Down the hall within the apartment, my grandmother's body lay cooling, veins full of fentanyl, life snuffed out. My poor mother wouldn't even get the chance to check on her—not after stumbling, literally, upon False Grandpa sprawled on the floor with a bullet hole neatly placed in the center of his forehead.

For a moment, I almost felt bad.

That feeling evaporated as I heard the clatter of keys unlocking the door. Creaking open just enough for my mother to step inside, something blocked it from swinging open fully. The subdued light made it hard to see her face, but I could imagine the confusion—and oh, how I hoped for horror! The thought of her reaction sent a thrill through me.

She reached for the switch, and the kitchen flooded with harsh fluorescent light. Her gaze landed on the body. She shrieked, a sharp, satisfying sound that echoed through the apartment.

"Oh—Oh my God!"

Then her eyes found mine. I smiled. Raising the pistol in her direction, I locked the hammer back.

Click.

"Hello, mother," I said cheerfully. "Shut the door and lock it. Let's talk. It's been *so* long."

She did what I asked, but rapidly started digging through her purse, presumably searching for her phone to call the police.

"No," I said, my voice light, almost playful. "You're not calling anyone." I flailed the .22 around as if reminding her of the circumstances.

My mother froze with her hand buried deep into her purse, like she was digging for treasure. I stepped forward, the barrel of the gun inching closer to her.

"Hand it over," I said calmly, leaving no room for negotiation.

Her hand slid out of the bag, dragging it down with her until she held it out to me. "Alright . . ." She whimpered as I snatched the purse from her grip, keeping the gun trained on her face. "Alright!" She snapped again, louder this time, like she was trying to reclaim some dignity.

With the bag in one hand and the pistol steady in the other, I placed the bag on the small table beside me, rummaging through her belongings until I found her phone. That's when I noticed her long, green coat. A perfect hiding spot for weapons.

Not that she'd expected me to show up today.

"Take off the coat and toss it aside," I ordered.

She hesitated for a fraction of a second before shrugging it off and letting it fall. It landed unceremoniously on False Grandpa's body, like some morbid fashion statement.

"What the hell are you doing here, Cassandra?" she asked, her voice wary. It had been years since we'd last spoken, but she recognized the look in my eyes instantly—the one that screamed this wasn't a social call.

I smirked. "Doesn't seem like you're in any position to ask questions, Maureen." My finger brushed the trigger with the kind of care usually reserved for a lover's touch. "I came for the family reunion."

She blinked, lips parting like she might say something—maybe a plea, maybe a curse—but nothing came. Instead, her gaze flitted around the room, scanning for an exit, a weapon, divine intervention. Unfortunately for her, divine intervention was booked solid, and I wasn't feeling generous.

"What family reunion?" The question was as brittle as dried leaves.

I nudged my head toward the hallway, smirking. "Can't you tell? False Grandpa was so excited, he decided to greet you at the door."

Her face drained of color so fast, I half-expected her to pass out. I watched as hesitation snuck into her stance, dread flickering in her gaze. She knew. She didn't need to look. The tremor in her fingers, the way her throat bobbed—it had already settled in her bones.

But curiosity was one hell of a thing.

She turned her head, the inevitable horror dragging her eyes toward the corpse. Her breath sputtered in her chest. Frozen in the doorway, her hands still levitated like I had personally slapped her into an arrest. But there were no cops here.

No flashing lights.

No Miranda rights.

No negotiable plea deals.

"Where's your motherly instinct now?" I mocked, stepping forward, gun steady as ever. "No lectures? No guilt trips? No melodramatic speeches about my 'failures'?" I clicked my tongue. "Oh, right. You only play the concerned parent when you've got an audience. Too bad the guest list tonight is looking a little worse for wear." I angled my head down to False Grandpa.

Her lips pressed into a line so tight it could've cut glass.

I laughed manically, intentionally letting the sound carry between us. "C'mon, Maureen. Don't be shy now! Tell me how you really feel. You always had so much to say when I was a teenager —so many critiques, so many insults." I tipped my head, amused. "Go on, say it. Tell me I'm a disgrace. Tell me I'm ruining my life."

She shook her head, her lips parting like she wanted to speak, but didn't.

"Nothing?" I stepped closer, my voice dropping to a chilly disposition. "No more speeches about how I was your biggest mistake?" I paused. "Funny. It almost seems like you're scared."

She swallowed hard.

"Because you should be."

Keeping the .22 trained on her, I gestured toward the couch with a flick of my hand. "Have a seat. Let's catch up—it's been ages, hasn't it?"

She hesitated, her eyes darting between me and the couch. Eventually she relented, shuffling past, lagging as if she was trying not to spook a bear. She sank into the cushions, her eyes never leaving mine, as if she thought staring hard enough into them might save her.

I flicked on the lamp, harsh light spilling across my mother's face. Moving to the window, I yanked the blinds shut just in case some nosy neighbor decided to play hero. Not that anyone could make out my features from this distance, but I wasn't about to take chances.

"Cassandra—" Maureen gasped, her voice cracking like dry wood. She stopped short as I leveled the gun at her, my grip tightening just enough to make my point.

"Ah, Ah!" I barked. "When I said, 'let's chat' it didn't mean with an open-ended conversation!"

She folded into herself, hands wedged between her knees. Bleary eyes darted anywhere but at me, head dipping low. She dragged a trembling hand through her brittle, greasy hair like she was trying to comb out her shame.

"Jesus. You look rough," I said, my laugh dry. It echoed in the room like a bad punchline. "I didn't think I'd ever see you again. Guess miracles really do happen."

Her gaze flicked up to meet mine, wide and terrified, but her head remained bowed like she was trying to disappear into the couch cushions. I stood over her, a gloom she couldn't escape, a reminder she couldn't ignore.

"You were never supposed to . . ." she muttered, voice trailing off into the kind of sadness that might've tugged at someone with a heart. She dropped her eyes back to her lap, and I smirked.

Crouching down, I placed the pistol between my knees, my finger still on the trigger; the barrel of the suppressor fixed on her face. She didn't move.

"You ruined my dad's life," I said with no bite whatsoever. "You took me away from the one person who would have protected me. You brought me here so Falsey—now dead by the door if you haven't noticed—could use me as a blow-up doll. You and the dead bitch down the hall both turned a blind eye to it." I nodded rhythmically as I spoke, my gaze sharpening with each word. "Then you brought me to Bristol where you yourself proceeded to continue the abuse, physically and mentally, then fucking left me to fend for myself!"

"You killed her—"

"Shut the fuck up!" I cried, throwing myself upright to dig the barrel of the pistol into my mother's skull.

Maureen began to sob.

"You don't get to speak! You wanted to be silent, so be silent!"

Her jeans darkened with tears, the fabric soaking up her grief like ink spreading across paper. I searched myself for even a flicker of sympathy, but found nothing—no trace of compassion, no room for forgiveness. My mother had spent her life pointing fingers, shifting blame onto everyone but herself. Every problem she faced was a consequence of her own choices, though she'd never admit it.

"Dad would have never treated me the way you did, the way you let other's treat me," I spat. "And now he's fucking gone. It's your fault he got so sick. You think I couldn't put two and two together? How did dad mysteriously always have bricks of cocaine? How did his friends just magically appear to snort it with him?"

"Don't—"

I dug the pistol deeper into her head. "I'm talking!" Tears formed in my eyes. "He could've gotten clean. He tried. He wanted to for *me*. But you wouldn't let him, would you?"

Maureen shook her head but said nothing. I pistol whipped her with as much power as I could issue in the face, right above her eye. Blood trickled from the wound, and she covered it with her hand to keep more of it from dripping onto her pants.

"Now would be a good time to answer while you still can."

"I didn't *force* him to do anything," she said through gritted teeth. "He made his own choices."

The gun came in contact with her face again, this time on the other side. A gash opened on her forehead, deeper than the one above her eye. She cried out, and I swear I felt euphoria as she did.

"Don't fucking lie to me, Maureen," I hissed, clenching my jaw. "You kept him hooked. You needed him strung out because when he was sober, he saw you for what you were. And you couldn't handle that."

My mother scoffed, continuing to avoid my stare. An edge of nervousness coiled within her voice. "You think you know everything, huh?" She shook her head, keeping it down. "You were a kid. You didn't see the shit we went through."

I took another step forward. "I saw enough."

My mother shifted further back on the couch, trying to put space between us. She breathed heavily through the pain she was assuredly feeling right then. "You don't get it. Your father—he was weak.

"Weak?" I shouted, taken aback that she'd actually say that about anyone other than herself. *How dare she!* I inched ever closer to my mother, the suppressor inches from her face. "You know what *is* weak? Deserting a teenager to fend for herself, with no explanation, no warning, no nothing. You didn't even check to see if I was okay!"

My mom continued to stare down the barrel, fear lining her face as she did.

"Dad was an addict," I continued. "You made sure he never got help, and I had to watch him die once I finally got him back."

My mother exhales heavily, shaking her head, the words husky as she struggles to breathe. "You came all the way here to tell me that?" She smirks bitterly. "Fine. You hate me. Get in line."

"I didn't come to tell you that," I said, my behavior switching swiftly from enraged to playful. "I could never hate you, but it's not fair you're alive and he's not. I'm here to change that." A smile crosses my face, while confusion crosses hers.

My mother frowned. "Then why . . . Cass—wait—"

Enough talking, cunt.

BANG!

BANG!

BANG!

Three shots.

One to wound, one to kill, and one just for fun.

The gunshots ripped through the apartment, crisp, unforgiving, like lightning bolts cracking through the sky. My mother jerked backward, a spray of red splattering against the yellowed wallpaper of the living room. Her body slumped onto the couch, blood soaking into the fabric, a slow exhale escaping her lips before she went eternally still.

I stared at her, gun still warm in my hand. My chest heaved with the remnants of rage that hadn't yet burned out. "I actually don't feel anything for you at all," I said, but the words felt hollow, like they were trying to convince me of something I wasn't sure I believed.

As I watched the life drain from her eyes, I remembered how they'd always been icy—like staring into a void that had never cared to hold anything but contempt. My anger still simmered, clawing at the edges of my composure. It wasn't the kind of anger that burned hot and fast—it was the kind that lingered, heavy and suffocating, refusing to let go even when the source was gone. She was dead, but the memories weren't. The years of torment, the manipulation, the cruelty—they still lived inside me, like ghosts refusing to be exorcised. Killing her hadn't erased them.

I shoved the weapon into my bag, removing the silencer and clicking on its safety with skillful precision. The motion gave my hands something to do while my mind wrestled with the storm inside. I turned off the lights as I left, the darkness swallowing the room and the wreckage I'd left behind. The nurse who came by to check on my grandmother would have the surprise of her life come morning. A gift to society, really—three wastes of flesh no longer able to breathe, to hurt, to exist.

But even as I thought it, anger began to shift. It loosened its grip just enough for something else to seep in.

Relief.

It was subtle at first, like the faintest breath of air after being strangled for too long. Then it grew, spreading through me like a medicinal balm, quieting the turmoil, and leaving behind a strange, unfamiliar calm.

And death, it seemed, had finally done its job.

My heels clicked against the pavement as I snuck back outside, each step a punctuation mark to the disorder I'd left behind. The black SUV waited like a loyal accomplice, its sleek frame promising escape. I paused to swipe on a fresh coat of crimson lipstick—a shade that felt figurative, given the blood spilled today. The act was a way to reclaim control, to remind myself that I was still standing, still intact, still me.

Thomas, ever the dutiful driver, pulled open the door, and I slid into the back seat with the kind of grace that only comes after a day of tying up loose ends. As the door shut behind me, I leaned back, letting my mind drift into a blissful haze—a serendipitous nirvana, if you will.

My abusers? *Gone.*

My past? *Dead.*

And me? *Still standing, lipstick intact.*

The SUV hummed to life, and as we pulled away, I felt the weight of it all lift off my shoulders, carried away by the wind like yesterday's trash. I didn't look back—why would I? The view ahead was far more promising.

Thomas glanced at me in the rearview mirror. "Eventful day?" He asked casually, like we'd just wrapped up brunch instead of a trio of homicides.

I quirked a smile, checking my makeup application in my compact mirror. "You could say that. Let's just hope the neighbors aren't too nosy."

Chapter 16

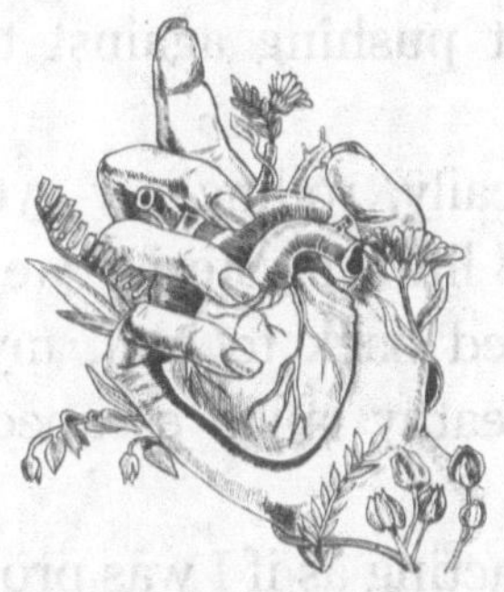

Barreling into the interrogation room like an incoming bomb, Detective James Hall was all force and fury wrapped in a too-tight coat he hadn't bothered to shed. His breath came uneven, laced with frustration. Judging by the tension coiling in his shoulders, I'd wager he was one harsh word away from snapping. He planted both hands on the table, looming over me, his shadow stretched across the metal surface, cloaking my face like some striking movie villain.

I offered him a lazy smile, easing back into my chair to put just enough space between us to simulate comfort. Not that it mattered. Even from here, his breath could kill a colony of wasps.

My chained arms rested limply on my legs, but in my mind I was lounging in a throne, draping my arms over the chair's back with regal pleasance. This interrogation room was no less my dais. My fingers twitched, aching to carve shapes into the air, but I anchored them to the seam of my jeans instead.

James remained standing, rigid. A man refusing to sink back into the familiarity of our game.

A silent staring contest ensued.

I jerked my head to the side—sharp, sudden, like the clash of gears grinding to a halt. "Mm. Rough day, James?" My eyebrows arched in imitative curiosity, a silent dare for him to speak.

He didn't answer.

Sausage fingers curled around the edges of the metal table, the strain rippling through him. The throb at his throat was unmistakable, each beat pushing against taut skin like a silent drum.

I sighed dramatically, rolling my eyes toward the ceiling, scanning it like all of life's mysteries were scribbled up there. Then my gaze snapped back to him, my amusement entirely misplaced. A little breathy laugh escaped—because really, this was just too much.

"Wow," I mused, acting as if I was probing him on a medical examination table. "You're breathing kind of heavy there. Let me guess—did you run all the way here? For me? Jamesey, I'm touched."

He didn't wince. Didn't blink. Just stared. "Cut the theatrics," he growled. "I know how you got into our systems."

I slapped a hand over my mouth, gasping so profoundly I should've been cast on Broadway. My other hand dangled loosely from the chain. Who needed symmetry in a crisis? Then, for added effect, both hands flew to my chest like I'd just heard the juiciest scandal, clutching invisible pearls.

"Oh, wow," I deadpanned, instantly bored again. "That's what we're talking about now? Really? I thought you'd finally work up the nerve to ask me about the hearts."

James gritted his teeth, his jaw twitching in resentment.

I let out a quick, biting laugh designed to get under his skin. I knew exactly how much it irritated him. He's dealt with murderers—the cold, calculated, remorseless types. He's dealt with liars—the ones whose voices tremble as they spin their fragile little tales.

But me? Oh, I was something else entirely.

I saw it in his eyes, the flinches of uncertainty. Part of his brain scrambled to figure out where to place me. Poor James. He didn't realize there wasn't a box for me quite yet.

Straightening my spine, each vertebrae locked into place like the teeth of a zipper. My gaze darted upward, eyes broadening, like I'd just been struck by some great revelation—something James, with all his training and bravado, had completely missed. Parting my lips, I moved them silently, forming phantom words that carried no sound. Not saying anything. Just *implying*.

Oh, the torment on his face as he tried to decipher my nonexistent confession.

His thoughts must have been racing: *What is she saying? Is she mocking me? Is this part of her plan?*

Then, as if a switch had flipped, I snapped back to reality, my grin sliding into place with automatic finesse.

"Detective," I purred, my head falling askew as my fingers brushed my chin. "Do the ones you've failed to save linger when you close your eyes?"

James's chest rose abruptly, betraying his composure.

"You know . . . Evan. Lile. Ben . . ." Their names floated around us, suspended like ghosts. "Do they speak to you?"

Again, silence. But his stare pinned me in place, scrutinizing every shift in my posture. I absorbed the gravity of it, but instead of faltering, I let it strengthen me.

"I'm surprised they didn't warn you," I continued lightly. "Then again, they were dead before they could. Lile was so sure I *wouldn't* get away with this." I sighed, faking sympathy. "Funny, isn't it? Considering I'm the one who *called* you here in the first place." I stooped closer, resting my elbows on the table, my smirk widening. "They're talking to me, James." In a hushed whisper, I trembled, simulating wonder. I glanced over my shoulder sharply, then back to him, my grin creeping ever wider. "They're here. Right now. Watching us."

I saw it then—a waver in his expression.

Was that . . . *intrigue?*

James finally sunk into the chair across from me, resting his folder under his hands.

I allowed my head to fall back, scanning the ceiling once more. Abruptly, I started humming—low, eerie, just off-key enough to sound unsettling.

"Tell me how you did it," James ordered, ignoring my ruse.

My head lowered; eyes gleaming in the light. My lips stretched into a languid, triumphant grin. "I thought you already knew, so you're going to need to be more specific, James."

James hunched over the metal table, his forearms pressing into its surface. His eyes fixed on me as if trying to drill information into my mind. I met his stare with a smile—the kind of smile that suggested I hold the pieces to a puzzle he hasn't even realized he's solving.

"You knew where they lived. Where they drank. Where they liked to sneak off with their side pieces when their wives weren't looking," James said, flipping open his folder with a skillful glare. The pages were a mess of scrawled notes, like a madman's grocery list. "You didn't just get lucky. Someone gave you access—police records, classified systems—you had help."

Dropping my head, my face portrayed wide-eyed innocence, like butter wouldn't melt in my mouth. "You really don't give me enough credit." Then I added, "Besides, Ben was divorced, and the other two? No wives, no nothing. But boy, did they *want* me. Followed me home like ducklings, they did." I held back, granting the graveness of what I'd said to settle. I leaned in just slightly, lowering my voice like I was about to tell him a juicy secret. "You'd be amazed what people will share when they think they're impressing you. Men love to brag." I exhaled like this whole thing was exhausting. "And let's be real, James—you guys aren't exactly subtle when you think no one's watching." Tracing my chin with a thoughtful finger, I continued my spiel, words flowing effortlessly under James's watchful eyes. "Honestly, I barely had to lift a finger. Except to, well, you know . . ."

His stare remained steady, impenetrable. He leaned into his words with the precision of a scalpel. "Who. Helped. You?"

I huffed roughly, dragging a nail across the tabletop in slow, random strokes, as if drawing out his question. Truth is, I already knew how this would play out. Like I've said before, I take all the credit for every decision, every action. Whether I borrowed Lonney's old hacking tricks or coaxed Zina into something—none of it mattered.

The glory was *mine*. If James thought I'd sell out a fucking dead man and my best friend, he's just as stupid as I'd expected.

"Your system is a joke." I dropped the volume of my voice, just a whisper above mute.

His jaw tightened, the muscle in his cheek flexing as my words land exactly where I want them.

"Do you really think your boys are untraceable? That your little blue wall is bulletproof? Please," I said, shaking my head with a faint smirk. "I had everything I needed before I even selected my murder weapon."

I cocked my head the other way, savoring the exquisite state of aggravation etched into his features; the cracks in his wannabe tough-guy cop routine. He tried so hard not to let it show. So hard, it was almost amusing.

"You don't hack systems, Cassandra," he said, strained, like he was trying to convince himself more than me. "You're smart, but you're not *that* smart."

Oh, excuse me? *Not that smart?*

Ahem—behold the woman who single-handedly dismantled three of your boys like they were flimsy IKEA furniture and probably could've kept going if I hadn't decided to be merciful to the rest of the department. I was furious, but I didn't let it show. Instead, I smiled slowly. The kind of smile that says, *Oh, honey, you've just made my day.*

"Did *you* attend Yale, Detective?" I asked, as if I actually cared what the answer was, because I already knew the answer was *NO.* "You continue underestimating me, and honestly, it's adorable." My lips curled further, sharpening into something ravenous. "Lonney taught me everything he knew—well, without ever realizing he was actually teaching me. Poor guy thought he was helping me. Turns out, he was just handing me the keys to the kingdom."

I paused to let the words hang in the air like smoke from the fire I'd just started. His entire body went still. The name was like a gunshot, and I knew I hit my mark. I fell back, satisfied, watching his reaction unfold in real time.

"You remember Lonney, don't you?" I asked, narrowing my eyes.

I know what I said about not implicating a dead man but come on—he didn't actually *do* anything. I'm the one who re-membered everything, the one who pieced it all together. Lon-ney wasn't here to lift a finger for me. If anything, James de-served this for thinking my intelligence stopped at my manicure or the crimson in my lipstick.

"Qualley's right-hand man," I continued. "The guy you idiots thought you took out of the game years ago. Oh, he told me all about that story. Turns out, all it took was the right incentives to get back in."

James's knuckles pressed into the table as his hand curls into a fist. "You're telling me *he* hacked into our system?"

I scoffed as if he just said the dumbest thing I've ever heard —because he did. "*He* didn't, James, because he's *dead*." I cocked my head as my lips formed a small "O" in mock surprise. I pressed my hands childishly on each side of my face. Think, *Home Alone.*

Recognition struck him like a cartoon anvil, crushing and inescapable. He finally understood. Realized someone—maybe an entire team of someones—had left the back door to his prized system propped wide open, practically inviting trouble in with a welcome mat.

Passwords? *Untouched.*

Firewalls? *More outdated than his operating system.*

The breaches were there, just begging to be exploited—and exploited they were. Long before anyone had a chance to slam the door shut, I'd already made myself at home.

"You ever notice how easy it is to get what you want when people think you're nothing but a pretty face?" I pressed closer, my voice took on a gentle, almost mischievous lilt. My chin lifted, eyes glinting, savoring James's peeved mug.

James shook his head, disgusted. His composure disintegrated with every passing second. "You're telling me *you* got into police files because someone left their login open?"

"Oh god no," I said, grinning wider. "I got access to police files because *your* whole damn department is a circus of fucking idiots. Lonney? He was simply an unknowing collaborator. I watched him access everything, memorized his passwords, copied his hard drives—it was child's play. I knew it'd come in handy eventually."

James sat back, swallowing his palatial rage. His eyes darted across my profile, as if aiming to calculate the damage I'd caused the precinct's systems. I chuckled under my breath, the sound a low rumble, mischievous—because honestly, the whole scene was comedy gold. A joke so brilliant it's only now dawning on him, like a delayed punchline delivered in slow motion.

"You should really thank me," I mused, coating the words in artificial sweetness. "I did you a favor. Now you know your department has holes. Big ones." I leaned in, cupping my hands around my mouth as if telling him a secret. "Including the one I dug for you in my backyard—with all your men inside it."

The air shifted then—sharp and chilly—like their ghosts had just popped by to stir up drama. Overhead, the lights emitted probably all the warmth of the interrogation room, casting jagged shadows across James's face. I watched him, my gaze steady, vulturine—though, let's be honest, I looked less like a lioness stalking her prey and more like a cat smugly watching a bird through a window.

Slowly, with all the theatrics of someone who's about to drop the punchline to the cruelest joke, I licked my lips. Not because I was hungry (well, maybe just a little), but because his visible discomfort was just so delectably . . . nourishing.

"See, James," I purred, "you think all I had was police records. But . . ." I picked at my fingers, peeling loose skin with an almost absent-minded focus. "I had access to everything. Medical histories. Prescriptions. Surgeries . . . conditions." My voice drips with malice masquerading as tenderness. Tracing invisible shapes on the tabletop as I spoke, each word slipped out like a taunt. "It's funny, really, what people think is private. What they assume is safe, hidden behind a fragile little password. All it took was a little observation. Men wear their intentions like mismatched socks—easy to spot if you're looking." I mimed typing on an invisible keyboard, then lift a single finger to my lips in counterfeit secrecy.

James's breathing remained controlled, but I caught the telltale signs of an impending explosion—his fingers curling tighter against the table again, his rigid posture. It was endearing, really, how hard he tried to keep his cool.

I smiled, letting out a quiet breath through my nose. A sound almost contented, if I'm honest. Watching him unravel was just too satisfying, and to push the knife in further, my gaze drifted downward, lingering on his chest. And no, this wasn't admiration—it was a look that said, *Are you sure you're ready for this? Because I don't think you are.*

"It must be exhausting," I said tenderly, "carrying a heart that fragile."

"Excuse me?" James snapped, drawing closer to invade my precious space, as if the close proximity was supposed to intimidate me.

Cute.

For the first time since he walked in, I saw just the crack in his disposition. Something unfamiliar twisted through him, crawling up his spine, and oh, I saw it! I saw it and savored it like the first sip of a good wine.

My grin widened. "Tick, tock. Tick, tock." I had sung softly, wagging my finger in slow rhythm, like keeping time on a metronome. "That's what it feels like, right? Every little flutter, every tiny strain, wondering if this is it—if this is the moment your whole world decides to crash down."

His face reddened, jaw tightening. Brows furrowed into something almost artistic. The scowl he tried to pull off was fierce enough to warrant applause—if he weren't so utterly predictable.

"You don't know anything," he growled, attempting to sound threatening.

"Oh, please," I teased playfully. "So you really didn't run here to see me?" I shifted slightly, my tone carrying an air of quiet amusement, as though revealing something meant to intrigue. "Your heart was racing before you walked through that door. Admit it, James—you missed me. You *enjoy* my company. You *enjoy . . . presents,* don't you?" I giggled—a quiet, childish, giddy sound that only deepened the thundercloud brewing on his face.

His scowl sharpened, composure fraying like an old rope about to snap. He was halfway across the table then, practically breathing my air, but I didn't flinch. I shifted in closer, matching his intensity, my voice dropping to a conspiratorial whisper.

"Tell me . . . does *your wife* know? Or do you hide the heart thing from her too?"

James slammed his fist into the table, a metallic clang ricocheting through the room as his chair crashed to the floor behind him. The sound was crisp, jarring—and utterly satisfying. But I didn't startle. If anything, his tantrum added a whole new level of entertainment to the itinerary.

"Why do you keep mentioning her?" he cried. I didn't give him the satisfaction of answering. That would come in due time.

I clapped my hands as much as I could in an applause, laughing—melodic, perfectly timed as he stared at me. He was shaken but trying to keep his composure. For a man with a heart condition, he really knew how to pile on the stress. *How ironic.*

Tracking his movements, my grin fixed to him as my eyes glinted like a wolf sizing up the weakest in the pack. He headed for the door, and I bent myself lazily into the chair, letting my head loll back over the edge like lounging poolside on a sunny afternoon.

"I wonder," I called after him dreamily but detached, "how much stress it takes to break a heart like yours."

James hit the button and stepped out without a word, leaving behind nothing but a soft echo of the door clicking shut.

<h1 style="text-align:center">Chapter 17</h1>

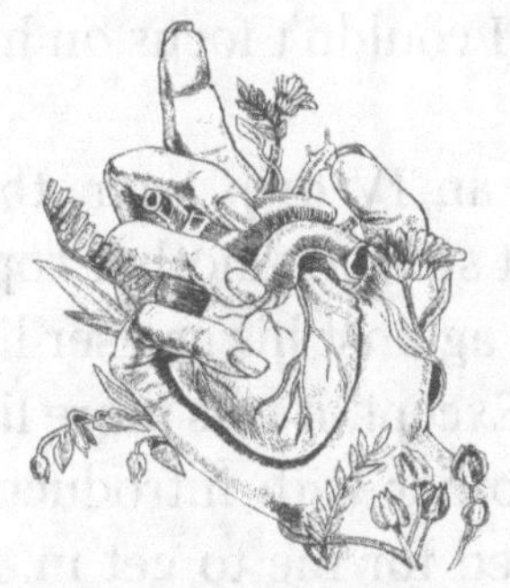

Do you really think Yale let me in for my charm? My dazzling personality? Please. It was my brain. My amazing memory. Sure, it was art school, and sure, I dropped out faster than you can say "student loans" thanks to my douchebag ex, but that memory of mine? It was my secret weapon. Every image I saw was already a masterpiece in my head before I even touched a brush. And beyond painting, my highly superior ability to recall every single thing that's ever happened to me or anyone I care about—made dissecting that court case a breeze. You know, the one where a whole squad of officers walked away scot-free under the banner of 'self-defense.'

Lonney's hacking systems? A *joke*. The guy used the same password for everything. It was like he wanted to be caught. When the authorities raided the house, they seized all their electronics, but guess what? I'd already cloned Lonney's hard drive onto my laptop years ago. He never even noticed, or he did and didn't say anything. I had everything I needed, neatly organized and ready to go.

However, before I could tap into what I'd acquired, I had to deal with the issue at hand.

The hospital had patched me up after passing out after being told Qualley was dead. I couldn't call Zina to check on her because she was still being grilled by the cops at the time. She'd been in the house during the raid, and from what I overheard, she was a wreck. Her name floated through Goldfinch's radio as the EMTs worked on me in the ambulance and I fell in and out of consciousness, but I couldn't focus on her then. I had my own mess to deal with.

A few hours and an IV drip later, the hospital discharged me. But freedom? Not so fast. Another cop waited for Goldfinch and I outside, leaning against his cruiser like he was auditioning for a bad cop drama. Except, it was more like *Super Troopers*.

He didn't even bother with introductions. Just opened the back door and gestured for me to get in. "We're not done with you yet." He said it as if *I* was wasting his precious time. I rolled my eyes but slid into the car without a word. Goldfinch followed in the front seat, looking cocky as ever.

The ride back to the station was a symphony of awkward silence, punctuated by an occasional crackle of a radio and the two officers' wildly inappropriate jokes about a female colleague mixed with random conversation. My whole world was crumbling and they're over here talking about someone who probably trusted them with their life in a derogatory way, wondering if there would be cake in the break room for officer whoever's going away party. I could feel eyes on me from the rearview mirror, but I ignored them, staring out the window instead.

The police car reeked of stale coffee and regret. My hands clenched into fists so tight my nails dug into my palms, but the pain was a lifeline tethering me to the present. I stared out the window, my reflection a ghostly overlay on the darkened streets of Bristol. The city blurred past, but my mind was stuck, replaying the moment I'd heard the words I couldn't unhear.

Qualley is dead.

Tim Fieldman had said it with all the passion of someone reading a grocery list. *Gone*. Like Qualley had just stepped out for a pack of cigarettes and might be back any minute. But I knew better.

Gone meant dead.

Gone meant I'd never hear his laugh again; never see that crooked grin he wore when he thought he was being clever.

Gone meant my life had just been ripped apart, and the pieces didn't fit back together anymore.

Blinking hard, I willed my tears, threatening to fall, to stay put. Not here. Not now. Not in front of dumb and dumber.

The officers in the front seat lowered their voices, suddenly reminded of my presence behind them. Their tone shifted; words muffled like they were trying to shield their conversation from my ears. The unidentified officer cracked a joke about something ridiculous, and Goldfinch laughed—a grating sound that made my blood boil hotter.

How could they laugh?

How could they sit there, so casually, so unaffected, while my reality was unraveling at the seams?

My chest throbbed with a grief that clung to me like an unshakable illness. I bit the inside of my cheek, the metallic taste of blood sharp on my tongue. Anything to keep the tears at bay. To feel like I'm still here, still alive. I wouldn't give them the satisfaction of seeing me break.

Officer Goldfinch glanced back at me, his eyes meeting mine in the rearview mirror. "You okay back there?" He asked perfunctorily rather than concerned.

I refused to react, though even if I wanted to, my throat was too tight to speak. I knew if I opened my mouth, either the dam would break, or I'd say something reckless and get myself thrown in jail for good.

He shrugged, realizing he wasn't getting anything from me, turning back around, attention already elsewhere. I exhaled slowly, fogging up the window. I traced a finger through the condensation, drawing a heart with a "Q&M" inside. I tried to focus on anything but the hollow ache in my chest.

Qualley was gone.

The words echoed in my mind, a relentless drumbeat I

couldn't escape. I wanted to scream, to cry, to lash out at the universe for taking him from me. But all I could do was sit there, silent and still, as the police car carried me away from the life I'd known.

My reflection in the window stared back at me, eyes red-rimmed but dry. I didn't recognize the woman looking back at me. This wasn't Cassandra Kessler, the woman who always had a plan, always knew what to do. This was someone else—someone lost, someone broken.

But the woman in the reflection seemed to say, "not for long."

As the car turned onto another empty street, I straightened my spine, my hands relaxing in my lap. Tears would come later, in the privacy of my own space. For now, I held it together. I had to.

Qualley might be gone, but I was still here.

And I wasn't done yet.

👁 👁

Back at the station, they peppered me with more questions. I gave them answers so half-hearted they were practically quarter-hearted. By 8 PM, nearly twenty-four hours after Qualley's death, they finally decided I wasn't their villain of the week and started the discharge paperwork. Goldfinch brooded as he typed on his computer, his little scowl firmly in place.

"You know you can't go back to that Chippen's Hill house for a few days, right?"

Way to condescend my ability to read the fucking room, I thought.

Rolling my eyes so hard, I nearly saw my own brain. I brushed past him, grabbing the bag of junk they'd confiscated during my arrest—sorry, detainment. Let me remind you, for absolutely no reason. I rifled through my handbag to make sure everything was there.

"I need a ride to my car," I said flatly, not bothering to look at him directly. Instead, I glanced at him from under my lashes, watching his reaction like a hawk.

Eyebrow arching, his lips tightened into a thin line. His expression seemed to say, "So?"

"I promise, the car isn't inside the house, Finchy," I said sarcastically, throwing in a shit-eating grin for appearances.

Goldfinch's self-complacency faltered for just a moment. "I'll have Jones take you to it, then." He reached for the phone.

I leaned against the counter. "Too busy ruining lives to chauffeur me yourself?" I savored every second of his discomfort.

He frowned, holding the phone to his ear as he stared me down. Someone on the other end answered, and his expression shifted to something more professional.

"Jones, I need you to take Miss Kessler to her car on Chippen's. Don't let her go inside," he said as if he'd been all business, and wasn't being a dick to me this entire day. I was pretty sure this was the same Jones he and the other officer had been cracking sexual jokes about. There was a short reply, and then he hung up.

My grin widened. "Can't even say please?" Teasing him and watching the squirm was the highlight of my day.

Goldfinch didn't take the bait, he just turned on his heel before disappearing down the hallway. I watched him go, wishing I had more time to get under his skin. But hey, life's long, and Goldfinch? He's not going anywhere.

❧ ❧

Lily Jones said nothing for the entire ride to my car. A woman after my own heart. No forced small talk, no tired clichés to distract me from the lingering headache they'd gifted me over the last twenty-four hours. She had stuck me in the 'criminal's seat,' as she bluntly called it, "for her own safety." Sure, I caught the flicker of regret in her eyes when she did. No doubt she'd seen worse occupants in her line of work, but at least she owned the decision.

After a parade of superiority complexes from her male colleagues, that human hesitance was refreshing.

Officer Jones was practically an anomaly. She carried herself with a quiet confidence that belied her petite frame and youthful face. Her sleek, no-nonsense bun was a work of art. A sculpted counterpoint to every flyaway strand that mocked my attempts at composure over the last day. Even her uniform couldn't hide her sharp cheekbones or warm, honey-toned complexion. Though she was shorter than most of her peers, her presence was magnetic, commanding attention in a way that spoke louder than shouting ever could. She didn't need theatrics. Her calm demeanor did all the heavy lifting.

She was the only one who seemed capable of empathy. And honestly, I wasn't sure whether that unnerved me or reassured me.

Throughout the drive, I caught her stealing glances in the rearview mirror. Her brows furrowed in faint concern; a silent puzzle piece wedged in between her stoic professionalism. She didn't say anything, and neither did I.

When she finally parked the patrol car behind my Mercedes, I sat there for a moment, still trapped in the 'naughty girl' seat. I'm not going to lie, Jones calling it that was both hilarious and borderline patronizing—but hey, she was consistent. I watched as she climbed out to open the door for me.

The evening air carried a brisk chill that bit at my skin as I stepped out of the car, my handbag slung over one shoulder. The door clicked shut behind me. I started to walk away, eager to escape yet another interaction with law enforcement. But her voice stopped me cold.

"Wait, Cassandra," she said, soft but firm.

Something about hearing my name, spoken with that mix of

warmth and authority, caught me off guard. It didn't happen often. I paused, turned back to face her, my keys clenched tightly in one hand while my bag slipped into the crook of my arm. One brow arched as I waited.

Jones stepped closer, resting her hand on the grip of her holstered weapon—not like she was preparing to draw it, more like the fact it was anchoring her. Her expressive brown eyes locked onto mine, filled with sympathy edged by something deeper.

Regret, maybe?

"I don't know all the details of what happened here," she said carefully, "but what the other officers did to you last night was absolutely disgraceful."

Disgraceful.

That was the word she chose? Like it was just poor behavior at a dinner party or an offhand insult someone could shrug off?

I scoffed, rolling my eyes dramatically. "Is that your professional opinion?" I asked, with enough sarcasm to drown a small village.

"No," she countered evenly, ignoring my disrespect. "It's a personal one."

A personal opinion. How quaint. It wasn't often I heard the words 'officer' and 'personal' in the same sentence without it being some sort of self-serving excuse. Still, her tone didn't carry the condescension I was used to. It was disarmingly genuine. A note I didn't quite know what to do with.

"No offense," I retorted, turning away from her, "but I don't need your pity."

Jones shrugged, unapologetic. "Maybe not. But I'm giving it to you anyway."

Her calm delivery was maddening, the lack of defensiveness catching me off guard yet again. It wasn't the pity that annoyed me; it was the sincerity behind it. The way her words didn't seem rehearsed or carefully calculated like everything else the department had thrown my way.

Empathy, real empathy, wasn't supposed to come from their ranks.

I let out a breath of irritation, continuing toward my car. Gravel crunched under my feet with each step until my fingers brushed the handle of the car door, eager to put this entire ordeal firmly in my rearview mirror.

"Qualley was a good guy," she called out, her words threading me into place. "Lonney too. They did a lot of good work to support this community. Work the department won't bother to acknowledge. I know because I was one of the students who benefited from the Wallis Scholarship when I was earning my Criminal Justice degree."

My lips pressed into a hard line as I stared at my reflection in the car window. The keys in my hand felt heavier than they should. I turned back to her, my expression unreadable.

"So why join the department that wanted to take him down?" I asked sharply, much sharper than I intended.

Jones sighed, her shoulders rising and falling as if they carried the weight of the question itself. "I didn't know," she admitted. "Not until I was assigned here after the academy. Not until recently, actually." Her gaze drifted toward the mansion, its grandeur now hollow and foreboding behind caution tape. "I thought about quitting or requesting reassignment, but then I figured, if I left, nothing would change. At least if I stayed, I'd have a chance to do something about it."

I nodded. "Thanks for the ride," I said, not bothering to regard her confession. "And for being the only person in your department with a brain."

Jones smiled solemnly but made no parting quip. She simply walked away, slid into her vehicle and drove off, leaving me standing there alone with only the mansion's looming silhouette and my own spiraling thoughts to keep me company.

As the sound of her engine faded into the distance, I stood rooted in place, her words echoing in my mind.

If I left, nothing would change.

That conviction she carried troubled me. There was a clear disconnect between her and the rest of the department, a division I couldn't ignore. Maybe she wasn't lying; maybe she truly believed she could make a difference. But it was hard to trust that belief and imagine one person making even a dent in the machine that was law enforcement.

I turned my gaze once more to the mansion, its once-pristine presentation now scarred and lifeless. It felt like a cruel metaphor for my own state—hollowed out, stripped bare, and left exposed for the world to see. I tightened my grip on the keys in my hand, the cold metal biting into my palm. Jones's belief in change might have been admirable, even noble, but it wasn't my reality. My world didn't just change; it burned. Her words didn't absolve the facts—the officers storming through the house or the ones who stood by and let it happen. And it certainly didn't absolve me of the promises I'd decided to make to myself.

Justice?

Revenge?

Maybe they were two sides of the same coin, but whatever it was, something had to happen.

Finally sliding into the driver's seat of my Mercedes, I didn't start the engine immediately. Instead, my gaze lingered on caution tape flapping in the breeze like some twisted parody of Halloween decoration. The memories of the last twenty-four hours clawed at me, vivid and relentless, but not with fear or regret.

No, what I felt was colder.

Resolution.

Gripping the steering wheel tightly, I let out a slow, measured breath, my eyes narrowing as I whispered, "They should've done a better job."

The thought sat heavy as I started the car, the engine's purr breaking the quiet. They might have stormed in and ransacked my life, confiscating everything they thought mattered, but in their arrogance—or maybe sheer incompetence—they hadn't searched my car.

The laptop in the trunk? Still there. Still untouched. My sanctuary wasn't this house anymore—not for now. But my temporary lair was out there, and I knew exactly where to find it. I knew exactly where I'd go.

Adjusting my seat, I drove off, not daring to linger. I needed refuge, somewhere invisible, inaudible, and untouchable. There was only one place that fit the bill.

And with that, I was already halfway there.

Qualley and Lonney's systems—both their lifelines and their Achilles' heels—needed to be wiped clean before the vultures circling their memory swooped in to feast on their secrets (if they haven't already). The investigators at the station had scrolled through my phone like it was a TikTok feed, dismissing me as nothing more than Qualley's girlfriend—a clueless bystander, wholly uninvolved in the operation they were so desperate to unravel. That underestimation? Their first mistake. Possibly their worst.

Laying low during the days that followed was like trying to hide a neon sign in a blackout. The night I was released from police custody, I logged into Lonney's digital labyrinth for the first time on my own. My laptop transformed into a portal to an ocean of secrets: buried reports, internal memos, personal records—everything the Bristol Police Department thought they'd buried beneath layers of encryption and firewalls.

Lonney had been the unknowing locksmith. A man without a conscience or concern for the systems he picked apart. And me? I was his shadow, the unintended apprentice to his craft. He had no idea I'd been watching him, memorizing every keystroke, every workaround. Or, maybe he did. He'd probably be proud, regardless. But the pride I felt? It was cold and dark, born of necessity, not triumph.

Once inside, I didn't rush. I studied James Hall, the lead detective, and his team the way a lioness studies her prey before a kill. Every detail became a puzzle piece, meticulously cataloged into separate folders: addresses, habits, routines, family members. Anything that made them seem human. Anything that made them weak. Their vulnerabilities were my ammunition.

During the days after my redundant detainment, I saved everything to an encrypted drive, erasing any trace of a digital presence in Qualley's and my lives like a ghost passing through hallowed halls. Later, as the ensuing court case found a resolution: *not guilty of two counts of murder*—my determination to infiltrate the lives of Qualley and Lonney's assailants hardened, intensified.

But still, paranoia crept in.

The apartment on Main Street became both my sanctuary and my prison. I had secretly kept it, just in case, and it was still in my late mother's name—a detail I'd never bothered to change, and the very reason no one looked too closely. To outsiders, Ms. Doherty, my mother, was still alive, and her devoted daughter dutifully took care of her. I'd kept the ruse alive for years, paying rent on time to avoid suspicion. The landlord, Mrs. Morris' daughter, Kathrine, managed the property now. She never asked questions. But whenever I sat in that dimly lit apartment, the walls seemed to breathe my secrets, whispering them into the void.

The chihuahua next door barked incessantly, scratching at the floor like it was trying to dig its way into my psyche. Footsteps echoed in the hallway—maybe a neighbor, maybe something worse. Every creak of the floorboards sent my pulse racing, but I forced my fingers to steady on the keyboard.

My fear was irrelevant.

My investigations were not.

Qualley's estate had passed to me swiftly thanks to his lawyer's efficiency. I hadn't even begun to comprehend the vastness of his holdings until it was all mine. Hidden accounts, investments buried under shell corporations—it was staggering. It was also a cruel irony. The wealth he left behind felt like a reminder of everything I had lost. Everything that had been taken from me.

I'd burn the whole sum if it meant having Qualley and our old life back.

The grief hit me like a tidal wave. One moment, I was staring blankly at the screen, and the next, I was on the floor, my knees buckling under the crushing weight of it all. Their laughter echoed in my mind—Qualley's easy grin, Lonney's sarcastic quips. They weren't just my friends; they were my true family. My lifeline in a world that had always seemed hellbent on breaking me. And now they were gone.

Murdered. *For what? Some law enforcement recognition or quota?*

No. For *nothing*.

Anger, burning hot and fierce, tangled with the grief threatening to drown me. I clenched my fists until my nails bit into my palms, the pain fastened and tethered me to reality. Questions hovered, swirling around me, each one sharper than the last. *How could this happen? How could they be taken so cruelly, so violently?*

My rage became a mantra, a promise.

Justice.

Revenge.

Retribution.

Whatever form it took, I would see it through.

I pulled myself back into a chair, the legs creaking under my weight as I leaned back, staring up at the cracked ceiling. The tears came fast and hot, blurring my vision, carving trails down my face. My body shook with the force of it, a dam finally giving way to the flood. I buried my face in my hands, letting the sobs wrack through me. And then, as suddenly as it started, it stopped, but the anguish didn't leave me. Not entirely. I merely locked it away, slamming a steel door on it deep inside my mind.

It would stay there, waiting, acting as fuel.

Reopening my laptop, my fingers moved with cold precision. The Bristol Police Department's network blinked to life on the screen.

James Hall.

Evan Matthews.

Lile Henderson.

Ben Prout.

The beginnings of a hit list.

I whispered their names as I pulled up their files, tasting each syllable like poison on my tongue. My rage burned brightly now, a guiding light in the strangling murk. Each keystroke was a nail in their coffin, every piece of data another weapon in my arsenal. The screen illuminated the room in a cold, luminescent glow, the only witness to the storm raging inside me.

I didn't flinch, didn't falter.

Their fates were sealed.

Chapter 18

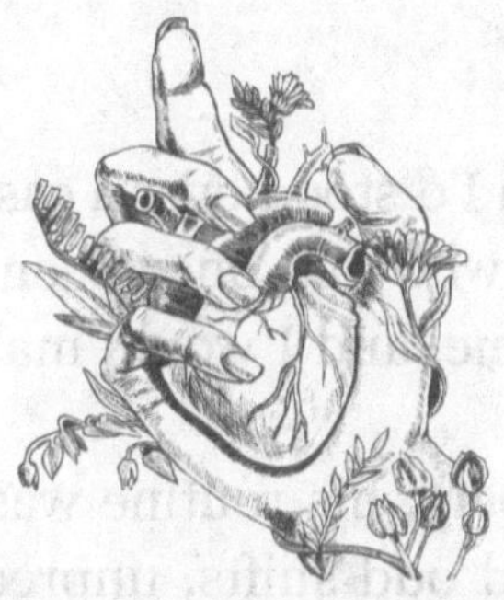

ile would suffer the most, that much was certain. He was the one who pulled the trigger that ended Qualley's life without hesitation.

The image of Lile standing over Qualley's lifeless body burned in my mind vividly. I could envision it as clearly as if I had been there. Qualley's eyes, wide with shock and pain, his body crumpling to the ground, the life draining from him in an instant. The thought of it made my blood boil, a searing fury threatening to consume me whole. It wasn't just the act itself—it was the choice. Lile had chosen to pull the trigger rather than extend due process. He had chosen to end a life that meant everything to me. He would come to understand the burden of his deeds in ways that would defy his comprehension.

Grief clawed at my chest, as it usually did, and it was disorienting. But I shoved it aside so I could concentrate. There was no room for it now. Grief was a luxury I couldn't afford. Instead, I let my anger sharpen into something glacial and precise. Lile's punishment wouldn't just be payback—it would be a tribute to the love I had for Qualley, to the depth of my loss, to the unrelenting ache that now defined my existence.

His death wouldn't just be a statement.

It would be *art*.

Unlike Evan, who'd simply been in the wrong place at the wrong time, accidentally pulling the trigger that ended Lonney's life, Lile's actions were intentional. He had made the choice to follow through—a life-altering, world-shattering choice.

The final shot.

A last breath.

He was the reason I'd stood over a casket, staring at the lifeless body of the man who had once been my entire world. Lile had stolen that from me, and I would make sure he understood what he had done.

But Lile was slippery, his routine was harder to crack than the others. He worked odd shifts, unpredictable hours, always keeping himself just out of reach. But even the most careful men have their weaknesses. And I found his.

An art studio, funnily enough.

It was in a makeshift garage—if it could even be called that. Perhaps it was more of a glorified storage shed with delusions of grandeur. Nevertheless, Lile had transformed it into his so-called sanctuary—his escape from reality. As if splattering paint on oversized canvases could ever mask his fraudulence. He called it therapy. I called it an insult.

Lile fancied himself to be an artist, the kind who believed that tossing color in chaotic bursts somehow equated to skill, to talent, or to meaning. But I saw him for what he was: a *pretender*. An intruder in a realm he had no right to enter. His art was supposed to be 'therapy', some fleeting release from guilt or a means to avoid facing the truth of his actions.

Art was creation.

Art was intention.

Art was mastery.

Lile characterized none of those things.

I imagined standing in the center of his garage, scanning the scattered bullshit around me—the splattered canvases leaning carelessly against the walls, the buckets of paint still dripping where he hadn't bothered to clean up, and the collection of mismatched brushes tossed into coffee cans like forgotten relics. Every detail screamed amateurism and lazy indulgence masquerading as artistic exploration. It was enough to make my stomach turn.

I could see it so clearly in my mind: Lile, strapped to a chair in the center of that studio, his wrists bound with layers of zip ties or chains that bit into his skin. The room, dimly lit, the shadows dancing across the walls. I pictured his face, twisted in confusion, eyes darting around the room—the moment of realization. I imagined myself standing over him, calm and composed, the very portrait of control—my hands steady, my gaze unflinching. I would watch as the fight drained from his eyes, as the weight of his actions bore down on him like a crushing tide. And then, I would begin. Slowly. Methodically. Each cut unhurried, each movement meticulous. I would take my time, ensuring every second was a reminder of the pain he had caused, the lives he had destroyed.

His death wouldn't just be an act of retaliation; it would be a masterpiece. A symphony of justice and retribution, composed with the precision of an artist and the fury of a woman scorned. It would be a *gift*. One he didn't deserve, but one I would give him, even so.

The day I contrived my schedule, the visions of his demise playing out in my mind, I felt a strange sense of calm wash over me. The storm inside me quieted, replaced by a frigid, premeditated determination. Lile would suffer, that much was certain. He would understand the depth of my loss, the weight of my grief. And when it was over, when the last breath left his body, I would finally find a smidge of peace.

But why stop with Lile when there were others involved?

Ben, on the other hand, was a drunk. An arrogant, self-serving son-of-a-bitch who laughed in Qualley's face the night before the raid, pretending to be a concerned cop while waiting for the chance to put a bullet in him. I remember him coming to the door, asking intrusive questions, trying to find his way inside. As he stood at the door that night, his questions grew increasingly intrusive, his demeanor more aggressive. He was searching for weaknesses, fractures in Qualley and Lonney he could exploit. But they stood firm, refusing to be intimidated by his tactics.

"Come back with a warrant," Qualley and Lonney had said. They knew their rights.

And of course we now know they had. The raid was swift, brutal, an assault on everything Qualley and Lonney had fought to protect.

Ben, who was so cocky and content the night before, just about halfway through the raid and just before Qualley and Lonney were murdered, had lost his momentum. He realized that everything went way too far. He fled, so he says, to ensure the FBI and all the other players knew the plan for reconnaissance. Ben didn't want to be anywhere near the violence, and the betrayal was complete; the consequences, devastating.

Ben had a wife—emphasis on *had*. Apparently, he'd been involved in a messy divorce that a brand-new baby in the middle of. A life built on a foundation of deceit.

He cheated . . . a *lot*. Somehow, he had many lady friends.

I found proof of that within minutes, buried in his phone records. Long, late-night calls to a woman named 'Sarah T,' which meant that there might have been other Sarah's in the alphabet. He made frequent expenditures to a hotel across town, I assumed, with Sarah T.

It wasn't just physical, either. He told her he *loved* her. I could tell from the messages. He spoke to her like she was the only thing keeping him breathing.

But the divorce had left him foolish, his once-perfect life now in shambles. His wife had finally seen through his lies, uncovering the truth about his infidelities. The baby was a constant reminder of his failures. Ben's world was crumbling, and he was desperate to regain control, no matter the cost.

Ben's life, that fraudulent abyss of a life, had finally caught up with him. His actions had torn apart families, destroyed lives, and left a trail of pain and suffering in their wake. I couldn't help but feel a twisted sense of satisfaction knowing that his own life was practically in ruin. He cheated, not just on his wife, but on everyone who had ever trusted him. And for that, he would pay dearly.

His weakness wasn't his schedule or his drinking, it was pretty, attractive women. It was portraying this self-assured hero character on the outside, but contained deep inside was a coward who let other people fight his own battles. I used that to my advantage—especially since he frequented the Zenith Bar—which was Zina's dining establishment.

I pictured the moment he'd realize that I was an easy lay, someone he could have fun with—or take advantage of. I wouldn't have to lay a finger on him. I could destroy him from the inside out.

He was the easy one, that is, and I'd save him for last.

Evan Matthews would be first. He had to be. I studied him with the precision of an artist before putting brush to canvas, breaking him down piece by piece. Every detail was another layer—color, texture, shadow, light. In many ways, he wasn't even a man to me anymore. He had a pattern, a routine, a carefully constructed rhythm that made him easy to predict.

6:00 a.m.—his daily five-mile run, always the same route, winding through the quiet suburban streets as though the monotony gave him comfort.

6:45 a.m.—a quick stop at the Orange Cat Café for coffee. Two sugars, no cream. Predictable to the point of absurdity.

7:30 a.m.—at his desk, rifling through reports as though his life depended on it.

8:00 a.m.—roll call. No deviations, no exceptions.

9:30 p.m.—home at last. A single beer, a rerun of some procedural crime drama on his ancient TV. I imagined him sinking into his couch, letting the lies of his profession feed his delusions.

But one detail stuck out more than the rest: his weekly visits to Blackwell & Co. Bookstore on Wednesdays and Fridays. There was something oddly figurative about it, the way he sought refuge in a place filled with stories when his own life seemed like a hollow fabrication.

As I scrolled through his file, my fingers brushing the edge of my laptop, I let my mind wander. I could picture the world that revolved around Evan Matthews so vividly. The rhythmic slap of his sneakers against the pavement during his morning runs, the way his breath must mist in the early morning air. The low hiss of steam rising from his coffee cup as he scrolled through his phone, his attention always divided, always elsewhere. I could see the faint glow of his TV casting shadows across his living room walls, the way his body slumped into the cushions, exhausted but blissfully unaware. I envisioned him in his most vulnerable moments—the fleeting slivers of time when the armor of his routine wouldn't protect him. Half-asleep in bed, his guard down as the soft hum of a fan drowned out the world. Standing at the kitchen counter, unarmed, absorbed in something as mundane as slicing an apple. Mid-shower, the sound of running water masking every other noise, leaving him utterly exposed. A bullet to the head as he stepped out the front door for his morning run—quick, efficient, leaving nothing but a body on the pavement and a trail of red smeared against the concrete. A knife slipping across his throat in the privacy of his shower, the steam mixing with blood, the tiles forever stained. A blade through his ribs as he stood in line for coffee, surrounded by strangers who wouldn't realize what had happened until it was too late.

There were so many ways to end him and each scenario played out in my mind vividly.

I thought about the stroke of a paintbrush—how careful, how final. I thought about the way each movement contributed to the completion of a masterpiece. Evan's life was nothing more than a canvas waiting to be painted, and I already knew exactly which strokes would bring the picture into focus.

I tapped my fingers against the laptop, the rhythmic motion grounding me. This wasn't just revenge. This was methodical. This was art.

For months, I played a role to perfection—the grieving girlfriend. The woman hollowed out by loss, barely able to keep herself together. I moved through the world like a shadow, hidden, sticking to the darkness. My interactions were sparse, my words even more so. To anyone watching, I was a woman shattered, a ghost of who I once was.

I barely spoke to Zina. Not because I didn't want to, but because I couldn't risk her. She was too close, too raw, and I couldn't afford to let my mask slip. The weight of my silence hung heavy between us. I told myself it was necessary.

On the surface, I was broken. But inside? I was sharper than I had ever been.

Every night, when the world went quiet and the darkness wrapped around me like a shroud, I got to work. My laptop became my lifeline, the glow of the screen illuminating the storm raging inside me. I pored over the files I had pulled from the Bristol PD network, dissecting every detail about my targets with surgical precision. Bank statements, social media posts, internal memos—I left no stone unturned. I peeled back the layers of lies, unraveling a narrative they had so carefully constructed. Every bullet fired, every order given, every falsified report—I absorbed it all, committing it to memory. The raid wasn't just an operation; it was a tapestry of deceit, and I was determined to untangle every thread. The more I uncovered, the clearer the picture became.

This wasn't just about Qualley or Lonney, it was about power, corruption, and the lengths people would go to protect their own.

Detective James Hall was the storm that dismantled my world, the force that turned love to ash and left ruin in its wake. Among the shadows of those responsible, his was the darkest, his presence etched into every fracture of my broken heart. Of all who played their part in the chaos, he stood as the one I craved to destroy most.

But he would be the toughest to crack.

The hatred I felt for him burned with an intensity that eclipsed anything I had ever known before. It wasn't just a fire—it was an inferno, relentless and all-consuming. Every memory of Qualley's lifeless body fueled the flames, searing the image into my mind. The senselessness of it all made the rage sharper, the grief deeper.

James wasn't just a man. He was an embodiment of injustice, the face of the system that had torn my life apart piece by piece. Every time his name crossed my mind, a wave of anger and sorrow followed. I could see him so vividly—his smug expression, the way he carried himself with that unbearable air of superiority. He always moved as though he were untouchable, as if the world bent to his will.

James Hall was the one who had orchestrated everything, who had dissected Qualley's life with relentless determination. Every step, every report, every whisper from his team—it all pointed back to him. He wasn't searching for justice. He was hunting for an excuse, a reason to bring Qualley down.

In my mind's eye, I saw him at his desk late at night, a fortress of case files surrounding him as he sat hunched under the dim glow of a desk lamp. His pen scratched across paper; his brow furrowed in self-righteous focus. I could imagine how he viewed himself—convinced of his own heroism, justified in every move he made. It was just another case to him, another victory for his record. But to me? It was everything. Everything I loved.

Everything I had lost. And it was all his fault.

James was meticulous, a man bound to routine and method, much like Evan. He lived his life in precise steps, always scheming, always anticipating the next move—but not necessarily with purpose. That was what made him so difficult to track, so maddeningly hard to corner. But no one is invincible, not even him. If he thought he could stay one step ahead of me forever once his men began to disappear, he was wrong. I wouldn't just catch him. I would dismantle him.

I spent hours imagining the gaps in his masquerade, the moments when he wasn't the unshakable detective he pretended to be. The exhaustion that must haunt him during those late nights in the office when even he questioned his own decisions. The doubt that shined unsteadily, no matter how briefly, in the solitude of his mind. Those were the moments I would exploit. I would find a way in, a way to make him pay. He would feel the loss that had consumed me. He would know the depth of my grief, my rage, my despair.

And as much as I loathed him, that hatred brought clarity. It sharpened my focus, drove me forward with a singular purpose. He had set the wheels in motion that destroyed my world. And I would be the one to bring his crashing down. There was no forgiveness for what he'd done.

The discovery of Detective James Hall's heart condition was a turning point, one that I hadn't anticipated. It began with a whisper, a fragment of information that seemed too insignificant to be true. But as I delved deeper, the pieces began to fall into place. I dug and dug, sifting through medical records, insurance claims, and any scrap of information I could find. It took time, patience, and a network of contacts willing to bend the rules, but eventually, I uncovered the truth.

James had been diagnosed with a severe heart condition years ago, one that required constant monitoring and medication. He had undergone surgeries, faced close calls, and yet, he continued to push himself to the limit.

The more I learned, the more I realized how deeply work consumed him. His dedication to his job was almost obsessive, a desperate need to prove himself and maintain control. He chose work over his family, prioritizing his career above all else. It was a decision that had cost him dearly, leading to a strained marriage and, ultimately, isolation from his children. Because of this, his health suffered, but he ignored the warning signs, convinced that his mission was worth any cost.

The knowledge of his heart condition added a new layer to my hatred. It was a vulnerability, a fissure in the exterior of a man who had caused so much pain. He was not invincible, and I would use that weakness to my advantage.

As I pieced together the route to his downfall, I felt a twisted sense of gratification. Detective James Hall, the man who had started it all, would finally face the consequences of his actions. And I, with a heart full of rage and a mind set on revenge, would be the one to deliver justice.

A realization dawned on me: I didn't need to put a bullet in his skull, strangle him in his sleep, or cut his throat in some back alley. I just needed him to break. *Stress. Fear. A perfectly timed event.* Anything that would send his body into overload, pushing his heart past its limits. Like the deaths of the people he cared about more than his own family: *his team.*

I imagined his face paling, his breath hitching, the sharp pain stabbing through his chest as he realized, too late, that he was dying. I could make him watch everything happen. I could be the last face he saw in his mind before everything faded to black.

This epiphany made me smile for the first time since Qualley's death.

My strategy wasn't just forming—it was alive, breathing, growing. A series of perfect strokes on a blank canvas, the image becoming clearer with every new detail. I had always been an artist, but now I was painting something new. Not with oils or pastels . . .

With *blood*.

And I'd take back every heart that was rightfully mine.

<h1 style="text-align:center">Chapter 19</h1>

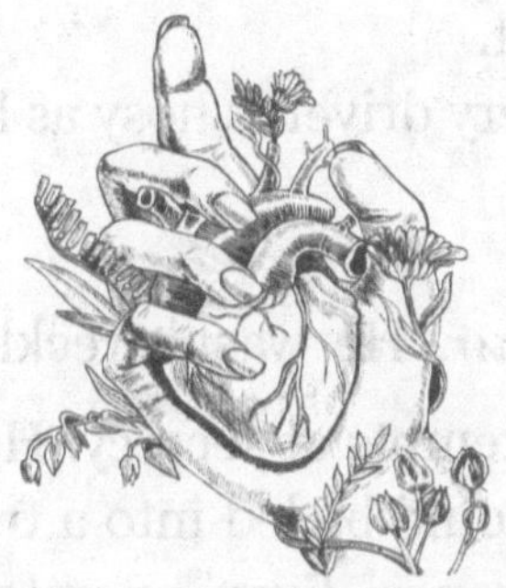

One mistake so many criminals make is waltzing into a hardware store like it's any other day, piling their carts with items that scream, "Hi, I'm up to no good!" They seem to forget—stores have cameras. Shelves have eyes. And worst of all, cashiers and customers have memories.

Imagine it: dozens of potential witnesses watching as Joe Schmo buys his rope, duct tape, tarps, and trash bags—all the makings of a lurid headline. At the time, maybe no one thinks much of it. But fast forward to the discovery of a body wrapped in tarp and bound with duct tape, and suddenly, authorities are revisiting those mundane transactions.

And Joe?

Well, Joe's sitting in a cell, clutching his head, wondering how surveillance footage of him grabbing a bright orange Home Depot bucket is now trending on YouTube. It's not even a good bucket—it's just a branded one with a legacy that outlived him.

It's comical in a way, but also a tragic lack of foresight.

Joe should've known better.

Buying supplies for crimes isn't just shopping; it's a confession waiting to happen. Which is why I'll never understand why they don't take a simpler route—*online shopping*. Specifically Amazon, or any number of faceless online vendors. No awkward glances, no judgmental looks from the cashier, and certainly no overhead cameras logging your every move. Just a knock at your door, your carefully curated package sitting neatly on the porch, unnoticed by anyone except the delivery driver who will forget you in two seconds flat.

Unless your delivery driver is nosy as hell.

Evan was no amateur. He wasn't reckless like Ben, with his clumsy, half-baked attempts at secrecy. He wasn't easily manipulated like Lile, who could be led into a trap with a breadcrumb trail of his own arrogance. Evan operated differently. He was careful, thoughtful. The kind of careful that made you want to throw your hands up because he left nothing to chance.

Recklessness or impulsivity wouldn't be his undoing—it was humanity. Even the most careful among us are creatures of habit. We repeat patterns. We carve ruts into the fabric of our lives, believing them to be invisible. And that's where the chinks in our defenses form.

Evan had his patterns and he thought they kept him grounded, that they made him untraceable. But patterns aren't shields—they're maps. All it takes is someone willing to look closely enough.

He was smart. Smarter than most. But even the smartest men could be fooled when their egos blinded them.

I couldn't afford to approach him first. That would be too obvious—too risky. Men like Evan thrived on their instincts, on the illusion that they're always in control and one step ahead. So, I made him notice me instead. I became a ghostly presence in his peripheral vision—a woman who seemed familiar but was just out of reach. Someone who lingered in the back of his mind, nagging at his attention but never fully clicking.

Evan had a type. Blonde hair, blue eyes, and the kind of polished, conventionally attractive aesthetic that read as effortless. It wasn't hard to piece together—his scarce social media accounts, the photos buried in private albums of old girlfriends immortalized in pictures he never bothered to delete.

I knew what he liked. And I was ready to become it.

Of course, that meant I had to change. Drastically.

I bleached my hair—platinum blonde, the shade that practically screamed "California dream girl." My beautiful, auburn curls, with their unique bounce and texture, were fried to a crisp in the process. I hated it. The vibrancy, the character that I used to see in the mirror—it was gone. Now I was someone new, someone painfully generic. And because the curls lost their life, I had to learn how to straighten my hair myself, spending hours watching tutorials just to keep it from breaking off in clumps. I dropped absurd amounts of money on products I'd never imagined needing—toner to kill the brassiness, leave-in treatments to salvage what little integrity my hair had left. I even bought a hair straightener that cost about as much as a down payment on a new car.

My transformation didn't stop there. The local Sephora staff probably knew me by name by the time I was done. *Buying copious amounts of make-up to completely modify my look wasn't suspicious, right?* The amount of makeup I bought could've kept their lease paid for a year. I learned to craft eyes that radiated just the right amount of sadness, the vulnerability men like Evan loved to see. My eyebrows were reshaped, darkened to frame my face, their arches perfected through countless hours of tutorials.

Then came the wardrobe. Gone were my colorful, eccentric pieces—the fabrics and patterns I'd collected from all over the world, each one a small part of who I was. They were replaced with something much simpler: girl-next-door attire. Cotton dresses, jeans, neutral tones that whispered effortlessness to most people, but to me it said, "you're fucking boring, aren't you?"

My tortoise shell glasses were swapped for colored contact lenses—a subtle shift to blueish green that added just the right touch of intrigue.

My cadence, my posture, even my perfume changed.

Everything about me was engineered into a woman like the ones Evan favored. Striking, but not too obvious. Beautiful, but 'naturally' so. The kind of beauty a man like Evan would assume wasn't because I was trying so hard—a mistake, really, because everything about me was calculated to a T.

Thanks to Lonney's hacking tricks, getting into the police records was the easy part. I found Evan's work schedule buried among department files—irregular, as expected, with shifts bleeding into his off-hours. Policing seemed to be a career that never truly clocked out, and his pattern was maddeningly generic: work, home, work again.

But his financials? That's where I found my way in.

His credit card activity told a story. Every Wednesday and Friday morning, like clockwork, he made the same small purchase—always at the same location.

It wasn't a bar, nor a gym. It wasn't even a coffee shop.

A *bookstore*. It was a goddamned bookstore.

Blackwell & Co.

After uncovering that pattern, I was on it, and for two weeks, I lingered there, lurking from a corner table in the café section. The coffee was terrible—bitter and burnt—but I forced it down as I observed. My face, hidden behind a book, glanced up only every few minutes to avoid suspicion.

And then, right on time, there he was.

Evan was always punctual, arriving at 8 a.m. sharp like clockwork. His presence was impossible to ignore, the way his tall, muscular frame seemed to shift the atmosphere of the room as soon as he entered. He moved with quiet authority; his broad shoulders cutting an imposing silhouette. His sharp features and angular jawline lent him a presence that demanded attention, even if he wasn't actively trying to claim it. It wasn't just his physique—it was the way he carried himself. There was a confidence in his movements, a controlled precision that suggested he wasn't a man to be taken lightly. I watched the way he adjusted his watch as he surveyed the room, and couldn't help but wonder: *Could his size and strength pose a problem when the time came to take him down? Would his physicality be an obstacle, or would it be his arrogance that made him vulnerable?*

My gaze lingered as I calculated, weighing the risks against the opportunities. He looked like the type who could snap necks without breaking a sweat—but appearances were rarely the full story. Evan might be built like a brick wall, but I'd learned that even walls have weak points, cracks you can exploit if you know where to look. And that's where my mind went: finding the leverage, the blind spot, the flaw hidden beneath the surface of his cool exterior.

Strength wasn't everything. Physical dominance could be countered with speed, cunning, and careful strategy. But Evan's presence carried an unnerving air of capability that left me wondering whether I had underestimated him. *Was his physique the biggest hurdle, or was it the unwavering confidence in his eyes that told me he'd dealt with worse than me before?*

Still, I didn't back down. If Evan was expecting brute force, he'd be disappointed. My strength was my mind—sharp, adaptable, and unrelenting. His size was intimidating, sure. But brute force was only as good as the strategy behind it. And if his plan of action relied on the assumption that his physical strength made him untouchable, then he'd already made his first mistake

Evan browsed the same sections every time: crime thrillers, history, philosophy. He never flirted with the barista, never made small talk, and always came alone. Even off-duty, he was immaculate—button-down shirts, dark slacks, the polished appearance of someone who never truly let his guard down.

But everyone has weaknesses. And his? I'd make sure that would be *me*.

I waited, letting curiosity do the work.

Until eventually, it did.

Chapter 20

One Friday morning, I made my move. I grabbed a book from the shelf—one I'd memorized cover to cover weeks ago: *Beyond Good and Evil* by Friedrich Nietzsche. It was intended, part of the show. Evan constantly had it in his hands, and if I wanted to catch his attention, I needed to play the part.

What better way to catch his eye than with something familiar?

Settling into a wooden table a few feet away from where he sat, coffee in hand, I casually began flipping through the pages. The noises of the bookstore wrapped around us—the distant murmur of the barista, the soft rustle of pages turning, the aroma of old paper mingling with freshly brewed coffee. It was serene, the kind of tranquility that made it easy to disrupt.

"That's not even what Nietzsche meant!" I grumbled just loud enough for my voice to carry, slamming the book closed with a frustrated huff. I let out an exaggerated sigh, shaking my head before smirking to myself, the kind of expression that invited curiosity. The kind that baited attention.

From the corner of my eye, I saw him glance up, his curiosity piqued.

Perfect.

I tilted the book slightly; the cover angled toward him and quirked an eyebrow. "You ever read this?" I tried to sound exasperated enough to garner some sort of response.

Evan hesitated for a moment, leaning forward to get a better look. He slid his finger between the pages of his own book to mark his place before responding. "Yeah. It's one of my favorites."

Of course, it was. Only someone like you would call Nietzsche a favorite. I bit back the thought, masking my inner disdain with a teasing smile.

"Is it?" I tilted my head, faking skepticism. "So what exactly do you think he meant?"

A playful edge danced in his eyes as he leaned back in his chair, intrigued. "I was about to ask you the same thing." A small smirk tugging at his lips.

Hook.

Pretending to consider whether he was worth the explanation, I reclined in my chair with an air of confidence. "He wasn't saying morality is meaningless," I began casually, as if we were old friends sharing a conversation. "He was saying people cling to outdated moral systems because it's easier than thinking for themselves. Context matters."

Evan studied me, his gray eyes narrowing slightly—not with suspicion, but curiosity. I could practically feel his thoughts shifting. In this moment, I wasn't just some random woman browsing the philosophy section in a bookstore, I was something more. Someone who knew exactly what they were talking about.

He nodded slowly. "Most people don't get that. They see Nietzsche and think he was advocating for chaos."

I laughed softly, shaking my head with a touch of bemusement. "Right? 'God is dead' and all that nonsense," I mocked, rolling my eyes. "Half the people quoting him haven't read a single page." That earned a chuckle from him.

He closed his own book completely, rising from his chair and crossing the short distance between us to sit across from me. He placed his book, *The Wealth of Nations* by Adam Smith, on the table.

And just like that, *line*.

"You really like philosophy, don't you?" I asked, mimicking curiosity as I spotted the title of his book. I didn't care, of course, but it was part of the act.

He shrugged, running a hand through his short, dark brown hair. His eyes swept the room, scanning like a detective in his element. Missing nothing, always aware. It was almost endearing, the way he seemed to assess every detail.

"You come here often?" He appeared genuinely interested.

I picked up my coffee, taking a slow sip so I could reflect on my answer. It was just enough of a lull in time to make him tilt forward, waiting for my response. Then I smiled—a small, enigmatic curve of my lips.

"Sometimes," I said finally. "Depends on who's here."

The faintest flicker of confusion crossed his features before it melted into intrigue. I winked at him over the rim of my cup, gauging his reaction—the slight angle of his head, his eyes constricting. He was trying to figure me out, to place me. He couldn't, and that was satisfying.

"And what kind of people keep you coming back?" He asked, his voice morphing into something flirtatious.

I dropped forward slightly, resting my chin in my hand. A teasing grin spread across my face. "The interesting ones."

The pause hung in the air delicately, and I could see the fleeting thought flitting across his expression like a whisper in the wind. This was something he'd dreamt of. An encounter made for stories and fantasies. He was the kind of man who likely believed in moments like this—serendipity wrapped up in intrigue, a stranger who seemed to stumble into his life with the perfect blend of mystery and allure.

His own hallmark Christmas movie.

I almost laughed at the realization, though I kept my expression steady. To him, I wasn't just a woman with a cup of coffee; I was the puzzle piece he never knew he was missing. A character straight out of his imagination, one he might've dreamed of meeting in quiet bookstores or bustling cafes. Maybe that's why he always came here, to meet the woman of his dreams.

It was amusing, really, the way he gradually got closer, wonder and hope mingling in his expression. For him, this was a meeting etched with possibility. For me? It was a game; one I played so well I could win without lifting a finger. He didn't understand that the dance we were doing was orchestrated entirely by every glance, every pause, every ambiguous word I tossed to him. He was already wrapped around the strings I held, and the best part was he didn't even know it.

Maybe that was why I couldn't help but play along a little longer. Watching the interplay of confusion and fascination on his face was far too satisfying to cut short.

Evan's lips curled into a genuine smile. It softened his sharp features, catching me off guard for just a moment. He chuckled lightly, leaning back and crossing his arms as he studied me.

"Is that your way of saying *I'm* interesting?"

What a loaded question.

If only he knew how utterly uninteresting he actually was to me.

I arched an eyebrow, lifting a shoulder in a slow, casual shrug. "I guess that depends." I allowed my gaze to linger on him for a while. "What's your take on *Beyond Good and Evil*?"

His hands clasped together; expression thoughtful. "I think you already have an opinion on it." There was a playful challenge in his voice. "I'd rather hear your take."

I let my lips curve into a lazy smile, cocking my head as if debating whether to share some grand secret. He was hooked. I could see it in the way his posture shifted, the way his focus zeroed in on me.

Running a finger along the edge of my book, I let my eyes drift to the true crime novel tucked under his philosophy book—

The Art Thief by Michael Finkel. How had I missed that before?

"You like reading about crime?" I asked playfully, just enough edge to make him pause from the subject change.

He followed my gaze, then shrugged nonchalantly. "I like understanding how people think. Why they do what they do."

A laugh bubbled in my throat, quiet and amused. The irony of his answer didn't escape me. *Understanding how people think? That's what he thought he was doing now, isn't it?* Trying to crack me open, dissect me like some academic exercise. If only he knew how far ahead I was in this ruse.

"Let me ask you this," I purred, resting my head on my hand. "Do you think killers are worth understanding?"

Evan's expression shifted slightly, cautious now. He was careful with his answer, as I knew he would be. "Most aren't as complicated as people like to think. Some act on impulse, some because of trauma. And some . . ." he paused, watching me closely, ". . . just because they can."

My fingers toyed with the edge of the book. "And what about the ones who think they have a reason?"

He studied me for a beat too long before responding. "Oh, well," he bobbed his head thoughtfully. "They're the most dangerous."

Dangerous. The word hung between us like smoke curling around my thoughts. *Dangerous is what he thought of people like Qualley, wasn't it?* People who challenged his authority, who threatened his illusions of control. And now he was staring at me, wondering what kind of danger *I* carried.

Our gazes locked, a silent clash that lingered between us, and I let a slow, devilish smile creep across my lips. I wanted him to feel it—that faint ripple of discomfort, the whispering doubt curling at the edges of his thoughts, questioning what kind of woman could pose a question like that and hold his stare so steadily.

When I finally broke the silence, my voice was light, teasing.

"You sound like you've spent a lot of time thinking about this. Podcast host? Cop?"

Evan stiffened. Barely, but enough for me to notice. He masked it well, his expression smoothing into something neutral. "Something like that."

I nodded slightly, simulating just the right amount of machination to keep a conversation going. My grin remained detached, almost lazy as my head dipped in a quiet, almost playful gesture of involvement in our conversation. I assessed him as if weighing his words against some invisible scale.

"Should I be worried?" I asked casually, almost disinterested, as though I was humoring him rather than truly seeking an answer.

He chuckled, shaking his head. "I don't think you have anything to worry about."

"Funny. That sounds exactly like the reassurance you hear before everything goes sideways."

A sly grin tugged at his lips, a spark of amusement flickering in his eyes. Clearly, he liked the comment.

The conversation unfolded exactly as planned, every word, every glance, a carefully placed step on the path I had laid out. Evan was hooked now, reeled in by the mix of intrigue and nonchalant indifference I had projected. And when I finally stood to leave, I did so with practiced grace, gathering my things with an air of calm detachment.

"I should go," I said, slinging my bag over my shoulder and stretching as if I had forgotten about an appointment. "I've got to be in Hartford in about an hour, and the traffic is always terrible this time of day."

Evan watched me rise, curiosity sharpening, his body shifting as though he was debating whether to let me walk away without saying anything more. For a moment, it seemed like he'd let me go, and I was almost at the door when his voice cut through the quiet hum of the bookstore.

"Wait!"

Sinker.

I stopped, glancing back over my shoulder. One hand rested lightly on the door frame as though I could step away at any moment. Evan hesitated even after I'd stopped, running a hand through his dark hair before meeting my gaze. There was something soft in his expression now, a vulnerability he probably didn't show often.

"Will I see you here again?"

I let my lips curve into the barest hint of a smile, angling my head as though mulling over the answer. For a moment, I let the silence hang between us, stretching just enough to create that perfect state of unrest.

"Maybe," I said at last, my tone light but enigmatic. "Depends on who's here."

Evan's brow furrowed slightly as I winked at him, the faintest hint of confusion flickering across his face. He probably wasn't used to being the one who chases, unless it's law enforcement business, and that's where we were alike. I didn't wait for him to respond. Instead, I turned back toward the door and pushed it open, stepping into the cool morning air.

Behind me, I could feel him lingering, the unanswered question hovering in his mind. He didn't try to follow. He wouldn't. But he'd be there next time, waiting, hoping for another chance to unravel the mystery I had left behind.

Everything was unfolding exactly as I intended.

The Orange Cat Café had always been my sanctuary, a place where the scent of freshly brewed espresso mingled with the faint notes of music, creating an atmosphere that felt both lively and intimate. The dim lighting softened the edges of the room, casting warm shadows over the mismatched furniture and the eclectic art on the walls. It was the kind of place where secrets could be whispered and forgotten. Where the world outside seemed to fade into irrelevance.

That evening, I wasn't there for coffee. I was there for the quiet, for the anonymity that came with my new look and alias. But as I sat behind my laptop, pretending to work, a shadow fell across my table, blocking the light from the rest of the establishment.

"I know you from somewhere," the shadow said, its voice familiar. I didn't need to look up to know who it was. That sound, though new to me, had already etched itself into my memory.

Slowly, I lifted my head, assembling curiosity, and let my gaze meet his.

Evan Matthews held two steaming cups of coffee and a small brown paper bag tucked between his fingers. The warm light from the café caught the sharp angles of his face, softening them just enough to make him seem approachable. The faintest hint of a smirk played at the corner of his lips, as if he already knew he had my attention.

I closed my laptop slowly, pitching forward slightly as I rested my chin between my fists. A flirtatious smile tugged at my lips. "Oh, really?" My eyes flicked to the coffee in his hands, and I pointed toward one of the cups. "Is that for me?"

He shifted his weight, his smirk deepening. "Depends," he said, with that same calm confidence I'd noticed before. "You never did tell me your name yesterday."

I raised an eyebrow, and with a playful tip of my head, I nodded toward the coffee. "I'll tell you my name if that's for me."

Evan tittered, pulling out the chair across from me as if he'd been invited to sit, and slid into it. He placed one of the coffees and the paper bag in front of me.

"Fair trade." He propped back into his chair. "Now, a deal's a deal—what do I call you?"

I wrapped my hands around the coffee, letting the warmth seep into my skin. For a moment, I savored the feeling, at the same time creating apprehension between him and I. I looked up, my smile methodical.

"Crimson."

His brow furrowed slightly, curiosity crossing his gray eyes. "Crimson?" He repeated it as if testing the name on his tongue, examining me with amusement. For a second I thought he wouldn't believe me, because really, who the fuck was named Crimson? But he seemed intrigued, not suspicious. "Like the color?"

"Yes, like the color."

He chuckled, shaking his head as he takes a sip of his own coffee. "Alright. *Crimson*," he said, coming to terms with my unusual alias. "Seems fitting somehow."

"Oh?" I said. "How so?"

He studied me, his smirk permanent at this point. "You give off a . . . boldness. Something striking. It's a bit hard to ignore."

Laughing softly, though it wasn't funny at all and actually quite irritating, I broke off a piece of the pastry I'd pulled out of the bag, popping it in my mouth. "You say that to every woman you meet in a bookstore café?"

"Only the ones who don't tell me their names right away."

Watching him, I sipped my coffee, savoring the moment and the subtle charge between us. He's interested . . . at least I hoped so—just as I intended.

"So," I said, tapping my finger on the table, "what do I need to do for *your* name?"

Hell could freeze over and there would still be absolutely nothing I would do for this man's name. I really didn't need it to put him in the ground, anyway. But, I had no choice but to humor him.

He raised an eyebrow, smirking as he leans back. "Now that's an interesting question."

"I like interesting, as we've already determined."

He pretended to think before responding, awkwardly gazing

into my eyes with his, trying way too hard to seem desirable. If he thought I'd actually find him charming . . .

"Alright," he said. "Impress me."

I bent a brow, fascinated with how wrong I was about his character. "Oh, okay. You're the one who came over to me with a bribe and now you want *me* to impress *you*?"

He smirked, taking a slow sip of his coffee before setting it down. "Hey, you're the one that asked what you could do for my name."

I pouted as I tore off another piece of pastry. "I must admit, I've never worked this hard to get someone's name."

"I wouldn't say 'hard to get'—just . . . selective," he chuckled, shaking his head.

"And here I thought I was the one being selective."

"Maybe we both are." He raised his coffee cup slightly in a mock toast.

A charged silence rose up between us, something unfolding between us. He was playing along, but he had no idea just how deep he had stepped in. The last thing I needed was for him to smell a scheme. He was a cop after all. I knew he was capable of killing an innocent man, but I wasn't sure of his ability to spot a threat.

I smiled, resting my chin in my hand again. "Guess I'll have to work for it then." I kept my voice light but with an underlying challenge.

He watched me over his coffee cup as he considered me. I met his gaze with a playful, unwavering stare, waiting for his response. The pause expanded just long enough to make me wonder if he'd keep this going.

With a small chuckle, he shook his head, angling forward slightly, lowering his voice as if he was letting me in on a secret. "It's Evan."

"Hmm . . . Evan," I repeated slowly, pretending to memorize the sound of it. "You look more like an Anthony or Gregory."

"Gregory?" Evan chuckled, raising his eyebrows. "In any case, now you owe me."

"Owe you?" I scoffed, crossing my arms on the table. "I don't remember agreeing to that."

He grinned and sat back with a confident, borderline cocky ease. "Oh, you did. The moment you asked what you had to do for my name."

"Touche," I said, laughing softly. I dragged my finger along the rim of my coffee cup, studying him. "Alright. What do you want?"

Evan acted out a thinking gesture, tapping his fingers on the table. "I'll let you know."

Taking another sip of coffee, my mind is calculating my next steps. He thought he was playing me, keeping his sense of command. But he had no idea—I'd already decided exactly how this would end.

Angling toward him, I dropped the volume of my own voice like I'm compelled by his arbitrary response. "Mysterious. I like it. But if you wait too long, I might just forget I owe you anything."

"I doubt that," Evan said, shaking his head. "Something tells me you don't forget much."

Over the rim of my coffee cup, I smiled, dipping my head in acknowledgment. He was annoyingly observant. Good. That made this all more fun.

"So, Evan. What made you come here tonight?"

Evan shrugged. "I guess I was curious." He was playing it cool and watched closely for my reaction. I didn't rush to give it to him. "I saw you through the window, and you didn't tell me your name yesterday. That kind of stuck with me, so I thought I'd say hello."

How nauseatingly thoughtful.

"And now that you have it?"

"Now I have more questions."

"Oh, yeah?" I asked, sitting up straight. "Like what?"

Evan examined me closely, studying my face. "Like why you're here alone. Why did you look so deep in thought when I walked up . . . And why you don't seem all that surprised that I'm here."

I pinched my eyes together as if considering whether to let him in on a secret. Like that would ever happen. The real secret would remain concealed until the time was right, but by then, Evan wouldn't know what hit him.

Cocking my head, I slouched in my chair, attempting to make myself look as innocent as possible. Coming into this cafe, I didn't think I'd be interrogated this early in this gamble of life or death.

Which in this case, death being the ultimate goal.

"Maybe I was hoping to see you somewhere other than the bookstore," I said, teasing him with the lie, making myself feel sick in the process. "But I'm usually here most evenings, working."

"Hmm," he said. "So you've been following me?"

Raising an eyebrow, my face fell. "Hey, you're the one who spotted *me* through the window and bought me a coffee and bear claw."

Evan's gaze lingered on me with increased intensity, like he was trying to figure out if I was messing with him or genuinely rubbed the wrong way. Before he had a chance to speak, I seamlessly steered the conversation in a new direction: *me attempting to leave.*

As I stood up, I swiftly threw on my coat. Reaching for my laptop and bag, I felt a hand grip my arm before I could slide the computer inside.

"Wait!" Evan cried, stepping in front of me. "I was just giving you a hard time, I didn't mean to offend."

My grip tightened around the strap of my bag, the tension in my knuckles mirroring the distaste curling in my gut. His hand lingered on my arm for a second longer than necessary before he let go, the warmth of his skin burning like an unwelcome brand. I resisted the urge to flinch, to rub the spot where his touch clung to me like residue. It wasn't just the contact—it was everything it represented. His confidence, his entitlement, the casual audacity of assuming he had the right to touch me. It made my skin crawl, a simmering disgust I struggled to contain as I forced myself to stand still, unmoving, unflinching. Letting him see my revulsion would've given him too much satisfaction.

I took a steadying breath, pretending the strap of my bag was the only thing anchoring me in place, even as the spot where his fingers brushed my skin seemed to pulse with irritation. His touch wasn't just intrusive; it was offensive—like a mark left by someone who didn't belong in my world. My gaze flicked to his hand, now hanging loosely at his side, as if it hadn't committed the crime of crossing my boundaries.

A self-satisfied air surrounded him, utterly oblivious to the loathing he'd planted in me with that simple gesture.

"I'm sorry." His eyes, once filled with amusement, now carry something else. Hesitation? Regret? Or maybe he was just fascinated.

"You're fine," I lied, pretending to brush it off with a lightness I didn't quite feel. "I should still get going, though. They'll be locking up soon."

Evan glanced toward the window where the streetlights cast a dull glow on the wet pavement outside. "It's late. Where's your car?"

I hesitated, weighing my options. *Could I really do this tonight?* I thought. My mind worked through the dilemma unraveling in real-time. I hadn't planned for Evan's demise to be this soon. In fact, not for another week, maybe. He was supposed to be a passing amusement, a distraction from the inevitable. But now, with him standing there, so willing, so unaware, I wonder—*could I?* The thought unsettled me, because I couldn't decide which answer I wanted.

I could lead him inside the house, pour him a drink. Let my fingers trail the curve of his throat before pressing in, squeezing until all that warmth disappears. I pictured the moment his easy smile turned to shock, the light in his eyes flickering as understanding dawns too late . . .

Or I could let him go. Let him stay floating between danger and desire, neither a target nor an escape. Then next time would be the dagger in his chest.

But what if there was no next time?

"A few blocks over at my house. I walked here."

"You shouldn't walk alone this time of night." Evan said.

I blinked up at him, and for a moment I thought he saw something there—an edge of darkness. But he didn't budge. He just looked at me, waiting.

"I'm a big girl," I said, mocking annoyance, yet smirking slightly. "But are you offering to walk me?"

He nodded; an ugly smirk carved into his face. There was a lazy confidence in the way he stood, like he thought he was safe.

He wasn't.

He shouldn't be.

We tossed our garbage into the bin as we left, the bell above the door ringing, a crisp chime cutting through a chilly night. I glanced down the street, weighing my options one last time—but the decision had settled in my bones. It had to happen tonight. It was too perfect. I couldn't risk him becoming attached to the thought of some sort of relationship. I also didn't want him to end up sniffing out my plot to end his life by discovering my true identity.

Evan's hands found their way into his pockets as he gave me that trademark grin. "You seem lost in thought," he mused. "What's on your mind?"

"Just debating whether I actually need to walk off this bear claw or if I should just let the sugar rush carry me home." I forced a soft smile.

He snickered, falling into step beside me as we traveled down the sidewalk. "I think you're fine. Besides, I wouldn't let anything happen to you.

"And what exactly do you think would happen?" I carefully glanced at him.

He shrugged. "It's late. Creeps come out at night." I bit my tongue against the irony of his words.

If only he knew.

"You don't seem too worried about yourself."

"Maybe I should be," he said, smirking again. "But I like to think I'm a good judge of character."

I exhaled a quiet laugh. "That's a dangerous way to think."

"Oh?" He raised an eyebrow. "Why's that?"

My gaze fixed forward. "Because sometimes people aren't who they seem to be."

The words tore free before I could rein them in—razor-edged, unfiltered—a flaw in the careful charade I had planned. The impact was immediate. A blunt force truth hanging between us, raw and too honest. A mistake. A rookie mistake. I knew it the moment his eyes turned toward mine. Inquiry struck like steel against flint, sparking with restless energy.

I clenched my jaw, forcing myself to keep my expression neutral, but inside, my thoughts churned. *Why had I said that? Why had I let him see even a sliver of the truth?* It wasn't like me to slip, to let my emotions bleed into the act. I was supposed to be in control, always in control. A hush deepened, and I could feel him studying me, dissecting the meaning of my words. I hated it—the way his gaze persisted, the way he seemed to peel back layers I hadn't meant to expose.

I tightened my grip on the strap of my bag, finding my footing in the physical sensation as I scrambled to recover. It wasn't too late to redirect, to deflect, to turn the focus back on him. But the damage was done. He'd heard the crack in my voice, the faint tremor that betrayed more than I intended. I forced a small, dismissive smile, hoping it would be enough to mask the slip.

"Just an observation."

Evan falls silent for a moment, like he's considering my response. Then he laughs lightly. "You're right. But something tells me you're exactly who you seem to be."

Oblivious, idiotic man!

I knew then I wouldn't have to worry about him catching onto much of anything.

"And who do I seem to be?" Peeking from the corner of my eye, I'm engaged despite myself.

He pivoted his head, studying me. "Smart. Sharp. A little guarded. Maybe even a little dangerous." The corner of my mouth twitched. He had no idea how close he was to the truth.

"Dangerous? Like, drinks at my house dangerous?"

Evan winked. "Perhaps, but also like the kind of person who doesn't take any shit."

"Maybe."

We walked a few more steps in comfortable silence, the muted activity of distant traffic and the occasional commotion of blinking streetlamps filled the gaps between us. The night air wrapped around us, carrying with it a stillness that feels almost conspiratorial.

I slowed my pace. My heels clicked softly against the pavement, and I glinted over at him. "So, *do* you want to come in for a drink?"

There was something beneath his smirk now—something tacit. Curiosity? Hesitation? It was fleeting whatever it was. Gone as quickly as it appeared.

"That depends," he said smoothly, his tone playful. "What's on the menu?"

A faint smile played peek-a-boo with my features, but I kept my it relaxed, steady. "Oh, I have plenty of options." I listed them off with just a hint of allure. "Liquor, beer, wine . . . maybe even something a little . . . sweeter."

His gray eyes narrowed slightly, as though trying to decipher some hidden meaning in my words.

"I owe you, remember?

Internally, my thoughts churned. He owed *me*, not the other way around—not in the way he thought. Not in the way his annoying smirk suggested, with its faint undertone of expectation. I would never sleep with him. I knew that's what he thought I meant. The very idea was repulsive. It was a violation of everything I stood for. Men like him—arrogant, conniving, always assuming they could charm their way into anything—were the reason I had built walls so high they were practically impenetrable. His touch, his gaze, his presence, all felt like an intrusion. A message of the power dynamics he thought he could exploit. I wasn't here to play *his* game. I was here to win *mine*. And if letting him think he had the upper hand was part of the strategy, so be it. I could endure his smirk, his judging eyes, his attempts to unravel me, because I knew the truth. He wasn't the predator in this scenario.

I was.

Allowing time to pass just long enough to keep him guessing, I turned toward the door, controlling my movements.

"Come on. Let's see if you can handle what's on the menu."

Evan's hesitation lingered for half a heartbeat, and then he acknowledged me. He bobbed his head, smirk deepening. "Alright. Lead the way."

I turned without another word, my steps robotic, the rhythmic echo of my heels on the concrete were like a siren's call in the quiet night. The shadows stretched long and dark ahead of us, swallowing the faint pools of light cast by the streetlamps. He followed without question; drawn by something he couldn't quite define.

I don't even think he registered where he was going.

It was almost canon. The way he trailed behind me, unaware that with each step he took, he was leaving the world behind. The charge in the air sharpened, crackling like static, and I resisted the urge to glance back. I don't need to see his face to know I have him.

As if he were enchanted, bewitched by some unseen spell, he walked willingly into the dark house with me.

Chapter 21

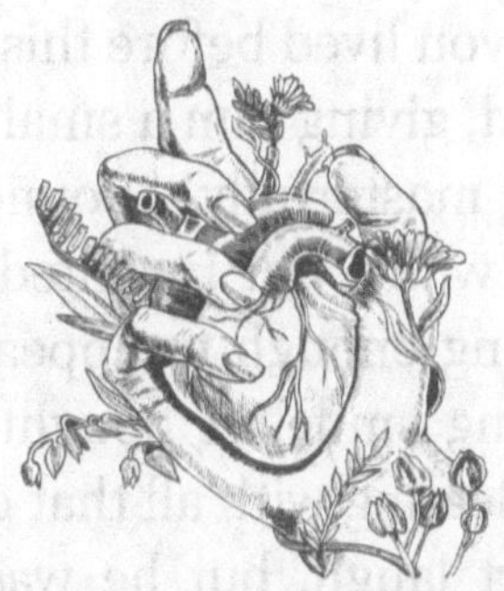

Stepping inside the threshold of the house, Evan's eyes sweep over the living room as I closed the door behind him. The space was diffusely lit, furniture steeped in the memories it had witnessed. I'd made small changes: new curtains, a different rug, subtle things that kept the ghost of Qualley from fully settling . . . or the three cops I was about to dispose of, remembering, then fleeing.

He really walked into this house willingly? Did he not remember busting through that same front door, dressed in his bulletproof vest, barking orders, and murdering someone who hadn't given anyone a reason to?

The audacity of it was *almost* impressive.

Evan turned slowly, his brows drawing together as he scanned the house from its entrance. The way his eyes roved—intent and meticulous, as though trying to capture everything—made it clear what was going through his mind. He wasn't just looking. He was *remembering*.

"I've been here before," he said, almost to himself.

I halted by the door, leaning casually against the frame, though my muscles coiled with apprehension. "Oh?" I allowed my voice to carry just the right amount of disinterest.

He nodded, stepping further inside, scanning the walls, the furniture, the shadows in the corners, like they might hold some forgotten truth he was trying to unearth. He turned to me, curiosity dancing behind his eyes. A curiosity that was starting to harden into something more. Recognition.

"Where'd you say you lived before this?"

"I didn't," I replied, giving him a small, effortless shrug. The lie slid off my tongue masterfully. "Bounced around New York City apartments for a while, but I wanted something more permanent." I paused, long enough to appear thoughtful, then offered him an easygoing smile. "I bought this place furnished. Didn't really feel like dealing with all that decorating nonsense."

He let out a short laugh, but he wasn't fully relaxed. His smile was thin, masking the gears turning in his head. "That explains why it still looks . . . lived in, the same."

My heartbeat quickened, though I kept my movements steady as I stepped past him, setting my bag down on the kitchen counter. I could feel his eyes on me, even as he glanced around the room again, his gaze snagging on the details that should've been forgettable if not for the serious event that happened here.

"I liked that about it," I continued, a hint of amusement coloring my voice. "Felt easier to just slide into a life that was already built, you know? I made a few changes here and there to personalize the spaces, of course." I peeked at him, watching for any flash of acknowledgment, any crack in his concealment of the truth. "Why? Do you know the old owners?"

Evan inhaled, rubbing a hand over his jaw. The gesture was thoughtful, yet distracted, as though his mind was elsewhere. "Uh, not personally . . ." He trailed off, his words hesitant with a distant gaze. His hand lingered near his jaw like he was trying to tether himself to the present. He wasn't convinced, not entirely.

And why would he be? This place wasn't just familiar to him, it was etched into his memory, perhaps his soul, deeper than he was willing to admit. Murder doesn't come with a clean slate; your subconscious is like an ex who just won't let you forget. I could see it in the way his shoulders stiffened, the way his gaze flicked to the staircase like it might hold the answer he was searching for. He remembered more than he was letting on. He might not have all the pieces yet, but the puzzle was taking shape in his mind. I'd underestimated how quickly he'd start connecting the dots, how sharp his instincts really were.

Forcing myself to keep moving, I kept my demeanor casual, unaffected. Letting him see any strain or my awareness of his unease would only confirm his suspicions. But inside, the pressure was mounting, a slow burn building beneath my calm exterior.

Evan was circling too close to the truth for comfort. For the first time in what felt like forever, doubt—annoying and unwelcome—nudged at the edges of my carefully curated confidence. Still, as long as he didn't suddenly piece it all together and bolt out the door like he'd seen a ghost, why should I care? If he remembered this was the house where he'd played God and pulled the trigger, well, that was his haunted bedtime story, not mine. I had enough skeletons to juggle.

Instead I nodded, pretending all was perfectly normal. I advanced toward the bar tucked into the corner of the sitting room, mentally cataloging the lies he fed me. He would never admit to murdering someone, especially not the someone who he believed lived in this house before me. And honestly, I didn't need him to. His denial was practically a given. Men like Evan didn't confess. Men like Evan rationalized, justified, and buried the truth under layers of delusion.

"Still up for that drink?" I asked.

His attention lingered on the staircase for a moment longer before turning back to me. "Sure." His gaze snagged momentarily, as if brushing against something hidden just out of reach.

I watched him, curiosity obscured by my practiced cheerfulness. *Why the staircase? Why did his gaze keep drifting there, like it was calling to him? Was he remembering something? A fragment, a shadow, a flash from the past year—or was he* merely searching for answers that refused to come?

Forcing a smile, I conceal my mind's formulation of demanding questions.

Did the staircase hold some significance to him—perhaps the vantage point from which he'd orchestrated his chaos? Or was his fixation on it simply another puzzle piece, hinting at a memory he hadn't yet placed? Whatever it was, I wasn't about to press the issue. Let him figure it out on his own. Watching him squirm under the weight of his own fragmented recollections was far more entertaining.

"Whiskey?" I asked as I pulled a drugged glass out of the secret compartment underneath the bar. I had stocked them for purposes like this, when the killer of my boyfriend came to hang out. "I don't have anything fancy, just Macallan and Jameson."

"Sure," he said, rubbing the back of his neck. "Jameson is fine."

Pouring two glasses of Jameson with ease, I was careful not to mix up the glasses so I didn't drug myself rather than him. As I handed him his glass, I couldn't help but wonder: *how long would it take before the memories clawed their way to the surface? Before he realized he wasn't just standing in a house that looked familiar—he was standing in the scene of his own crime? Surely he knew that, right?*

The thought made me smile. A small, private thing I hid behind the rim of the glass. Let him remember. Let him piece it together. It wouldn't change his fate.

As I poured, he wandered the sitting room, fingers trailing the edge of a bookshelf. His eyes traveled over the space like he was perusing an exhibit at the MoMA—appreciative, but not in any real rush, and blissfully unaware of what coiled in the depths of the house.

Slipping another pinch of white powder into the drugged glass, tasteless and harmless in small doses, it infused easily into the whiskey. A gift from one of Qualley's more resourceful associates. It wasn't potent enough to knock him out cold—no dramatic collapses tonight—but just enough to fog his mind, loosen his tongue, and ideally, turn him into a more pliant version of himself.

Less interrogation.

Less pushback.

More blind trust.

He was a cop, sure, but I was banking on the fact that his senses weren't quite in the drug-sniffing-dog category. If they were, well, I'd cross that bridge when I got to it.

I swirled the glass carefully, watching as every last grain of powder disappeared into the amber liquid. Satisfied, I turned and handed it to him. "Here you are! Enjoy!" He took it without a single shred of hesitation.

If I'd had a tip jar, I might've left it out—his faith in me was downright touching. Or it would've been, if I wasn't so busy poisoning his drink.

He took a sip, and I carefully watched the moment it crossed his tongue, the way his throat bobbed as he swallowed. He made a small sound of approval.

"Damn. That's smooth."

I lifted my own glass to my lips, letting the whiskey warm my mouth before swallowing. "That's Jameson for you. Nothing special, but gets the job done."

With a hum in agreement, he drank, moving and circling the room with a newfound ease. Clearly, he relaxed by degrees since we had entered the house, unafflicted by the fact he was involved in murdering two innocent people. It was as if he was all of a sudden in a completely different, unfamiliar place.

All that he needed was a little liquid courage.

It didn't take long—fifteen minutes, maybe less—before the subtle shift began. His inhibitions peeled away like wet wallpaper.

"Must've cost a fortune. What do you do to afford a place

like this?"

I smirked, handing him another poisoned glass after he'd chugged the first one. "Trust fund baby."

He let out a short laugh. "Seriously?"

Cocking my head, I shrugged. "My parents had money, but I try not to lean on it too much." I took a sip of my drink, letting the warmth settle in my chest. "When they passed, I inherited both of their fortunes. But now I sell and collect art. Originals, mostly. Some commissions. I love it."

He lifted the glass to his lips, pausing just before sipping.

"You know, for a trust fund baby, you sure don't scream 'old money.'"

"That's the point." I smirked, hanging over the counter.

"So, you're an artist?"

"Something like that." Exactly what Qualley had told me when I had asked him what he'd done for work.

"What kind of art?"

"Portraits. I like capturing people the way they *really* are."

Evan chuckled, unaware of the context of my words. "That sounds a little intense. I have a colleague that's into art."

Lile.

I swirled the whiskey in my glass, ignoring his mention of his 'colleague'. Engaging on that now could potentially unravel everything.

"You'd be surprised how much people reveal when they don't realize they're being studied."

He hummed, thinking it over, and grinned. "So, am I about to become your next masterpiece?"

I met his gaze, smile unwavering. "If you're lucky."

As spiked whiskey settled in his system, I observed him, waiting for the change. The way his shoulders dropped just a little more, a casual looseness in his stance. It happened gradually.

His fingers dragged lazily over the back of the couch as he walked, occasionally gripping it for support. His smirk lingered just a beat longer than usual, as if everything felt good or amused him.

"This stuff is hitting harder than I expected," he muttered, rolling his neck like he struggled to shake something off. "You sure you didn't spike my drink?" He laughed, but an edge of haziness crept into his voice.

Sipping my own drink, I beamed, wise to the early signs of a drugged state. "Wouldn't need to. Apparently you're just a lightweight."

He scoffed, unbothered to argue. *Did I hit a nerve?* Oh how men hate being called lightweights—it's practically a universal truth. Give a guy a couple of beers, and he's suddenly a philosopher-slash-sports-commentator, yelling at a pool table like it owes him money. Hand him tequila, and he's halfway to making a clumsy pass at the girl he's been side-eyeing all night, convinced he's irresistible.

But instead of defending his fragile honor, he stepped closer, brushing the edge of my personal space. "So, tell me something," he slurred, his words weaving slightly. "Why'd you really invite me here?"

The way he says it—like he's expecting some flirtatious, coy answer—almost made me laugh. He thought he was in control, that this was unfolding on his terms.

Angling my head, I stride past him, trailing my fingers along his arm as I proceeded toward the hallway. Winking at him I said, "Why don't I show you?"

And oh, he *bit*.

He followed me like a puppy chasing a treat, utterly spellbound. His brain was firmly lodged in cartoon-land complete with heart-shaped thought bubbles popping above his head and floating behind me down the hallway. The drug worked beautifully, easing down his defenses, making him susceptible to anything I did to him.

The drug made him . . . compliant.

That's all I really needed anyway.

When I opened the bathroom door, the light gave a dramatic little flicker—perfect ambiance for murder . . . if I'd been that kind of person. Steam curled lazily from the bath as I clutched the knife holstered under my skirt, grip steady like I was auditioning for the role of 'totally-not-about-to-stab-anyone'.

Quickly, I shoved the blade into a basket of hand towels, burying it beneath the fluffiest one, because if anyone found it later, at least it'd feel cozy.

By the time Evan turned to face me, I was already smiling and perfectly composed. I was someone who'd just innocently reorganized a basket of hand towels and definitely not someone who'd hidden a knife in it moments ago. I was definitely not standing there considering 'Plan B' if things went awry . . .

Resting against the wall, Evan blinked slower than before. "You had this ready for me?" He smirked at me as if he thought he was charming.

Spoiler alert: *he wasn't.*

The water was hot, inviting, but all I could think about was the last time I'd gone through this ritual. Back then, it was for Qualley—smooth-talking, cologne-reeking Qualley—who'd always insisted on eucalyptus salts and "the perfect temperature" like he was royalty. I'd stand there, dutifully stirring the water like a witch brewing a potion, while he'd call me his "bath artist." Now here I was, drawing a bath for another man. It was so . . . unethical, like I'd accidentally slipped into some twisted sequel to a bad romance novel. I hated the setup, the familiarity, the way my muscles seemed to remember every step of the process even though my brain was screaming, *never again.* Still, I plastered on a smile, the kind that screamed, *I'm totally not plotting your doom.*

"Of course," I said sweetly. "Only the best for you." His

guard was so down, it was practically underground. I had to run with it. "I like to be prepared." I turned to him, my expression unreadable. "Wanna relax with me?"

He exhaled a small laugh, rubbing a hand over his face. "I don't know, I—" He wobbled slightly, catching himself on the door frame.

My fingers closed around his wrist, steadying him. "You're fine," I murmured, almost a whisper. "I'll take care of you."

He swayed slightly, his attention slipping in and out of focus as though he was trying to piece together who I was. "Relax, huh?" He asked, pupils dilating.

My hand rose to his face, fingers brushing the stubble along his jawline, the warmth of his skin unsettling against my palm. I hated every second of it—hated the intimacy, hated the pretense —but the gesture was necessary, a calculated move.

"Trust me," I whispered, words like honey despite the bitter taste they left in my mouth. My thumb grazed his cheek as I held back the urge to recoil. This wasn't affection; it was strategy.

If this was what it took to keep him pliant, I'd play the part for as long as I had to.

And he was pliant as fuck!

I helped him peel off his shirt tentatively, like we were starring in the world's most awkward slow-motion sex scene. His shoes followed, then his pants and underwear, which he discarded with all the grace of someone tossing laundry into a hamper whilst drunk after a night out. He stepped closer, emitting a heat so war, he could have been a human radiator. He leaned in for a kiss.

Ducking, I simulated to adjusting my footing clumsily, and his lips landed somewhere in the vicinity of disappointment. Undeterred, he tried again, and I turned my head just enough to make it look like I was inspecting the drywall. *How did this dent get here? Were the walls always this yellow?*

We shuffled into a masterclass in accidental avoidance, and

he didn't even seem to notice.

By the time he gave up, I was already steering him toward the tub, my hand light on his arm. He followed, blissfully unaware that I was playing dodgeball with his attempts at romance. I kept my gaze carefully fixed ahead, refusing to let my eyes wander to places that might distract me—or worse, make me feel something I didn't want to feel. The proximity was smothering, unwelcome, like an itch I couldn't scratch.

Steam curled upward as the water's warmth rose. Its surface rippled as he lowered himself in. A low groan escaped his lips, the sound grating against my nerves even as the heat seeped into his muscles. I loathed the closeness—the unsolicited brush of skin against mine as I steadied him, the misplaced trust he offered so freely. Each touch only deepened my disdain for the act I was forced to maintain, but I buried it as best I could, keeping my actions smooth and cloaked in calm indifference.

"Oh, this *is* nice," he said, exhaling.

I crouched beside the tub, trailing a fingertip through the water. "Better? The bathtub is heated, so the water won't go cold."

"Yeah . . . nice . . ." Evan's eyes slipped shut for a moment as he sighed.

I stood, fingers curling around the object tucked discreetly behind a stack of folded towels on the large, wooden shelving that held them.

"Good," I whispered.

The cord in my hand was cold, coiled like a waiting serpent. I slid forward, jerking my head as I inspected him—the way the water flowed delicately around his shoulders, the way his fingers traced absently along the rim of the tub.

He didn't see it coming.

And by the time he did, it was far too late.

Preparing everything long before Evan ever set foot in the bathtub (some things before he even entered the house) I excused myself pretending to go to the bathroom. I filled the tub, ensuring its warmth and comfortability, mostly inviting—which was kind of the point. Scents of lavender Epsom salt curled within the steam.

Water shimmered under the low flicker of candlelight—soft, golden, intimate. But the bath wasn't just for relaxation. The Epsom salt that dissolved into the water would ensure every inch of it became a perfect conductor.

Weeks of research were spent making sure the setup was flawless. The GFCI outlets? Gone. I replaced them with old, standard ones, the kind that wouldn't save a careless fool from a lethal mistake. The circuit breaker was rewired, bypassing any automatic shutoffs within the bathroom. There would be no interruptions or sudden cuts of power. I could possibly get a job as an electrician's apprentice with all the videos I'd watched on the subject.

And the final touch?

A space heater I found at a Goodwill. Heavy, solid, reliable. *Old.* The newer models would never work, considering most of them also had automatic shut offs just as the GFCIs. I'd ripped open the plug a bit, exposing some of the wiring which would cause a direct surge of electricity to flow the moment it hit the water.

After all that, it was just a matter of getting Evan in the tub.

Evan stretched his arms along the sides of the porcelain, sighing as warm steam wrapped around him. His head lolled slightly as the drug lulled him between relaxation and detachment.

"You're right," he muttered slowly, words garbled. "This is exactly what I needed."

Beside the tub, I relaxed my chin in my palm. Waiting. "Told you," I purred. "I'm good at knowing what people need."

"You're full of surprises."

My fingers glided along the edge of the tub, skimming the water just enough to feel its warmth. "Perhaps, though I'd say I've got a pretty good read on you by now."

Evan's head tipped back against the cool ceramic; eyes closed. His chest rose and fell in deep movements. He seemed so comfortable.

And completely unaware.

Reaching behind me, my fingers wrapped around the heavy heater plugged into the wall. The cord slithered off the counter, taut in my grip. It stayed rooted in the outlet, unmoved.

I stood in one, fluid motion.

Evan barely reacted as I lifted the heater. Maybe he thought I was just shifting things around, adjusting something, getting myself naked to join him in the tub. His drugged mind probably couldn't quite make sense of why I was suddenly looming over him, why I was holding something so out of place.

Then, I let go.

The old heater plunged into the water with a splash, descending on top of his crotch and crushing his dick.

I almost felt bad about that.

For half a second, nothing happened. Only the sound of water settling, and the theatrics of Evan sucking in a breath as confusion and pain flashed across his face—*then the electricity hit.*

His body jerked violently, muscles locking, and his back arching against the sudden, brutal current. Water sloshed over the rim as his hands shot up, fingers clawing at nothing. His mouth opened in a silent scream, eyes going wide with shock—literal, searing shock—as the charge tore through him.

The bathroom lit up in sharp, erratic bursts, like a haunted house or Fourth of July fireworks. A wondrous display! The exposed wiring crackled, sending ripples of white-hot energy through the tub. A stench of burning skin rose, mixing with the humid air and clinging to the walls. His hands twitched, spasming before they went limp. His chest heaved once. Then stilled. Lights flickered once more. Water settled.

Then finally, dark silence.

Chapter 22

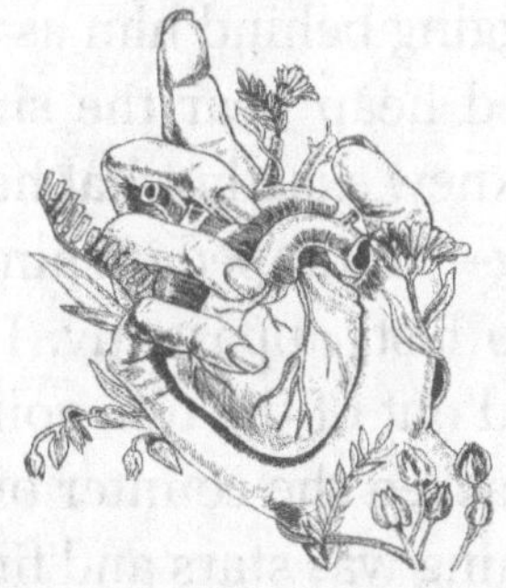

The last remnants of life appeared to drain from Evan's face. His limbs floated slightly, his head fell morbidly to the side; lips already turning blue, just barely parted as if he had one last question he'd never get to ask.

Just as casually as I'd invited him inside, I spun away to go turn the power to the bathroom off from the sub-panel in the garage so I wouldn't be barbecued when I returned to remove the space heater.

Downstairs, as I worked to turn off the power, a *thud* echoed from the bathroom. Then another.

I stilled.

Fuck.

I bolted up the stairs, practically tripping over my own feet, erupting back into the bathroom. From the doorway, I saw it: Evan's pale hand gripping the tub's edge like he was auditioning for a zombie flick. Somehow, against all odds, he'd hauled himself out—smoking, trembling, but still alive.

How could he have still been fucking alive?

"No!" I hissed, channeling every ounce of dramatic flair as I launched myself into the dark bathroom and delivered a round-house kick straight to his face. It was a move worthy of an action movie, except for the part where Evan collapsed onto the tile, coughing like he'd just inhaled a lifetime's worth of bad decisions.

Thank god for those self-defense sessions with Zina.

His skin was mottled and scorched in patches from what I could see, one leg dragging behind him as he crawled toward his pants—a sad, crumpled heap near the sink. His hand reached into the pocket, and I knew exactly what he was going for.

"Don't you fucking—" I jumped on him faster than I thought humanly possible. Too fast, apparently. I slipped on the water spilling off of Evan and out of the tub, going down like a sack of potatoes. My head smacked the counter on the way to the floor. For a moment, everything was stars and fireworks. I couldn't tell if the throbbing in my head or the bruising of my ego hurt worse.

Meanwhile Evan, ever the opportunist, fumbled with his phone like a drunk raccoon, his bloodied fingers smearing streaks across the screen. He hit a button—I didn't catch which one—but the unmistakable sound of a ring confirmed it.

A call.

Rookie mistake 101: always confiscate the damn phone. I mentally kicked myself, though the physical kicking would have to wait until I wasn't sprawled on the floor seeing constellations.

How could I have been so careless? Nevertheless, I hastily recovered and was on him in seconds, my heel slamming into his ribs, sending the phone skittering across the floor. Unfortunately, Evan didn't stop. He *crawled* after it.

Remembering the knife I'd stashed in the wicker basket of towels, I shuffled to grab it from the vanity. My heart pounded, not from fear, but with wrath so hot it could've electrified the bathwater all on its own. This was supposed to be clean—like a noir film where the villain takes one last soak before fading dramatically into oblivion. He was supposed to die in the water. Peaceful, poetic, like some kind of twisted baptism.

Instead, here he was, alive and dripping, ruining my plan and the fancy white tiles with every shaky breath he took. How hard was it to just . . . die? Honestly, he was making this unnecessarily complicated, and I started to regret all the effort I'd put into creating the perfect murder ambiance.

Candles? *Wasted.*

Steam? *Pointless.*

The flickering bathroom light? It was working harder than he was at actually dying . . . and it was off.

Now I was stuck improvising, and let's be real—I'm not exactly the 'wing it' type when it comes to murder.

I pounced on him, knife in hand, yanking him back by the hair like I was trying to win a tug-of-war championship. He screamed—a sound so piercing, it was as if it was trying to claw its way into my soul.

"You ruined everything!" I snarled, my voice sopping with the kind of anger that might scare the boogyman. "You fucking ruined everything!"

Honestly, I couldn't believe how much effort he was making me put into this. Especially considering my plan's simplicity—a one-and-done kind of deal. But no, he had to go and complicate things, dragging me into this chaotic mess like some amateur. I mean, who even survives a perfectly planned bath murder?

No matter. I plunged the knife downward, aiming for something vital, but in the pitch-black bathroom, it found his shoulder instead. He gasped a sharp, startled sound.

"Fuck," I shouted, squinting uselessly into the void at my missed mark. The power outage had turned this into a literal stab in the dark, and I started to think the universe actively rooted against me.

Evan writhed beneath me, clutching his shoulder like I'd just ruined his day—which, to be fair, I had. The lightbulb that had been my moody accomplice earlier was now as dead as my patience, leaving me to fumble through this mess like a clumsy newbie.

I never envisioned *this* to be my grand moment.

As Evan flailed around, barely keeping his limbs under control, he flopped down like a fish out of water, and I seized the moment. With a satisfying *schlunk*, I plunged the knife into his side. To think—if he'd been wearing clothes, this whole ordeal might've been ten times harder. I made a mental note to be thankful for silver linings.

Finally, I battled his twitching body around to face me, and with a grim sort of determination, drove the blade deep into his chest. He wheezed, blood bubbling at his lips like some sort of grotesque soda fountain, but my attention was snagged else-where—the phone on the floor. Still blinking. Still connected.

A muffled voice drifted through, male and impatient. "Evan?" It said. "You okay? Hello?"

Panic ripped through my veins. *How had he been so quick to call someone? How long had it been connected? Was he se-cretly a speed-dial soldier of fortune?* I stepped away from the mess on the floor—the mess being one bleeding out Evan—picked up the phone slowly. I stared at it like it was the final boss of the night, the kind that shows up when you're out of health potions and your controller's battery is dying.

The screen glowed, mocking me. The call was still connect-ed. I half-expected the voice on the other end to start narrating my failures like a sports commentator: *"And she fumbles the murder attempt! What a dumb bitch!"*

Without a word, I pressed the red button to hang up, ending the call with a beep so final it felt like punctuation for the entire night's topsy-turvydom. Not satisfied with just cutting the con-nection, I tossed the phone into the tub, watching it sink with all the grace of a brick to the bottom. The steam swirled lazily around it like it was taunting me, my murder ambiance wasted on electronics.

I directed my gaze to Evan's crumpled form on the floor, his chest rising and falling slower and slower, mouth open in what I assumed was his final, wordless protest. His eyes stilled.

Finally.

This time, I didn't smile. Oh no, there was no room for premature celebration. I wasn't going to be fooled by some last-minute gasp or surprise resurrection. Leaning down, I checked his pulse, my fingers pressing firmly against his neck to confirm a very welcome absence of life. No pulse. No movement. No more goddamned problems.

"You're clean now," I whispered, as though it was some great figurative ending. In truth, it was more like the closing line of a sitcom episode gone horribly awry. Frankly, I couldn't help but think: if there was a version of this where I *didn't* end up grappling slippery tiles, a stubborn victim, and a now-water-logged phone, I'd like to live in it.

Pivoting sharply, I exited the bathroom and made a beeline for the electrical sub-panel to restore the power after removing the heater from the tub and wall socket. It was bad enough I couldn't see what I was doing when it was taking place, but I wouldn't deal with the aftermath of my impromptu slaughter in total darkness.

On the way back to the bathroom, I snatched a stack of tarps from the shelves that, in a perfect world, would've been neatly laid down before butchering someone. *But no,* Evan had to go full zombie on me, derailing the well-orchestrated murder setup I'd envisioned. Now, instead of preserving my floors like a responsible killer, I had to clean up a mess that was destined to seep into every nook and cranny. The grout? *Absolutely ruined.*

Staring at the tarps in my arms, I couldn't help but curse myself. If only I'd followed step one of any DIY murder guide: *Protect the flooring, you idiot.* Now I was going to spend hours scrubbing, all because Evan couldn't just politely stay dead in the tub.

I also grabbed a mason jar, mostly because it looked useful, though at this point I wasn't sure if it was for evidence, improvisation, or sheer panic collecting. A roll of duct tape landed on my wrist as well, like a makeshift bracelet—practical and stylish, if you ignored the impending horror-show cleanup.

When I reentered the bathroom, I situated the jar and duct tape onto the counter and slapped the plastic tarps onto the floor with all the enthusiasm of someone who'd just given up on caring about ruined flooring. Water danced with blood smeared across the tiles like some avant-garde art installation, but cleaning that was a problem for future me. Present me had bigger issues—like figuring out how to roll a 250-pound dead guy onto the tarp without pulling a muscle.

I turned back to Evan, his lifeless body sprawled out like he was on vacation, leisurely ruining my flooring one drop of blood at a time. The once vibrant pink of his skin had faded to a ghastly greyish blue; the electricity and blood loss having drained every last spark of life from him. Grabbing his arm, I gave it a tug, only to realize that rigor mortis hadn't kicked in yet, which meant he would still be floppy—like trying to wrestle a giant, uncooperative noodle. I huffed, repositioning myself for better leverage, but all I managed to do was slide him an inch closer to the tarp.

"Seriously, Evan?" I groaned, glaring at his unhelpful corpse. "You couldn't have been, I don't know, *lighter*?"

After several failed attempts, I resorted to rolling him like a burrito, grunting and cursing under my breath as his limbs flopped around like they had their own agenda. By the time I finally got him onto the tarp, I was sweating, my back was sore, and I was seriously reconsidering my life choices.

Glancing down at him, I couldn't help but think: if there's a hell, Evan owes me a spa day for this nonsense.

And new goddamn flooring!

When Evan was finally sprawled onto the tarp after what felt like an Olympic event in corpse wrestling, I let out a breath I didn't realize I'd been holding. My fingers slid over the bloody knife on the counter, the cool metal steady in my grip.

I glanced at the countertops, now smeared with blood like some macabre abstract art piece. *Great,* I thought. *There go the countertops too.* At this rate, I was going to need a full bathroom remodel, and I doubted 'murder cleanup' was covered by my home insurance.

It was Evan's blood, smeared across my once-pristine home, that sparked the perfect idea. Funny how destruction can be so inspiring.

For a moment, I just stood there, staring at him. His lifeless form laid still, finally not causing me any more problems—except for the glaring logistical nightmare of getting him out of here. My mind wandered to the absurdity of it all. This wasn't how I'd pictured my evening.

Hmm, pictured . . . I thought.

I sighed, letting the knife rest at my side. "Well, Evan," I whined, "you've really outdone yourself this time."

Even the knife wasn't part of the original plan.

It was supposed to be quick, efficient—just a plunge, a shock, silence, then straight to the backyard. But something about the way he looked at that moment, the way death had claimed him so beautifully, made me hesitate. Not out of guilt. Out of curiosity.

Turning the blade between my fingers, I witnessed the reflection of the bathroom light shimmer against the blade. The thought of simply disposing of his body felt . . . wasteful. There was more to be done. A slow smile pulled at my lips as an idea took shape.

Squatting beside Evan's body, my free hand trailed lightly along Evan's chest, my touch featherlight. I followed the curve of his ribs, the dip of his collarbone. I imagined the canvas he could become, the possibility of what I could depict from his cooling flesh. For a moment, I explored his body, studying him with the solemnity of an artist about to ruin their studio.

This was going to be messy—no way around it. But hey, all great art demanded sacrifice, right? And at least I had tarps now, which meant my floors might survive this creative endeavor. Probably. Maybe.

Okay, not likely, but a girl can dream.

Easing the knife into his sternum, I thrust it in just above the top of the rib cage. I didn't rush. The blade bit in further, parting skin with a controlled precision. Red bloomed in a magnificent comparison to his pale form and dripped like crimson tears down his chest.

Some might have called it a chaotic mess, and I foolishly overlooked that gloves would shield my hands from the sticky warmth of his blood. Before I got too absorbed in my task, I recalled some I stashed in the closet after dying my hair. Hurriedly, I washed my hands to avoid spreading the blood any further; warm water mingled with scarlet, flowing down the drain.

Once I protected my hands, I got back to work. Fingers pried through muscle and sinew, carefully carving into his chest until I attained the treasure beneath. His heart, once strong, beating, was silent. A useless lump of flesh.

But maybe it didn't have to be.

Lifting Evan's heart from its cavity, I observed in fascination as the last remnants of blood dripped into the mason jar, swirling like ink in paper fibers. Holding it up to the light, I realized it was beautiful in its own way, soaked in the last thing that made Evan human.

Another surge of inspiration gripped me. This wasn't just a kill. It was creation.

Leaving the heart on the counter in its jar, along with some of the blood, I stepped back, examining myself in the mirror. I wiped my hands absently along my reflection.

The dim bathroom light projected sharp shadows across my face, highlighting dark smears of blood that streaked my cheekbones, my jaw, the bridge of my nose. Blood clung to my gloves, drying in thin, flaking rivulets that spiderwebbed down my wrists. I extended my hand again, pressing my palm to the cool glass, smearing a bloody print over my reflection. My lips parted slightly as I angled my head, studying the woman staring back at me.

She was different. Or maybe she wasn't.

Maybe this was always who she was, who she was meant to be—just waiting beneath the surface, beneath the pretense of normalcy, beneath quiet smiles and careful conversations.

I trailed my fingers down the mirror, leaving streaks like veins. Tears followed, stinging my eyes as Qualley returned to my mind.

I'd replicate this day two times over . . . hopefully with less exuberant and unexpected events.

I breathed, slow and steady, and then, despite my tears, smiled.

Tonight, I will create something beautiful, I thought.

Standing by the grave I dug large enough for three bodies in preparation for its new tenants, I examined the naked body of Evan Matthews. The duct tape placed tightly over his chest helped contain anything leaking out of the incisions I created. All his personal items were stored inside his chest cavity.

I might be homicidal, but I'm no kleptomaniac.

Hauling this man's body out of the bathroom, through the kitchen, out the back door, across the deck—nearly busting my ass down the stairs—to my current location was fucking absurd . . . but totally worth it.

I shoved him closer to the gaping hole, aligning his lifeless form with its edge. With a swift, forceful kick, I sent him plummeting into the abyss, tarps and all, giggling as he disappeared into the darkness with a thud. He rested there, motionless, of course, in the dark chasm of the hole, and a sense of pride washed over me. But I didn't have much time to admire my handiwork. I wiped sweat from my forehead with the back of my wrist and got to work covering him up.

The thick blue tarps came first; dragging the edges inward and folding them like a makeshift shroud before shoveling in a few layers of dirt. I placed bricks, already weathered and caked in dirt, around its edges, stacking them carefully to form an uneven, yet natural-looking barrier. I threw in a few cracked stones for good measure and by the time I finished, it looked like nothing more than a forgotten corner of the yard. A kind of place weeds will reclaim in no time.

You know . . . *gardening.*

That's what I would've called it if anyone asked. A little landscaping project where I'd plant bushes first since its winter. Maybe I'd even throw in some flowers before spring, like tulips. Something that spread fast, with roots tangling deep.

But my mind wasn't on the grave anymore once Evan's body was hidden.

My thoughts focused on what waited inside my art studio, blocking the view of my mock grave from anyone looking on from the deck of the house. I crept over to check the accuracy of that theory, finding my calculations correct—you can't see shit.

I shook out my arms and rolled my shoulders, lolling my head in circles. My hands were sore, my body exhausted, but none of that mattered. Now the easy part of my night began.

Without pausing to clean up or catch my breath, I rushed back to the bathroom. Evan's heart still sat in its jar on the counter, a gruesome, twisted reality I found myself in. The mason jar was crusted with blood, so I took a moment to rinse it off in the sink, washing my hands in the process. Once I finished, I headed back outside to my art studio.

A vast, untouched canvas loomed on the easel in the corner of the room, because I'm always ready; my tools meticulously prepared for the moment inspiration strikes. Brushes awaited my attention but remained unused.

Instead, I employed a more . . . intimate approach.

I tilted the mason jar with two fingers over the top, ensuring Evan's heart wouldn't topple out and spray paint and bodily fluids everywhere before I was ready. Blood poured onto my palette in a slow, viscous stream, pooling like molten rubies. Careful, precise, I didn't waste a single drop. The heart trembled in its jar as I set it back down, slick, glistening, a fresh relic of my devotion.

Dipping my fingers into the thick warmth of paint and blood, I spread the liquid between them, savoring the texture; the way it clung and stained, seeping into the whorls of my fingerprints and sinking into my skin like it belonged there. This wasn't just paint—it was essence, sacrifice, and the purest form of creation.

I smeared my first strokes across the canvas, crimson streaks spread like open wounds upon its surface. The first strokes were erratic, instinctive blots of red across the white expanse. I let the blood dictate the composition, painting the echoes of final moments. Raw energy of life leaving a body. Frenzied marks with severe imprints of my fingers.

A macabre masterpiece.

I decided not to immortalize Evan in this portrait, shifting instead to the one person I'd kill a man—a cop—for.

Qualley.

Soon enough, I thought. *I'd collect my other two trophies with which I'd create more pieces to preserve Qualley's memory and show people who these bastard cops died for.*

Additionally, they took *my* heart, so it was only fair I took *theirs.*

They'd be my *crimson keepsakes.*

Chapter 23

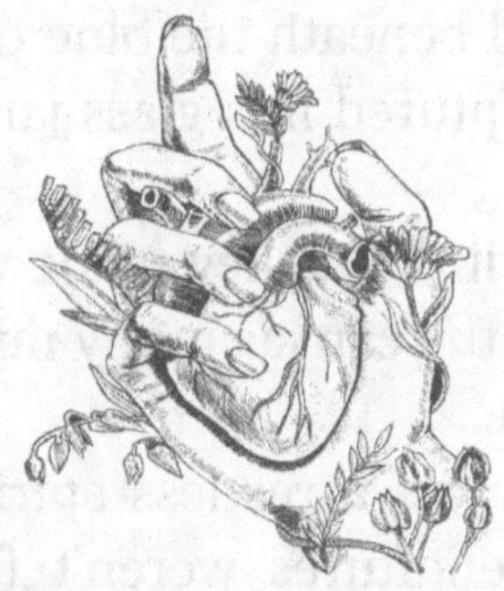

Mortal enemies exist for everyone. Sure, some people might simulate forgiveness, their bitterness cloaked with an air of sanctimony, but let's not kid ourselves —that's a crock of shit. Beneath civilized facades lies tempests of unresolved anger and seething frustration. Deep down, they crave retribution, longing to unleash restrained fury and put their adversaries in their rightful place.

For me, that place was six feet under.

I never imagined anyone could have eclipsed my bitch mother and those she allowed to hurt me from their throne of cruelty, but then Qualley was murdered. During that time, her malice seemed almost benign in comparison. Besides, their ship had long since sailed, a literal ghostly specter in the distance.

Consigning my mother's memory to the fathomless depths of my past, Lile Henderson became the object of my obsession. Police reports I secured whispered the dark truth—he was the one who murdered Qualley.

Evan decayed at the bottom of my backyard grave, his presence a gaping void beckoning from the shadows. He claimed Lonney's life, and without Zina ever having to lift a finger, I'd secured the vengeance she never even knew she needed. When the dust finally settled, and truths revealed themselves, I hoped Zina would be the one to understand. Maybe even, in some small measure, feel a trace of gratitude—not that I was holding my breath. Dwelling on an innocent party's reaction to my actions was unreasonable. Focusing on my next move—one that would establish Lile sprawled beneath the blue tarp behind my studio, his heart and blood captured in a glass jar, was my main priority.

The newest portrait of Qualley made with Lile's fresh blood already took shape on the canvas in my mind, each brush stroke fueled by the inevitable.

Unlike Evan, Lile was a restless spirit never tethered to a single place. His expenditures weren't flooded with frequent bookstore or cafe trips, nor did he linger in bars. Instead, he moved throughout the state like a shadow on the move, leaving behind only whispers and fleeting impressions. This made it awfully difficult to contrive how I'd lure him into my familiar abode to secure his entrance into hell.

During a deep dive into Lile's life, I'd discovered he frequented art galleries across Connecticut—his preference: *The Hartford Gallery*.

How fucking convenient.

Becoming best friends with social media for my research, Instagram in particular, I stalked his pictures, analyzing every carefully curated caption, and pieced together the locations of his usual haunts like some kind of art-loving detective.

It was just my luck that the person I loathed more than anything in this world was probably the only one who could've shared my passion for art . . . if I ever desired to 'bond' with the creature . . .

Spoiler alert: *I didn't.*

Semantics of our mirroring hobbies were irrelevant, nothing more than a mildly irritating coincidence.

When I said plotting the downfall of the officers involved in the raid since the trial was a meticulous venture, I meant it. Every word. Every detail. I left no stone unturned, and yes, I even altered the signature on my paintings—small touches for grander schemes. My alias, Crimson, became the embodiment of my wrath, a blood-soaked symbol of everything I was about to unleash.

The real challenge?

Getting my artwork showcased in the gallery without unmasking my true identity as Cassandra Kessler.

Maybe *Crimson* was my true identity—hard to tell, honestly. Either way, I had to bite the bullet, enlisting Zina's assistance so I'd have better chances at pulling this ruse off stealthily. Her razor-sharp instincts and, let's face it, morally flexible attitude were critical to my success. I would merely redact the truth of what I'd been up to in our conversation.

And that Evan was dead in the backyard.

Convincing Zina to help wasn't easy. Gone were the days of cigarette and Cheeto bribes—though I kind of missed the simplicity of those negotiations although cigarettes were still a preferable compromise. Nowadays, her greed had evolved to the point where sushi, liquor, and cash money were the currency of persuasion. Regardless, I dialed her up, promising a girls' night fueled by sake and sashimi, and prayed she'd bite. Knowing Zina, she would. After all, she'd been greedy since the day we met, and while that trait was exasperating at times, it was also oddly reliable.

👁 👁

Ultimately, persuading the parasite that was Zina with a promise of food and wine worked like a charm. Knowing her penchant for fine dining, she was probably halfway there already once I'd called.

Truth be told, I wasn't in the mood for company. A sleepless night and a frantic day spent finishing the piece that I hoped would grace the gallery with its presence, had left me utterly drained. But friendship had its dues, and I forced myself to plaster on a happy face for her sake.

Inviting Zina into my studio was a peculiar move for me; I never allowed anyone inside, not even my closest friends or fellow artists. It was strange. The studio was my sanctum, a space where creativity blossomed free from outside interference. The sole exception was Qualley, both my muse and the architect of this refuge. His presence was a constant, reassuring, comfort and almost sacrilegious to consider expelling him.

But he wasn't with me anymore.

I couldn't risk Zina discovering my first trophy and painting —the very thought sent a shiver down my spine. As I awaited her arrival, I hurried to drape a linen sheet over the canvas I'd painted with Evan's blood, concealing its sinister depiction. I tucked it away in the cramped supply closet. The canvas stood out, a ghost among its taller, more innocuous neighbors, so I hid the rest of them under the sheet as well.

Turning my attention to the heart, its presence is a severe reminder of my deed, I jostled it behind a row of dusty paint tins, placing one directly on top of the jar and arranging it as if it were just another color in the bunch. With a sense of urgency, I retrieved a grimy, old washcloth from the laundry basket, throwing it over the tins. I hoped it would be enough to mask the horror hidden beneath.

Zina was one of the nosiest individuals in the state, possibly the country. In order to keep up my con, minding my wits was essential.

The door of the studio swung open just as I shut the supply closet and in danced Zina, radiating the nightclub energy that didn't belong in my paint-splattered lair. Her short, jet-black hair curled softly against her neck; bangs styled in a pure '90s flare. It bounced gracefully as she moved.

She wore an ivory faux fur coat, its ends tinged a few shades darker, over a black mini dress that clung to her enviable curves. Despite the night darkening outside, her oversized sunglasses remained perched on her face, amplifying her dramatic entrance for what was supposed to be a casual sleepover. Her bag, also black and comically large, could easily fit a week's worth of groceries for a family of four. Hopefully it also contained something she could sleep in.

Just in case she tried to sneak out and drive into the abyss, I planned to secure her keys quickly to prevent any chance of another DUI on her record . . . a tale that wasn't mine to tell.

Zina stopped in the threshold of the door, crossing her arms. Pulling her sunglasses down the bridge of her nose, she eyed me up and down. "Okay . . . what the hell is this?" Her New England dialect, strong as ever, only meant she'd already started drinking.

I smirked, running my fingers through my newly dyed soft pink hair. "A change." I flashed a flirty wink, as if she was hitting on me. I flipped my hair from side to side.

Unimpressed, her purse slid to her hand as she plopped it beside the door. "You look like a fuckin' pop star." The gum in her mouth smacked with each word.

Adult Zina reminded me of a stereotypical girl from an 80's movie—think *Grease* or *Dirty Dancing,* or Claire from *The Breakfast Club*. Despite our rocky past, she kept things interesting, and I couldn't help but be charmed by her. She had an uncanny ability to light up a room or make parties more fun wherever she went. That ridiculous accent only added to her appeal. All she needed was one of those long ass cigarettes to complete the picture.

"Maybe I felt like standing out." I laughed, shrugging.

Zina scoffed. "You? Standin' out?" She narrowed her eyes. "You've spent years blendin' in, Cass. *I'm* supposed to be the exuberant one. This isn't just 'a change'." She uses finger quotes and gestures at my own outfit, as if punctuating her point. "You don't just wake up one day and decide to look like this unless . . . oh God . . . this is a fuckin' crisis if I ever seen one."

"Maybe I just got bored." I kept my voice unconcerned, attempting to pivot from any serious questioning.

"You don't do things just 'cause you're bored." She regarded my shelf full of paper mâché projects behind her, then swung back toward me, meeting my eye. "You know . . . every time I see that stuff, I think about how much Lonney loved your weird little projects. He said you made 'ugly beautiful'." Zina's tone shifted, softer now, laced with something almost mournful.

The sudden mention of Lonney landed akin to a punch in the gut. "I miss him too," I murmured, quieter than I intended.

Supporting herself on the counter, Zina crossed her arms, as if the gesture protected her feelings from bursting through more than intended. "And Qualley. Damn, Cass, sometimes it feels like yesterday we were all just . . . whole. It's been so long now."

A loaded silence hung between us, thick with loss and a thousand unsaid things. My chest ached. I sought to push down the emotions clawing their way to the surface.

After a beat, Zina's lightheartedness returned, and she scanned me up and down again, forgetting she ruined the whole vibe of the room seconds ago by bringing up the boys.

"Alright, spill it. What's the real reason I'm here? It's not to see your hair or eat sushi, that's for damn sure."

I presented her with a playful smirk. "Maybe you don't know me as well as you think."

"I fuckin' doubt that!" She cried incredulously, sucking her teeth. "I know when you're up to shit!"

"So . . . you don't like it?"

Zina flew over to me then, fixing some hair in my face. "I never said that!" She fluffs my hair again carefully. "You know . . . it does bring out your complexion . . . wait, are you wearin' contacts?"

"Guilty!"

"Alrighty, you got my attention." Zina coasts around the front of the studio, studying the paintings hanging on the walls. Nervous that she'd discover my secret in the closet, I followed her around as she spoke whilst touching all my shit. "Now tell me why I'm here. There better be drinks involved. Talking about Lonney and mischief makes me feel weird."

I pouted, swirling my hair in my finger. "Can't I just show my friend my latest creation?"

She raised a skeptical brow, chewing on the arm of her sunglasses. "You never ask me to see your work . . . well, unless it's at the gallery. And especially not lookin' like this." She gestured at my pink hair. "So cut the bullshit, Cassandra. What do you want? I'm *hungry!*"

Chuckling, I step over to her, grabbing her hands. "I need . . . a favor." I threw on the best manipulative face I could conjure.

Zina sighed, rubbing her temple after letting go of one of my hands. "Of course you do. You ignore my calls and texts for weeks and now you need a favor . . ." She trailed off looking me up and down. "Is it illegal? Last time I did you a favor, I ended up in—well, let's not go there."

I cocked my head, shrugging. "No, nothing illegal. Unless using a pseudonym to enter a piece of art, and my amazing and beautiful and perfect best friend transporting it to the gallery is illegal all of a sudden. You know I'll make it worth your while."

Watching me close, Zina shifted into me as if telling me a secret. "Isn't that like . . . traffickin' or somethin'?" She straightened her torso, and her composure became serious. "Wait, so . . . let me get this straight. You want me to take this to Hartford Gallery, tellin' em' some mystery artist painted it?"

I nodded, pushing the canvas toward her a smidge. "Yes."

Zina raised an eyebrow, stepping around the painting to take a look at it. "C'mon Cass. This is sketchy. And fuckin' weird . . ." She stopped, considering the fact it sounded like she was demeaning my painting. "Sorry, not the paintin' that is. I mean, you submit stuff under your real name—why the sudden need for secrecy?"

Sighing dramatically, I acted as if I was frustrated. I knew this girl would ask me a million questions. She hated doing shit that didn't benefit her, but that didn't mean I'd quit buttering her up.

"Z, please?" I begged, batting my lashes at her. "You know how these galleries are. They put artists in a box. I want a fresh start. None of the usual expectations, no preconceived notions. Crimson is . . . untethered. Darker. Rawer."

"Crimson?" She scoffed, throwing her head back. "That's your fancy new name? Why not Fuchsia? Your hair is fuckin' pink!"

I passed Zina a pleading look, overlooking the jest about my current hairstyle.

Zina groaned, throwing her head back dramatically. "Cassandra, what the actual hell is wrong with you?"

"You know I need you," I said, letting a hint of desperation creep into my voice. "You're the only one I trust to pull this off."

Zina tilted her head, eyes narrowing. "You trust me? Or you know I'll cave if there's sushi and booze involved?"

"Why can't it be both?" I teased, grinning.

She sighed heavily, rubbing her temple like she was already regretting every decision that had led her to my door tonight. "This better not blow up in my face, Cass. I swear to God . . ."

She pondered my explanation for my unorthodox request, considering the painting again. "Darker, hm?"

I revealed the piece painted with blood in mock flair. If Zina ever found out about that detail she'd shit herself. Thankfully, I'd sealed it with a polyacrylic varnish so people didn't touch or smell the blood directly. No one would ever know.

"It's dark for sure, I'll give you that," Zina continued. "Damn, this piece *is* intense. Feels almost . . . personal."

"You know all art is personal."

Zina studies me for a moment. "This isn't just about art, is it?"

"Z, I know this sounds silly, but I need you to trust me." I threw my arm around her, planting a kiss on her cheek. "I need you to be my proxy. You just have to take it to them. Tell them you're handling submissions for a reclusive artist. They eat that shit up. Tell them I'll make it worth their while, too."

"What about *my* while?" Zina groaned, rubbing her temple. "I swear to God, if this comes back to bite me, I'm gonna—"

I placed my hands on both of her shoulders to interrupt her impending anxiety attack. "It won't, I promise. It's *just* art. I'm only trying something new. A social experiment, if you will. You don't need to give them *your* real name either. And when they love it—because they will—you'll have been the one who discovered Crimson."

If there was anything that hadn't changed about Zina through the years, it would be her love of being the center of attention. Therefore, I was willing to give her the spotlight in this case, because here soon, it would be all about me and the other portraits I'd create with precious supplies donated from my lovely, stiff friends buried in the backyard.

"Do I need to dye my hair blue?" Zina joked.

I huffed a laugh, resting my head on her fuzzy shoulder, and although I couldn't see it, I could practically detect Zina rolling her eyes.

"I hate that you always get your way. You're lucky I love you. Even though you fuckin' ignore me."

"I'm sorry. I've been busy." I peeked up to her, my head still resting on her shoulder, "I love you, more. Trust me."

Zina rested her head on mine. "You're insane."

"You have no idea." I said, winking as we make eye contact.

Holding Zina's hand, I lead her toward the door. "Let's go get ready to eat; food should be here soon."

"Good. I'm SOOO hungry." Zina groaned theatrically.

Collecting her oversized purse, I reach inside searching for her car keys. I plucked them out, tucking them into the pocket of my jacket, zipping it closed with a sense of security that my best friend would be safe another day. Zina didn't resist as I handed her the bag—minus her keys. Instead, she sent me a silent acknowledgment of gratitude for keeping her in check and safeguarding her from herself.

As I turned off the studio lights, the room plunged into darkness. I closed the door, locking it behind me with a soft click. My thoughts lingered on how much I wished I could show Zina the depths of my love . . . starting with what was hidden in my closet, and the man who had killed her sweet Lonney, now decomposing just a few yards behind us.

Sending Zina all the fabricated details the next day—an artist bio and a statement that articulated profound themes behind the painting, emphasizing its emotional depth—all under 'Crimson's' carefully crafted identity, each word was calculated.

A brushstroke in the portrait of my deception, if you will.

Reinforcing the illusion, I unearthed an old, unregistered phone, setting up a fresh email account, and creating a new number to serve as my so-called 'business' line. Communicating with the gallery through this deception sent a thrill coursing through a precarious dance on the edge of exposure. It was bold, sure. But fear had never stopped me before and I didn't stop there.

I encrypted communications made with anyone involved in the procurement of my painting, routing them through secure networks attached to systems Lonney utilized long ago to mask digital footprints. Every interaction was a tightrope walk, balancing the need for authenticity with the imperative of secrecy. If my disguise was blown, there would be no way to trace my location—I'd just have to dye my hair back to its original color. Easier while it was pink.

There were a few late nights before the gallery show opening that I spent rehearsing my alibi and dissecting possible flaws in my plan. I arranged for the painting to be delivered anonymously, paying in cash—$1,500 to be exact—ensuring the courier didn't ask any questions. Zina would've brought the canvas, she'd said, but her Porsche 718 Cayman—sleek, compact, and utterly impractical if you ask me—couldn't accommodate anything beyond her designer tote and massive ego.

The Hartford Gallery—those insatiable leeches of the art world—grudgingly agreed to feature my painting for a fleeting weekend. Two ephemeral nights of patronage, charging an exorbitant $5,000 for each night. They wield their financial demands like a double-edged sword, knowing full well the desperation that clings to every artist's heart. It wasn't the first time they'd succumbed to such an offer; they had done it before for artists draped in wealth and superficiality, whose canvases were mere facsimiles of true creativity.

Yet, the Gallery, ever the capitalist vulture, would stoop to showcase an eggshell, a fragile remnant of the mundane, if the price was right, touting it as 'the latest in modern art'. They'd spin tales of transcendence and innovation, turning the ordinary into a spectacle, an illusion that only those blinded by gold could truly appreciate.

But as I handed over payment to the driver transporting my painting, a mix of indignation and resignation swirled within me. My painting—so uniquely mine, a visceral extension of my soul—deserved more than to be a momentary exhibit for those with bottomless pockets. Nevertheless, in the harsh reality of the art world, recognition often comes with a hefty price tag, and I was prepared to pay it if only to see my creation bask in the spotlight, even if for but a moment.

But this wasn't solely about the art, of course; it was about the ambush subtly hidden beneath its guise.

Each phase was another layer in an intricate web I'd woven, guarding prying eyes from glimpsing my truth. Yet, a nagging thought lingered: *was there something I'd overlooked?* Every detail, no matter how insignificant, were potential threads that could unravel everything. The walls gave me the impression that they'd observe me as I cautiously covered my tracks, their silent judgment a constant reminder of the stakes at play.

The more I immersed myself in Crimson's identity, lines blurred between her and Cassandra. The personage was a phantom, already making me do unmentionable things. Both the puppeteer and the puppet, orchestrating performances where one misstep could bring the curtains crashing down. The gallery believed they were interacting with an enigmatic artist, and I intended to keep it that way.

After all, mysteries were always more captivating than vague, boring details, and I needed all eyes on the art—not the artist behind the mask.

Chapter 24

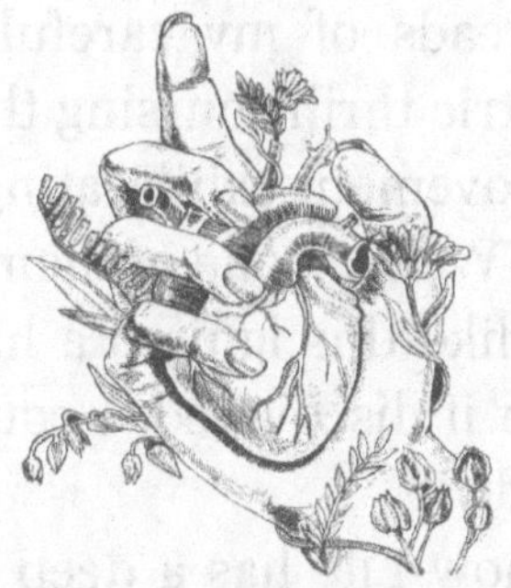

Entering the Bristol Police Department's domain was unquestionably one of my most audacious moves yet. Not only was this the one place where my very presence could unravel my meticulously crafted scheme, but the possibility of encountering Detective James Hall, Lile, or Ben added another layer of peril. The mere sight of my face would be enough to obliterate everything. They could never know my true identity.

Still, I had no choice but to plant the seed of curiosity in Lile's mind, convincing him that an art show in Hartford was a perfect way to while away his weekend. To accomplish this, I'd infiltrated his territory, leaving an irresistible lure.

With painstaking precision, I crafted and printed a mock flier; its vibrant colors and bold fonts designed to catch the eye . . . unless one is colorblind. This subterfuge had to be flawless, seamless.

As I approached the police department, a surge of adrenaline coursed through my veins, my heart pounding like a war drum. My head remained low and my movements inconspicuous, each step careful yet calculated. The air was thick with rising pressure, every shadow a potential enemy.

I located Lile's ridiculously large, lifted truck midst a sea of law enforcement cruisers. How did I know it was his truck, you ask? It was all he fucking posted on social media.

My mind spun with the dire consequences of exploit—caught red-handed, the flier falling into the wrong hands, unraveling the delicate threads of my carefully woven plan. Yet I couldn't deny the electric thrill coursing through me, adrenaline making each covert movement exhilarating. Perhaps remnant of Evan's cause of death. Well . . . one of them.

Sneaking around like this ignited a hidden spark of excitement within me. Even if discovered, I could potentially write it off as a gesture of goodwill.

"Oh, don't you know Lile has a deep appreciation for art?" I'd say.

I could explain that I had specifically targeted him with the flier because I believed he would genuinely enjoy the exhibit. After all, he had an eye for creativity and a penchant for immersing himself in the world of fine art, at least from what I could tell. It was precisely why no one else received fliers.

"A mutual friend had sent me on a mission to put the flier on his Decepticon of a truck. Tell him, 'be there, or be square'."

This cunning (borderline ridiculous) explanation would serve as a plausible cover, deflecting any suspicion and allowing me to maintain my deceit. Knowledge of Lile's passions and preferences would lend credibility to my story, painting me as an innocent enthusiast rather than a covert operative. My actions, seen through this lens, appear as a thoughtful invitation rather than an act of subterfuge. This calculated risk, while dangerous, might provide me with a slim yet vital chance of escaping unscathed.

Let's hope it didn't come to that, I thought.

In the back of my mind, I also harbored hope that my artistic ruse would appeal to Lile's sense of intrigue. The cryptic message and its allure of a hidden masterpiece could easily captivate his curiosity, drawing him to the gallery under the guise of meeting others with a shared passion for art.

As I crept around the truck, my breath hitched as an echo of footsteps grew louder, each one punctuating the silence. A bad horror movie cliché, except I wouldn't run *to* the assailant. I pressed myself against the wall, melting into the darkness as if I would magically become one within it. My heart pounded so hard, I wondered if it'd give me away—some kind of traitor sound system. Time slowed to the type of agonizing crawl in which makes you wonder if the universe is secretly laughing at your expense.

Every creak, every shuffle, became its own dramatic event in my symphony of panic. I strained my ears so hard I could practically hear my own thoughts screaming.

Don't move, don't breathe, definitely don't sneeze.

Then came the worst moment: the footsteps stopped. Frozen in place, I waited, every muscle in my body clenching in protest. *Was this it? Was I about to be found because my own lungs refused to breathe quietly?*

A bead of sweat leisured down my temple—it had all the time in the world to mock me. I hoped if it dripped on the ground, it wouldn't make a splashing sound as if I'd just jumped into a pool. My mind raced through absurd solutions: *Should I fake a ghostly wail? Pretend to be part of the scenery? Offer them a snack and hope for friendship?*

A soft shuffle, followed by an exhale was close enough to rustle the hair on my arm. *Oh great,* I thought, *we're playing the 'how close can you get before I pass out' game.*

Everything around me stilled, but my brain betrayed me with entirely inappropriate thoughts: *What if they're just looking for snacks? Everyone loves snacks. The intruder would probably settle for some chips and leave. That's logic, right?* Logic didn't help when the tension threatened to snap like a bad rubber band. So there I was—stuck, sweaty, and on the verge of either brilliance or total disaster.

A car door slammed, and the footsteps faded into silence, leaving me crouched behind the truck like I was auditioning for a low-budget spy film. I relaxed a fraction—just enough to retrieve the crumpled flier from my pocket. A shameless attempt at guerrilla marketing.

Sliding closer to the driver's side window, I muttered to myself watching the stranger enter the building. "Alright, Cass. You're basically James Bond. If James Bond were promoting a gallery exhibit instead of saving the world. Totally the same vibe. Wait . . . didn't he go to a gallery in Skyfall?"

The waning streetlights cast ominous shadows slithering across the pavement, while the distant hum of late-night traffic on North Main whispered of a world oblivious to my silent plight. The faint scent of rain mingled with an earthy aroma of the nearby park, heightening the chill in the air.

Cloaked in a fitted leather jacket and dark jeans, I was a silhouette of total black. My long, now pink, hair secured in a tight bun on the nape of my neck, a necessity to avoid obstruction. Black leather gloves shrouded my hands, ensuring no trace was left behind, and to protect from the biting cold. My boots, crafted for silent strides, barely stirred the still night.

The flier fluttered in my hand as the wind suddenly kicked up, threatening to escape. I scowled at it as though it had personally betrayed me. "Stay with me, you little traitor," I slapped it against the window with perhaps too much vigor.

My fingers quivered slightly as I meticulously placed the flier under the windshield wiper of Lile's comically colossal black monstrosity on wheels. The paper rustled in the breeze once it was placed, and I willed the rain to withhold its descent until Lile grasped the communication: the art gallery's address and a cryptic message.

Only the boldest brush strokes reveal the hidden masterpiece. 6 PM. Hartford Art Gallery on Maple Street

Soon footsteps drew near again, and my heart's frantic

rhythm quickened once more. I pressed myself against the un-yielding, rough surface of the brick wall behind me once more, shielded by the fender flares of the truck as I sunk behind it, longing for my form to dissolve into obscurity.

The footsteps halted, and I held my breath, covering my mouth with my gloves. The moment felt suspended in a dread-laden void, until the footsteps resumed in the other direction, fading into the night. Exhaling with measured restraint, my breath coalesced in the frigid air. One final glance at the flier confirmed its secure placement, and I melted away behind the other vehicles, bound for my house.

Just as I turned to scuttle away, my foot caught on a stray rock, and I stumbled, nearly taking myself out in my rush to escape. I froze mid-recovery, heart pounding as I imagined Lile emerging like a wrathful deity to smite me for my crimes.

Embarrassing yourself when you're up to no good should definitely be illegal.

No one came, nor did they see me nearly eat shit. Thank god. The truck remained as silent and imposing as ever. I sighed in relief, patting myself on the back (mentally, of course) for my daring escapade. "See, Cass? You nailed it. Could've gone viral if anyone had been recording."

By the time I slunk back into the shadows, I was already dreaming up my next marketing stunt. But as the adrenaline wore off, one thought lingered: *Was it necessary to risk public humiliation just to stick a flier on a truck?*

Absolutely.

My mission, for now, had been fulfilled, and I wasn't going to wait around to see if Lile would receive my message. The clock ticked on. This had to be done before the weekend, or my entire plan would be jeopardized. If it failed, I'd be forced to rethink other techniques to lure Lile into my booby trap (and no, not my actual boobs. Pervert).

Failure was not an option and I prayed he'd bite the hook.

At the Hartford Gallery, the atmosphere was refined, the lighting dimmed just enough to highlight the artwork adorning the walls. A rich aroma of aged wine mingled with a faint scent of polished wood floors, creating an olfactory tapestry that heightened the senses. Soft murmurs of conversation wove through the space as guests nursed glasses of expensive liquor from the bar, lost in contemplation of the art before them. Gentle clinks of crystal glasses added an auditory layer to the symphony of the evening, punctuated occasionally by genuine laughter or hushed whispers of admiration.

Disguised as my alias Crimson, I lingered beside my featured piece. A foreboding, yet captivating, painting drenched in red and deep shadows, its subject just ambiguous enough to stir curiosity. The textures of the brush strokes, alive under the subtle play of light, invited viewers to lean in closer, brows furrowing in concentration to decipher layers of meaning.

My heart raced with a mix of pride and nervous anticipation.

Would anyone guess this was actually painted with blood?

Traveling from one guest to another, I scrutinized them, catching snippets of their silent dialogue with the piece—some standing with arms crossed, deep in thought, while others tilted their heads, analyzing the dark hues and hidden shapes. Every appreciative glance toward my painting fed my inner fire and disastrous ego.

I recalled Qualley's eyes lingering onto the very dress I was wearing, curious and quietly appraising, as though the color itself had mesmerized him. He'd joked that night about how navy-blue was supposed to be "safe," but somehow, on me, it seemed to spark trouble. I'd laughed—not because the joke was particularly clever, but because he delivered it with such easy confidence that I couldn't help myself.

This was before I had gotten drunk and completely forgot his name.

In that moment, the dress wasn't just fabric; it was a kind of alchemy, transforming a casual encounter into something electric. Qualley's charm, his self-assured grin, had made the evening unforgettable. And as the memories floated back, his absence felt sharper, heavier, like the dress had taken on the weight of all the moments we'd never get to share.

The gallery was no longer the magical place it had once been.

Pulling myself from the swirl of emotions, I ran my fingers lightly over the silk, letting the texture steady me. The world buzzed with life all around, but that memory of Qualley—the way he had smiled, the way his presence had felt larger than life —would always linger.

This was all for him.

Subtle vibrations of footsteps through the polished floorboards resonated in my chest as I readied myself for who I came here to see. That is, if he bothered to arrive.

Thoughts of inspiration for the piece shimmied through my mind. Memories of midnight musings and fevered sketches— murder—the emotional turmoil that poured into each stroke. I found myself wondering if anyone else could see the shadows of my soul hidden within the depths of the bloody paint or sense the unspoken stories that pulsed through the canvas.

A sudden, gentle touch on my elbow brought me back to the present. Twisting around, I met the eyes of a gentleman, his face etched with the lines of a life well-lived.

"A remarkable piece," he said, his voice a gravelly whisper.

I offered a grateful smile in response, the corners of my lips lifting with genuine warmth. "Thank you."

Feeling a thrill with the recognition wash over me, in that moment the gallery, with all its sights, sounds, and sensations, blurred into the background. It left only the shared connection between an artist and an admirer.

Except this wasn't just any admirer, he was my next victim. The motherfucker whose face I'd unfortunately never be able to forget.

Lile Henderson.

When Qualley had first stood before one of my pieces offering his quiet, heartfelt praise, it had felt disarming in the most delightful way. His voice, soft but confident, had carried the kind of awe that could make anyone's heart swell. He hadn't just been admiring the work; he was speaking to its soul—and to mine.

Though similar, the words delivered in Lile's gravelly tone grated on my nerves like nails on a chalkboard. His admiration felt sharp-edged, as invasive as a brain worm, as though it was less about the art and more about imposing himself into my space. Where Qualley's praise had been like a warm embrace, Lile's felt like a predator's calculated growl.

Masking my disdain with an artist's poise, I meet his regard, but inside anger frothed, threatening to boil over. I wanted to laugh at the audacity of his feigned sincerity. *A remarkable piece? Gag!* I thought, even as I nodded graciously. His admiration wasn't real. It couldn't be. Not from a man like him.

As he continued speaking, I found myself fixating on the difference. Qualley's words had breathed life into me, made me feel seen in a way that lingered long after he was gone. But Lile? He didn't deserve to see me—not the artist, not the person, and certainly not the darker truths I kept hidden. And as I smiled through the moment, I let that anger simmer. After all, it wouldn't be long before I showed him what 'remarkable' truly meant.

I knew exactly how to play this. Lile was a man of discipline, careful, and always aware of his surroundings. I needed to make him feel like he was the one in control, like he had the upper hand. So, when our eyes met, I smiled—just a hint of amusement in my expression, as if I'd been expecting him all along.

Lile, with his perfectly pressed suit of deep charcoal, seemed almost out of place in the warm ambiance of the gallery. His crisp white shirt opposed severely against his olive skin, and the meticulously knotted tie in a muted, sophisticated shade of navy spoke volumes about his attention to detail. Ugh, it even matched my dress, like we were heading to the high school prom. I wanted nothing more than to go home and change. If fortune favored me, I could bring Lile home to stain it with a shade of red.

His hair, light brown and slicked back, framed a face marked by jagged, angular features as if chiseled from stone—though not the pleasant kind you'd admire in a museum. No, his features had the harshness of a statue someone hastily sanded down with a grudge. Every angle of his face irritated me further: the sharpness of his jawline that screamed *vain perfectionist,* the high cheekbones that practically demanded attention, and those piercing eyes that I was convinced were judging my existence. It all added up to a face tailor-made to annoy, like the universe had, again, conspired to create the human embodiment of smugness.

He was the kind of man who probably spent more time on his reflection than I spent painting. The sheer arrogance it radiated made me want to reach for a bottle of hairspray and sabotage it.

If stone could roll its eyes, it would've been his face. And oh, how I hated it.

He navigated the room around me with measured steps as he pondered my work, his posture rigid and upright. It was clear he was assessing every detail—the layout of the space, the positioning of the artwork, and the people mingling within it. Even with the soft lighting and muted colors, his eyes—an intense, piercing shade of hazel—seemed to cut through the shadows, taking in everything with laser-like focus.

I needed to make him feel at ease, to coax out that illusion of safety and control. Lile had always been a connoisseur of the arts, so I've read. A man who found solace in the strokes of a brush and layers of meaning hidden within each piece. He appreciated the subtleties and complexities of fine arts, often finding reflections of his own experiences within them. So he said on social media.

This painting, with its raw emotion and violent undertones, seemed to have resonated with him, unless, it was me he wanted to assess more. Perhaps it reminded him of a past he couldn't quite escape (I wonder what *that* could be?), or emotions he had buried deep within—familiar, haunting, and inescapable.

Ironic, considering he'd be buried deep really soon if all went well, and I don't mean sexually.

But beneath my composed exterior, a storm brewed.

Lile was a puzzle, a carefully constructed enigma that I had to decipher if I wanted to get close enough to him. The thought of his shrewd nature and the coldness he exuded made my skin crawl. *He* murdered Qualley, after all. The fact alone made my fingers twitch with an urge to throttle him right there in the gallery. Alas, I had to act interested, warm even. I couldn't afford to let my true feelings slip, not yet. He had shown up tonight out of sheer curiosity, drawn in by the flier like a moth to a flame.

And now, here he was, standing before my work with a strange sense of kinship, as if the painting whispered secrets only he could hear. The irony of it all nearly made me laugh. *Oh, you feel connected to this piece? That's cute. Let's see how connected you feel when you're six feet under.* I could see it in the way his gaze lingered on the painting, the way his brow furrowed ever so slightly as if he were trying to unlock its secrets. He probably thought he was so clever, so insightful. Little did he know, the real masterpiece was the trap I had set for him.

Maintaining my smile, I let my eyes soften, closing in on him with an air of nonchalance. The game had begun, and I had to play my part to perfection. Every momentary look, every word, had to be carefully orchestrated to draw him in, to make him believe he held the reins.

But beneath the mask of amicability, my true intentions simmered—hidden from view, yet ever-present. *Oh, Lile, you're a poor, oblivious fool. You think you're in charge, don't you? That you're the predator in this little exchange?* I nearly smirked at the thought. *Just wait until I get you home. You'll be the one hanging on my wall—metaphorically speaking, of course. Or . . . maybe not.*

"You painted this?" he asked, nodding toward the haunting canvas.

I crossed my arms, ensuring my posture was just provocative enough to keep his attention. "I did. But you already knew that." I said it sweetly enough to mask the irritation bubbling within my chest.

Seriously? I thought, biting back an urge to roll my eyes. *What did he think I was doing here—selling overpriced candles?* The question itself felt like an insult, as if he couldn't fathom that someone like me could possess actual talent.

I forced a smile, though inwardly I was imagining all the ways I could creatively end him. *Oh, Lile, you're lucky I need you alive right now. Otherwise, I'd be showing you my talent in a much more . . . permanent way.*

Lile frowned slightly. "What makes you think that?"

My smirk deepened. "Because you're looking at it the same way I did while I was painting it. Like you understand something no one else does."

That was the temptation that made him pause. It wasn't flirtation, not really, not on purpose. It was a shared understanding, an unspoken bond through art. He had seen violence firsthand, and so had I—or at least, that's what I wanted him to believe. It's too bad Lile had to die. He would've made an exceptional art enthusiast partner—if he weren't, you know, a sociopath. The thought almost made me laugh. *Imagine us at gallery openings, sipping overpriced wine, debating brush-strokes and symbolism. What a dream team.* Except for the minor detail that I despised him with every fiber of my being. I mentally threw my hands up in exasperation. *Of course the universe would make my mortal enemy the one person who actually gets my art. Typical.* It was almost insulting how he lingered by the painting, his brow furrowed in what looked like genuine appreciation. *Oh, you like it, Lile? That's adorable. Too bad you won't be around long enough to see the rest of the collection.*

Lile uncovering the rest of my collection was inevitable, especially if he dared to set foot inside my house.

Seconds persisted before I spoke again. "It's about loss."

"It looks more like vengeance," Lile said, repositioning himself to get a better look. His glass found its way back to his mouth

Raising my eyebrows, I appeared surprised. "Same thing, isn't it?

He studied me instead of the painting. The way I carried myself—confidence, intrigue, the perfect blend of mystery and accessibility. Perhaps he could tell I wasn't a typical artist. There was something darker about me, something real. He was a cop, privy to human behavior.

I let our conversation drift into the safe, impersonal waters of artistic inspiration—anything to avoid the minefield of questions about myself. You know, those pesky 'past choices,' the ones that cling to you like glitter after a craft project gone wrong. The gallery's ambient music was my silent accomplice, a soothing background track that helped mask an occasional awkward pause. I might've looked like I was pondering brushstrokes and color palettes, but in reality, I was imagining how satisfying it would be to metaphorically (or literally) pull the head off the man. Because Lile—bless his oblivious little soul—probably thought this was the beginning of some grand connection. *Oh, Lile, I mused internally, if only you knew. You're not bonding with me; you're auditioning for a spot in my backyard grave-yard collection.*

Spoiler alert: *you nailed it.*

Speaking of the intuitive emotions that drive an artist—the demons that claw their way out and spill onto the canvas, each tale was crafted with painstaking precision, designed to resonate with the dark places lurking in one's mind. I watched Lile close-ly, noting the flashes of recognition in his eyes. His guarded de-meanor softened ever so slightly, as if my words had cracked open the fortress he'd so carefully built. I analyzed his move-ments—the unhurried adjustment of his tie, which he probably practiced in the mirror before leaving the house, the way his gaze darted between the painting and me, like he was trying to figure out if I was more fascinating than the art. *It's the paint-ing. By a landslide.* When I spoke of the inspiration behind my work, I spun it as if it were an unstoppable tempest, a force be-yond control.

"The paintbrush fell into my hand," I said exaggeratedly, "and I simply couldn't rest until my soul had transferred to the canvas." Overkill? Maybe. But he ate it up, so why not? "You know," I said, my voice a whisper that only he could hear, "there's a kind of art that speaks to the darkest corners of our minds, that gives voice to the things we dare not say aloud."

His eyes narrowed slightly, and I knew I might have struck a chord.

I leaned in, my smile veiled. "It's as if the artist reaches into your very soul and lays it bare for the world to see. And some-times, that's the only way to truly understand ourselves, isn't it?"

Lile's jaw tightened, a brief sputter—fear, recognition, or maybe indigestion—crossed his features. He took a sip of his drink, the glass trembling ever so slightly in his hand. "Sure."

I just *loved* a man with so many words, but it was more likely that he had no idea what the fuck I was talking about.

The walls around him seemed to close in, the inescapable reality of his own emotions bearing down with relentless force—or perhaps it was just me forcing him into this awkward little dance. Every carefully chosen word was another step deeper into the labyrinth, with me holding the only thread of escape.

"I'd love to pick your brain more about this," I said, swirling my wine in a way that screamed casual sophistication. "But it's hard to have a real conversation in a room full of people."

Lile glanced around, suddenly aware of the noise, wandering eyes, movement. The unfortunate man didn't realize he was the star of my personal little tragedy.

"If you're up for it, you should see my private collection. More pieces that . . . well, delve into themes like this. I have others as well if you need something more uplifting."

I gave him the out, and he took the bait like a fish desperate for a shiny lure. It wasn't outright seduction—it was intrigue, trust, and the tiniest sprinkle of challenge. And Lile, cautious, calculated Lile, nodded like he had nothing better to do than follow me home.

Could I have single-handedly wrecked my entire scheme just by opening my mouth? Absolutely. The thought occurred to me the second the words left my lips, like watching a glass fall in slow motion—too late to catch it, just bracing for impact.

But I needed something to make it seem like Lile was making the choice himself, rather than me subtly steering him toward it like some sort of social chess master (which, let's be real, I was not).

Was it manipulation? Not exactly. More like carefully orchestrated fate . . . which sounded suspiciously close to manipulation now that I was thinking about it.

"Alright, why not? Show me what you've got," he said, nonchalant, as if agreeing to visit the private collection of someone he barely knew wasn't screaming "poor choices."

I could practically see the mental gymnastics going on in his head. He probably thought this was a stroke of luck—an exclusive chance to peek behind the curtain of an oracular artist's world. *Oh, Lile, sweetie, if only you knew.*

As I led him toward the exit, I caught the faintest trace of a smirk on his face, as though he believed he was playing me. With each step, my collection would gain something new—a very special piece, one that required no varnish and no frame. Only a jar and a canvas.

We walked side by side along the street in the direction of the parking garage adjacent to the Hartford Gallery; the late evening city streets a distant symphony that mingled with the soft rustle of chilly early winter in the gentle breeze. The cool air carried a faint scent of snow, a prospect of a storm yet to come. Our footsteps scraped on the concrete, a rhythmic counterpoint to the far-off wail of sirens and the occasional honk of a taxi.

Streetlights cast long, wavering shapes, turning us into spectral figures moving through the urban twilight. The faint glow of the city skyline shimmered on the horizon, the bustling city just beyond the gallery's serene layout. As we walked, the importance of unspoken words hung between us, dense and lingering, like dark clouds gathering in the sky. Our breaths steamed in ringlets throughout the cold.

The chill seeped through my thin coat, raising goosebumps on my skin. I glanced at Lile from the corner of my eye, noting the tension in his jaw and the way his hands were clenched into fists. He was lost in thought, his face a mask of determination and unease—he must have come to the realization that he was walking with a stranger . . . or *worse.* I knew he was wrestling with emotions stirred by the evening's events, memories unearthed by our conversation. Every step felt like a journey into the unknown, the path ahead shrouded in uncertainty.

The soft glow of the gallery's lights receded behind us, a beacon of warmth that seemed worlds away now. The depth of our shared history, the secrets we both carried, and the unspoken truths that bound us together loomed large, coiling around us.

"You've got an eye for this," I mused, refraining from peeking over at him.

Lile snickers, wagging his head. "Not like you do. I love art, but I'm not that great at it myself."

Fascination curled into my smile. "Oh? You say that like you know me."

"I know artists. The real ones, anyway." He exhaled through his nose, amused.

"My name is Crimson," I announced, turning slightly toward him, extending a hand. "Now you officially know me."

Lile's gaze swiped to mine, assessing if danger lurked in the act, but after a beat, he took my hand. His grip was firm. "Lile."

I held onto his hand just a second too long. Enough to make it feel intentional and borderline uncomfortable. My thumb brushed lightly over his knuckles before I let go. "Lile. Strong name."

"Yours is . . . dramatic, honestly." He pulled his hand away, examining me as we continued down the street.

I let out a soft, playful laugh. "So I've been told. My parents named all us kids after colors. Perhaps that's where I get my affinity for the arts."

"So, Crimson," he said, nodding toward the parking garage, "where do you live?"

"Bristol. Right on Chippen's Hill behind the Orange Cat Café," I said casually, as if the statement wouldn't set off alarms or raise red flags. As if he wouldn't react to the fact my residence is on the same street he murdered someone.

Lile paused, brows knitting together, subtle but noticeable. A glimmer of suspicion tightened his expression . . . as expected. "Bristol?" he repeated, his tone carefully neutral. "Chippen's

Hill?"

"Mm. Yeah. Funny, right?" I said, wrapping my jacket tighter around myself in a great show, as if I wasn't bothered. "I suppose you know because people get weird when I tell them I live where murders happened."

Lile swallowed hard, as if the truth started to appear and he was pushing it back down. "And that doesn't . . . bother you?"

I shrugged, smiling at him lazily. "It's a beautiful house. Tragic history, sure. But aren't most places haunted by something?" I lifted my gaze to in front of me. "Besides, if I'm being honest, I like ghosts." I quickly reached out, grabbing his arm as if trying to scare him.

Lile huffed a quiet breath, half a scoff, half consideration. "Most people would run the other way. How do you even afford a place like that?"

"I'm not most people," I said, tipping my chin. "I'm a trust fund baby. I saw the listing, and I couldn't resist. Bought literally everything, especially the paintings and the furniture. It had everything I wanted—big windows, space to paint, a view. It wasn't until I'd already moved in I found out about the murders." I let the words hang in the air for a moment before suspiring, leaning just slightly closer, our proximity charged with turbulence. "The past is just that, isn't it? The past?"

Some dismiss the past as something neatly packed away. I know better—it doesn't just vanish, and it certainly doesn't forget.

Sometimes the past brings on consequences.

Lile didn't answer right away, but I saw his lips press together at the second mention of murder. The spark of something aphotic crossed his eyes, a shadow of thoughts he kept hidden. For a moment, I wondered if he'd press further, delve into the secrets of which I had just hinted, find out what I knew. His silence lingered, brimming with unanswered questions and traces of a past we both understood should remain untouched. I sensed the conflict within him. A struggle between his inherent curiosity and caution that had probably always guided his actions. His eyes bore into mine, searching for any hint of deceit, any crack in the deception I had so carefully constructed.

The parking garage's soft lighting cast a halo around us, turning our interaction into a silent duel of wills. My heart raced in my chest; each beat a message of the stakes at play. I needed him to believe me, to trust in the story I was weaving. But the truth threatened to rise, like a dark tide creeping ever closer

Lile's fists tightened, his knuckles whitening with the pressure. His eyes narrowed slightly, and for a moment, I thought he might break the silence, challenge me, demand answers. But then, he simply nodded. A small, almost imperceptible gesture of acquiescence.

"Yes," he finally said, his voice retrained, low, "the past is just that."

Relief washed over me, but I didn't let it show. Instead, I leered, as if we had just shared a secret understanding. The game continued, stakes growing higher with every passing moment. And as we stood there, locked in our silent exchange, I knew that the true battle was only just beginning.

I switch topics seamlessly, giving him no chance to dwell on his unease. "Shall we take your car, or would you prefer mine?"

Chapter 25

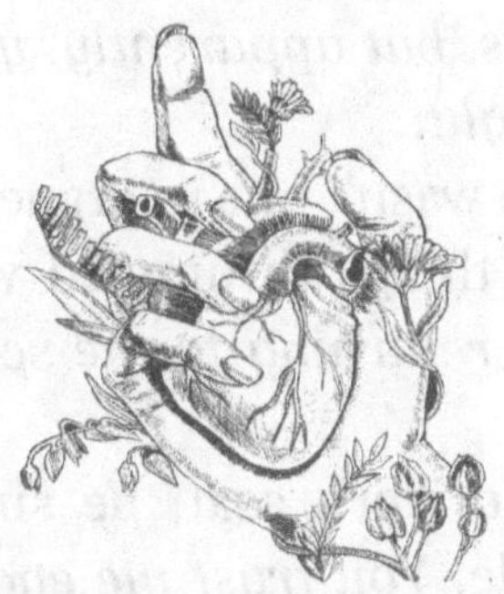

Pulling into my long, winding driveway on Chippen's Hill, my car's headlights cut through the darkness, illuminating the grand, yet ominous, presence of my house. Gravel crunched beneath as the vehicle eased to a stop. Stillness enveloped us for a brief moment as the engine cut off.

The choice to take my car instead of Lile's behemoth of a truck seemed casual enough, but it was far from arbitrary. We stood outside in the parking garage; my sleek, white Mercedes gleaming under the streetlights, a complete opposition to Lile's imposing pitch black truck.

"Let's take mine," I suggested excitedly, inviting inflection. "It's really fast! Plus, it has a certain . . . elegance to it, don't you think? We'll come back for your truck later."

No we wouldn't, I thought.

Lile hesitated for a fraction of a second, his gaze darting from his truck to my car, as if weighing the option. Or determining if I was actually trustworthy. I mean, who agrees to ride all the way to Bristol with a stranger?

Go on, I silently urged, holding my most charming smile. *Say no. Insist on taking your obnoxiously large truck, complete with the whale-sized ego parked right behind it. You'll die either way.*

But instead, he surprised me. "I suppose it does." A faint smile peeked through the corners of his lips.

Well, well, well, I thought, suppressing the urge to laugh out loud. *You've officially disappointed me, Lile. Not only do you have bad taste in suits, but apparently, your survival instincts are worse than I thought.*

I surmised that he wasn't one to argue over such trivial matters—not when other things thrummed within his mind. Like, oh, I don't know . . . *returning to the scene of the murder he committed.*

Sinking into the driver's seat, he simultaneously climbed into the passenger side. *You trust me enough to carpool, Lile? Adorable.* I shook my head slightly, almost amused. *Don't worry—you'll regret it soon enough.*

He was completely silent the entire ride to Bristol, and it was *excruciating.* Not the kind of peaceful silence where you can enjoy passing sceneries or lose yourself in thought—no, this was the awkward, tension-filled kind that made every second feel like an eternity.

I glanced at him out of the corner of my eye, hoping for some sign of life—a cough, a sigh, *anything.* But he just sat there, staring out the window like a brooding statue. *Oh, come on, Lile,* I thought, gripping the steering wheel a little tighter. *You're not auditioning for the role of 'Mysterious Passenger #1.' Say something. Anything. I don't care if it's about the weather or your favorite brand of toothpaste—just break the silence before I lose my mind.*

Turning on the radio, I hoped it would fill the void, but of course the only station that came through was playing static-laden country music. I turned it off with a huff, muttering under my breath. *Great. Now it's just me, you, and the sound of my own spiraling thoughts.*

By the time we hit the halfway mark, I was practically begging for him to speak. *Ask me why I chose this route. Complain about the air conditioning. Tell me I'm a terrible driver.* But no, he just sat there completely oblivious to the fact that his silence was slowly driving me to the brink. *If this was how he planned to act the entire time, I should've just let him take his stupid truck. Or just took him down right there in the parking lot.* At least then I wouldn't have to sit here wondering if he's plotting my demise or just really bad at small talk. When we finally pulled into Bristol, I let out a sigh of relief so loud it probably startled him.

"Well, that was fun," I said sarcastically. He glanced at me, raising an eyebrow but still said nothing.

The strong, silent type. My favorite.

In the dim lighting of the car, I caught the subtle shift in Lile's behavior—the way his fingers drummed absently on his thigh, a classic tell of discomfort. It was almost amusing, watching Mr. Stoic start to unravel. Even in the shadows, the stiffness in his shoulders screamed louder than a soap opera monologue. His gaze blinked up at the mansion, wide-eyed, like he was about to star in a low-budget ghost story.

The mansion loomed. Its grand exterior, illuminated by the headlights, cast dramatic silhouettes doing their best to audition for 'Creepiest Setting Ever.' I had to admit, it did look menacing, the kind of place where you'd expect to hear floorboards creak even when no one was walking on them. I glanced at Lile, whose stare was locked on the house like it might lunge at him. *Please don't faint,* I thought. *I don't have the upper body strength to drag you inside and then outside again.*

My eyes followed his, taking in the imposing structure that once dripped with opulence and grandeur. Now it stood like some kind of Gothic caricature, its darkened windows gaping back at us like hollow eyes. The house had a way of making you feel like it knew all your secrets—and in Lile's case, it definitely did.

The oxygen in the car deepened with each passing second, filled with the contemplations that danced around his mind. *Are you really going back in there? Wasn't one murder enough for one lifetime?* Honestly, if he didn't snap out of it soon, I was going to have to start charging him for a therapy session.

With a soft sigh, I turned to him, unraveling the stillness with the kind of nonchalance that bordered on theatrical. "Well, here we are," I said the words so casually, they could've walked itself into a party uninvited. "Château Crimson! Shall we go in and have a drink?"

Lile's jaw ticked, an elusive but oh-so-telling giveaway of the havoc seething beneath his carefully controlled exterior. For a moment, he just sat there, staring at the house as if it had leaned down and whispered, "*Remember me?*"

"Oh, the house won't kill you," I quipped. "C'mon!"

I half-expected him to fling open the car door and sprint down the driveway screaming. Instead, he was frozen in that perfect mix of dread and indecision that made me want to roll my eyes and say, *Oh, for heaven's sake, grow a spine.*

"Lile," I said, brushing an imaginary speck of dust from my coat, "if you're going to let a little house intimidate you, maybe we should just turn around now. Or—better idea—you can sit out here while I enjoy a drink and admire the fact that this charmingly haunted mansion doesn't seem to scare me."

For a second, I thought I saw his tenacity stiffen, but knowing Lile, it was probably just his ego coming to his rescue. "Fine," he said, his voice clipped. "Was just . . . uh . . . admiring its beauty. Of course. Let's go."

Sure you were.

As he reached for the door handle on the passenger's side, I smirked to myself. *Well done, Lile. You've almost convinced me you're not utterly terrified.*

I exhaled, relieved but still wary. *Good choice, Lile,* I mused internally. *Because let's be honest, if you tried to bolt, I'd have to kill you anyway. And frankly, I don't feel like cleaning up a mess in the driveway where people are bound to see.*

As he stepped out, I followed, my countenance serene but

my thoughts anything but. *You're walking into your own personal haunted house, buddy. And guess what? I'm actually the ghost.*

As we approached the mansion, dread prickled at the edges of my mind, a subtle warning that tonight would demand every ounce of my cunning. The house seemed alive with memories, lingering remnants of choices I could never undo and waiting to pull me back into the past. But I had no time for nostalgia or regret—not when my plan was teetering on the edge of execution with so many variables threatening to spiral out of my control.

"Hell of a place," Lile mumbled, forcing a smirk that didn't quite reach his eyes. It carried an edge. A restrained undercurrent that would have been easy to miss—if I wasn't observing him like a hawk.

"You okay? You look like you've seen a ghost," I asked, my head inclined gently as I faced him. "Remember, I've got whiskey inside. Works wonders for anxiety."

Lile exhaled—a sound that was supposed to be a laugh but landed somewhere between uncomfortable and painfully human. "Yeah. I mean . . . that sounds nice." His response was as scattered as his expression, and I knew I had him right where I wanted him: caught between pride and fear, too distracted by his own psyche to anticipate the trap and sputtering like an idiot.

"Come inside," I said coyly. "I'll show you my studio, too. A couple drinks, and maybe you'll forget whatever phantoms are lurking in that head of yours."

His jaw worked itself in circles as he rubbed it—a man trying to iron out his own stress. But eventually, as I knew he would, he agreed, giving me a reluctant smirk. "Alright. Let's see what kind of trouble you get into with a paintbrush."

Trouble, Lile? You have no idea.

Inside, soft lighting pooled like liquid gold, spilling from carefully placed lamps that enhanced the warmth of recently polished floors and expensive furniture. A classical melody hummed faintly from hidden speakers—my intended choice, designed to ease his worries and disarm suspicion. The room carried a faint tang of oil paint, intertwined with something richer—something darker.

"Cozy," Lile remarked as he stepped inside, his gaze flitting from the staircase to the foyer's artwork. His eyes landed on an ornate painting near the hallway. "You paint these?"

I shook my head, watching him absorb the space with something almost approaching awe—or maybe discomfort. "No. They came with the house. Well, I purchased them with the house. I couldn't see them go. All my own works are in my studio." It wasn't a lie, but it wasn't the full truth either, which somehow made it feel more satisfying.

As I guided him through the dim entryway, he followed closely behind, his movements cautious. His eyes scanned the space like someone accustomed to danger. It was clear he was sizing things up, thoughts circling any risks. Which was why I necessitated every word, every gesture, to be flawless.

"You really know your work," Lile said, genuine in his impression as we entered the sitting room. His gaze caught on a canvas splashed in visceral shades of red, his lips pressing together. "Oh . . . this . . . It's intense."

Chuckling, I join Lile where he stands, running my fingers along the textured surface and letting it speak for itself. "Art should make you feel something, shouldn't it?" I turned to face him. "Do you feel anything, Lile?"

His lips parted slightly as he paused, caught between wanting to answer and fearing that his response would reveal too much. That pause—that single breath of indecision—was all I needed.

"Come on," I said, my tone slipping lower. I walked toward the far side of the room, where the flooring changed subtly, concealing the truth beneath. "I want to show you my latest piece.

It's still unfinished, but I think you'll appreciate it."

I could feel apprehension rolling off him in waves, see quivers of inquisitiveness sparking in his eyes as he followed. No, he didn't seem suspicious of *me—yet*. My performance had been seamless so far, the role I inhabited as natural as breathing.

But then again . . . My stomach knotted with something between excitement and dread. *Perfection only matters until the moment it falls apart.* I couldn't afford any missteps, no miscalculations—not tonight. Not with Lile.

Not like Evan refusing to die and almost calling for help.

I still didn't know who he had called that night. It could have been Lile for all I knew. What I did know for sure is that I got incredibly lucky, for whoever it was, didn't trace the call and come sticking their noses in my business.

This time, every word, every movement was a balancing act between keeping Lile fascinated and ensuring he didn't bolt at the wrong moment. Sure, he could've tried to run, but where would he go? I'd already decided that if he lost his nerve, I'd kill him anyway. I was always packing. But I wasn't about to let it come to that—not when the real art was still waiting to be revealed.

So keep walking, Lile. You're almost there.

The trapdoor had been Qualley's secret weapon—a clever, albeit sinister, piece of engineering that served his drug and weapons-dealing empire. Hidden beneath the mansion's polished floors, it was used to stash contraband, cash, and anything else that needed to disappear in a hurry. If the authorities ever came knocking, Qualley could activate the mechanism, sending incriminating evidence into the depths below, where it would be nearly impossible to retrieve without knowing the exact layout. It also doubled as a security measure. If someone tried to cross him or steal from his operation, the trapdoor could be used to 'dispose' of them—though whether that meant a literal fall or just a scare tactic depended on Qualley's mood. Usually, because his clients and associates respected him, it never came down to that. But, alas, there were always those select few that just had to test their chances.

The mansion itself was a fortress of secrets, and the trap-door was its crown jewel.

A sharp, startled gasp left Lile's lips as he plummeted. I positioned him perfectly, the door opening as I pressed the button activating it on my keychain. His arms flailed, body twisting; the sound of his fall swallowed by the shadows below. A solid thud followed by a grunt of pain echoed up through the twenty-foot gaping hole in the floor.

I laughed as I leaned over the edge, peering down at him.

Lile groaned, shifting around in the dim space. Dust settled, and his breath was heavy, ragged. His hands scraped at the concrete walls of the pit—too high and too smooth to climb.

"What the—" he groaned, strained. He was cut off as he tried to move, but at the moment he inhaled deeply, a mist filled the air as I pressed the second button on my device. A controlled dose of chloroform from a motion activated device used for room fragrances—just enough to make him sluggish, to take away the precision of his movements. Another one of Qualley's innovative security measures.

Pitiful (Literally, because he was in a pit!).

I continued squatting by the edge, watching him struggle to get up to avoid the noxious fumes.

"You always struck me as the careful one," I called down to him. "But even careful men make mistakes. Or are you just stupid?"

Lile let out a slow, shuddering breath, shaking his head as his limbs grew heavier. He couldn't force himself to his knees, he had to have broken something, and his balance was off.

"You—" he started, blinking up at me through the haze. Realization dawned in his eyes.

"Me . . . what?"

His breathing deepened, panic slipping in as he struggled to keep himself alert. I stood, my figure framing the dim sitting room lights. Veering away, I left him down there to marinate in his confusion, in his growing helplessness.

He had no idea what was coming, and that was exactly how I wanted it.

Before Lile could find an opportunity to climb even a few inches out—although, the fact he was losing consciousness might hinder that chance anyway—I slammed the trapdoor shut.

I would've kept it open, but I didn't want to take the chance of chloroforming myself.

Although, the nap *would* be nice.

His shouting cut off, muffled by thick wooden boards and soundproof materials that made up the trap.

Click. The lock snapped into place with satisfying finality as I pressed a third button. The seamless floorboards gave no hint of a hostage hidden beneath them—a perfect illusion.

I didn't leave the scene immediately. Instead, I crouched by the door, straining to hear Lile's cries fading into silence. The chloroform had done its job, and for now, everything was under control. I tugged the Persian rug from the foyer, dragging it over the trapdoor which added an extra layer to muffle any stray sounds that might escape. Just as I finished smoothing it out, the doorbell rang.

FUCK!

Freezing for half a second before springing into action, I shuffled hurriedly to the kitchen counter. My bag landed on its surface with a *thud*, and I tossed my keys inside with a precision that would make the WNBA proud. My heels clicked furiously against the floor as I darted around, straightening anything that seemed even slightly out of place. Of course, I nearly tripped over the damn rug I'd just laid out.

I cursed under my breath as the doorbell rang again—this time with a kind of impatience that could only belong to one person. I didn't even need to look outside to know who it was.

The door groaned open, and there she was—Zina, perched on the porch in one of her signature 'effortlessly chic' ensembles. Her hair was artfully tousled, and her jacket screamed designer without even trying. Her gaze swept over me, probing, her brows knitting together in a way that practically spelled out *What have you been up to?*

"Cassandra," she bit out, stretching my name out like she was auditioning for a soap opera. "I called you TEN TIMES! What are you even doin' up this late? You're not exactly a card-carryin' night owl."

Without waiting for an invite—because why would Zina ever *wait*—she breezed past me, leaving me teetering on my heels. She shoved me aside like an inconvenient coat rack.

Her nose crinkled like she'd just walked into a crime scene— or maybe my living room qualified as one. "You're in a dress," she announced, her eyes narrowing in accusation. "So you've definitely been out. And why does it smell like . . . paint thinner and regret in here?"

I blinked, wrestling with an urge to physically shove her back out the door. "Zina. It's—what? —one in the morning? What are you doing here?" My voice was calm-ish, but my hand was twitching for the nearest excuse to banish her. Maybe my cat could help? Zina was scared of them.

But wait . . . I didn't have a cat.

Fantastic. Now I'm inventing imaginary pets to cope. What's next? Pretending I have a dog named Sir Barksalot to keep her distracted?

"Oh, please. Like you've never randomly decided to check in on a friend in the middle of the night. And don't give me that look." She strode further into the foyer, already scanning the room like a detective in one of those bad crime dramas. "I just . . . I don't know. I was thinkin' 'bout the boys. Worried 'bout you . . ."

I sighed, shutting the door behind her with an exasperated *thud*. "We've talked about this, Z. I'm trying to move on. Qualley is gone and there's nothing I can do about that. I miss him, but —" I threw my arms out for emphasis.

Zina tipped her head, an epitome of judgmental disbelief. "Oh, are you?" Her lips curled into a sly smirk. "Because you're standin' here in a house full of dark, moody art, smellin' like you're either coverin' up a crime or havin' that midlife crisis we spoke about. All while in your favorite dress need I remind you."

I let out a sharp laugh, if only to keep from visibly panicking. How did Zina always know what I was up to? She probably bugged my house with cameras the last time she was here. "Midlife? Please. Not even close. And as for the art, it's called ambiance. You wouldn't understand." I stepped closer, gently taking her by the arm. "Now, as much as I love our little heart-to-hearts, it's late, and I have . . . things to do. Important things. Alone things."

Zina raised an eyebrow. "Important things? At one in the mornin'? Cass, you barely stay up past ten. What's going on? Is someone *really* here?"

I could feel my patience fraying, thoughts lingering dangerously close to what I might do to my best friend if she ever found out about my recent escapades. "I appreciate your concern, but if you don't leave, I'm going to—"

"Oh my God." She gasped, eyes widening. She stared at the Persian rug I'd hastily arranged. "Wait, *did* you decide to see someone else? Like, actually see someone. Is that why you've been actin' so weird? Dodgin' my calls? Why you're dressed up!"

I blinked, momentarily thrown off by her accusation. "Seeing someone?" I repeated a little too high-pitched to sound convincing. "What are you talking about?"

"Oh, please," Zina said, rolling her eyes. "You've got that look. The one you get when you're tryin' to hide somethin'. And don't even try to tell me it's work-related, because we both know you're not that dedicated to your job. He's here, ain't he? Let me meet him!" She tried to scoot around me, but I blocked her path before she could.

I laughed nervously, my mind racing for an excuse that would get Zina out of the house before she started asking questions about the rug's new position—or worse, why I covered up the trapdoor beneath it.

I pulled Zina by the sleeve back towards the front door. "Okay yes, I'm seeing someone. Are you happy? But it's one in the morning and you need to get your ass out of here right now, you fucking cock block!" I let out a sigh. I wanted her to think that by telling her that information, I was liberated and hoped it would get her off my back for another few days.

"Oh. My. God. BITCH!" Zina squealed, crossing her arms. "I'm your bestie, and you can't even tell me you've been fuckin' someone else? Especially since we literally just spoke about how we missed our boys."

I pinched the bridge of my nose. Stumbling over my words, I tried to figure out what I'd say. There's no lifetime in which I'd ever think of seeing or even thinking about anyone other than Qualley. "I just want to feel something other than pain, Z. He's helping me with that so . . . how can I do this when you're barging in. I'm about to, you know . . ." Trailing off, I grasped Zina's hand and don my most pleading face. "I love you, okay? But I really need you to leave. It's late. I promise to call you tomorrow."

If I was done cleaning up a crime scene by then.

Zina bobbed her head, her expression shifting from suspicion to amusement as I lead her back to the front door. "Fine. But I expect details. It's about time you started seein' other people. We won't forget them, but Qualley and Lonney have been gone for ages, and we're not gettin' any younger. Ask him if he has a brother who likes Italians!"

Smiling tightly, I rolled my eyes, resisting the urge to slam the door in her face. "Goodnight, Zina."

As Zina finally strutted off into the night shouting, "USE PROTECTION!" like it was her civic duty, I thrust the door shut, twisting the lock with a little more force than necessary—because, really, who needed subtlety at this point? I leaned against it, letting out a breath so heavy it felt like I'd been holding it since she arrived.

Seeing someone. A dry laugh gargled up despite myself. If only she knew the truth. It's not 'seeing someone' so much as *haunted by someone,* and that someone is Qualley. Always Qualley. It's him or eternal solitude with a side of Persian rugs.

My attention snapped toward the rug in question, stomach twisting. *Please stay unconscious, Lile. Just for a little while longer.* The thought of him waking up and clawing his way upstairs was enough to make me break out in a cold sweat.

Glancing at the abandoned whiskey bottle on the counter, I considered whether I should pour myself self a drink—or pour it over the rug and set the whole thing on fire.

❧ ❧

Lile groaned, breaths coming in as ragged gasps. Assuming by its position, his leg was most assuredly broken, he couldn't move the way he needed to. He must not have been able to think straight past the white-hot pain and residual chloroform searing through his body.

Dust and splinters settled around as he struggled to push himself up. I uncovered the trap to ensure Lile was still immobilized, and crouching at the edge, I studied him. A monster contemplating its way forward.

"Help me up," Lile snarled through gritted teeth, hoarse, strained.

I considered it with a hum. "Help me up," I cooed, smirking. "Please?"

Lile's fingers dug into the dusty floor, attempting to shift his weight. Fresh waves of pain crashed over his face. He was, for sure, trapped, injured. Even if he could stand, climbing out was impossible. I hadn't spent days setting this trap up for it to be flawed.

That would just be irresponsible.

I stood, stepping back from the hole and cool air brushed against my skin. A faint, musty smell of the old cellar infiltrated my nose, and I turned, strolling away.

Panic flared in Lile's eyes. "Come back—"

Securing the trapdoor and simultaneously silencing Lile's protests once more, I pulled the rug back into place. A soft thump of the fabric muffled the secret beneath. Distinct clicks of my steps echoed through the house, and I made my way toward the bottom floor. My eyes adjusted to dim light filtering through the narrow basement window. It cast long shadows across the uneven stone walls.

Each step rippled; the sound of my approach clinking off the concrete. A countdown to the inevitable. I moved toward a rickety wooden staircase at the far end of the room, the boards creaking under my weight as if protesting my very existence. I gripped the splintered railing for balance, the rough texture scratching against my palm. A minor inconvenience compared to irritation bubbling in my chest was that my guest was still alive.

As I descended the staircase, darkness swallowed me whole. It wrapped around me like an unwelcome hug. The atmosphere grew colder and damper with every step, sending shivers down my spine.

Perfect. Just the ambiance I need for dealing with the world's most insufferable man.

A faint dripping of water somewhere in the distance added to an eerie vibe, but I barely noticed. More ambiance for Lile to enjoy. My mind was too busy replaying every smug comment, every infuriating smirk he had ever thrown my way. *Oh, you'll pay for all of it. Every single time you thought you were clever.*

Every time you made me want to scream.

I replayed the nonsense I'd fed Zina to get her out of the house. *Seeing someone? Really?* I rolled my eyes at myself. *Of all the excuses, is that the one I really went with?*

Honestly, Zina should be thanking me for sparing her the details. What was I supposed to say? *Oh, yeah, Zina. I'm seeing someone. He's unconscious in my basement right now, but don't worry, it's not serious?*

Making it to the bottom step and through the narrow corridor, floorboards creaked as if alerting my prisoner of my arrival, tattling on me. The aroma of aged wood and dust wafted through the space, tinged with a distant, melancholic scent of sorrow. I was obsessed with it—so much so I wanted to bottle it and make my signature fragrance. *Eau de salauds assassinés* —'Water of murdered bastards,' I'd call it. French sophistication and just the right amount of menace.

I reached a heavy oak door at the end of the hall; the tarnished brass doorknob cool under my fingers. Pushing the door open, it groaned in protest, revealing a hidden entrance to the basement's lower level.

This is it. Time to face the music—or, more accurately, time for Lile to face me.

My fingers brushed against the cold metal shelving lining the walls, laden with forgotten jars and cobwebs. I navigated through the labyrinth of shadows, my senses heightening, every sound amplified. The metallic taste of anticipation lingered on my tongue as I close in on Lile's prison.

The door to where Lile lay, broken, creaked open.

"You . . ." Lile cried, edged with command. "Don't you fucking leave me down here!"

"Oh, don't be so dramatic," I called back, my voice carrying down the basement walls. "I'm right here. I wouldn't leave you like *this*."

With a flick of a switch, dim yellow light flooded the basement. Lile squinted, adjusting to the sudden brightness. It took him a second to register what he was looking at.

The walls were lined with plastic, chains extending from them and bolted into the concrete. They snaked onto the floor, winding from behind where Lile fell. A single chair sat waiting ominously in the center of the room, including a table of various tools: knives, pliers, needles . . . things one may not wish to identify.

Lile exhaled through his nose, nostrils flaring. "You've got some fucking nerve."

I grinned. "So I've been told. Most artists are bold after all."

Closing the distance between us, I retrieved my gun from the holster on my thigh, pressing the barrel to his forehead. "Now, let's make this easy, shall we?"

Before he could react, I move fast. Lile reached to shove me away, but his broken leg betrayed him. He wailed in agony, collapsing to one side.

That's when I struck.

A stiletto punctured into his ribs as I kicked him—sharp, precise—knocking the breath from his lungs. He barely registered the cuffs from the wall biting into his wrists until it was too late. I go for another crisp movement—a heel against his back. This time, it punctures through his ridiculously thick suit coat. *What is this thing made of? Kevlar?* I turned my eyes heavenward. *Of course Lile would wear something obnoxiously over-prepared, even for an art exhibition.*

He moaned, folding over to brace himself, and I couldn't help but smirk. "Calm down, it's not that serious," I grumbled, crouching down to grab the plastic restraints and empty his pockets, happy to find his phone had broken from the fall. His ankles twitch as he tried to kick me, but his leg is destroyed in an angle even a yoga instructor would call excessive. "Yeah, that's not going to work, buddy." I tightened the restraints with a satisfying zip that nearly breaks skin. "You're not exactly in peak form right now."

As I finished securing his ankles, I stole a moment to catch my breath. "You know," I said conversationally, "if you'd just been a decent human being, we wouldn't be here. But no, you had to go and be . . . well, *you*." I glanced at his face contorted in pain, and add with a mockingly sweet tone, "Don't worry, though. This is just the beginning. You'll have plenty of time to reflect on your life choices. You just might not be alive to do so."

I towered over him, brushing off my hands. I took a step back to admire my handiwork. "Not bad," I said out loud to myself, swiping my attention up and down his mangled body. "You look like really unpleasant spring roll"

"You . . . bitch—" Lile snarled, thrashing within his restraints.

"Careful," I purred. "You'll make me think you don't want to be here."

Lile hollered in pain, jerking against the bindings, but it was useless. No one could hear him. He was completely immobilized, and his broken leg and potentially bruised body was useless to do anything but submit at this point. I couldn't guarantee as a cop he would comply to my abuse willingly; that he wouldn't try to put up a fight.

Squatting beside him, I hold my .22 with suppressor firmly in my hands, ready to use it if things go south. I brushed a strand of hair from Lile's sweaty forehead. "Now," I crooned, my voice both silk and steel, "why don't we have a little chat?"

Chapter 26

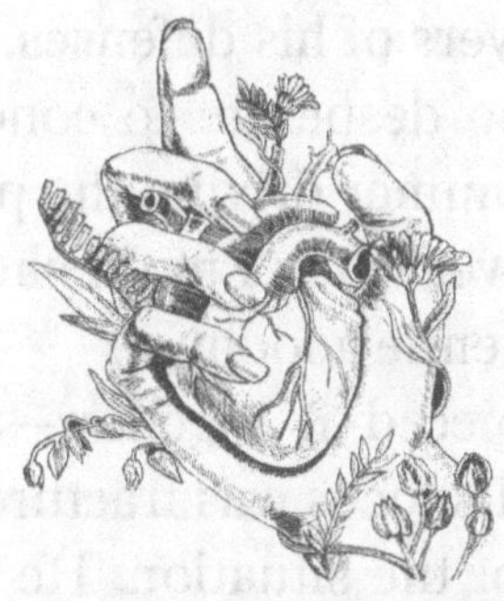

For a while, menacing silence lingered between us. I reveled in its embrace. Lile shifted, his breaths brisk and defiant as he strained against the restraints in which his limbs were bound—unyielding, unforgiving—just like me. His instincts roared for an escape, desperate to claw his way out of the basement.

I knew better.

No one ever got out of the trap.

My tools gleamed resting in perfect order on the rolling tray, their metallic edges a promise of the purpose they had yet to fulfill. They were well within reach but far from where he had plunged through the floor during his spectacular failure.

Hovering nearer, my breath whispered against his clammy skin. I traced a slow, gloved finger around the circumference of his face, stubble scraping against the latex as I slid it down. Brushing over his mouth and cheek, I savored the quiet agony radiating from his every movement.

"It's funny, isn't it?" I asked with as much vitriol as I could possibly muster. "How quickly the balance of power shifts. One second, you're on top—gun in hand, control in your grasp—and the next? You're nothing but prey. Weak, broken, and at my mercy." My nail scraped his chin once more, just enough to make him flinch.

A hiss slipped through his gritted teeth. "What the fuck…"

he growled, choking on his discomfort, "are you talking about?"

I smirked, my gaze locking onto his with unrelenting ferocity, peeling back the layers of his defenses, and exposing the raw vulnerability he was so desperate to conceal. "You," I intoned darkly, each word a hammer driving the point home, "are going to greet death like a lover when I'm finished with you. And trust me, I don't believe in gentle goodbyes."

Lile still hadn't pieced it together—my true identity, the heart of his torment. His focus was fractured under his pain, and the sheer wrongness of the situation. He squirmed, but was so weak, he couldn't move much more than an inch. His body betrayed him with every wound. A haunting promise of those still to come.

Lowering myself beside him again, I ran a scalpel's blade along my gloved palm, its icy edge pressing firmly against the material. Its sharpness seeped into my skin, and I considered the power it held. A thrill coursed through me. Shivers of dark satisfaction that I didn't bother concealing. The corner of my lips curled into a sinister grin as I surveyed him, my head cocking slightly, eyes alight with a blend of wicked amusement and frosty disdain. I hated him—hated everything he represented: his arrogance, his content superiority, his belief that he could control everything and everyone, including me. That hatred was fuel feeding every decision I made, every sharp word, every moment I stole from him in this umbrageous hell.

Lile's shallow, rasping breaths mingled with the rhythmic ticking of a clock countdown to his inevitable demise. And I was going to enjoy every second of this intoxicating torture. Even if someone burst through the front door like a budget action hero, they'd never find us down in that prison. Lile would be long gone—well, not gone exactly, but definitely not among the living —before they even knew where to look. If they even *thought* to look. I was determined to avoid another fiasco similar to Evan's utterly catastrophic bathroom blunder. That one still gave me secondhand embarrassment.

Savoring the way Lile's body tensed under my gaze, I recognized the sweet, metallic scent of blood filling the air, mingling with a sharp tang of sweat protruding from his body.

"Do you know why you're here?" I asked gently, almost a whisper. The question floated around us longer than I'd wanted—dragging like a bad song stuck on repeat. I sighed, patience waning with every second his silence persisted. I slapped the scalpel onto the rolling tray with a satisfying clink.

"Take your time, Lile," I said scornfully. "I've got all day—or at least until you don't."

His lips parted, but no words came, just a strangled breath that grated against my nerves. My gloved fingers tapped lightly against the tray, a sound that broke the stillness as I waited, the rhythm steady and unhurried.

I stepped closer, letting my shadow fall over him. Light caught a glint in my narrowed eyes. "You know," I crouched low enough for him to feel my breath against his ear, "stalling is cute, but it won't save you."

Every flicker of the fluorescent light above, every shuddering breath he took, fed my dark satisfaction. I grabbed the scalpel and dug its edge lightly against the skin on his cheek, watching with cruel fascination as a thin line of red welled up. His eyes widened in terror. I couldn't help but let out a soft chuckle.

"Don't worry," I said, though he had much to worry about, "this is just the beginning. I'm going to take my sweet, precious time with you. You've earned it for that night you took everything away from me."

Lile coughed. "What . . . night?"

I almost laughed. The way his voice wavered, his hesitation stretching with each word. It was like he thought I'd actually believe him. The darting eyes, the tremor in his tone—he knew exactly what night I was referring to. The sheer audacity of pretending otherwise? It was offensive, almost insulting, like he thought I'd fall for his pitiful act. The truth was written all over him—his nerves had betrayed him long before he stepped foot in here (Or should I say, fell in here). The way he'd hesitated on the porch, taking just a second too long to follow, the way his hands twitched as I led him to the trapdoor. Every move screamed apprehension and guilt. A man walking toward his own funeral. And now, here he was, lying to my face, literally. It was intriguing that he thought ignorance might save him.

"Lile," I said, "You've been rehearsing that line since you got here, haven't you?" A fresh bead of sweat slipped down his temple. "You and I both know that's not going to work."

The fear in his eyes deepened, his chest rising and falling in short, panicked bursts. Good. Let him feel it. Let him know he couldn't worm his way out of this. Not tonight. Not with me.

Softly—mockingly—I said, "Don't tell me you've forgotten whose house this once was. *You* killed *him*. Simultaneously stealing everything from *me*. You're a cop, right? Don't you know stealing is wrong?"

For a moment, I observed Lile with genuine fascination. He resembled some tragic character in a poorly written play—trembling breaths, the single, theatrical tear sliding down his face. A whole pitiful display. Honestly, it was almost touching. *Almost*.

But then I caught the faint sound of his restraints creaking as he squirmed, and my sympathy evaporated faster than his fleeting will to live. My fingers kept tracing the scalpel's edge as I edged closer, fighting the urge to roll my eyes. *Really, Lile? A single tear? This isn't the Oscars, and you're definitely not winning Best Actor.*

The room exuded the essence of a gothic nightmare: the dim flicker of the light casting erratic shadows, the air thick with foreboding, and the faint, sour tang of decay creeping in from Evan's resting place beyond the walls. Perhaps the scent lingered just for me, a sinister motivator to finish what I'd started

—after all, Evan wasn't meant to spend eternity alone. It was practically begging for a slow zoom and melancholic soundtrack. But Lile? He just laid there, trembling like a kitten caught in the rain. Panic masqueraded him as a tragic figure, but anyone with an artist's eye could see through the illusion—he was far from heroic.

"You know," I mused, "if you're going to greet death with this much melodrama, maybe I should hand you a script and charge admission."

His body tensed again, as if he thought he could summon the strength to fight me. Adorable, really. I shook my head, the corners of my lips curling. *Keep squirming, Lile. I could use the entertainment.*

As I slithered closer, his chest heaved, each breath shallow and frantic, as though the very act of breathing had become a betrayal. His wrists strained against the restraints. Faint creaks of leather cut through a deafening stillness. Sweat gathering at his temples slid down in uneven trails, his body betraying the fear he refused to voice.

Eyes darting wildly, Lile searched for any escape, but they didn't exist. His attention locked onto mine. There it was—the flare of realization: no amount of desperate thrashing could alter his fate.

The stars aligned only for me that night.

His lips quivered, barely opening as if to form words, yet none escaped. Instead, a low, guttural sound escaped his throat, half a growl, half a plea, as his body recoiled instinctively from my approach.

The room stretched and twisted around us, swallowing everything in its suffocating embrace. I enjoyed the way his muscles clenched, his entire frame coiled like a spring, ready to snap —though we both knew there was nowhere for him to go. His eyes broadened. Bloodied fingers curled against his bonds. He knew now that this wasn't random. This wasn't some sadistic stranger playing games.

"There it is," I said, examining the discernment bleed into his expression. "The moment it all clicks."

Lile panted like a dog for air. His eyes zipped around the room, avoiding mine. His mind must have been screaming at him, trying to put it all together.

And then—he saw it.

The painting.

It was propped against the far wall, partially covered, but the details were unmistakable. The exact face he's seen before caught in a moment of anguish, blood streaking his lips, eyes frozen in that final second before death. Qualley: the painting I made just after euthanizing Evan. His rich, viscous, opaque blood he so willingly allowed me to have made the perfect medium.

Lile's stomach lurches, its contents spilling out next to him.

"No," he choked, heaving. He shook his head as if denying it would make it untrue. His gaze jerked back to me, darting over my face; the way I reveled in this moment, but disgusted with the fact he just vomited all over the floor. It smelled terrible and my own stomach threatened to puke as well.

I was a sympathetic puker.

Tightening my expression, I ignore the smell and conceal the satisfaction that bloomed within me. My gloating smile was gone, replaced by a far more intimate hunger I didn't bother to hide.

"Say it," I murmured, leaning closer until my lips barely brushed his ear. My voice was velvet, soft but uncompromising. "Say my name."

He swallowed hard, his Adam's apple jerking painfully as though he'd choked on the very air around us. The struggle etched itself across his face. Finally, his voice, raspy and strained, came through: "Cassandra."

I beamed, genuine this time. Hearing him rasp my name

was a symphony of control and vindication, a melody crafted just for me.

"Perfect," I whispered, savoring the moment. "Now, let's make it interesting. Say *his* name. You couldn't even bother to remember it, and you're in his house!"

The command sliced through the fragile quiet like a blade, my tone laced with insistence. His lips trembled, and I waited, every second dragging lusciously in the hot space between us.

Until the silence dragged out much too long.

My smile faltered, patience thinning like a thread stretched too far. I tightened the distance between us. "Say it, Lile. Say his name!"

Lile's jaw tightened, his lips pressing into a defiant line. He stared at me, his silence louder than any words he could have spoken. The challenge in his eyes was a spark, daring me to ignite.

My expression darkened; the amusement in my eyes was replaced by something malevolent.

"You think this is strength?" I hissed, words slashing through the muteness like the snap of a whip. "You think silence absolves you?"

Lile's breathed shallow but steady. He didn't flinch, didn't waver—even as my hand shot out, gripping his chin with a force that made his resolve falter for just a moment.

"You don't get to rewrite the story," I said, trembling with restrained fury. "You don't get to erase him like he was nothing. Say his fucking name."

Still, he said nothing.

Then, something inside me snapped.

With a snarl of rage, I drove my knee into his stomach, doubling him over with a grunt. Before he could recover, I slammed the front of my heel into his face, kicking him like a soccer ball. Lile collapsed to the other side, coughing, retching.

"Say. It. Now!" I wailed, punctuating each word with another brutal kick to his ribs, his jaw, his temple. He curled inward, gritting his teeth against the pain, but still refused to speak.

Breathless, I loomed over him, chest heaving. My foot pressed down against the side of his face, grinding it into the icy floor. "Coward," I spat, my voice shaking with ire. "You can't even face the truth of what you've done. You're not strong. You're pathetic." Tears I refused to shed burned behind my eyes. I shoved Lile away with a snarl of disgust, sending him sprawling.

Turning away, my fists clenched, and shoulders shivered as I fought to regain control. But the storm in my eyes betrayed me —fury and pain swirling together in a tempest that refused to be tamed.

Behind me, Lile groaned. Blood stained the concrete floor beneath him. His voice, ragged and broken, barely rose above a whisper.

". . . Qualley."

I froze, my back still to him. Qualley's name lingered in the air like a ghost. For a long moment, I said nothing—but the cruel smile that slowly curved my lips as I twisted around to face Lile said everything. A sigh released from my lips in mock ecstasy. The sound is almost musical, a distorted lullaby as I knelt to lean into him, closer. My breath was warm against his bloody ear.

"Now *that's* a good boy, Lile."

I could practically feel the terror radiating off him, thick and intoxicating. It was exhilarating, really—the way his body betrayed him, shuddering like a leaf caught in a storm. I savored every twitch, every shallow breath, every ounce of dread etched into his face. The room responded to this fear, growing algid, the shadows stretching greedily toward me as if they, too, wanted a taste of his despair. My gloved finger traced a tear on his cheek, wiping it away like it was some precious treasure.

"Oh, Lile," I said with counterfeit sympathy, unable to hide the grin tugging at my lips. "You're making this far too enjoyable. Keep trembling for me, won't you? It pleases me."

The thrill that coursed through me was electric, a heady mix of power and anticipation. His fear wasn't just satisfying—it was invigorating, a reminder that in this moment, I was the one in control. And I intended to savor every second of it.

"Don't be afraid," I lied, falsifying sweetness. "This will all be over soon. It will only hurt a lot."

The scalpel glinted in the subdued light as I plucked it from where it had fallen on the floor during my tantrum. It was crusted with blood from his cheek, but I urged it lightly against his skin again over the wound I'd made earlier, just enough to draw a thin line of blood, creating an 'X' shape. He hissed through the pain, and I could feel his pulse quicken beneath my touch.

"Do you understand the gravity of your situation?" I asked. "I mean, gravity *is* what got you here." He made a despicable effort to speak, but the words caught in his throat, choked by fear. Curving my head gently, I contrived inquisitiveness. "No? Well, let me enlighten you." Lounging back, my eyes never left his. "You see, Lile, this is your reckoning. Every sin, every lie, every betrayal—it all lead to this moment. And I, my dear, am your judge, jury, and executioner on this day. Just as you were Qualley's on that fateful day."

The room enveloped us as the walls pressed in with a suffocating weight. His eyes floundered, searching for an escape. I reveled in his despair, the way his hope crumbled to dust.

"Now," I said, "let's continue, shall we?"

Attempting to wipe hair away from his face, Lile jerked his head away, snarling. "You think this is gonna last?" He hawked up blood, attempting to spit it at me, but I dodged the attack before it could make its mark. "Someone's gonna find me," he continued. "You're not as smart as you think you are."

I chuckled. "No?" I moved past him, my heels echoing against the plastic-lined floor. From the table, I pick up a serrated scalpel. Its blade sparkled under the muted lights. "Enlighten me, then, officer. Why hasn't anyone come looking for your accomplice, Evan, hmm?" I twirled the blade between my fingers. "Did you even know he was missing?"

Lile gaped at me, silent.

"Come on," I urged, playfully. "Tell me how this ends for me exactly."

But he said nothing.

The absence of words conveyed everything, a desperate attempt to maintain some semblance of power. He must not have known about Evan's disappearance, or he did and just didn't think he'd find himself in the same situation.

Lile's eyes quivered with uncertainty, scanning the room as if searching for an explanation. I visualized wheels turning in his mind as he tried to piece together the puzzle of his predicament. My presence hovered over him like a guillotine, an admonisher of his helplessness. A cold shiver ran through him, his body revealing the delightful fear he tried so hard to hide. The faint sound of dripping water echoed in the background through the basement, each drop a cruel countdown to his doom.

Taking a step closer, the soft click of my stilettos against the floor broke the overbearing hush.

His chest rose and fell with increasing urgency and difficulty. I could almost taste his fear, bitterness, lingering, but welcome.

"Do you understand now?" I asked, a low, almost sinister mussitation. "Do you see the truth that's been staring you in the face? Do you see that *no one* cares, and *no one* is coming? *No one* will find you until I *want* you found."

The look in his eyes shifted from confusion to dawning horror, as pieces fell into place. He shivered, another tear escaping, tracing a path down his cheek. I examined him with a mixture of amusement and satisfaction, relishing the power I held over him.

"Poor Evan," I continued, mockingly sympathetic. "He never

saw it coming. His death, that is . . . *it* being me." I shook my head, looking down at the scalpel in my hands. "His death was truly *shocking*."

With practiced calm, I knelt beside him, careless that my favorite navy-blue dress would now be coated with dust, blood, vomit, and whatever else was in this basement; the scalpel hovered just over his arm.

"Did you hesitate? Even for a second?" I whispered, my words almost reverent.

Lile froze as the scalpel rested against his bicep. My gaze locked onto his, demanding the truth. But as always, he stayed mute. It was vexing, each second feeding the fury that churned within. My jaw clenched, betraying the storm of impatience raging beneath my skin. Was it too much to ask for him to explain why Qualley had to die? Why they denied him the chance to testify, to save himself by speaking out?

"I bet you didn't hesitate," I answered for him with a mix of anger and sorrow.

Memories of Qualley flooded my mind—his laughter, his kindness, the way he always believed in justice, believed in change for his career, his work. He was more than just a name on a list; he was my friend, my confidant, the one person who understood me.

Moisture gathered at the corners of my eyes, heavy with sadness. With a blink, I banished them, sealing away the vulnerability that threatened to surface. Weaknesses, I vowed, would not claim me.

"You took him from me," I continued, my voice almost breaking. "You took away the one person who mattered. And for what? To protect your secrets? To silence the truth? Because you could?"

Lile's eyes swelled, and for a moment, I saw a flicker of regret. But it was far too late for remorse. The damage was done, and the void left by Qualley's absence is a wound that will never heal.

"I loved him," I confessed softly. "And you took him away without a second thought. You didn't even give him a chance to fight for his life, to testify and bring justice to those who deserved it." My grief smothered down on me, so I took the time to expel the emotion by pressing the scalpel a little harder against Lile's skin, drawing more blood. "You owe me an explanation," I demanded, stripped of all pretense or emotion, my words blunt and void of sentiment. "Tell me why. Tell me why he had to die. Tell me why and I won't make this a painful death!"

Once again, he didn't answer, choosing his fate undoubtedly. Accordingly, I moved to make the next cut—which, I suppose, was more of a slice. The scalpel struck clean through his skin, parting it with surgical precision. Lile's body jerked, his jaw clenching so hard it might snap. A sharp hiss escaped through his teeth, so tight it threatened to crush them. But he still refused to cry out.

I watch his blood pool beneath him onto the tarp. "You're holding back," I said. "But for how long?"

Lifting the scalpel, I pressed it into his neck, bringing my crimson lips to his ear again and whispered, "Because you're the one who killed him, I'm going to take my sweet, sweet time with you."

I returned back to his bicep, and lodged the blade deeper, dragging it up his forearm in a slow, intended motion. Lile's entire body shuddered. Sweat slicked his forehead, his lungs worked overtime, but still he refused, refrained, from screaming.

I wanted that pleasure so badly.

"You're tough," I said, clicking my tongue. I admired the bright scarlet streaks I created; the way it beaded and trailed down his arm. "I can respect that, but that makes this no fun. I want you to feel. To scream."

Rising to my feet, I let the motion of choosing my next tool linger, drawing attention to the tray beside me. The mason jar stood resolute, almost taunting in its stillness. Inside, I envisioned Lile's heart floating. My grim trophy; a truth he had yet to face. I could see the question forming behind his eyes, the quiet torment of wondering what purpose the jar held. And oh, I wouldn't dream of denying him the revelation waiting to unfold.

I shifted slower as I returned to him with my scalpel and jar. I sliced through the fabric of his shirt, the blade gliding with almost surgical precision. I barely grazed his skin, but it's enough to leave a thin, angry line down the center of his chest—a whisper of blood gemmed at the surface. Lile jerked under me instinctively, a hoarse gasp ripping from his throat. His muscles twitched in helpless spasms, eyes wide and glassy with pain and panic. He tried desperately to speak, but only a strangled whimper escaped his lips.

I sat back on my heels slightly, admiring my work. Observing him bleed was like watching the first crack in a dam—small now, but full of promise.

He shivered forcefully, chest rising and falling in shallow, frantic spurts. His fingers clenched uselessly at his sides as he, unsuccessfully, willed his broken, numbed body into action.

Dragging the flat of the blade gently across the fresh line I made, I smeared the tiny pearls of blood.

"You felt that, didn't you?" I cooed. "Good. I *want* you to feel it."

Lile groaned, squeezing his eyes shut against the sting. More tears escaped, sliding down his temple.

So many beautiful tears.

The sight of them initiated a strange sensation in my chest—not pity. Not guilt. Something deeper. Older. A satisfaction that tasted like iron on my tongue. I turned to him, studying him like a scientist with a pinned-down specimen.

"You deserve so much worse than I can ever provide you," I said woefully, pouting. "So, you should be grateful." I smirked, raising the jar between us, shaking it just enough to make the glass glint in the light.

The gesture captures Lile's attention and he rotates his head toward it, confusion warring with something deeper—like dread.

"See this?" I asked softly, sweetly. I gave it another little shake. "With this, I will keep what you stole from me. Can you guess what that is?"

A flash of resistance glares in his eyes, but he didn't speak. It was as if speaking was excruciating. I saw what he wanted to say in the way his hands curled into weak fists against his restraints; the way he struggled to breath when I showed him where his heart would be kept.

I'm glad he understood.

I angled forward, the cold glass brushing against his bare skin. Right over the spot where his heart beats strongest. "Do you know what it feels like," I whispered, "to have your heart ripped from you? To watch the one thing keeping you alive slip through your fingers?"

Hanging the scalpel lightly just above his sternum, I allowed the blade to rest there without breaking the skin—at least not yet. Lile exhaled sharply through his nose. Still defiant and pretending this doesn't scare him, pretending it doesn't hurt.

Smiling at him, I extended my other hand to stroke his face, the scalpel inches from his flesh. "Don't worry," I lied, my grip tightening on the handle. "You're about to."

With that, I placed the mason jar to the side, stretching over to take the lid off so it was ready for its new tenant. I shifted back to Lile, taking a moment to admire his last breaths, building the tension so his mind swam with what would come. I knew I'd never get answers from him, and even if I did they'd be lies to save his skin.

"Hm, I wonder," I said. "Should I open you up and make you watch?"

Lile didn't answer, but his entire body tensed, muscles coiling like a live wire. The chains rattled violently as he jerked back, a snarl of panic twisting across his face. He tried to scramble away, tried to press himself through the floor, but the cuffs held him tight to the cold concrete. His breath came fast and shallow, nostrils flaring.

His eyes locked onto mine—wild, unblinking. No smugness now. Just raw, silent terror.

I stepped closer. He thrashed harder, legs kicking, shoulders straining, veins popping beneath the skin of his neck as he fought against the steel that refused to give. Sweat beaded along his temple, sliding through a smear of dried blood. He didn't scream. He didn't speak.

He just fought like an animal that finally understood it was trapped.

Reveling in his terror, and as much as I wanted to watch him squirm and fight for his life, I wanted him dead even more. Therefore, without a second thought, I gripped the scalpel, stabbing it into his throat. I left it there as if it were a plug keeping bodily fluids from flowing out of his neck. Lile choked on his own blood, his eyes enlarging, bulging. He must have realized that this was the moment he wouldn't come back from. A moment he wouldn't survive.

"Just kidding," I revealed, "Taking your heart will be a private moment for me."

A wet, strangled gurgle broke free from his throat as his body jerked against the restraints. His muscles instinctively fought against the inevitable, but it was useless. Lile's skin darkened, veins protruding from his neck as his breath comes in desperate, garbled gasps.

"What? What's that?" I asked, laughing, mocking him like he was trying to tell me something but couldn't.

I cocked my head, observing him the way I might study an unfinished painting, assessing composition, textures, brush strokes.

The scalpel quivered where I left it, lodged deep in his

throat. Steel that stained slick and glistening with his life. Curling my fingers around the handle, I twisted it slowly—not enough to end it too soon, but enough to watch his body react. His back arched, his mouth opening and closing in silent, frantic attempts at breathing. His chest heaved, the tendons in his neck strained.

I angled my lips near his ear for the last time, feeling heat radiate off his dying body. "You're feeling it now, aren't you?" I whispered, syrupy with satisfaction. "Tell Lucifer who I am."

His eyes, glassy and losing focus, tried to meet mine. There was no fight left, just a trembling, fading shell of the man who pulled the trigger on my world, trying to stay alive.

I ran a fingertip down his chest. He was coated with blood, seeping slowly from the wound in his neck. I wanted to experience the last, erratic beats of his heart beneath it. Then, with a single, decisive motion, I ripped the scalpel free.

Blood poured out, spilling in thick, glistening ribbons down his chest. It pooled beneath him in a dark, spreading halo. His head lolled weakly, limbs jerking in broken spasms, as the last fight drained from his body.

I plucked the mason jar from the floor with a shaking hand —whether from adrenaline or anticipation, I couldn't tell—and steadied myself, the jar cool and solid against my slick palms. I held it against his chest, scooping blood into it with the flat edge of the scalpel. Each scoop sent warm, sticky liquid running over my fingers, I could feel it through my gloves. It dripped from my wrists in hot trails.

A strange calm overtook me, cold, sacred clarity.

As his body shuddered, his final breath rasping from cracked lips, a profound stillness filling the space between a silence so dense it nearly choked me. And then, with a slow inhalation, I took what was rightfully mine while Lile still clung to life.

I worked quickly; my hands sure despite the feral pounding

of my own heart. The scalpel bit through skin and muscle like silk, splitting under the blade. His chest cavity divided, exposing a glistening maze of bone and organs; the steam of his fading life curled into the cool basement air, the scent, metallic, primal. It flooded my senses, grounding me, anchoring me.

At some point, my body moved on instinct alone—I fetched the bolt cutters from where I left them against the wall, their grim steel jaws waiting for me like loyal old friends. I had a difficult time with Evan's ribcage, using only a knife to get to what I wanted. This time, I brought in better tools so I didn't have to work so hard. I positioned them, and with a firm squeeze, Lile's ribs cracked open, parting like the red sea before me.

His heart, once defiant and thrumming with life, now fluttered its last twitches. A bloom of flesh framed by ruin. It waited for me—silent, defenseless.

Reaching in without hesitation, my fingers sunk into the wet heat, navigating through torn tissue and shattered bone. The resistance was fleeting. A shudder raced through me as I curled my hand around the heart, feeling it spasm weakly against my palm—one last whisper of defiance before surrender.

Slowly, reverently, I pulled it free.

Arteries stretched, snapping one by one. Sickening little sighs of defeat. Blood sluiced down my arms, soaking into the fibers of my dress. It dripped onto the floor in rhythmic, hollow plinks. I cradled the heart like a relic, something sacred, something earned.

I placed it into the mason jar filled with Lile's cooling blood, flesh thudding against the glass with a heavy, wet sound that reverberated through my bones. Sealing the lid tight, I lifted the jar to eye level, turning it slightly. I let the basement's dim light catch the swirling tendrils of blood and tissue inside.

An involuntary breath escaped me—half sigh, half moan—an exhale of pure, unfiltered satisfaction.

This wasn't just revenge.

It's rebirth.

It's liberation.

Lile's heart floated weightlessly in its crimson tomb, and I smiled through the red dripping from the spaces between my fingers—because something broken inside me felt whole again.

Chapter 27

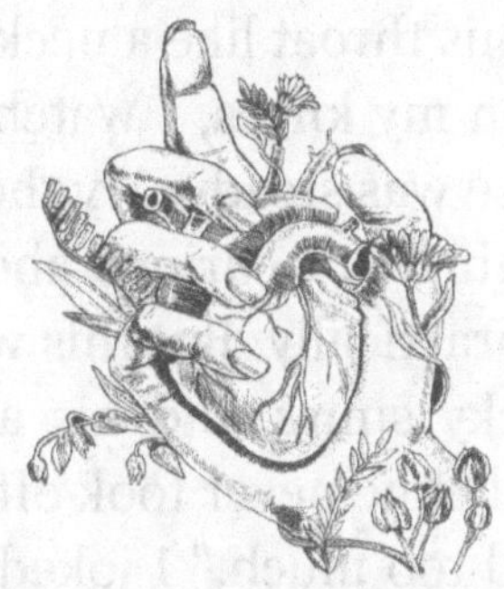

Getting Lile's body into the backyard behind the studio was ridiculous and hell of a lot more difficult than dragging Evan's down the deck stairs. Evan had been lighter, much to my surprise, and easier to maneuver—Lile was dead weight in every possible sense. He was bulkier, more rigid, and the pooling blood from inside his open chest cavity made everything around him on the tarp slick.

I had already packed him up nicely, stuffing all of his personal items inside the hollow of his ribs—his broken phone, his wallet, even the badge he didn't think I knew about—before sealing it with thick layers of duct tape. Everything that made him reduced to an unnatural little package inside his own person.

But getting him outside? That was an entirely different challenge.

I crouched beside him, assessing my options. Dragging him straight out the front door was out of the question. The back entrance through the cellar was my best bet, but it required hauling him up a stone flight of stairs. The last thing I needed was for his body to slip from my grip and come crashing down, splitting open like a grotesque piñata, spilling his neatly packed souvenirs all over my floor.

Before I even got him outside, I had an intrusive thought.

The body was still warm.

Lile's head lolled to the side, chin slick with blood that had trickled from his mouth during the spasms. It was starting to dry, flaking at the edge where his beard had caught some of it. The rest pooled down his throat like a necklace carved in red.

With my elbows on my knees, I watched the glossy film set along his skin. My pulse was steady. My thoughts, less so.

There was something . . . curious about it. I'd seen blood, sure. I'd bathed in it, practically. But this was different. This was *his*. Lile, with his cocky smirk and his awful breath and that stupid patch on his jacket he never took off.

"You always talked too much," I joked. He was the most infuriatingly quiet person I've ever met.

The copper scent filled my nose. Strong. Intimate. My tongue touched the corner of my lip and—on a strange, wild impulse—I leaned closer and dragged a slow lick along the curve of his cheek.

Warm. Metallic. *Alive*, somehow, even in death.

And then—*disgusting*. I pulled back, gagging, wiping my mouth with the back of my glove.

"Jesus Christ," I coughed. "Okay. No. I'm not that kind of psychopath."

I stood up, brushing my dress off, mentally checking vampire off my list of future occupations and tried scrubbing the taste from my memory. "Fucking gross," I grumbled, heading toward the sink.

After throwing up and taking a moment to head back upstairs to chug the whiskey still sitting on the bar to get the taste out of my mouth, the issue of getting Lile's body out of here still lingered, so I improvised. I pulled the edges of the plastic tarp tighter around him, rolling him like an oversize burrito. I guaranteed the plastic hugged his form as snugly as possible, the key being keeping everything contained—no unnecessary mess, no loose ends.

I reached for duct tape, wrapping it around his torso first, then securing the tarp just below his arms. I wound it around his neck and head in tight, overlapping layers. With his arms pinned to his sides and his legs wrapped up tight, he was nothing more than a human parcel, ready for delivery.

Testing my grip, I took a deep breath before heaving him forward. The weight of him resisted at first, a stubborn anchor refusing to be moved. My fingers dug into the layers of plastic as I braced my stance, using every bit of strength I had to drag him across the floor, but the friction slowed me down. Plastic caught on uneven concrete a few times, and the occasional speck of blood that had congealed on the floor.

"Come on, Lile," I grunted through gritted teeth, adjusting my hold and yanking harder. "Uncompromising even in death!" He didn't respond, of course.

I laughed at the joke lingering in my head. "Of corpse."

Finally, as I reached the cellar stairs, the incline loomed ahead of me in silent challenge. One wrong move, and his body would tumble backward, and I would have to start all over again.

At least if he bashed his head it wouldn't kill him.

I dug the heels of my feet in, now bare, pulling with everything I had, step by agonizing step. My muscles burned, my breath came in sharp exhales, but I didn't stop. I couldn't. Every time I felt the weight shift in a way I didn't like, I adjusted my grip, squeezing the tarp tighter to keep him from slipping free.

At last, I reached the top, emerging into the cool night air with a victorious gasp. Now, the backyard stretched before me, bathed in soft moonlight and a biting early November chill, but it was a welcome situation, especially after scaling the stairs was like carrying a body up Mount Everest.

Freshly disturbed soil waited for its newest occupant, the hole in the ground gaping. A mouth waiting for its next meal. I let go of the tarp for a moment, rolling my shoulders and shaking out my arms.

Almost there.

Gripping the plastic once more, I dragged Lile's body the

rest of the way across the yard. The hole was deep, ready, waiting. With one last pull, I lined him up with the edge and took a step back, admiring my work.

"Time to tuck you in," I sang and with a swift, final shove, I sent him tumbling into the abyss.

I brushed dirt from my hands, exhaling through my nose as I stared down at Lile's bundled corpse crushing Evan's. It was a fucked-up sleepover, bodies lying motionless in the pit, their plastic-wrapped forms barely visible in the dim moonlight.

Just another piece of trash, buried in a landfill.

Rolling my shoulders to loosen remaining aches after hauling dead weight up the basement stairs, across the yard, and into his final resting place, I planned out what I would do next.

Grabbing the nearby tarp, I cover the grave as I did the first time I shoved Evan's body inside. Satisfied, I took a step back, assessing my work.

A slow smile curved my lips.

Tension that had been coiled tight in my chest finally unwinds. My muscles relaxed, adrenaline still humming faintly beneath my skin. I closed my eyes for a brief moment, savoring another victory.

Back at the house, I stepped through the cellar doors and into the house. The smell of blood still lingered in the air, blending with a faint metallic odor of my latest keepsake.

I practically floated through the dimly lit basement where Lile's execution took place, locating the tray that held the bloody tools, reaching for the mason jar containing Lile's heart. Blood had settled at the bottom, thick and dark, a perfect shade of red. I lifted the jar, rolling it between my hands as I appreciated the organ floating inside.

"You took him from me," I said tenderly. "And now, you're mine."

From the basement, I made my way to my studio, another portrait of Qualley forming in my mind.

Chapter 28

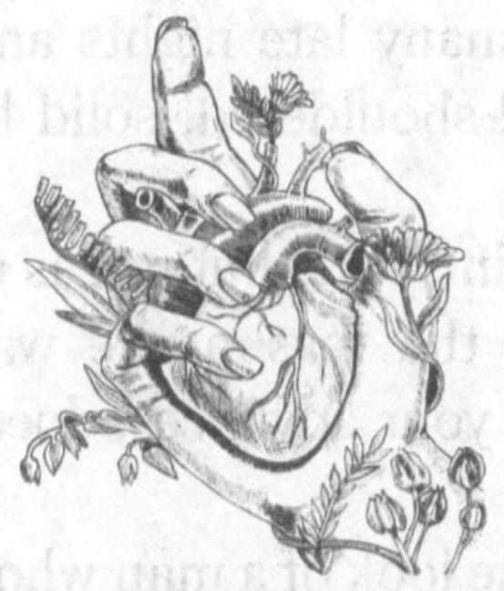

When you have an assortment of your favorite food, you save the best for last, right? If you're eating trail mix, you don't go for the chocolate first. You might usually eat the boring stuff like raisins or nuts before moving onto the good stuff. Most people wouldn't start with something easy, or good. They complete the difficult things first, moving onto the simpler things after. It's more satisfying that way, at least in my opinion.

Ben Prout was my favorite.

He was the chocolate in the trail mix.

It's really a shame he had to die.

Ben would have had potential if not for the fact he had a hand in murdering Qualley and Lonney, which made him significantly more unpleasant to me when I remember that fact.

He was conventionally attractive, but also the kind of man who thought he was more handsome than he actually was. He had a rugged charm, which was fading—the kind of look that once turned heads in his adolescent years but now relied on confidence more than natural appeal. At thirty-three, his divorce and his work, perhaps, accelerated the decline of the ladies-man he saw in his head. And yet, he had a strong jawline, stubble-covering his chin from lazy grooming, and his dark blonde hair was always a little unkempt, not in an effortlessly cool way, but in a 'didn't bother to style it' kind of way. His piercing blue eyes lost some of their sharpness over the years, where light crow's feet gathered at the corners of them. In my opinion, they displayed a sign of too many late nights and too much drinking, considering his broad-shouldered, solid build, carried the look of too many bar visits.

Women noticed him, sure, but not as often as he might have thought, and not for the reasons he wanted. Just because a woman acknowledges your advances, doesn't mean she'll follow through with them.

Even so, he had the look of a man who had peaked five years ago—or in high school—and still coasted off that confidence, unaware that the charisma had cracked.

For me, his arrogance made him even easier to manipulate.

The headlines were almost laughable. *Bristol Police disappearances!* The media was buzzing, the police force scrambling, patrols doubling down as if their vigilance could somehow undo what had already been done. But their oversight was glaring—searching in the wrong places, considering the wrong suspects. Qualley's former team? Gang initiation?

Oh, please.

I was the one they should've been looking for, and I tried not to take that insult to heart. I was the woman who had walked into their lives and erased them from significance (not that they were *that* significant before) with precision, with purpose. And yet, here I was, watching the confusion unfold from a safe distance, untouchable and unseen. It was slighting how easily they'd been misled, how quickly they'd latched onto the wrong narrative. But it was also . . . satisfying. Watching them chase shadows while I stood in the light, unbothered, was a reminder of just how far ahead I was.

Still, the reality of my choices lingered, pressing against the edges of my mind like a dull ache. Evan and Lile weren't just names on a list—they were pieces of a puzzle I'd spent a year trying to solve. Their disappearances weren't random, weren't impulsive. They were calculated and necessary. As much as I wanted to feel triumphant, there was a smoldering truth edging closer to revelation. Anger. Not at them, not at the police, but at the world that had forced me into this position, at the circumstances that had made this my reality. I wasn't proud of what I'd done, but I also wasn't ashamed, either. It was survival, plain and simple. Essential. They'd made their choices, and I'd made mine.

As the city speculated and feared for their lives, I felt a strange mix of emotions—relief, satisfaction, and a resentment that refused to fade. Let them search. Let them theorize. Let them waste their time chasing ghosts. I'd done what needed to be done, and I wasn't about to let their incompetence ruin the clarity I'd fought so hard to achieve.

All of it was fine by me, Qualley's boys would be vindicated once this was all over.

I hadn't been suspected . . . yet, thanks to my alias, disguises, and careful planning. But I knew if I wanted to carry this mission out further, I needed to keep my head down and think smart. Relying on Ben's lack of situational awareness, or his habitual routines to keep me safe in this particular instance would be another rookie mistake. I considered his status as a cop meant he could sense a scam, was able to read a dishonest face, and conclude if he was in danger or not.

Luckily for me, he was a *dumbass*. Look in a dictionary, you'll see Ben's name there.

A few weeks is all it took to arrange the murder of Ben Prout. This was, for sure, the most thrilling one of all the officers, and I didn't have to work as hard to get the conclusion I wanted.

See? Save the best for last.

Ben was a bachelor—a *divorced* bachelor—who's ex-wife had been, according to my research, given custody of their new baby because of his alcoholism. The fact he was always working didn't help his case either.

By the looks of it, the BPD was on their last straw with Ben Prout too, and his childish, reckless behavior.

Saving Ben for last was quite strategic, too, might I add. Evan and Lile were more connected within the force, making their deaths more urgent in my schedule of events. Taking them out first disrupted the department, making the remaining officers paranoid and distracted. Ben was a lone wolf, preferring to do things on his own. Plus, his disappearance wouldn't send shockwaves through the BPD the way the first two did. Considering his pending termination, no one wanted him there anyway.

Luckily for the Bristol Police Department, I'd do the termination for them.

You're welcome!

Another advantageous detail shocking me at first: Ben hated Evan and Lile for their highly distinguished careers. One thing they skimmed over in court was Lile and Evan, allegedly, got all the recognition for the raid, while Ben was left in the shadows.

According to Ben's dissertation, he alluded to Lile and Evan botching the job, which, if they hadn't, should have resulted in Qualley and Lonney being apprehended rather than killed. Even so, Ben was the one working behind the scenes to make sure everything having to do with the raid was covered up properly, probably in order to get back on James Hall's good side again. He made calls, planted extra evidence, and silenced witnesses—but none of that got him the same promotion.

Sad thing is, if Ben had just simply not done anything, or testified entirely against his rogue team members, his life would've been spared, rather than forfeit.

My idea was to make it look like it was Ben who was responsible for Evan and Lile's disappearances, but that was too far-fetched, I think. As much as I wanted to take credit right away for all the hard work I was doing, everything would fall into place eventually. And the piling corpses in my backyard were nothing compared to my last and final scheme that would dispose of their leader, James Hall.

However, before I even considered what that scheme would be, I had to create the itinerary for Ben's impending fate.

Therefore, I requested Zina's help. *Again.*

The Zenith Bar bore many marks of its origins—modernized under Zina and Lonney's ownership yet infused with echoes of their ambitions. Located in the heart of Bristol, it carried an air of casual sophistication that contrasted with the shady undertones of its clientele. A long, polished bar stretched across the room, its glossy surface reflecting a muted glow of overhead pendant lights. Rows of liquor bottles lined the bamboo wall behind the bar, arranged meticulously by type and label, their colors shimmering like jewels in the warm lighting.

High-backed stools with sleek metal frames and faux leather cushions lined the bar's edge, their design inviting yet practical, a perfect spot for long conversations—or discreet deals. The floor was a mix of dark hardwood and sections of worn black tile, hinting at the space's transformation from a forgotten dive to its current status as a bustling hub. Booths hugged the walls, their plush upholstery in shades of deep green and charcoal gray offering a degree of privacy to those who preferred their conversations kept off the record.

The air carried a blend of familiar scents—whiskey, beer, faint notes of smoke from an outdoor patio, and the occasional hint of citrus from fresh cocktails. The soundscape was a medley of low laughter, the occasional clink of glassware, and the rhythmic hum of an ambient musical playlist carefully curated to set the mood without overwhelming it.

Above the booths, framed photos and small memorabilia hinted at Zenith's historical mix of portraits capturing its owners, Zina and Lonney, alongside grainy snapshots of past patrons. For those who knew the space intimately, the décor told a quiet story of loyalty and remembrance.

The bar was alive with its usual energy, drawing in its peculiar mix of clientele. Ben Prout sat in one of the corner booths, his laughter rising above the gentle commotion, his confidence amplified by the whiskey in his glass

Beside her glass of water, Zina stood in her element, the faint smile on her lips betraying nothing of her thoughts. The bar was more than just a business—it was a battlefield, a sanctuary, and a stage where her heightened perception of people thrived. I couldn't help but notice a subtle strength in her posture, the way she leaned into the bar with both authority and ease, swirling the water in her hand like she was ready for anything.

For me, every detail mattered—the dim lighting, the mirrored walls that reflected Ben's movements, the worn booths that held secrets long spilled. It wasn't just a bar; it was a snare, and that night I had every intention of using it to deceive my prey.

Zina smirked at me, her eyebrow arching in question. "I don't get it. That's the guy you're interested in? He's not even that cute."

I laughed softly, keeping my eyes on Ben. He's sat in a booth, talking too loud, his confidence dripping with whiskey. When he glanced our way, he catches us staring. I quickly glance down, playing it off.

"It's not like that. I just need to get him alone for a bit."

"That doesn't sound sketchy or anythin'," Zina deadpanned, swirling her glass of water with an almost bored precision.

"It's not, I swear," I lied, sighing, shaking my head. "Look, I'll tell you, but you can't judge me."

Zina moved in closer, her interest piqued but still guarded in the way she moved—a subtle distance that I couldn't quite name. Her tone, though playful, carried an edge I could feel, needlelike and pointed. It wasn't like her, not entirely. I get it—things had been tensing since Lonney died. Tense in ways neither of us have fully acknowledged. But still, her bluntness stung more than I liked to admit.

"Well, I hope you do, bitch, or I'm passin' and you're on your own," she said, her voice teasing but just shy of affectionate.

"What happened to 'we're in this together,' hmm?" I asked lightly, though the question was genuine.

"We are," Zina whined dramatically, gripping my forearm with her hand. Her expression didn't quite match her playful delivery. "But only when it comes to Qualley and Lonney stuff. You know that."

I tried not to let her words settle too heavily, though they dug deeper than I would've liked. Everything that mattered most to her had been tied to Lonney, and because he was gone, the pieces that remained were jagged and untouchable. Still, there was a part of me wishing she'd let me in, let me bridge the distance instead of keeping me at arm's length. Maybe the few months of me distancing myself from her and dodging her calls and advances had set me up for failure rather than provide a friend who would trust me.

I glanced around, sneaking another peek over at Ben, who was doing the same. I lowered my voice. "This *is* Qualley and Lonney stuff. He has answers to questions I have."

Zina narrowed her eyes, skepticism adorning her expression. "Answers? Wait, hang on." She leaned closer, voice dropping to a whisper. "Is this the guy from the other night? You know, when I showed up and you were actin' shady?"

My pulse quickened, though I didn't let it show. I kept my grip firm on my martini glass, swirling the drink lazily. "No," I said smoothly, carefully casual. "That was someone else. Totally unrelated."

"Unrelated, huh?" Zina's gaze didn't falter. "You practically shoved me out the door. Didn't even let me get past the front hall. Doesn't feel 'unrelated' to me."

I exhaled softly, forcing a laugh to disarm her. "Look, Zina, that really was different. Trust me. This guy—Ben—he's important in a different way. He's got information I need, okay?"

Zina didn't look convinced, not entirely. Her eyes tracked Ben briefly, then back to me, her lips pressing into a thin line. "You've been actin' weird ever since Qualley died," she said flatly, carrying more bite than I expected. "Months of weird that have me wonderin' what the hell is really goin' on with you."

My jaw tensed at the mention of Qualley, his name cutting through my composure. It had been a year since the raid, since everything fell apart—since I lost him, and she lost Lonney. A year wasn't enough to patch up those kinds of wounds, but Zina had found a way to move forward, throwing herself into running the bar and keeping her head above water. She wasn't out here doing . . . this. Not like me.

"You don't need to wonder," I replied firmly, but it wasn't defensive. "We've been talking a little already. Tonight's the night."

"For what?" Zina pressed, refilling her glass with tonic water.

Reaching into my purse, I pulled out a vial wrapped with a ten-dollar bill. I adjusted it in my palm, then slid it across the bar to Zina. She paused, her fingers hovering over it like she wasn't sure she wanted to touch it.

"There's a lot more where that comes from," I said.

Zina didn't pick it up. Instead, she folded her arms, leaning against the bar and leveling me with a look that saw through all my deflections. "Cassandra," she said slowly, her voice low. "What are you doin'? What is this really about?"

I sighed, my fingers tracing the rim of my glass. "I told you. This is Qualley and Lonney stuff."

"Don't give me that," Zina snapped quietly, though her tone wasn't harsh—just frustrated. "Qualley and Lonney stuff ended a year ago. We all lost people, okay? You don't see me—" She gestured toward the vial, her words hanging heavy in the air. "You don't see me doin' . . . this." I stared at her, my jaw tightening as she continued. "It's been a year, Cassandra. Why now? What's so important that you're cozyin' up to this guy and pulling me into whatever this is? And don't lie to me."

Her words struck deeper than I cared to admit, and for a moment, I considered telling her everything—about the anger that still hadn't faded, the questions that haunted me, the desperate need to know. But instead, I hardened my expression, forcing myself to stay calm.

"He knows something," I said finally, my voice quieter but still firm. "Something about what happened that night. About why everything went down the way it did."

"And you think spikin' his drink is the way to get it?" Zina asked, incredulous. She gestured to the vial again but still didn't pick it up. "I mean, what's the plan here? I need more than this cryptic 'Qualley and Lonney stuff' you keep throwin' at me."

I glanced at Ben, who was now nursing his beer and glancing at the TV screen like he didn't have a care in the world. A pang of anger flared in my chest at the thought of how easy his life seemed, how unbothered he looked while I clawed my way through the wreckage he and his colleagues wrought.

"He's involved," I said simply, harder now. "I know he is. And he's not about to hand over answers out of the kindness of his heart."

Zina studied me, her expression softening slightly but still guarded. "And if he doesn't have the answers you think he does?" she asked. "What then?"

I didn't answer right away, because it's something I hadn't considered. What then? I didn't want to think that far ahead, and I guess it didn't necessarily matter considering my true end game. For now, all I could focus on was what I needed to know, the pieces I needed to fit together before I could even start to make sense of the rest.

"I wouldn't ask if it wasn't important," I said, reaching for her hand, covering it gently. "Please, Zina. I need this. You know I wouldn't pull you into something unless it mattered."

A long silence stretched between us as she stared. I could feel the weight of her hesitation, the way she was trying to reconcile the person she knew with whatever I'd become. Finally, she exhaled sharply, glancing at Ben, then back at me.

"Lord God," she muttered, rolling her eyes. "First that weird paintin' situation, and now this? You're lucky I like you."

A smile tugged at my lips as I picked up my drink and mimicked a cheers motion her way. "You *love* me."

Zina shook her head but took the small vial, her fingers gripping it loosely as if she still wasn't sure about the whole thing. She blinked, her brow furrowing deeper as she stared at the vial, her hesitation palpable. "So . . . what? You want me to knock him out with this so you can interrogate him?" she whispered, glancing around the bar even though no one was close enough to overhear.

I laughed, shaking my head. "That's the idea. You know how men like him are. They talk big, but then you get them in the right space, and they start spilling their guts."

Zina's skepticism deepened, her lips pressing into a tighter line as her gaze flicked between me, the vial, and Ben. "And by 'right space,' you mean . . . .?"

"Just somewhere quiet."

"Such as?"

This gave me pause, but only for a moment. I couldn't tell her I'd bring him to my house—not after the way she'd looked at me the other night when I shoved her out the door before she could step inside. She hadn't seen anything, but her suspicion had been written all over her face. As far as she was concerned, the mansion had been a mausoleum since Qualley died, untouched and unvisited. Other than the guy I was 'seeing'.

"His house, I suppose," I said breezily, grinning and sipping my espresso martini, leaving a crimson mark on the rim. The lie slipped out effortlessly, though the tightening in my chest reminded me that Zina's sharp eyes weren't something to take lightly.

She studied me for a long moment, her hesitation still perceptible. "Cass," she said slowly, her voice almost pleading. "I don't know about this. It feels . . . off."

"I wouldn't ask if it wasn't important," I begged, softening my tone as I placed a hand over hers, still covering the money and drugs. "This guy—he was involved in . . . he knows things, and I need to know them too. Please, Zina."

Zina couldn't hide the concern in her eyes, not completely. If anyone knew what I went through—losing my lover, my best friend, my Qualley—it was her. She'd been through her own pain, her own loss, but she hadn't taken the same path I had. And maybe, on some level, she knew it. She shook her head but took the small vial, her fingers gripping it loosely like she still wasn't sure about the whole thing.

"I'd like to buy that guy over there another beer and cover his tab. He's cute," I joked, as if we hadn't just had a conversation about him. I pointed toward him in flamboyant fashion, putting on a show, making a big deal of it so as to catch the attention of my victim.

Ben looked over toward me as Zina made her way to prepare his drink. Leaning back, I lifted my drink to him, winking, before bringing it to my lips in seductive fashion. I wasn't expecting him to leave his seat, walk over toward me, and place himself next to me.

Zina startled, her eyes widening as she worked to finish Ben's drink before getting caught spiking it. But he didn't even notice her there, or what she was doing. He was too busy putting all his attention onto me.

"Can I offer you another martini?" Ben asked, folding his

arms over the table. His hand grasped his glass as if someone might take it from him.

Or drug it.

It was plainly, almost painfully, obvious that Ben probably would've just followed me home like a mosquito chasing the scent of O+ blood if I'd asked him to. He was completely sloshed, reeking of alcohol, but still competent enough to make my acquaintance after a few weeks of light smiles and passing glances.

Some would call it stalking, I would call it opportunistic pursuit. Right place, right time. Perhaps coincidence.

Zina made a show of filling the drugged glass to the very top, froth almost overflowing onto the counter.

"No," I said, denying his offer. "But my friend here just poured you a round on me."

Ben gaped at me in surprise, then smiled, reaching for the freshly drugged beer and setting it in front of him.

He watched, confused, as Zina removed the unemptied glass he was sipping from, dumping the rest of its contents in the sink and placing the glass in a bucket. She scurried away before he could question her through floppy doors leading into the kitchen of the pub, leaving me to my business.

The pub wasn't loud, and it was uncharacteristically slow for a Friday night. Customers were tucked into their perspective corners, participating in their own intimate conversations. The atmosphere closed in onto Ben and I as the volume of music and voices dissipated into dull murmurs. It was as if we were the only ones in the room at that moment. No one else mattered. Nothing else mattered. It would have been endearing if he was a lover and not my next casualty.

"What? A woman can't buy a man a beer?" I asked playfully.

"Of course she can," he said. "Just never happened to me before."

I winked at him again, sipping my almost empty martini.

"Then today's your lucky day."

"Ben," he said, introducing himself and offering an out-stretched hand.

My hand met his, and I smiled. "Crimson. Nice to meet you."

The handshake took me by surprise, and I thought that maybe he knew my name wasn't Crimson and the drink sitting in front of him would knock him the fuck out. But I didn't spend precious moments becoming paranoid. And that became simple enough when Ben started gulping his beer into his face.

See?

Dumbass.

After draining almost half the laced pint I'd bought him, Ben swiveled his body in my direction. "What kind of name is Crimson? Sorry . . . I mean like, origin. It's unique. I like it."

I feigned a coy smile. "Not sure. But I got it for my birthday, so . . ."

Ben burst out in a disturbing, boisterous cackle, apparently finding my dry joke hilarious. Zina stepped out into the service area of the bar at the same time, holding a rack of clean glasses, fixing her attention to us as Ben continued to giggle. My eyes locked with hers, and she gave me an "is this guy serious" kind of look, to which I offered her a shrug.

I swirled the remnants of my drink, watching the lone coffee bean dance around in the liquid. Ben had finally stopped laughing and was now asking me dozens of questions about my personal life, to which I gave false answers. Acting interested in him served to be rather difficult, and it was a good thing he wasn't too bad to look at otherwise this mission would've been fucked from the start.

The conversation started to take a turn about twenty minutes later when Ben's speech started to slur more than it already had been when he placed himself next to me, and his statements started to piss me off. I let the bar atmosphere cover the moment his body started to go limp, his head drooping slightly, his eyes blinking sluggishly.

Sending a quick **"SOS"** to Zina through text, I babysat Ben who wasn't completely unconscious right then—just too disoriented to resist. I needed to make a scene, but one where the others within the bar wouldn't be alarmed.

"Ben, hey—are you okay?" I asked, stroking his shoulder like a concerned lover. To everyone else, it just looked like a drunk guy with his girlfriend or date. Ben tried to respond, drooling a little, his words absolute nonsense.

Zina, who still had no idea what I was really planning, helped prop Ben up. "He's wasted," Zina sighed, playing along.

"Well, this is a bar and he was drinking," I quipped as we lifted him off the stool. Zina tossed me a "no shit" kind of look. "I'll get him home." I attempted to sound promising as we propped him on our shoulders.

Zenith's newest bouncer, Gordon, glanced over as we passed.

"Be right back," Zina promised him. Seeing a woman and his boss helping the woman's 'boyfriend' out of the bar was nothing suspicious, so he turned a blind eye.

As soon as Zina and I positioned Ben into my Mercedes, we buckled him in, ensuring he wouldn't fall over. I hoped he wouldn't puke on the way to my house. I didn't need more mess to clean up than I'd have later

"I hope you know what you're doin'," Zina said, skeptical of my plans for Ben.

I pulled her into my arms, and she returned the embrace. I wished I could tell her what I was doing . . . what I'd already done for her and I, but the less she knew, the better.

"Don't worry," I assured her, holding onto the sides of her shoulders. "He won't remember a thing." I made my way around to the driver's seat. "Thanks for your help. I love you."

"I love you, too," Zina replied, crossing her arms around

herself.

Zina and I had an unspoken agreement: I'd let her in just enough to keep her from asking the dangerous questions, and she'd look the other way on the finer details. Though, most of the time, she liked to push that boundary. It wasn't perfect, but it worked—our own little balancing act. I'd feed her fragments, bits of truth wrapped up in lies or half-explanations, just enough to keep her satisfied. She never pressed for more than I offered, and for that, I was grateful. The less she knew, the safer she was. For her own sake, there were things she was better off not understanding. A fragile arrangement, one I occasionally felt guilty for exploiting, but Zina wasn't blind. She knew the game we were playing, even if she didn't know the rules in full. And yet, she helped me anyway. Whether it was out of loyalty to Qualley and Lonney or something closer to love for me, I wasn't sure. Maybe both.

From the rear-view mirror, I noticed her standing there watching me. Though it was dark, I saw that worried face she gave me, similar to the one she gave when I passed out from mono many years ago.

Who wouldn't be concerned after being an accessory to drugging someone, and soon, murder, or watching your best friend spiral, making secret plans and avoiding your presence? The only feeling I felt when it came to my best friend was sorrow.

Sorrow for her loss of Lonney.

Sorrow for putting her through these roller coaster of emotions with all my sneaking around.

Sorrow because this was the last time I'd see Zina as a free woman and had to act like I'd see her tomorrow.

Sorrow that she'd have to learn her best friend is a killer.

By the time Zina noticed Ben's absence from the bar he liked to frequent, I'd be gone.

Chapter 29

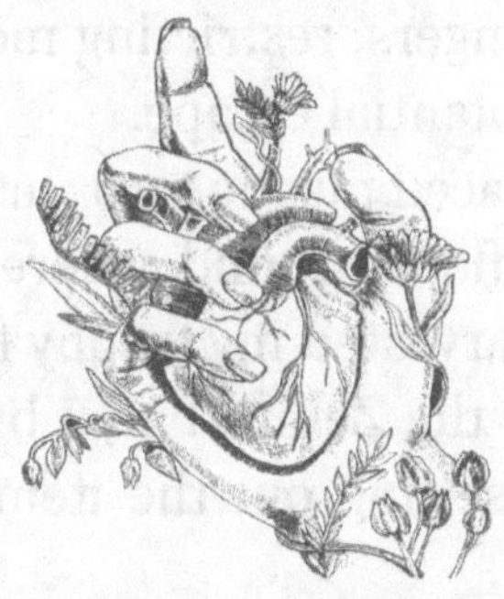

Reaching my house, Ben was barely aware of his surroundings. He fumbled as I pulled him out of the car, nearly falling onto the pavement and taking me with him. Thankfully, he was still somewhat cognizant, so I hoisted his arm over my shoulder and dragged him inside. Adrenaline pumped through my veins, making it easier to carry him, and I thanked myself for doing those extra arm workouts this month.

A chair sat prepared in the guest room, as cold and impersonal as it needed to be—plain beige walls, recessed lighting from the ceiling casting harsh, unflattering light over the space. No decorations, no distractions. Just the chair, bolted firmly to the hardwood floor at the center of the room, and a small side table stacked with carefully selected tools and restraints. The faint smell of bleach lingered, a scent becoming all too familiar. This was a room stripped of anything human, designed for one purpose.

The drugs, combined with the alcohol in his system, would keep him under for hours, giving me more than enough time to prepare.

Ben practically fell into the chair and I worked to position him, maneuvering his limp weight with proficient efficiency. He was slumped over like a rag doll, and I could feel the warmth of his body against mine, heavy and uncooperative. Multiple leather, belt-like straps pinned Ben's arms, legs, and torso into place. I stuck extra straps around his forehead because I'd be damned if he tried to head-butt me when he woke up. Duct tape wrapped around his fingers, restricting movement, and preventing the capability of potential escape.

Once secured, I placed plastic tarps around the area to cover the perimeter of the floor around where Ben sat. It made for easy clean up once I harvested my trophy from his body.

Before arriving to the Zenith bar, I brought my rolling tray into the guest room, setting out the items I'd need to kill Ben Prout.

As the girlfriend of a late drug lord, I always kept my distance from Qualley's business dealings, steering clear of the mayhem that surrounded him. But Lonney's programs—his knack for slipping past network hurdles and finding people most wouldn't dare approach—had left me with tools I couldn't pass up. Using what he'd built, I tracked down someone who could provide exactly what I needed: a combination of drugs to create a makeshift lethal injection. It wasn't easy, but desperation has a way of sharpening your focus.

The thing I loved most about drug suppliers: they didn't ask questions so long as you paid the price. That price just happened to be a collective forty-five thousand dollars for all three drugs.

Some may have simply passed away spending that much to murder someone, but to me, the termination of the team who took Qualley away out of my life was priceless. I'd give up everything to see them hanged in the streets.

Next to the drugs, I'd placed my trusty scalpel and bolt cutters, freshly sanitized after being soaked in Lile Henderson's blood. They sat beneath a hand towel, hidden from view. People tended to freak out when they saw knives—something primal about the glint of the blade and the promise of pain. So, for now, they would stay concealed, waiting for their moment.

Beside it, a box of black latex gloves rested on the table and I pulled a few out, laying them neatly beside the other tools. I wasn't worried about fingerprints—no one would find Ben's body, let alone trace it back to me until I was ready. But the smell of blood? That was harder to scrub away. Evan Matthews's murder had taught me that much. His death had been messy, chaotic, and far too personal. I wouldn't make the same mistake with Ben.

I glanced at him slumping, unconscious. His head lolled to the side, breathing slow and shallow, the drugs and alcohol working together to keep him under. He looked so harmless like this, so pitiful. It almost made me laugh.

The truth was, I didn't hate Ben—not the way I hated the others. During that fateful raid, he'd stuck to the plan, refusing to shoot anyone. For that, I had a sliver of respect for him, but respect wasn't enough to save him. He was a coward, plain and simple. A coward who'd let James Hall blackmail him into silence, who'd planted evidence and paid off false witnesses instead of standing up for the truth. He could've vindicated Qualley and Lonney, could've saved his own life. But he didn't. And now, his cowardice would kill him.

I reached for the roll of silver duct tape in the dresser beside me, pulling it out with a sharp rip. The drawer held other supplies I might need—my .22 pistol with suppressor, loaded with untraceable bullets. I checked it briefly, the weight of it familiar in my hand, before setting it back down and sliding the drawer shut.

My rolling chair jerked as I sat, wheels squeaking against the hardwood floor. I rolled over to the bed where I'd placed my handbag, pulling out my phone to check the time: one thirty in the morning.

I texted Zina, telling her we'd arrived at his place, and sending her the address. **"Save it just in case,"** I wrote, though I assured her I'd be gone the moment he was asleep. I added a lie about being busy at the gallery tomorrow, hoping it would keep her from poking her nose into this mess. The last thing I needed was for her to get involved. It would be a shame to have to kill my best friend, especially not this close to the end.

I turned off my phone, tucking it back into my handbag and hiding it under the bed. Then, while Ben was still incapacitated, I rifled through his pockets, pulling out his phone and wallet. They joined the pistol in the drawer, untouched. I didn't care about his money or his contacts. The only thing I wanted from Ben beat inside his chest. His belongings would be buried with him, just like the others.

Everything was ready. The three needles sat lined up on the table, filled with the concoction I'd carefully prepared. The anesthetic would keep him unaware, his body paralyzed as it shut down. It was a merciful death, all things considered. I wasn't heartless—not entirely.

I rose from the rolling stool, grabbing my book off the dresser. The chair in the corner caught my eye—Qualley's favorite. It was a deep, worn leather armchair that had softened over time, molding itself to his shape like it belonged to him alone. The arms were slightly scuffed, the rich, dark brown fading where his hands had rested countless times. It was as much a relic of him as anything else left in this house, a piece of him I hadn't been able to let go of.

Settling into the chair, it was like sitting in his shadow, enveloped in the memory of him. He used to lean back here, drink in hand, with that signature smirk on his face that made you feel like he knew something you didn't. The kind of smirk that made you believe he was invincible. Closing my eyes for a brief moment, I could almost imagine him here, as if his presence was stitched into the very fibers of the chair.

A pang of something distinct but fleeting hit me, grief maybe, or guilt. *What would he think if he could see me now, using this same space, this same chair, for something so far removed from the life we shared? Would he be proud, or horrified?* I didn't linger on that thought for long. The 'what if's' weren't something I could afford to carry despite my fortune.

Opening a book, I placed the bookmark between my fingers, though my eyes weren't really on the pages. My mind kept drifting back to Ben, slumped unconscious across the room. I'd gone through this process enough times to know what came next: the groggy confusion, the slow dawning realization of where he was, the fear. And then the words—pleading, bargaining, maybe even screaming if he could muster the strength. I'd let him speak, let him say whatever he thought might save him, but there'd be no saving himself.

"What will you say, Ben?" I mumbled to myself. "What pathetic excuse will tumble out of your mouth when you realize it's already too late?"

I gripped the book harder, the edges of the cover pressing into my palms. I needed to stay calm, composed. There was no room for chaos here, not like with Evan or Lile. Ben deserved a cleaner death—not out of kindness, but because the mess would serve no purpose. The anesthetic would do most of the work— he'd feel nothing, slipping into paralysis before his heart stopped. Efficient. Uncomplicated. Still, I knew it wouldn't stop the words, the accusations, or the weight of it all pressing down on me.

Corpses were easier. They didn't argue, didn't plead, didn't force me to confront the moral gymnastics of what I was doing. But the living . . . they were harder. Ben would wake, and I'd have to look him in the eyes and deliver the truth—or my version of it—before it all ended.

I let out a breath, forcing my gaze back to the book. I needed to stay focused, to let the quiet of the house and the comfort of Qualley's chair hold me together until it was time.

Shifting slightly, the leather croaked beneath me, and I glanced, again, toward Ben. I rose from the chair, crossing the room to inspect the tray I'd prepared earlier. But as I bent down, something caught my eye—tucked beneath his coat, half-hidden under his thigh.

A flash drive.

I plucked it free, turning it over between my fingers. No markings. No label. Just smooth, matte plastic. A strange sensation settled in my chest—curiosity, yes, but also unease. Things like this didn't feel random.

I crossed back to Qualley's armchair and reached for my laptop nestled in the side drawer. The laptop wasn't connected to the internet—never had been. It was strictly for things I didn't want traced, a relic of Lonney's paranoia that I'd inherited. I almost smiled at the memory of him lecturing me about "digital footprints" and "unnecessary risks." *What would he call this— necessary?*

The screen lit up, casting a pale glow across the room. I plugged in the drive, my fingers steady despite the adrenaline coursing through me.

Three folders appeared on the screen.

/OBSERVATIONS
/PHOTOS
/VOICE_LOGS

I clicked *OBSERVATIONS* first, the cursor hovering for a moment before I pressed down. The folder opened, revealing a series of text files. I clicked the first one, and the words spilled across the screen like a punch to the gut.

TARGET: "CASSANDRA K."
Initial contact: Zenith's Bar, 4 weeks ago. Subject friendly. Approachable. Possible seduction tactics.
Theory: Cassandra is responsible for Evan Matthews and Lile Henderson's disappearances. No forced entries. No signs of struggle.

Well, *shit.*

Words blurred for a moment as my mind raced. Four weeks ago. Zenith's Bar. *That was when Ben first approached me, wasn't it?* Friendly, charming, a little too eager to strike up a conversation. I'd thought it was coincidence, a chance encounter. But now, staring at the screen, it was clear he'd been watching me long before that night.

We were both there to stake each other.

I wondered what Ben's termination meant if he was undercover. *Was it dependent on what Ben found out about Evan and Lile's disappearances? How could they possibly suspect me?*

I crushed the flash drive beneath my foot into a dozen pieces, flushing them down the toilet.

From across the dimly lit room, Ben stirred within my periphery. He attempted a sharp inhale, but what followed was a long, shaky exhale. The drugs were wearing off, but the paralysis clung to his limbs, making his movements sluggish. His fingers twitched and jerked, wrists strained, arms pulled, but the leather straps held firm. Then, he moved his legs—or at least, he tried to.

I smirked, leaning back into the armchair across the room, a glass of red wine cradled in my hand. I always preferred watching them realize they're fucked; the first spark of confusion, the realization, the terror. I watched Ben let out another ragged breath, his eyes scanning the room. He took in the high ceilings, the towering bookshelves, the grand chandelier overhead: a mansion, not a basement. This wasn't some dingy hideout. It was a home.

"Wha—" Ben's voice was hoarse, his tongue thick in his mouth. "What the hell is this?" He narrowed his eyes, squeezing them a few times, and searching around the room again as if that would make his vision better.

Popping up out of my armchair I made my way over to park myself in front of Ben, crouching down before him. I offered him a shit-eating grin. "I was beginning to think you'd sleep forever."

He jerked at his restraints, testing them, but I secured them well. Not that I had any doubt that they would fail. His gaze fell to the tray, his face paling. Clarity was blooming into his field of vision.

"Crimson, listen—" he started, panic creeping into his tone.

"If you haven't already guessed, I'm not who you think I am . . ." I said, expression hardening into a scowl wiping away any pretense of friendliness. "And considering what I found," I held up a piece of the flash drive that I'd saved, "you *know* that's not who I am. So quit the act."

He looked at me in surprise, then confusion, and finally, the realization hit him like a freight train. His eyes widened as he took in the room, the restraints, and, most importantly, me.

"Cassandra?" he asked, as if my name itself was a revelation. "Kessler? Oh! Oh . . . shit."

"Impressive," I said, winking at him as I stood up, turning to grab my rolling tray and seat. "I was starting to think your reputation as unit dunce was true."

Rolling the tray closer, the faint squeak of the wheels cut through silence. His attention darted to the tray, then back to me, his face paling as clarity began to bloom. I could see the gears turning in his head, the panic continued setting in.

"You've been busy, haven't you, Ben?" I said, snapping on a pair of black latex gloves. "Carrying around little secrets in your pocket, thinking no one would notice."

His lips parted, but no words came out. I leaned forward, my gloved fingers brushing the edge of the tray as I locked eyes with him.

"That flash drive," I continued, "what's on it. Observations. Photos. Voice logs. You've been keeping tabs on me, haven't you?"

Ben's breathing quickened, his chest rising and falling in uneven bursts. "I—I wasn't spying," he stammered, his voice cracking. "It's not what you think—"

"Oh, it's exactly what I think," I said, my smirk returning. "You've been watching me. Following me. Writing your little reports, taking your little pictures. Did you think I wouldn't find out?"

His eyes darted around the room. "I was just doing my job." His voice was barely above a whisper. "I didn't mean—"

"Your job?" I snapped, cutting through his excuses. "Your job was to cover up the truth. To protect people who pulled the trigger. To bury Qualley and Lonney's names under a pile of lies. And now, because of that, you're here. I found you *first*. And now you're strapped to a chair."

"I didn't have a choice! James—he made me do it. He threatened me. I didn't want to—" Ben's face twisted in desperation, his voice trembling as he tried to reason with me.

"Save it," I said coldly, cutting him off. "You think I don't know that? You still had a choice, Ben. You could've told the truth. You could've stood up for what was right. But instead, you chose to be a coward."

I straightened up, grabbing the first syringe from the tray and holding it up to the light. The clear liquid glinted in the dim glow of the chandelier.

"You know," I mused, "I wanted to make this last longer. Make it hurt. But I'm feeling generous tonight. You'll get a peaceful death, Ben. Consider it my final act of mercy."

He thrashed against the restraints, his voice rising in a panicked plea. "Please, Cassandra—don't do this. I can help you. I—I have a daughter. She needs me!"

I'd known about his daughter for months. Her name, her day care, even the way she liked her peanut butter sandwiches cut into triangles. But he didn't know that I knew, and I wasn't about to let him off the hook so easily.

"A daughter?" I echoed; my tone laced with mock curiosity. "How sweet. And *now* you're thinking about her? Now, when you're strapped to a chair, begging for your life? How noble of you, Ben."

His face crumpled; desperation etched into every line. "She's innocent! She doesn't deserve this—please, Cassandra, I'll do anything!"

I leaned in closer, my smirk malevolent. "Anything?" I repeated. "Funny, because I don't recall you doing 'anything' to save Qualley or Lonney. I don't recall you doing 'anything' to stop James Hall from tearing apart everything I cared about. But now, suddenly, you care? Spare me."

Ben's breathing quickened, his chest heaving as he struggled against the restraints. "I didn't have a choice! Hall—he threatened me. He made me do it!"

I straightened, crossing my arms as I studied him. "And yet, here you are, all alone. No backup. No James swooping in to save you. Makes me wonder . . ." I let the words hang, watching the flicker of fear in his eyes. "*Does* he really know you're here? Or were you just trying to play detective, hoping to win his approval?"

Ben's lips trembled. "I was working alone tonight, yes. He doesn't know—he doesn't know anything about this."

I chuckled softly, shaking my head. "Of course he doesn't. Because you're not just a coward, Ben. You're expendable."

He flinched at my words, his gaze darting to the tray beside me. His panic was wonderous, the realization sinking in that there was no escape.

"You know," I said gently, "I've been thinking about your daughter. About what she'll grow up to be without you around. And you know what I realized?" I paused, watching for his reaction. "She'll be better off. Better off without a father who lies, cheats, and sells his soul to protect murderers."

Ben's eyes widened, his breath catching in his throat.

I smiled. "Oh, Ben. I know everything. But don't fret. I'm not in the business of killing babies."

The latex gloves sipped on easily, and I got to work prepping my injections. One might wonder how an artist learned the ways of phlebotomy. Well, I had once been around drug dealers and users, and I learn visually. Besides, it's not like I had to worry about infections or air bubbles or other dangerous outcomes. I'd kill him anyway.

Ben realized what I was doing and started babbling. "I—I know you're mad, but I wasn't the one who shot him."

Turning my head in his direction, I continued to work as we spoke. "You think this is just about the trigger being pulled?"

I could swear I heard Ben's heartbeat pounding in his ears. "Lile and Evan, they—they were reckless," he stammered. "I tried to keep things clean. That's why I didn't take credit. That's why I didn't—"

I sighed, reaching for the tourniquet as I finished with my needles. "That's why you're here." I got up from my seat to stand at his side, leaning into him so I could whisper in his ear. I began to wrap the strap around his arm. "You covered it up, when you could've easily told the truth. Funny thing is, in retrospect, your team should've killed *me*. Qualley would've never done something like this."

My fingers worked with delicate and careful precision as I wrapped the band around his arm, pulling it tight. Ben thrashed, the chair creaking under his weight.

"No—NO! Cassandra, please—"

"Gosh, you're much louder than the others. Scream for me, Ben!" I moaned, rolling myself and the tray of drugs over to his side, and grabbing his arm. He had nice veins, and I found them with ease.

Ben started to thrash around as I brought the first needle to his flesh. "Please . . . please!" He cried out, straining his muscles as if he was strong enough to break through my leather restraints. I was able to work with his movement and the needle pierced his skin. Ben sucked in a sharp breath. I slowly pushed the plunger down, watching as the clear liquid disappeared into his bloodstream.

"In the end," I explained, grinning and brushing a strand of hair from his sweaty forehead. "You still don't deserve my time, but I'm willing to make you comfortable. And by the time this anesthetic flows into your veins, you'll be unaware of your impending paralysis and your upcoming heart attack."

A sick, garbled sound escaped his lips. "C-Cassandra—"

"Don't worry," I said, sticking a new piece of duct tape to muffle his cries and screams. He was giving me a fucking headache. "I'll take good care of your heart once it stops beating."

He still attempted to yell through the tape, which muffled his cries. The second syringe rested in my palm and I rubbed his forearm, soothing his nerves.

"Shh. It's just a paralytic. I promised this wouldn't hurt."

He gasped for air that wouldn't come, and I felt his muscles lock, and heartbeat slow. Surprising since the last injection wasn't administered as of yet, and this would be the one to stop his heart completely. He couldn't move at all, the paralysis drug making quick work.

His eyes fluttered, but I could see him watching me. According to my research, his vision should be darkening at the edges, as his heart thudded sluggishly in his chest.

Sighing, I placed the last needle between my fingertips. "I'll make sure they find you . . . eventually. I've got one more thing to do before then."

A tear fell from his eye, and I took some time to lick it off of his face. I don't know what compelled me to do something like that again, but Ben's tears tasted so much better than Lile's putrid blood. Salty, yes, but still pleasant.

Ben could no longer respond with speech or movement, so I removed the tape from his mouth as a courtesy—not that anyone would hear him scream for help. His eyes closed, and I took my time administering my last, most fatal injection. Pulling the syringe out, I set it neatly back onto the tray.

Ben's head lolled against the head restraint, eyes glassy, lips parted just slightly like he was about to speak—but he wouldn't. Not anymore. The syringe dangled from his arm, still trembling slightly from the final push. I watched the last bubbles float in the chamber, watched the life drain from his face like paint rinsed from a brush.

Then, with arctic precision, I wandered over to the dresser and removed my knife.

The chair creaked as I stood, my boots echoing across the hardwood. I stepped into the bathroom down the hall, flicking on the light with the back of my wrist. I leaned over the sink, catching my reflection in the warped medicine cabinet mirror. A smear of eyeliner had betrayed me—sweat, maybe, or a tear I didn't remember shedding. My composure had slipped for only a second, but that wasn't acceptable. Not tonight.

On the counter, a container of cosmetics sat, and I pulled a black eyeliner out to repair my destroyed makeup. I lifted the knife, angled the blade toward my cheek, and let the point hover under my lower lid. With a clean drag, the wing of my eyeliner sharpened back into place, one flick at a time. The blade knew its place. Just like Ben should've known his.

In the reflection of the knife, my gaze met itself.

One more gone.

One step closer.

I walked back toward the corpse chilling in the chair. I didn't feel guilt. I didn't feel anything.

Just the rush of a job well done.

Chapter 30

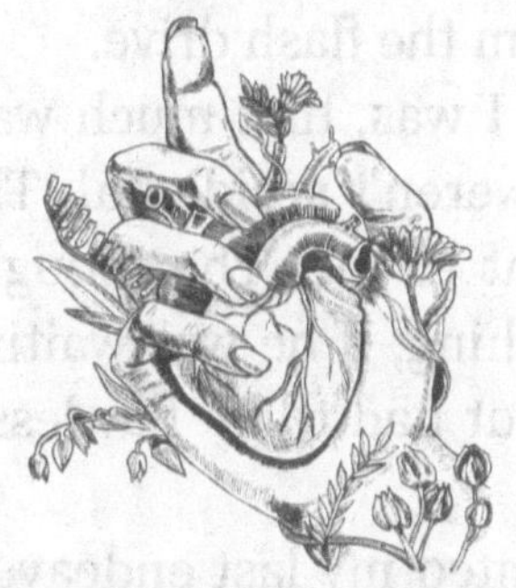

A brand-new mason jar, dripping with blood, sat on my tray. Ben Prout's heart floated motionlessly within it, the crimson liquid whirling as I adjusted it. I worked quickly to duct tape the long incision I'd made along his chest, sealing the cavity where I'd stored the vials of drugs used to euthanize him. The tape wasn't perfect, but it would hold long enough. Not that Ben was in any position to complain about shoddy craftsmanship.

I stood, stepping over Ben's lifeless body. The air was thick with the copper scent of death, the candlelight cast long shapes across the walls. I reached for the jar, holding it up to the light and surveying Ben's heart inside. It was smaller than I'd expected, almost underwhelming. But it wasn't the size that mattered —it was the message. And this one? Oh, it screamed.

I'd collected them all, the whole set, and yet, something gnawed at me. A seed of doubt planted by what I'd found on Ben's flash drive. The folders, the photos, the voice logs—they'd been meticulous, damning. But they'd also been incomplete. There were gaps, questions left unanswered. *Had Ben been working alone, as he claimed? Or was James Hall pulling the strings from the shadows, waiting for the right moment to strike?*

Exhaustion crept in, but I refused to let it settle. There was too much to do before sunrise, too many loose ends to tie up. I placed the jar back down and turned to Ben's body, grabbing the plastic tarp. As I hunched over to wrap him, my mind raced, replaying the details from the flash drive.

James knew who I was, that much was clear. Breadcrumbs Ben had left behind weren't accidental. They were trails meant to lead James straight to me. The thought made my stomach churn. If he was watching, if he was waiting, then every move I made from here on out had to be flawless. There was no room for error.

Especially if I wanted my last endeavor to go down without miscalculation.

Casting my worries aside until later, I dragged Ben's body through the hallway and into the kitchen, the tarp sliding smoothly over the floor. But as I reached the back door, I hesitated, my grip tightening on the tarp. *What if James wasn't just watching? What if he was planning something of his own?* Paranoia clawed at me; each question more suffocating than the last.

Fuck! I had to focus, so I shook the thoughts away.

The six-step wooden staircase loomed ahead, a potential disaster waiting to happen. I could drag him across the deck easily enough, and Ben's head slammed against each step as I carefully maneuvered down, the dull thuds echoing in the quiet night. I winced at the sound, glancing over my shoulder to ensure no one was watching. Once I reached the grass, I exhaled in relief. He was still secure, though he'd slid toward me slightly.

"Sorry about the stairs, Ben," I said, half-smirking. "Guess I'm not as gentle as I used to be."

I made my way toward the woods in the direction of my studio and the trench where the others rested, rotting. The thought of leaving Ben's body there, pouring dirt over the grave, and planting blood-red roses in Qualley's memory was tempting. The bodies would make excellent fertilizer. But Ben's information changed everything. My plan needed to adapt, and that meant keeping the bodies accessible—for now.

A light dusting of snow had settled on top of the blue tarp, and I swept it off with the broom I'd left nearby. Folding the tarp back revealed the trench below. The cold preserved the bodies somewhat, but the stench was still awful. Evan, killed two weeks ago, smelled the worst, I supposed. Lile, a week into his decay, wasn't much better. Ben would join them, his secrets buried alongside him—at least for now.

I slid Ben toward the edge of the grave, crouching down to look into his vacant eyes. "You always wanted recognition, Ben," I murmured, my voice soft, almost affectionate. "Well . . . now you'll be remembered."

With a grunt of effort, I shoved his body over the edge, into the rotting pile of Evan and Lile beneath him. A dull, wet thud echoed through the woods as he landed. I kicked the bloody tarp in after him, watching it settle over their pale, soulless faces.

"Tell Qualley I said hello . . . Oh, who am I kidding? You wouldn't even get past the gates to wherever he is. They don't allow cowards in."

I cackled at myself, but as I began to cover the grave, a new thought struck me—one that sent a chill down my spine. James wasn't just waiting for me to slip up. He was planning something of his own. Ben's information had been incomplete, yes, but the gaps felt intentional, leading me toward a trap.

I clenched my jaw, my hands trembling as I placed the bricks back around the tarp. If James thought he could outmaneuver me, he was sorely mistaken. I'd tip the police when the time was right, ensure they found me, the bodies, and the clues I'd left behind. But first, I needed to deal with James directly. He was the real threat; the one loose end I couldn't afford to leave dangling.

As I made my way back to the house, the mason jar waiting for me on the tray, a new plan began to take shape. Ben's death had been necessary but wasn't enough to complete my healing.

If I wanted to send a message, I needed to go bigger, bolder. And James? He'd be at the center of it.

 Killing Evan, Lile, and Ben had their moments, sure—there was a certain satisfaction in the precision, the artistry of it all. But destroying James Hall? That would be a masterpiece.

Chapter 31

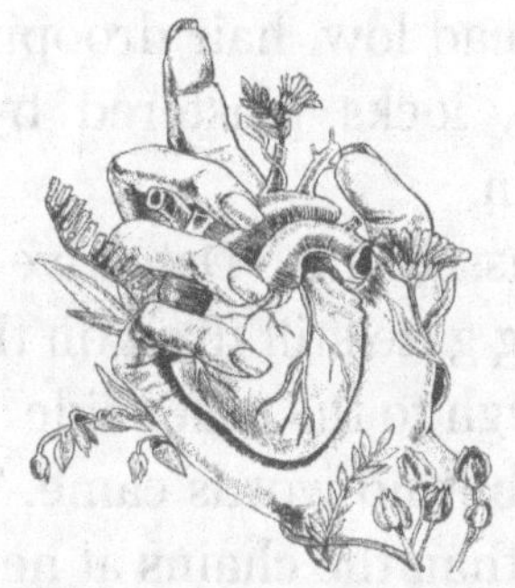

Detective James Hall

The metal chair screeched against the linoleum floor as Cassandra Kessler threw her weight back, kicking out her legs violently. The cuffs on her wrists clanked against the table, sending hollow echoes through the cramped interrogation room. Her curly red hair was a mess of snarled knots, caked with dirt and streaked with debris.

"You think you're so clever, don't you?" she spat as she inclined toward the two-way glass. "Sitting there, watching me like I'm some damn show!"

Her breath fogged the glass as her eyes bore into its surface. Her pupils were wide, shadowed, as if the flickering fluorescent light overhead couldn't touch them. She barked out a laugh—sharp, deranged—before slamming her palms against the table, the cuffs digging into her skin.

"Why don't you just come in here, huh? Afraid of me, James? You should be!" Her voice cracked mid-shout, though it didn't dull the malice in her tone. "You think dragging me out of my own backyard makes you a big man? You think it means you've won?"

Her head snapped to the side, strands hair clinging to her cheek, as if she'd heard something the others in the room couldn't. Then, without warning, her shoulders slumped, her body folding inward like the fight had been siphoned out of her all at once. She hung her head low, hair drooping into messy chunks in front of her face, locks plastered by the snow and dirt smeared along her skin.

Thirty minutes passed since Detective James Hall exited the room, but her piercing gaze still fixed on the two-way glass, as if she saw straight through to the other side. Her lips twitched—almost imperceptibly—but no words came. The sudden silence in the room felt heavier than the chains at her wrists. The fight was gone from her movements, but it was there in her eyes—conniving, ready.

James had left Cassandra in the room to formulate another plan to get more information out of her. Psychosis had started to take hold, and she sunk further into a two-faced madness James didn't know how to manipulate. She was completely off-center—her behavior warping rapidly, more intense and maniacal than that she'd arrived at the precinct with hours prior. It was as if she developed two personalities: one who convened her actions as a result of her ploy for revenge, the second, spoke in tongues, manifesting random outbursts that ended with thrashing and screaming.

Cassandra's crimes were some of the worst James had ever seen in his thirty years on the force. In fact, because the crimes were so brutal, and it had been his team slain, he was desperate for answers, even the minute details. James just wanted to understand. *What would lead her to that place, down a morally forbidden road?*

Three Murders, ripping their hearts out as she left—literally.

James leaned against the doorway of the interrogation room, his shoulders slumped, tie loosened just enough to suggest he'd given up on looking professional hours ago. His eyes were red-rimmed from a two-day sleep drought, but he didn't seem to notice—or care. Not when Cassandra Kessler sat just feet away, her hair plastered against her face like some demented mask, staring through the two-way glass with an unnerving stillness.

James made coffee as he prepared new questions for his next session with Cassandra; the fourth cup of his twenty-four, technically, forty-eight-hour shift if you count the time he's been on the premises. He was thankful to have a coffee maker in the room, avoiding the walk back to his office to make some. He wanted to avoid getting distracted with other various interruptions.

"You look like hell, James," Officer Neil Beckett said as he approached through the door, a half-hearted attempt at humor. "Not that that's anything new."

James didn't respond immediately, his gaze locked on Cassandra's faint reflection in the glass. "You guys talk to her yet?" he asked finally, his voice gravelly and strained.

Beckett shook his head. "She scares the hell out of us. We figured you'd handle it better—this is your thing, right? These psychos."

James snorted, taking a long sip of his coffee. It burned his throat, but at least it gave him something to focus on that wasn't Cassandra's lifeless stare. "Yeah, my thing," he echoed. "What does that even mean?"

Beckett shifted awkwardly. "It means you're the guy who figures them out. You don't flinch, don't crack. Hell, James, you don't even go home." The last comment stuck with James for a beat too long, and Beckett cleared his throat. "Speaking of which, you should call Lynda. She's was blowing up the station phone earlier asking for you way before we brought in Kessler. She even tried Fieldman."

"Did she leave a message?"

"No, but—"

James waved the suggestion away like it was an irritating fly. "She'll be fine," he said gruffly. "She always is."

Beckett frowned. "She called twice. Doesn't sound fine to me."

"She knows how I work," James shot back. "If it's urgent, she'll leave a message."

"Man, the way you 'work' is gonna cost you someday. Maybe not your sanity—but probably your marriage."

James turned to Beckett, finally peeling his gaze away from Cassandra's motionless form. His expression was measured, his tone firm. "Marriage isn't my focus right now, Beckett—not when we're dealing with this. She's murdered three men that we know of, possibly more. And based on her patterns, she could have had plans for others. Perhaps conspirators. Calling the police on herself? That's calculated, not impulsive. She left enough evidence to implicate herself, yet she's sitting in there like none of it touches her. My priority is to extract the truth from every detail, every motive. I don't have time to answer personal calls, and if I need marriage counseling, Beckett, I'll see a counselor, not *you*."

Beckett raised his hands in surrender. "Alright, alright. I get it. But seriously, James, don't let her get under your skin. You're a good detective, but you've got a habit of taking these cases too personally."

James laughed bitterly, like it had been dredged from the depths of his exhaustion. "Too personally? Beckett, she didn't just kill our coworkers. She made it personal the moment she dragged them into that hole and stared back at us like she's daring us to figure out why."

Before Beckett could respond, a sudden shout erupted from the interrogation room, loud enough to make both men flinch. "You think I care about what you think, Jamesey?" Cassandra's voice sliced through the quiet like a blade, her tone rising with each syllable. "You sit out there, hiding behind glass like you've got me all figured out—well, you don't! You're next! You never will!"

James's jaw tightened as he turned toward the glass, his coffee cup forgotten in his grip. Cassandra was on her feet now, kicking at the table, her wrists jerking against the cuffs. Her wild hair framed her face like an untamed storm, her eyes blazing as she glared into the glass. "You're all just puppets, dancing for the truth you'll never find! You think you're better than me? You think you're smarter? You're nothing!"

Beckett took a step back, visibly unsettled by the sheer ferocity radiating from the other side of the glass. "Yeah . . . you might have a point about her making it personal," he said.

James didn't even glance at Beckett. His eyes were locked on Cassandra, his expression unreadable. "She wants *us* to take it personally, too," he said quietly, more to himself than anyone else. "She wants us to react, to lose control, because that's when she wins."

Cassandra let out a sharp, mocking laugh, her voice echoing through the room. "Go ahead, James! Take your notes, build your little case. But you'll never understand me—not really. That's why you'll always lose. That's why they'll never trust you."

James lowered his coffee cup slowly, his gaze hardening. "You're wrong about one thing, Cassandra," he muttered under his breath, his voice low and dangerous. "I don't lose."

Beckett cleared his throat awkwardly, shifting on his feet as Cassandra's laughter faded into silence. "Well . . . she's definitely trying to get under your skin."

James straightened, taking a deep breath as he finally turned to Beckett. "And that's why I won't let her. She's calculating, Beckett. Everything she says and does—it's all a game to her. But I'm not playing."

"Yeah . . . sure," Beckett said, unconvinced.

James took another long sip of coffee, his jaw tightening as he turned back to the glass. Cassandra hadn't moved—not an inch—but her presence filled the room, suffocating and deliberate. "You know what the worst part is?" James added quietly, almost to himself. "She wants us to figure it out. Wants us to see every twisted detail of what she did—and what she's planning next."

Beckett didn't respond, didn't dare interrupt the silence that followed. Instead, he clapped James on the shoulder and left the room, leaving him to his coffee, his thoughts, and the lunatic behind the glass.

James's knuckles whitened against the cup. He wasn't going home—not tonight, not anytime soon. Not until Cassandra Kessler's secrets were laid bare, her twisted mind unraveled thread by thread. He'd sleep in his office again if he had to. Because people were right—his investigations were usually successful. And with Cassandra? He couldn't afford to fail.

☙ ❧

James Hall enters the interrogation room slowly, his footsteps heavy against the tile floor. There's a stillness in the air, the kind that lingers after a storm—after Cassandra's outburst, her manic laughter. She doesn't flinch, and sits motionless, her wrists chained to the table, head tilted slightly downward. The only movement is her fingers, tracing lazy, invisible patterns onto the steel.

James exhaled slowly, steadying himself. He'd spent years interrogating killers, seen the worst humanity had to offer, but Cassandra Kessler was something else entirely. She wasn't like the others. There was no telltale remorse masked by bravado; no misplaced righteousness dressed up as justification. She was a puzzle with pieces that didn't quite fit—an enigma, scattered and jagged, designed to cut anyone who dared try to solve her.

And then there was what she'd said, slipping it in randomly like he'd miss it with all the other words she spoke.

You're next.

It shouldn't have rattled him, not after everything he'd heard in this line of work—empty threats from people desperate to feel powerful in a losing game, but this felt different. Cassandra's words didn't carry desperation, they were calm, cool, and unafraid like she wasn't bluffing. He had no doubts about that.

Leaning against the table, his fingers drummed absently against the surface as the thought gnawed at the edges of his mind. He didn't scare easily, but the timing of her words, the way she'd spat them with venomous precision, made him wonder how much she really knew about him, more than she's already revealed, more than he was comfortable with. That much was certain. *And if she did know more, what did that mean for him? For everyone around him?*

Cassandra had butchered three men, left clues behind, and called the police on herself, then sat in a chair as though she were untouchable. Maybe she was—at least in ways that mattered only to her. She didn't seem to care that we had her locked up. She didn't care that the evidence against her was damning. All she cared about, it seemed, was James Hall and the message she was trying to send.

But what message? That's what he couldn't shake. *What was he missing? Was she trying to provoke him, unnerve him just enough to make him falter? Or was it more than that? Was he truly next—not just metaphorically, but literally?* The questions settled over him like a lead weight, a silent challenge issued from the other side of the glass.

He didn't have the luxury of ignoring her words. She hadn't wasted anything—not her actions, her choices, or her words. And if she said he was next . . . he believed her.

Attempting to adjust his tie, his fingers felt stiff. As he pulled out his chair, the metal scrapes against the floor. Cassandra's head lifts just a fraction, her lips curling into a small, predatory smile.

"Took you long enough," Cassandra murmured. She bit the cuticle of her fingertip but remained in her hunched position as she spoke. James didn't respond right away, but instead, watched her; the way her pupils dilated slightly as she looked up at him; the way she shifted forward, as if this game—is what she lived for.

Finally, James sat, folding his hands in front of him, spinning his wedding ring on his finger to keep himself from wringing her neck.

"Tell me about the hearts," James ordered, slanting forward slightly, swallowing hard. He kept his voice measured and free of too much emotion. "I've got to ask, out of all the ways you could've left your mark . . . why hearts? Why take *them*?"

"Finally!" She cried, smirking, eyes unblinking. "Why not? Hearts are symbolic, aren't they? The seat of life, love . . . betrayal."

"Betrayal . . ." James said, pausing. He narrowed his eyes and leaned back in his chair. "You think what we did to Qualley was betrayal? He was a criminal! Dangerous. He—"

"He was *human*," Cassandra said icily. "And he had a heart, just like the rest of you. But you tore it out of him when you stormed into his life. You killed him like he didn't matter."

James's jaw tightened but he his voice remained steady though he was growing cross. "And that's your justification for taking the hearts of the men who were doing their jobs and following my orders? You think that makes you some kind of avenger?"

"You can call me Thor if you want," she said, cocking her head slightly. "Oh, Jamesey, it's not about avenging. It's about balance. You took what mattered most to me, so I took from you. From them. Heart for a heart."

James exhaled deeply and became visibly frustrated. "You're sick, Cassandra. But you already know that, don't you?"

She nodded. "Who isn't sick? Anyway, do you like poetry, James?" Cassandra hunched over, a drawn-out, malicious grin creeping across her lips as she watched for James' reaction. Her voice was a gentle, sing-song whisper, laced with amusement and something far darker.

"Three hearts I've stolen, yet none are mine to keep.
Hidden where the past and present meet.
Where justice is blind and order stands tall,
They wait in silence, for Detective James Hall."

She observed the shift in James's expression, waiting for the realization to creep in. "Tell me, Detective," she cooed, "how strong is your heart?" Cassandra traced a fingerprint on the table and hummed before speaking again. "Three of blood, tied in fate, one by choice, the others by hate."

James frowned. "You mean the cops?"

Cassandra chuckled, shaking her head. "You're so focused on *now*, Detective. But the past—oh, the past is where the fun began. She paused as if reminiscing about something long before this.

"Are you admitting to more murders, Miss Kessler?"

"You think your boyfriends are special? I've been cleaning up messes since I was a teenager. Some filth takes longer to scrub away."

James squinted his eyes. "What messes?"

"Family matters."

"You are absolutely remorseless, aren't you?" James hunched in further, glaring into Cassandra's eyes. "Do you even know what loss feels like?"

Cassandra's face darkened as she fell back in her chair. "Are you fucking kidding me? That's why we're here, Detective. I lost people twice over. Once when they walked away, and again when I put them down."

James stilled. "Put them down?"

Shrugging, Cassandra's smirk returned. "People forget—sometimes mercy and punishment look the same." She whispered something like a song under her breath, barely audible to

James.

> *"Grandmother, mother, a man at the door,*
> *Three little bodies lay cold on the floor.*
> *One was sick, one was mean, one liked to take,*
> *Now they all rest, for their own earned sake."*

James shifted his weight, the chair beneath him creaking faintly. His fingers tapped a slow, uneven rhythm against the edge of the table, a subtle betrayal of the strain coiling in his chest. He fixed Cassandra with a measured stare, but his eyes betrayed a flicker of something deeper—uncertainty, unease.

"What was that you just said?" He hesitated for a fraction of a second, his lips pressing together in a thin line before he followed up, more directly. "Are you admitting to killing your family?"

Cassandra dropped her head further, her hair cascading over her shoulder like some macabre curtain. "Just an old song from home," she said, her tone syrupy sweet, but the smile she wore was razor sharp, enough to gut him where he sat.

James stiffened, his pulse pounding in his ears. Holy shit. *Was this a confession? A clue? Or worse—was she baiting him?* He couldn't afford to assume. If Cassandra Kessler was tied to the Queens murders he'd found out about when researching her, then his work wasn't just about Evan, Lile, or Ben exclusively anymore. It was bigger than he thought—much bigger—to include another whole jurisdiction. And somehow, he was too far behind.

Cassandra was finally quiet, watching him try to put it together.

Before James could respond, the interrogation was interrupted as the door swung open. Officer Goldfinch darted inside, his face pale and expression grim. He hesitated, clearly reluctant to interrupt James for the fear he would, figuratively, kill him once they stepped into the hallway.

"Sir, you're going to want to come with me."

James glanced at Goldfinch, annoyed, while Cassandra rested against the back of the chair. She ogled Officer Goldfinch as if he were a lover—hooded eyelids, biting her lip, teeth flashing.

"This better be *very* important," James barked through gritted teeth.

Goldfinch gestured toward the door with his head, his hand still holding the handle.

James collected his folder, peering at Cassandra while standing up. She gawked at Officer Goldfinch who lingered hesitantly in the interrogation room, his face sickened from Cassandra's eyes flicking up to him with a slow, lazy amusement. James could sense the tension rolling off him, the way he shifted uncomfortably under her gaze. Goldfinch was nervous, uncertain, and Cassandra thrived on that.

She let her tongue glide over her bottom lip, catching it lightly between her teeth. Her eyes darkened, trailing up and down his figure in an exaggerated once-over, as if sizing up her next meal.

Goldfinch cleared his throat, clearly trying to focus on James when Cassandra let out a soft, sultry sigh, shifting in her seat just enough to make the chains at her wrists clink faintly against the table. A delicate sound, but one that made her control over the situation undeniable.

As Goldfinch hesitated, clearly struggling with the news he was bringing to James, Cassandra's smile stretched just enough to show too many teeth—like a predator playing with its food.

"Oh, come on, Finchy," she purred, mock sympathy dripping from her voice. "Spit it out. It's not every day you have to tell a man his heart's been ripped away."

Goldfinch's eyes bulged, his expression wavering between confusion and unease. James also looked back at her as he reached the door where Goldfinch stood. But Cassandra just watched them, her eyes glinting with something unreadable—something too knowing.

She sighed dramatically. "Such a shame." She lowered her lashes just slightly, her fingers tapping against the table in mock impatience. "I always wondered what kind of woman could put up with a man like Detective Hall."

James stilled, his posture going rigid. Goldfinch paled.

A sly smile tugged at Cassandra's lips, radiating quiet triumph. "You know, James . . . I do know a thing or two about grief," she said, sinking further back in her chair, almost enough to fall out of it. She exhaled through her nose, as if this was all so amusing to her. "It's like your heart . . . stops."

James and Goldfinch shared a disoriented look, but James swiftly remembered he was upset that he was disturbed while in interrogation. He pushed past Goldfinch, stomping into the hallway of the station, leaving him in the breeze he left behind.

Cassandra lifted her chained hands to wave at them with her fingertips, her maniacal laughter the only sound that escaped through the cracks.

❧ ❧

Cassandra's cackle echoed through the door as James Hall and Officer Goldfinch stepped into the adjacent room beside the interrogation chamber. The door slammed behind James with a force that rattled the frame. His jaw was tight, his pulse hammering against his throat. He barely spared Goldfinch a glance before turning away, hands on his hips after slapping the folder down onto the counter. His breaths came fast and sharp, like a man who'd just had his lifeline yanked from his grip.

"Are you fucking kidding me?" James growled under his breath; his eyes locked on the glass separating him from Cassandra. Through the window, he watched her with an intensity that bordered on feral.

Her forehead was pressed to the table; arms limp beneath it.

Despite her stillness, the haunting sound of her laughter lingered in his ears, mocking him. His fingers twitched at his sides, caught between the instinct to clench into fists and the urge to grab the nearest chair and hurl it across the room.

Goldfinch shifted uncomfortably; guilt etched across his face. He glanced at James, then at the floor, his discomfort perceptible.

"Detective—"

James whipped around, eyes blazing. "Do you know what you just did?" His voice was venomous as he jabbed a finger toward the window in Cassandra's direction. "I had her. She was talking. You don't interrupt me when they're talking."

Goldfinch flinched but held his ground, though his voice faltered slightly. "I wouldn't have pulled you out if it wasn't important, sir."

James froze for a split second, confusion sliding across his face before it hardened into something darker. "What the hell are you talking about?" he barked impatiently.

Goldfinch cleared his throat, quieter now. "It's your wife, sir. She's . . . Fieldman and Jones found her. I guess your daughter called Tim, worried, so they went to your house and . . . well . . . her throat was slit. We're still piecing it together. She's deceased."

James stared at him, disbelief clouding his expression as the words struck him like a punch to the gut, knocking the breath from his lungs. "Murdered?" The question seemed to linger in the air in front of him like a challenge he didn't want confirmed.

Goldfinch nodded, swallowing hard. "Yes, sir. Chief Douglas sent me to fetch you. He said to bring you to him. It's . . . bad, sir."

James's jaw tightened, but for a brief moment, vulnerability made its appearance. He turned back to the glass, his gaze locking on Cassandra. She was no longer slumped over the table. Her head was lifted now, her eyes fixed on him, an unreadable expression etched into her features as if she could see him through the glass. It's like she knew where he was without having to be in her presence and it disturbed him.

He thought back to her earlier words, the cryptic taunts she'd thrown into the room: *You're next.*

Was it a calculated move to rattle him? Or something far worse—a harbinger of what was to come? The timing was uncanny, her laughter meticulously placed, and the unease it left simmering in his chest was impossible to shake.

"I need a moment," James said finally. His restraint hung by a thread. He turned away from Goldfinch, his steps erratic, the energy in his stride crackling with tension. "Take over here," he added firmly enough to stop questions before they could form.

Through the window, Cassandra bobbed her head just enough to draw attention. Her narrowed eyes seemed to pierce the glass, as though examining whoever she imagined might be staring back. The atmosphere in the precinct seemed to close in, heavy and suffocating, like the building itself had absorbed the gravity of what had just transpired—and was bracing for the ensuing developments.

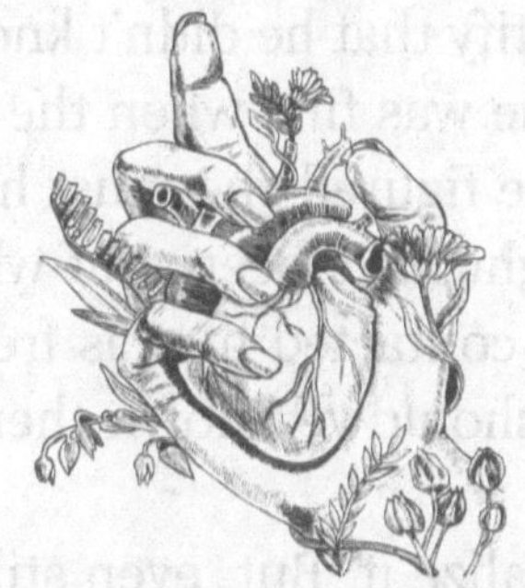

Chapter 32

The ride to the precinct was a blur as James Hall automatically, robotically, made his way through the empty streets of Bristol. He had just left the funeral home where his wife lay mutilated inside a mahogany casket, the one he had to choose for her because no one else could.

How he'd overlooked any moment where she wouldn't be safe, where she'd find danger within the home they'd shared for 35 years, was a mystery. He thought about how he shouldn't have been on that twenty-four-hour assignment; he should've picked up the phone when she'd called, but of course he never did. She always asked what he thought were stupid questions or she requested something that he couldn't just leave right then and there for. He stopped answering her calls altogether whilst at work to avoid the headache.

Lynda *had* really needed him then—the three voicemails were evidence of that. She was scared, alone. She told him to come home as soon as he could, or to answer her calls. He assumed she was only being paranoid, sending her a text that she'd be fine and leaving it at that. A grave mistake considering that had been the last text she had read or received from him before she died. Or worse, she had already been dead. No "I love you," no sentimental statements; her soul left this earth knowing her husband didn't fucking care.

James tried to justify that he didn't know how dire the situation was, assuming she was fine when the phone calls and texts eventually stopped. He figured she must have figured out whatever her dilemma might have been, but when he thought about it, when had she ever contacted him as frequently when he was on call that day? He should've known then that something was very, very, wrong.

He tried to rationalize it. But, even still, he was a cop, a detective; arguably one of the best in the state he might add—so why had he failed so miserably?

James had been consumed by Cassandra Kessler, her case, her many interrogations. He'd been consumed with how willingly she incriminated herself with her truth. She left out not a detail. He knew *everything* about his teammate's murders, more than he ever wanted to know. Putting her behind bars meant more to him than anything he'd dealt with in his career before.

He didn't know what it was about her that made him so uneasy compared to any other homicidal sociopath he dealt with. He wanted to find out with desperation, willing to offer everything he had to understand. Cassandra tried to break him; he couldn't and wouldn't let her. Even with the funerals of his team and wife on the horizon, she hadn't chipped at his spirits. He didn't feel damaged at all, other than the pain of losing those he cared for. She hadn't sent him to his knees begging for forgiveness. He knew, just like her, the apathy she showed for her crimes, he wasn't sorry about eliminating Qualley either.

Qualley was just as, if not a great deal more, sinister than Cassandra. According to the case evidence and Cassandra's claims, he fed her so many lies which she ate for breakfast, lunch, and dinner. Qualley had consumed her whole life, all the while he only cared about one thing: Qualley. If only she knew why his team was there at 9942 Chippen's Hill; what they caught

Qualley and his associate, Lonney, doing with that young woman—she'd have regretted everything she'd said and done. But what's the fun in revealing the truth to a psychopath when she'd just killed three police officers, and apparently her family too? She confessed to it as if it was her pride and joy in life.

Even if Cassandra *did* know what really went down at the Chippen's Hill mansion that day, she was so fucked up in her head that she still wouldn't have cared. This was all a game to her. She was perfectly content with ruining lives—even her own—for a bit of what she thought was revenge. Somehow, though, James still lost himself in the case of this sadistic woman. He wanted so badly to see her locked within bars containing only a small cot and toilet; the rest of her life spent in solitary confinement.

Cassandra did not have a soul on her side now, but James realized, neither did he.

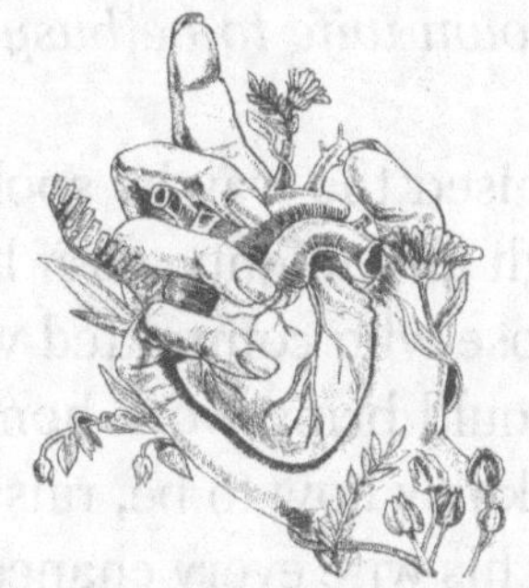

Chapter 33

Parking his car within the empty lot of the station, James comprehended how alone he truly was. It was ten at night, and he'd picked up another night shift because he didn't want to be in the house where his wife had been murdered. Though he knew he'd have to return eventually.

James checked his phone: no missed calls; no messages. His children hadn't even contacted him. The four of them were all on their way, traveling to Connecticut for the funeral scheduled in two days, which James thought was unusual to say the least. His kids never paused their lives for anyone, especially James. But for Lynda, he supposed they'd do pretty much anything.

Gemma, their eldest, had always been her mother's shadow; the boys: Connor, Owen, and Taylor, wanted their mother's approval over any their father could ever give. James, rarely home even as they grew up—similarly to recent times—assured that Lynda acted as both parents whilst he worked and worked some more, making a plethora of excuses as to why he couldn't be home. Lynda never complained. She loved the company of her children, and she figured her husband would be home eventually. But their four kids understood James cared more about his job than family.

Some hypothesized James only agreed to have children with Lynda so she wouldn't be alone. *Was this true?* James thought. *Did he just want his own wife to be busy, so he didn't have to deal with her?*

The children despised the way he spoke about those he apprehended, acting high and mighty, as if better than them, barraging them. Even those who committed victimless crimes were all belittled. James would bring work home, acting like the police detective he only knew how to be, raising his voice, depreciating his children and his wife every chance he got.

Nothing was ever good enough for James Hall, according to his children, though they were all successful adults leading their own lives with their own families. The children felt like those criminals many times, but they never let it affect them knowing their mother thought the world of them.

Lynda led life with love, telling their children she was proud of them, letting them know they could do or be anything they wished throughout their lives. She'd love them no matter what. James didn't offer that same sentiment. Their children didn't even get a glimpse of pride because James only showed them resentment. Even when Gemma received a full ride to Stanford with four other acceptances to Ivy League schools; when Connor received a basketball scholarship to UConn, or when Owen was accepted to MIT, or Taylor, their youngest, accepted into Texas A&M . . . even then, no congratulations, no pride in his children's achievements drove him to offer any hint of satisfaction in their successful lives or any hope for their futures.

James admitted, especially now, Lynda was the flame of their children's success. Of all their accomplishments, she was the reason they're all bright, intelligent, and secured everything they've set out to do.

What would he do without her now?

James suspected his kids wouldn't stay in the same vicinity as him for long, nor would they stay in the house. They probably wouldn't give him the time of day at all. All he knew was that they were coming for their mother's funeral, and that's about it. He pondered sending a group text to make plans, but he didn't know how to do that. If he called them individually, they'd never answer, neither would they call back—unless he left an urgent message telling them their mother was dead.

But even then he had to beg for responses.

To his kids, it all depended on the gravity of the situation. The forlornness he felt didn't constitute their attention. Nor did he deserve it, he understood that for sure.

He wished he hadn't had to have been the one to call them to relay the grim news, aware his children would despise him even more now; the conversation being, "Well, if you didn't work so goddamn much, mom would have been safe!" He hoped that maybe they'd have a bit of sympathy, but he didn't count on it.

As James crept out of his Chevy Tahoe, his thoughts dissipated a bit as he slid onto the pavement with his lukewarm McDonalds coffee he poured into his thermos to keep warm. He noticed a young woman sitting on a bench near the entrance of the station. He couldn't make out her features from the distance other than her shoulder length curls gathering within the hood of her beige jacket.

He didn't have his glasses on him, but he swore Cassandra was sitting there. Of course, it couldn't be.

He hated how much that damn bitch Kessler infiltrated his life, consuming his mind.

"Dad," the woman said, rising from the bench, and pinching her purple scarf around her slim neck.

James stopped before her, ice crunching beneath his feet from snow that had fallen yesterday. "Gemma? What are you doing here?"

Gemma looked down, brushing loose curls from her face. "I'm here for mom's funeral." She looked up at the sky as if it would speak to her. James could tell she was trying not to cry.

"I know, but it's not for another few days," James corrected, "and it definitely is not held here at the precinct."

"Gosh, dad, thanks, but no shit!" Gemma growled, rolling her eyes at her father's natural sarcasm. "I'm sure you'd have had it here if you could, just so you'd be able to work during the eulogy."

James pushed past his daughter, heading to open the door of the station. "If you came here to start shit with me, I'm not interested. It's been a long few days. I just want a hint of normalcy before I have to bury my wife of thirty-five years."

Gemma shook her head. "She was my mother more than she was ever your wife!" she cried, shaking her finger in James's face. "You act like you cherished her. You never saw the way she'd cry after you'd called her, telling her you'd picked up another twenty-four-hour shift. You never saw how she'd break down when you'd miss Connor's basketball games, or Owen's science fairs, Taylor's performances in the theater, or even my debates or dance competitions. We didn't care if you weren't there, but *she* did."

"Gemma! Enough, I—"

"No! Dad, you don't get to talk this time! I didn't come here for this, but . . ." she cried, pausing. Tears saturated her cheeks. "She *needed* you. Where were you? She called me, scared, you know. I tried calling you, too. But did you care to answer? Of course not! It's all about James Hall and his precious job. The crooked cop who went on trial for manslaughter on basis of self-defense. We all know you got away with murder, dad. Mom was always there for you though, even though you never were for her, or my brothers and I!"

James pointed his own finger now into his daughters face. "You know nothing of what happened that night, Gemma, or what happened after. My whole team is gone. Dead! You have no idea the pressure I've been tasked with to find the person who did this to them!" James spat. In his fury, his thermos slipped out of his tremoring hands, toppling onto the mat covering the entrance to the police station. Coffee splattered all over as the lid popped off.

Gemma grinned through her tears, but she wasn't happy. "Oh, I see. You're so caught up about your *team*, huh? What about finding who murdered my mother? Is that what you're here to do, or are you here to get in your mystery machine, eat Scooby snacks with your partner, and find monsters in masks? The only monster I see here is *you*. So I guess I've solved the case for you!"

"Jesus Christ, Gemma, I don't have time for this!" James roared, grabbing his now empty thermos and pulling open the door of the precinct just as another officer came rushing out to see what all the commotion was about.

"Everything alright out here?" the officer asked, holding the door open for James as he shoved himself past him, charging inside.

Gemma smirked, tears pouring from her eyes. "Oh yeah, peachy. Just James Hall being James Hall. Having no time for his daughter nor any family issues for that matter." She turned, heading the other direction where her rental car was parked. She got in, slammed the door, and sped off into the night, leaving the officer still holding the door bewildered and confused.

James reflected upon Gemma's words: she needed you. Where were you? for the remainder of his shift. He despised that she was right—everything she said was true. Maybe he *was* a crooked cop, but not in the way she had meant it.

How could he forget Gemma had called him too?

He wasn't sorry for the Qualley debacle, that was what it was, but he'd never live another day without regretting not being there for his wife, or his kids. James didn't blame Gemma for her anger. He'd deserved the way she'd spoken to him, even though he'd always demanded respect from his children. He knew why he wasn't getting that respect, but what could he do now that what happened, happened? He couldn't change anything about the situation without making it ten times worse. He sure as shit couldn't make them listen or talk to him for that matter. He has had multiple chances to talk in the past, and he took none of them.

I'm not a crooked cop, but I am a terrible father and husband, James thought.

The night wore on slower than normal and James's mind wandered constantly to Gemma. She had come to see him for something, leaving furiously. He wanted to call, apologize for his behavior—something he never did—but it was two in the morning, she'd likely be asleep. He'd call at some point that morning, if he could gather the courage to do so. Face to face would be preferable, but he had no idea where she was staying, he didn't think to ask during their argument.

Other than that, James dreaded going home. He hadn't been home, even after he'd been pulled out of his interrogation with Cassandra by Jeremy Goldfinch. A part of him didn't believe it. He felt like he was being punked. That the Ashton Kutcher fellow would jump out of a bush at any moment as a wicked joke organized by his family as payment for being unreachable. Perhaps this was a setup, making him realize how much he's missed out on since marrying Lynda. He couldn't fathom who'd set up such a stage.

Lo and behold, this was unquestionably a real scene straight from a horror movie or novel to which James Hall was the anti-hero.

He didn't kill her, but he also hadn't braced himself to save her either, even with her cries for help. *How shit of a person do you have to be when a person who's not the husband of your wife breaks down in tears before you ever do?*

The notion kept repeating in his mind.

Chapter 34

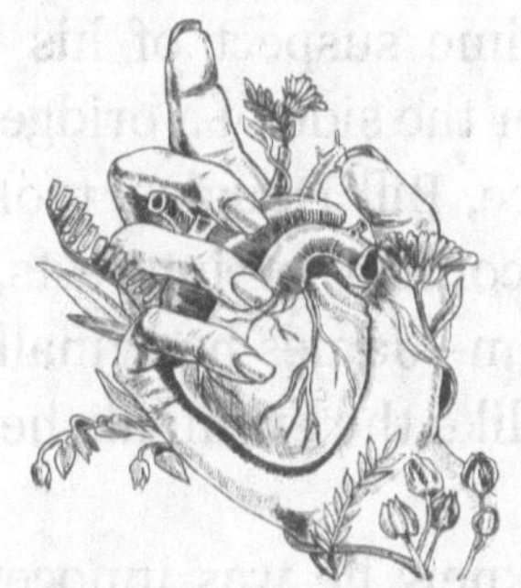

James reminisced the moment Jeremy Goldfinch, that asshole junior officer, knocked with furious vigor on the door to the interrogation room. He thought the bulletproof door would fall off the hinges. Then he just barged right on in.

He'd been continuing an inquisition to secure information he needed from Cassandra Kessler, for her case. James rose from his chair the moment the door of the room opened, Cassandra smirking as she eyed the encounter, chained to the floor. Jeremy nearly pulled James out of the room, mentioning how dire it was that he leave with him. James wanted to fire the stupid prick right then and there for the interruption, until the young officer spoke the words he'd never forget for the remainder of his life, "*. . . she's deceased.*"

At this point, James detected something within himself that he'd never experienced or, at least, hadn't felt for who knows how long: *remorse*. The emotion wouldn't fade, even after Lynda's body had been brought by a coroner to the medical examiner's office for a team of forensics specialists to collect evidence.

Not long after, the precincts bio-hazard remediation technicians took care of Lynda's blood in the house, along with any other areas soiled by bodily fluids. James wasn't allowed to enter the house during any of the investigation, which pushed him further into a spiral of melancholia and despair before he eventually became the prime suspect of his wife's murder, which merely tossed him over the side of a bridge.

The Chief of Police, Bill Douglas, took over the case to ensure there were no conflict of interests, monitoring James's phone, questioning him—James had finally experienced what it felt like to be treated like the criminals he had put away for the past thirty years.

Although James knew he was innocent, he felt guilty. The whole station knew now about his wife. They knew about the calls and texts she had made to him, which he ignored and the fact he slept on his office couch, not wanting to go home. He still couldn't go home and face it. They saw his blank expressions, that he didn't shed a tear. He was James Hall and James Hall didn't let his emotions show. He practically levitated through the halls of the police station like a ghost following his wife's brutal homicide. Miserable. James was distracted and delusional during investigations as all eyes were on him.

When he actually dozed off at night, he only ever saw Cassandra's face. That smirk she'd given him as he left the room with Jeremy, the cackle that followed as the interrogation room door shut.

He tried to think of his wife, dream of her. Lynda, the beautiful person who'd loved him unconditionally, raising their children with grace as he wasted his life in the goddamn precinct. She molded their children into successful human beings as he spent his time with people who'd replace him as soon as he dropped dead. James wanted to picture her short grey hair, again, with the streaks of blonde peeking through. He wanted to smell the scent of her ridiculously expensive perfume he'd always complained about being ridiculously expensive, loving it anyway, afraid to tell her so. James wanted to touch the lines that crossed her features as she smiled up at him, marking the many years they had spent together.

James didn't get that perfect version of Lynda when he closed his eyes. Instead, she was a mutilated version falling onto the bed, throat slit open. A nightmare that forced him to witness her death over and over and over again: *She'd cry out to him, pleading for him to stop sitting there. Help her! But he didn't. He sat as a dark figure he couldn't recognize bested his wife, stabbing her, over and over, leaving her to die. The figure eventually took shape. James's vision cleared so he could make out who it was. Standing there before him was himself, Detective James Hall, his badge strung around his neck, a knife dripping blood in one hand, a gun in the other.*

It was the same dream since he'd been notified of her death. James would wake up in cold sweat, breathing heavily, thankful it was only a dream. He *didn't* kill her, he wouldn't. He repeated that to himself over and over. Lynda *had* actually begged for help in reality, but he hadn't done anything to prevent her demise. He considered the fact that even his subconscious was being truthful, its point being, he *hadn't* helped her. He was no better than the murderous James in his dreams. *God, why hadn't he helped her? Why hadn't he gone home?* Perhaps she'd be alive now if only he had taken her seriously.

The irony of wanting that person to do that annoying thing they've always done, that always put you off—is that they're gone.

Chief Douglas eventually cleared James, accepting his alibi: he'd been working Cassandra Kessler's case at the precinct, locked in the interrogation room with her during the time Lynda was discovered and didn't coincide with her time of death. James overheard Tim Fieldman, his partner, speaking to Chief Douglas through his closed office door as he walked by. "Of course Hall didn't murder her, he never leaves this place. You'd think he's married to the job, sir."

James couldn't be upset with his partner of ten years as

much as he wanted to. Like his daughter, Tim had only spoken the truth. James's inability to turn off cop mode had really fucked up his life, affecting his children and everyone he cared about in the process.

He was only to blame.

James shoveled fresh ground beans into the filter of the coffee maker in his office, pouring water into the reservoir, and closing the lid. It bubbled and steamed to life. Muddy brown liquid slowly filled the pot. He watched it *drip, drip, drip,* his vision warping, visualizing the blood that covered his wife's neck and body.

A wave of nausea hit. He shook his head, the vision of his wife dissipating. He fell back onto the leather couch behind him to ease the dizziness surfacing through his system, his heart racing. He had to confront his issues before they consumed him or killed him, it was the only way to feel like he wasn't responsible for any of this. He wanted the support of his children, so he had to take a leap of faith—he just hoped it wasn't right off a cliff.

James checked his watch: 6:30 a.m. He hoped if he called Gemma now she'd be awake, so he fetched his cell phone from his pocket. The screen illuminated displaying a picture of Lynda and their kids behind the lock screen.

Dialing Gemma's number after breaking from the stupor of his heart palpitations, James took a deep breath. He rested the receiver of the phone onto his ear as it rang, and rang, and rang —he felt as if hours had passed since he'd dialed the number. But, just as he thought he'd have to leave a message, a soft, husky voice answered on the other end.

"Hello? Dad?"

James could tell he might have woken her, grogginess still prevalent as she spoke. He let himself smile, relieved his daughter answered even after their fight. "Hey, Gem. I'm . . . uh . . .

sorry to wake you." He stuttered, not really knowing what he was going to say next. He'd let Gemma and her attitude during this conversation decide where he'd go with it.

Gemma yawned from the other side of the receiver. "It's fine. Monty is teething so we haven't been sleeping much. Need something?"

James swallowed hard, feeling as if sandpaper had been lodged in his throat. He was nervous. This was his moment to make things right. A sliver of hope to make amends with the family he had pushed away.

"I—I—Uh, gosh," James stumbled over his words, not sure of what would be the right thing to say. "Listen, Gem, I don't really know how to do the whole apology thing. I know I don't deserve pity or forgiveness, but . . ." he paused again, throwing his hand over his bald forehead.

"Dad, I get it. I'm sorry too." Gemma said, sighing. "I shouldn't have made those comments to you, it wasn't fair. I know how much pressure falls on you in there so, yeah. But I was really angry, exhausted from the trip and Monty's teething and sleep regression . . . I just wanted to see how you were doing and knew you'd be at the station, so I left the kids with Mitch and met you there. The things you say sometimes just throw me off and upset me."

James exhaled slowly; the phone pressed tightly to his ear. His free hand ran across his face, the roughness of his palm grounding him as he processed her words. The tension in his shoulders eased, but only slightly. He leaned back against the desk, while his gaze fixed on the floor. Guilt gnawed at the edges of his conviction.

"God, I know, Gem," he said finally, his voice quieter now, tinged with regret. "I didn't mean to upset you. I just . . . I don't always know how to say things the right way. You know that." James breathed heavily into the receiver, close to tears.

His fingers tapped absently against the desk, the rhythm uneven, betraying the conflict simmering beneath his calm exterior. He wanted to say more, to explain himself, but the words felt trapped and tangled in the weight of everything he carried. Instead, he let the silence stretch, hoping it would say what he couldn't. Why was apologizing so hard for him?

"But some of the things you said, well, they're not wrong, hon," James continued. "I mean, I have dedicated myself to my work way more than I should have. I haven't been there for you kids or your mother. Now she's gone . . ." He stopped, a shudder escaping from his chest.

James never cried: not on his wedding day; nor when any of his four kids were born; nor when they all graduated high school and went off to college; not when Owen had open heart surgery, or Connor was involved in a hit-and-run by a drunk driver; not when each of his children scored high paying, prestigious jobs; not when Gemma or Taylor got married; not when his first grandchild was born.

None of it.

The only time James had ever shed a tear was the first day he wore a badge during his initiation thirty years ago. His own father looked him in the eyes telling him how proud he was. James had never heard any sort of sentiment from his father in his life. Feeling moved with the tears in his own fathers eyes—a man that had made the military his entire life, making it a point to never show emotion, he couldn't help but shed some too. However, after learning everything he knows about life from his own father, he couldn't help but feel his life crumble around him. He thought, perhaps, he had made the wrong decisions, giving too much credit to his own because he didn't know anything different.

Maybe if he had tried to form connections with his kids, experience more with them, verbally support them, and not try to be his father so much, he wouldn't be in this situation right now. Maybe he'd still be a successful cop and detective—or not—but at least he'd actually have memories with his family: vacations, school events that he always missed, memories made with his wife . . .

Everything fell down in shards around him, like that cracked picture frame scattered around his deceased wife's body in the crime scene photos he was shown.

He hadn't even shed a tear then.

Completely unbreakable, he still wouldn't cry as he spoke to his daughter. But he felt the fissure.

"Dad, please," Gemma's voice was subdued as she broke her father's silence. "Let's just pretend last night never happened for now, okay? I showed up last night because I wanted to know if you'd like to stay with us here at the Airbnb. I mean, you haven't seen the kids in a few years, never met Monty other than face-time. We'll order pizza and catch up. Maybe discuss the arrangements for moms funeral. I've got some ideas."

James couldn't help but smile at his daughters selflessness, sensing Lynda's calm, unconfrontational demeanor in her. He'd never felt close to his daughter before. He supposed this was one of many steppingstones into improving his relationships with his kids.

Why must it have taken Lynda's death for him to realize what he could lose if he kept going through life like he was? He merely lost his job after the Qualley Wallis case went down, his team accused of murdering him and Lonney D'Amato—but he didn't want to dwell on that. The precinct and the courts all knew that Qualley and Lonney's deaths were self-defense.

If he had lost his job, would he have felt the disconnect then as he does now from his family because of his wife's death? Would he have cared in the same way he does now? Why couldn't he differentiate those feelings between his job and family? Was his job really that much more important to him?

He was driving himself crazy with these thoughts.

"Of course, Gem. I'd love to spend time with you and the

kids," James pulled himself out of his spiral of self-reflection, rubbing his fingers over his dry eyes despite feeling so much grief. "I just need to finish up here, get my bereavement leave set up, then stop by the house to make sure it's good to go . . . grab clothes."

He could hear Gemma's breathing on the other end of the line. "Okay, dad. I'll call up the brothers to see if they'd like to join us. We have plenty of room for everyone."

"No, don't call them," James insisted. "I will. If you call they'll feel obligated to come—I don't want them to feel pressured."

"Oh, dad. They're not like that," Gemma assured, a sliver of pity resting in her tone.

"Gem, please. I'm sorry it's taken the death of your mother for me to realize how disconnected I really am from you kids," James confessed, feeling a tightness in his chest and throat. "If I'm going to improve any of this between us—which I want to do —I have to be the one to rectify it."

Gemma let out a hearty sigh. "Alright. I'll text you my address. You can give it do them when you speak with them. Oh, and dad?"

"Yes, Gem?"

"I love you," she sniffed. "I'm sorry you have to go through all this. Maybe you weren't the perfect father, but you don't deserve this. I hope you know that."

James sighed, an abundant gust of air escaping his nose as he smiled through Gemma's sentiment. "Thank you, Gemma. I love you, too."

He still didn't let himself cry.

Chapter 35

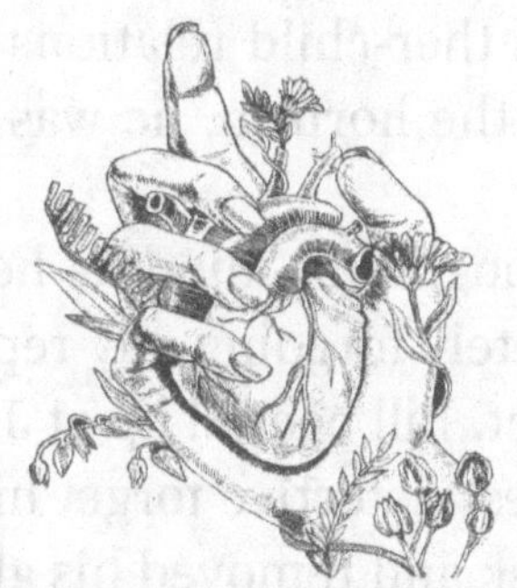

Detective James Hall

Owen, Connor, and Taylor all agreed to join James at Gemma's Airbnb that evening for dinner to discuss preparations for Lynda's funeral. He was overjoyed, surprised all three of his sons had answered their phones when he called, and even more so that all three conversations were somewhat enjoyable despite the dark cloud hovering over their heads. He was sure to text them Gemma's address immediately after, which he had sent via group text, after asking one of the younger officers how to do so.

As James proceeded to Bill Douglas' office, he was chuckling to himself as all four of his kids sent childish memes and GIFs to each other, like they had been close in his life longer than a day. James savored the feeling, hoping it wouldn't fade for the rest of his life. He knew that there would be copious amounts of invisible wounds to heal, but it was worth the work.

James' kids would be the most important things to him from now on.

To think Cassandra Kessler, after murdering the team James had built and had worked years to earn James's trust and loyalty, really thought she had succeeded in dismantling his whole world. Believe it or not, his family was his whole world—

just took him a while to realize it. Yes, he cared for his team, but they were only half of who he was. Now, with his kids safely back into his life, healthy father-child relations with each of his children materializing in the horizon, he was confident he was the one who won this.

He kept those thoughts in mind as he entered the Chief of Police's office, completely forgoing any reporting procedures set in place by the precinct. Bill peered up at James over his glasses, surprised to see his best detective forget his bearings. He set his pen down onto his desk and removed his glasses.

"I'm hoping your lack of sense entering my office without permission is mainly a result of your current situation," Bill propounded, a thick chuckle lurking in the back of his throat. "So, James, what'll it be?"

James bounded across the room, stopping at the window to peek out through the blinds. A rush of sunlight flooded his eyes, sunspots burring his vision before turning back to Bill who appeared to be struggling with his patience waiting for James's reply. Bill folded his hands over the papers he'd been working on.

James took a seat on one of the leather chairs that faced the front of bills desk, crossing his leg over the other, and stretching his arm across the back.

"Oh yes, do get comfortable James," Bill said flatly, watching his every movement. "It's not like I don't have your wife's case to figure out."

James dragged a hand down his face, rolling his eyes—a new, undignified reflex he could credit to the slow mending of hip relationship with his kids. "Would you fuck off, Bill!" James surprised himself, realizing just what he said as Bills face contorted into what Mr. Potato head would look like if you put his body parts in all the wrong holes.

"Well excuse the piss out of me," Bill spat, pointing his pen towards James's face as he spoke. "You come into *my* office, omitting proper respect to your chief, and you tell *me* to fuck off? After I've done everything to keep your ass out of jail? After I allowed you to interrogate Cassandra Kessler since your team were the murder victims? What the fuck is your problem?"

James didn't deny anything he said. Bill *did* do all those things. He just sat there in front of the Chief of Police, like a young, defiant boy. He was going absolutely crazy. He wouldn't have, in a million years, told Bill Douglas to "fuck off." He supposed he was exhausted—out of sorts with emotions he'd never felt before. Everything he was experiencing felt like a dream. The worst part being, he couldn't tell if it was good or bad.

Good because his kids didn't push him away like he thought they might—bad because his loving wife, who'd given him 35 wonderful years, had been murdered.

Perhaps he was in some dream purgatory of which he didn't know which way to go that'd give him the best ending or clarity. Just had to take the chance and see where he'd end up.

"Yes, Bill. Sorry, you're right," James said.

"You're sure as shit sorry," Bill boomed, reclining back into his chair and playing with the pen in his hands. "I'm going to assume your mental health at the moment is what made you lose some common sense. However, even though you've pissed me off, I'm feeling charitable. What do you want?"

"I'm resigning." James heard himself announce those two little words as soon as Bill finished his last word. Bills eyebrows rose with his body as he sat up. Anger and frustration had left him, replaced with concern. He studied James, who had been his most loyal officer for three decades.

"Well, retiring," James corrected.

"Retirement, James? Are you serious?"

"As a heart attack," James posed, nodding. "I want to spend more time with my family. This job has consumed me far too long. With what happened in the past week, I don't want to be unavailable again. It's about time I collect my pension and focus on them rather than myself."

Stunned, Bill sat back again, scratching the back of his head. He brought his fingers to his eyes, rubbing the bridge of his nose. James didn't know for sure but guessed the thought of James retiring stressed Bill out. He was one of the best in the station—if not *the* best. Bill would likely agree to that. But James didn't want to let life pass by more than it already had. His wife wasn't here to experience it anymore, so he'd try to go wherever life was going with his kids.

Maybe he'd move to Germany to live near Gemma and her kids, or to Colorado—smoke some weed like he'd always wanted to do. He didn't care where he went, he just didn't want to be here in this office anymore chasing down criminals and ignoring everything else around him. He wanted a fresh start to improve himself and his relationships with those around him.

Bill would just have to understand.

"James, Kessler's case is going to sentencing. It's going to take a while, though. We need more information," Bill informed, opening a folder on his desk. "The prosecutors are going for life without parole. They want to reject plea deals regardless of Kessler's reciprocity."

James stared at him, confused. Cassandra had confessed to everything, even rejected an attorney. What could she have put forth that he hadn't known about?

"What is she asking?" James queried. He'd put in so much time and effort into it already, arguably too much time.

"She's not asking anything. She's withholding information." Bill handed over a transcript that was printed out. "Tim went to visit her earlier. She's asked for you."

"Why me?" James asked, feeling like he might already know the answer. He was the one who got them all into this mess, she knew this. "Bill, I can't continue to put anything else into this case. She's already confessed everything she did. What more can I get out of her?"

Bill lowered his eyes, shaking his head as he pulled more

transcripts from the file in front of him. "She's unrelenting, James. I try to understand why she'll only admit the truth to you, but I'm guessing Qualley has something to do with it. There may be more victims out there she's not telling us about.

"There are no more victims," James countered, not sure if he believed what he was saying. "She went after my team, thinking she'd make me suffer since I'm the one who investigated Qualley Wallis. Cassandra doesn't seem like the type of person to hold anything back. She was quite comfortable relaying her acts to me in great detail."

Bill nodded, considering James's words. "I wouldn't be so sure, James." He reached out for the transcripts, and James handed them back to him. Bill tucked them into the folder, stood, and stepped over to the cabinet to his left, opening the bottom drawer and shoving it into a slot. Bill pulled up his trousers before heading back to his seat.

"James, I know the past week has been hard on you and your family, but after your bereavement leave, we—I—need you to finish up this case," Bill implored as he sat down. "Once Cassandra is behind bars and we know for sure there are no more victims, or anyone else involved for that matter, we will happily send you off with party hats and horns."

James thought about that, but didn't like the sound of it at all. He didn't want to give any more time or energy to the diabolically insane, "Queen of Hearts," as she started calling herself. He wanted to celebrate Lynda's life with his kids, getting to know them in the process. The more he thought about that, the more desperate he was to leave, but he owed Bill so much, he'd really come through for him.

"Fine. I'll give you a few more months, but I want a few extra days off to be with my kids while they're here," James said, lifting himself from the chair to his feet.

Bill nodded, looking up to James. "Done. But, before you go, I just want you to know that investigators looking into the evidence of Lynda's case may have found a link between the scene and previous members of Qualley Wallis's gang."

James turned over to him just as he was about to open the door to leave. "You think Qualley's boys did this?"

"We don't know for sure," Bill said. "Investigators and specialists think this was retaliation of some sort from one of the aligned groups. Many members of Qualley's bunch jumped into their jurisdictions. It's part of their gang initiation, perhaps even justice for their late drug lord."

James ran his hand over his head, considering the information. He wasn't so sure that was true. "My wife was the victim of a gang initiation?" He didn't want to believe that. What was with these damn people and their lust for revenge?

Bill stood, ambling over to James where he rested his hand on his shoulder.

"James, we will find whoever murdered your wife and ensure the greatest punishment for their crime," Bill promised, gripping him firmly. "Now, why don't you stop by and see our friend Cassandra, then head out to be with your kids, yeah? I'll keep you posted, rest assured."

James nodded as Bill opened the door from behind him, practically pushing James into the hallway where officers hustled by to start the daytime shift. Bill offered James a sympathetic nod before sinking back into his office and closing the door. He left James to process the information he had just received, alone.

Despite his boss requesting more of his time and his thoughts of Lynda festering around his conscious, James was gratified with his approaching visit with his kids. He hoped that his change of heart wouldn't fade, like the Grinch when his grew three sizes, realizing the true meaning of Christmas. James wasn't green, nor a fictitious character from a children's book, and hadn't experienced any palpitations other than the usual ones he had that would constitute his heart growing—but he still felt like something surfaced within him which determined he was ready to be a better person. He figured it was never too late to start making amends.

James lingered in the hallway, his gaze drifting across the precinct he'd called home for decades. The hum of activity surrounded him—officers rushing to their desks, phones ringing, the faint murmur of conversations blending into the rhythm of the station. It was all so familiar, yet distant, like he was watching it through a pane of glass. He'd spent years here, chasing justice, sacrificing time with his family, and now as he prepared to leave it all behind, the weight of those choices pressed heavily on his chest.

He walked slowly, his eyes tracing the worn floors, the scuffed desks, the bulletin boards cluttered with case files and memos. Every detail seemed sharper, more vivid, as if his mind was cataloging the space for the last time. He paused by the break room, where the coffee machine sputtered and hissed, its bitter aroma filling the air. How many nights had he stood there, clutching a cup of coffee, trying to stay awake long enough to crack a case? Too many to count.

James stopped by his desk, his fingers brushing the edge of the wood. The surface was cluttered with papers, pens, and a framed photo of Lynda and the kids. He picked up the frame, his thumb tracing the glass as he stared at their smiling faces. The ache in his chest deepened, but he forced himself to set it back down. He couldn't dwell on what he'd lost—not now. He had to focus on what he still had.

The precinct felt heavier than ever, the air was thick with memories and regrets. He'd spent his life here, chasing criminals, solving cases, and now, as he prepared to walk away, he couldn't help but wonder if he'd given too much of himself to this place. But it was time. Time to let go, time to start over, time to be the father his kids deserved.

Later in the interrogation room, Cassandra sat across from him, her posture relaxed and expression unreadable. James leaned forward; his hands clasped tightly on the table. "So you won't speak to anyone but me, huh?" he asked, voice steady despite the tension coiling in his body.

A slow smile crept across Cassandra's lips. "Why not?" she replied, almost playfully. "You're the one who understands me, Jamesey. The only one who sees the truth."

James's jaw tightened, his frustration simmering. He didn't want to be here. "If you have information, you need to share it. No more games."

Cassandra's smile widened, eyes glinting with something dark. "Games? Oh, this isn't a game. It's a story you're desperate to finish. But I wonder . . . do you really want to know how it ends?"

James leaned back slightly, his mind racing. "What do you know, Kessler?" he asked intensely.

Cassandra's fingers tapped idly on the table. "Lynda," she mused, drawing out the name like it was a melody. "If I had killed her, I would've made it quick. Clean. No mess, no fuss. But that's not my style, is it? You know that better than anyone."

James's fists clenched, his nails digging into his palms. "Stop playing games, Cassandra. *Did* you kill her?"

Cassandra shrugged, her smile never faltering. "Who's to say? Maybe I did. Maybe I didn't. Maybe I just know things you don't. Isn't that the fun part, Detective? The not knowing?"

James stared at her, his pulse quickening as his thoughts spiraled. *Could this be tied to Qualley's gang? Retaliation for the takedown of their leader? Or worse—had Cassandra orchestrated it herself, setting the pieces in motion like some twisted puppet master?* The timing was too perfect, her words too planned. He couldn't shake the feeling that she was pulling strings he couldn't see.

Cassandra jerked her head further, smile sharpening as she studied him. "Why don't you go sleep it off, James?" she said snidely with fake sympathy. "I'll tell you tomorrow. I'm done talking."

James's jaw tightened, his frustration boiling over as he stared at Cassandra. Her posture relaxed as she watched him with that maddening smile that never seemed to falter. She knew exactly what she was doing—keeping him on edge, dangling answers just out of reach.

His hands clenched at his sides, every muscle in his body taut with the urge to press her for more. But he knew better. She thrived on this—on pushing him to the brink, watching him struggle to maintain control. And right now, control was slipping through his fingers like sand.

James pushed back from the table abruptly, the chair scraping against the floor as he stood. He towered over her for a moment, his glare heavy, but Cassandra remained unmoved, her smile widening ever so slightly. She'd won this round, and she knew it.

Without a word, James turned and strode toward the door. As he reached the threshold, he paused, his hand lingering on the doorknob. He took one last look over his shoulder at her, still sitting there, her fingers tapping idly on the table as if she hadn't a care in the world.

"Sleep well, James," Cassandra said. "I hear eternal sleep is the most peaceful kind.

James stiffened, his grip on the doorknob tightening, but he didn't respond. Instead, he pressed the button, yanking the door open and stepping into the hallway as cool air hit him like a slap. The door swung shut behind him with a dull thud, cutting off the sound of her faint laughter that lingered like an unwelcome echo in his mind.

Chapter 36

James Hall

The house stood as a husk of what it once was, its former warmth buried beneath the quiet void. He couldn't sense Lynda's famous chocolate chip with bacon cookies anymore, nor could he taste the chili and cornbread she'd make on Friday's. There wouldn't be any more lunches packed for him, or sticky notes shoved between the sandwich and snack bag of baby carrots telling James she loved him.

He now had to worry about his suits being wrinkled and his watch being unpolished. His office desk was always clean, tidy, clutter whisked away into its proper place, a glass of bourbon waited for him next to his chair when he returned home so he could relax before supper. James would forget things if Lynda hadn't left it for him by the door or waited for him with the very thing he was about to leave the house without.

None of which he always took for granted would ever bless his life again.

James wandered through the house as if it were a museum from some other time. He told himself he'd never make the same mistakes again. Yes, Lynda wasn't here to see or experience the new, more attentive person he promised to be, cursing himself for that—but he'd do anything to make her proud.

A buzzing sounded from the pocket of James' trousers. He

pulled out his phone, thinking it might be his kids posting another inside joke to the group chat. Instead, Tim Fieldman's name illuminated the screen with an unread text message. James returned his glasses from the pocket of his coat to his face to read it out:

> **James, Bill told me you'd gone back to the house. Came to see you this morning. Forgot to let you know; we found a gift that was marked to you under the tree. Forensics team cleared it — nothing looked amiss. Looks to just be from Lynda. Enjoy your time with the kids. -Tim**

James read the text a few more times and shoved the phone back into his pocket. Lynda hadn't mentioned a gift at any point before she died—she usually mentioned things like that. She was the type of person who couldn't wait to give a gift. He also didn't remember leaving for his twenty-four-hour shift with a gift under the tree. Then again, Christmas was in a few weeks—Lynda could've snuck it under when he left. He considered, maybe, it might be from someone at the precinct offering condolences. *Not likely.* People didn't really care enough about him to do something like that.

He stepped through the kitchen, realizing everything had been cleaned to spotless perfection. Usually the crime scene cleanup team didn't do this good of a job, but he figured Bill or Tim might have slipped them a bonus to hook him up. He'd thank them later for that.

The refrigerator caught James's eye. He paused, inspecting pictures held up by magnets shaped as cats. He never liked those magnets, calling them childish. But the pictures that hung beneath them were of the children that would say the magnets brought back fond memories of their mother's silly personality, always ready for a joke, to laugh—she didn't take life too seriously. Not as seriously as James.

In one of the pictures, Gemma smiled, holding up a trophy. James couldn't recall what it was for or when the picture was taken. Another photo that hung under a silly cat butt magnet of the high school varsity basketball team that Connor had been a part of caught his eye.

Was this the championship game? He cursed himself for not knowing for sure.

Owen and Taylor filled the next picture with big smiles of which they were known for, arms thrown around one another's shoulders in a pool. James, once again, had no idea who had been the owner of said pool.

The final picture depicted Lynda and their kids, James nowhere to be found, in front of their house. One of Gemma's graduations—maybe high school? Perhaps Stanford? *Why didn't he know the difference?*

These few photographs were a fraction of proof that James was very absent from their lives but represented the rest of the family's perseverance to live on and enjoy each other without him. He couldn't be upset with his family; he had made the choice not to be there. Who was he to say they shouldn't have done things without him? He wanted to be angry. He *was* angry, but only with himself. The feeling gave James the courage to admit that he needed to change, and he would. He had to.

James took down the pictures, placing them on the counter, along with his phone so he wouldn't forget them when he left for Gemma's Airbnb. He'd bring them with him to show her and the boys. Maybe his grandsons would get a kick out of seeing their mother and their uncles so young. He'd have to see if he could locate the other photos his wife stashed within multiple memory boxes throughout the house. James hoped he could cheer his children up with memories of Lynda—beautiful memories—to which they probably didn't even need the frozen moment in time to remember, they'd lived it. James, however, needed any help he could get.

James made his way into the open family room taking in the sight of the gift Tim had mentioned in his text under the Christmas tree. Metallic green paper surrounded an oddly shaped package; a red bow tied around its circumference. A tag marked: **To James, With Love<3** hung from where it was tied from the back of the large bow. He didn't recognize the script from the tag to be Lynda's—she had written him all those notes in his lunch box—he'd know her handwriting anywhere.

James ran his finger along the back side of the gift where the paper was taped almost professionally, as if it was brought to one of those gift-wrapping places in the mall. He untied the ribbon and it slid down, drifting onto the floor. James watched it fall as he tried to lift the gift and turn it around. As he did, he realized there were multiple items wrapped up as one, and a piece of cardboard or something sturdy supporting the bottom.

Knowing he'd probably never use this paper again—something his wife liked to do, save wrapping paper—he ripped the paper right down the middle.

He didn't know what he was looking at as he lowered the paper further off the table, but it felt as if he'd been looking in a mirror. In front of him sat a painting of . . . himself. Red paint of various shades made up a bust of his face and torso. It looked to be the same posture from the picture on his wedding day that sat on his wife's side table in their bedroom. He hadn't smiled in it; he never usually did, and he had hair at the time. Before James could study the picture further, he noticed a small stack of paper that had been attached onto the corner of the canvas.

James's confusion vanished as he realized who this gift was from.

Dread set in recognizing the style in which his features were painted. He reluctantly lifted the canvas, hoping to get a closer look, when he heard something fall over from behind it. He held the canvas to the side, peeking around it, where three mason jars sat.

They all looked to be full of uncooked meat.

They had all been murdered in three separate ways. Yet each man's chest had been carved wide open, hearts taken from their bodies before being disposed into their shared grave ...

The canvas fell to the floor, along with an envelope. James fell to his knees as he took in the sight of what he now knew to be his murdered teammates hearts—all in jars marked with their names on the lid in the same script James's name had been written on the tag attached to the bow of this . . . gift.

Vomit rose to his throat, but he choked it back. His eyes began to water, skin heating with horror discovering what this all meant.

James remembered the papers that were once in his hand, which shook with such vigor as he picked them back up from the floor where he dropped them. He didn't think he'd be able to open it to display it's content the tremors were so bad.

His heart started to race, pain radiating in his chest. He went completely numb.

But despite his panic, he slid out the papers, revealing the handwriting he'd been seeing all along:

Dearest James,

Let me begin by saying this: you think I don't know about Zina, the woman with Qualley and Lonney that night, but rest assured, she'd have been well taken care of if your team hadn't barged in and ruined their fun. She went willingly, you know. That's why she never testified—not because she was frightened. Lonney meant the world to her, and you took him away . . . just as you took Qualley away from me. Wouldn't you know, Zina and I have been good friends since high school!

She had nothing to do with what I've done here, of course. I wouldn't let her take credit for any of it. She's off somewhere now, trying to forget that terrible night you forced upon her. But that's old news. Something I'm willing to let go of now that the truth has come to light and I've had my reprisal. But tell me, how does it feel knowing that what you did—murdering two innocent people—was all for nothing?

I suppose we're even now.

So, as a gesture of goodwill, I've left you a little gift. Something to remind you of those you loved most: Ben Prout, Lile Henderson, and Evan Matthews. Your team. The family you chose to care for instead of your own. A jar of hearts—ones I took because you took mine.

Qualley was my heart, my soul, my everything.

I have no use for them now, though. I'm on my way to a new chapter, a new residence. So, take care of them for me, would you?

You're probably wondering why I didn't take your wife's heart and preserve it in a jar, too. But first, tell me—do you really think you deserved her heart all these years? Poor Lynda, who gave you 35 years of her life while you gave her nothing but neglect. Married to the mission, right? It's okay, don't be too upset. I've painted a stunning portrait of you using her elegant blood. A fitting tribute, don't you think? After all, you've always loved yourself more than anyone else.

No need to thank me. I did it because I love painting with all my heart. It's just too bad you don't have one. That's why I never took yours either—it would've been an empty cavity filled with black, chalky dust. Not my style.

If I had killed you, though, I'd have done your wife and kids a favor. You were never home anyway.

Better off dead, I'd say.

And Lynda . . . oh, James, she was the best medium of them all. Her blood was so rich, so vibrant. A true masterpiece. But you should've heard her, James. How she begged for you.

I'll tell you everything, James. Every detail. How her voice cracked as she called your name, how her hands trembled, how her blood spilled like liquid rubies onto the floor. I'll describe it all—the way her eyes widened in terror, the way her breath hitched as she realized there was no escape. You deserve to know, don't you? After all, it's your fault she's dead.

Chapter 37

Scoping out your residence required meticulous care—and a healthy dose of patience. Detecting any form of security surveillance was crucial, so I began by observing the neighborhood from a distance, noting the streets' layout and the placement of nearby houses. With my car parked a few blocks away, I walked the rest, blending in with the early morning joggers and dog walkers in my best fitness gear. I even threw in a few stretches for good measure—nothing says "I'm harmless" like a convincing hamstring stretch.

I took my time, making multiple passes by your house at different times of the day, either in person or driving by. The lack of visible security cameras struck me as odd for someone in your position. A police detective without cameras? Bold move. But then again, maybe you thought your badge was enough to keep the bad guys—girls—away. Lucky for me, it wasn't. Still, I remained cautious. Overconfidence has a way of biting you when you least expect it.

Studying the windows, I surveyed them for any signs of motion sensors or alarm systems. I observed the doors and gates, noting their locks and potential points of entry. To gain *a deeper understanding of your security measures, I decided to get creative.*

Posing as a door-to-door salesperson one afternoon, I armed myself with a clipboard, a friendly smile, and just enough charm to make it believable. Audacious? Absolutely. But necessary.

When Lynda answered the door, I introduced myself and launched into a harmless spiel about home security services. Her initial hesitation made me wonder if she suspected anything, but I kept my demeanor friendly and professional.

"Are you interested in TruSafe's home security monitors and cameras?" I asked, clipboard in hand, channeling my inner salesperson.

Lynda reached to close the door. "Sorry, we aren't interested."

I stepped forward, placing my foot in the doorway like a seasoned pro. "Please! May I ask, are you at least protected, ma'am?"

*She paused, her eyes narrowing with suspicion. I could practically see the wheels turning in her head as she weighed her options. "My husband works with the Bristol Police. **They** are our home security."*

Crafting a blend of false care and curiosity, I pressed her further. "That's great to hear! But you know, even the best police officers can't be at home all the time. Does he have any plans for additional security measures? Cameras, perhaps?"

Her expression softened somewhat, possibly reassured by my apparent interest in her well-being. "Well, he mentioned cameras once, but we never got around to installing any. Our neighborhood is quite safe, and we haven't had any issues so far."

My head dipped, pretending to take notes on my clipboard. "I understand. It's always best to be proactive, though. You never know when something might happen. Our system is quick to install and very affordable."

Her grip on the door loosened, and she seemed to consider my words for a moment. "Thank you, but I think we're fine. My husband would probably laugh if he saw me talking to a security salesperson. He's very confident in our safety."

"Of course, ma'am. I'm sure you're in good hands with him," I said. "Welp, you were my last stop of the day! Have a good one!" I bowed before walking away. She watched me as I practically skipped down the street, elated. I twisted back, noticing her still in the doorway. Waving, I smile so wide it could've been mistaken for genuine friendliness.

As I walked away, my heart raced with a mix of excitement and satisfaction. Lynda had unwittingly confirmed that your house lacked additional security measures. Her confidence in you and your department's protection gave me data I desperately needed to pull this off. An absence of cameras or alarms made your residence vulnerable—a crucial piece of information I could easily exploit.

After that confirmation, I scoured social media and online resources to learn more about Lynda's routines and habits. Did you know she had a penchant for sharing her daily activities on platforms like Instagram and Facebook? She'd post about her morning yoga classes, visits to the local farmers' market, and coffee dates with friends. I couldn't help but marvel at her dedication to oversharing—it was like she was handing me a roadmap.

I also monitored public records and community events, noting frequent times and locations where Lynda was likely to be found. One of which was a Thursday night book club she attended weekly at her friend Hillary's house in Southington. Armed with this collection of facts, I staked out these locations for a few weeks, tracking patterns and attempted to remain unnoticed.

Timing her arrivals and departures with precision, I built

a comprehensive profile of both your residence and your routines. With this knowledge, I felt confident in my ability to anticipate your actions, all while remaining undetected.

To confirm my intel on your work schedule, I noted days when you pulled those grueling 24-hour shifts. Thankfully for me, they were a regular part of your demanding job, leaving you exhausted, less vigilant, away from home—a perfect opportunity for me.

On the day I planned to break in, I monitored you closely. I followed as you left for work early in the morning, observing your vehicle pulling out of the driveway and disappearing down the street. I knew you wouldn't be back until the following morning, and that information alone gave me a substantial window of opportunity.

Waiting patiently, I confirmed your absence by cross-referencing the precinct's schedule and staking out the station from the Orange Cat Café. It had the perfect vantage point—plus, their lattes weren't half bad. Once I saw you stroll into work, your bald head gleaming under the sunlight like some sort of misplaced lighthouse, I knew the coast was clear. Occupied by your duties, I made my reappearance to your residence later on that day after Lynda left for her book club.

Dressed in my finest "I'm definitely not up to anything suspicious" attire—black long-sleeve shirt, skinny jeans, and boots—I approached your house under the cover of night. My Mercedes was parked discreetly down the street, ready for a seamless getaway. Slung across my shoulder was a suede green side bag containing my trusty .22 and a collection of tools I'd picked up.

1492 Preston Street stood like a monument to Georgian elegance in Connecticut, its stately exterior practically begging for admiration. Palladian windows lined the walls, their intricate designs casting delicate shadows across the pristine white outside. The slate-gray roof and dormer windows added a touch of timeless grandeur, while the manicured lawn and shrubbery gave the place an air of suburban perfection.

Honestly, the only thing I liked about you was your taste in architecture—although I'd bet good money it was Lynda's doing, not yours.

I made my way to a side window I'd previously scouted as a weak, less visible link. It had a window fan—an odd choice for late December, when the air outside could freeze your eyelashes. Using a slim jim, I carefully pried the window open, and the fan tumbled into the flower bed below with a muffled thud. I winced at the sound, but the plants didn't seem to mind.

With the window open, I hoisted myself inside, relying on the strength I'd honed from, well, murdering three grown men. Not to brag, but I'm stronger than I look. But despite that, as I slipped into the house, my heart pounded like a drum solo, restlessness coursing through me in waves. Every creak of the window frame felt deafening, and I froze, listening for any sign that I'd been detected.

Nothing.

So far, so good.

Once fully inside, I moved with the precision of a cat burglar—or at least, that's how I imagined it. Each movement was as quiet as a whisper, a dense quiet enveloping the room, its dim recesses swallowed by the encroaching dark. I couldn't tell where I was—maybe a bedroom? Maybe a study? Either way, navigating the space felt like walking a tightrope over a pit of scorpions.

Adrenaline sharpened my senses to an almost unbearable degree. Every creak of the floorboards, every rustle of fabric, felt magnified. It was as if your house itself was conspiring against me.

My mind raced with contingency plans, each one more elaborate than the last. What if you or Lynda came home early? What if the neighbors heard something? What if I tripped over a rogue ottoman and knocked myself out cold and you discovered me there? The stakes were higher than ever, and failure wasn't an option.

This was it. The culmination of weeks of planning, of careful observation, of sacrifices made in the name of vengeance. Evan, Ben, and Lile were gone, their hearts preserved in my workspace, but you—oh, you were the **true** prize. Everything hinged on this night, on how quickly and efficiently I could execute everything prior. There was no room for doubt, no margin for error. I had to stay focused, no matter how much my nerves threatened to betray me.

👁 👁

The interior of the house was just as I'd pictured it—immaculate, almost obsessively so, yet brimming with subtle contradictions that told a quiet story about its inhabitants. The faint tang of lemon polish lingered in the air, an invisible badge of Lynda's unyielding commitment to order and cleanliness. The walls wore soft, neutral tones, calming and serene, and their surfaces were adorned with strategically placed photographs of smiling faces and golden memories.

As I studied the frames more closely, a glaring absence struck me—**you** weren't in them. Not a single frame held your face. It didn't take much to figure out why. You were probably holed up at work, knee-deep in evidence logs or barking at some poor rookie to follow the chain of custody. Lynda's sanctuary of a home seemed to carry on without you, polished and perfect, as though she'd built a world that didn't need your constant absence explained.

Venturing further into the house, the gleaming hardwood floors reflected the warm glow of tasteful sconces, their shine practically begging for admiration. Still, beneath the charm and meticulous effort, subtle flaws began to surface. Small acts of rebellion were tucked here and there—little telltale signs of *your obsessive work habits barging in uninvited.*

That's when it hit me—I was suddenly standing in your office. And let me just say, the space was so tangled and messy it made an unhinged suspect look composed. Front and center was the desk, a hulking mahogany beast drowning beneath the disarray of open files and scattered papers. Sticky notes clung desperately to its edges, curling up at the corners as if trying to escape their fate. A coffee mug with a faded logo rested precariously near the edge, leaving behind a faint ring on the wood— an offense that probably made Lynda twitch every time she walked in.

Towering bookshelves loomed on either side of the room, crammed with law books, manuals, and crime scene guides. Their cracked, battle-worn spines were an unrelenting counterpoint to the neatly dusted shelves they occupied—evidence, perhaps, of Lynda's quiet intervention. But as I scanned the shelves, I couldn't help but notice glaring omissions.

No books on empathy.

No guides to basic human decency.

Certainly nothing titled "How Not to Kill People Without Due Process: A Detective's Handbook."

Honestly, it was a shame—those might've been the most useful additions to your collection. Instead, it seemed you preferred volumes that reinforced your relentless pursuit of making others' lives miserable, even if it meant trampling over the very principles you were supposed to uphold.

Ignoring your lack of positive professional development, my attention fixed above the doorway where a vintage clock hung, its rhythmical ticking filling the silence. Each second a countdown to time slipping through your fingers. The credenza near the window carried Lynda's unmistakable touch, polished silver photo frames arranged with care. But they stood in blunt contrast to the desk's chaotic sprawl of pens, notebooks, and paper clips. A perfect visual of two lives perpetually out of sync.

Then there was that absurd corkboard on the wall—a shrine to your tireless pursuit to the disposal of anyone you deem criminal. Notes, clippings, and photographs were pinned haphazardly, connected by a web of red string that looked like it had been spun by a spider on a caffeine binge. It was hauntingly fastidious, a clear visualization to your late-night obsessions, and yet, Lynda's fingerprints lingered faintly in the order she had tried so hard to impose.

I smirked as my eyes scanned the bizarre display of suspects, connections, and half-baked theories. "What's next—are you going to interrogate the string? Seriously, where'd you learn your detective skills—an episode of *Law & Order*?" I murmured to myself, imagining the melodrama that had to have gone into this setup.

My fingers drifted lightly over the surface of the desk, brushing against the keyboard and the stack of legal pads covered in shorthand scrawls. It felt invasive, touching these fragments of your life—pieces you had no idea were now mine to examine. But wasn't that the point?

I wanted you to feel violated.

I needed you to know that your safe little world had been breached by something far darker than the criminals you spent your days chasing.

A framed photograph sat to the right of the desk—a picture of you, Lynda, and what I assumed were your four kids at what looked like a summer barbecue. Their smiles were bright, effortless. But when I tilted the frame in my hands, my gaze fell on you.

You were there, front and center, but you didn't smile. Not really. Your expression was tight, restrained, as if you'd been dragged into the moment against your will. Shoulders squared, arms stiff at your sides, you barely leaned toward Lynda or your children. It was subtle, but it stuck out like a sore thumb among the carefree joy of everyone else.

I scoffed, turning the frame slightly to study you more closely. "Really?" I muttered to the glass. "You couldn't even fake it for them? For her?"

The longer I stared, the clearer it became. **This wasn't your life.** Not really. You were always somewhere else—at the precinct, buried in a case, married to your job instead of your family. I could see it in the way Lynda smiled, brighter than anyone else in the picture, as if she were trying to carry the weight of happiness all on her own.

"You don't deserve this life," I whispered to the frozen faces in the frame, my grip tightening on the edges. For a moment, I considered smashing it, letting the glass shatter and scatter across the desk. But no. That would be too easy. Too impulsive.

Instead, I set the photograph back down carefully, stepping away. You didn't deserve the family in that frame—but you were going to lose the perfect life you'd taken for granted anyway.

I couldn't help myself but explore the room more, satisfaction surging through me like a drug. The weight of your life unfolded in severe detail around me—a perfect storm of discipline, obsession, and the occasional betrayal of disorder. This was your sanctuary, your war room, the place where you transformed into the detective everyone feared and respected. Yet, as much as the room fascinated me, I couldn't afford to linger. Time was my enemy, and I still had work to do.

Advancing tactfully toward the hallway, the dim glow from the living room guided me forward, the space opening up beyond the office like the yawning mouth of some great beast. The house was unnervingly silent, save for the occasional groan of old floorboards, as if the house itself were sighing under the weight of its secrets—or just letting me know it was tired of your shit, too.

It was warmer inside than out, carrying a faint scent of

aged wood, stale coffee, and something oddly sterile—printer ink, maybe, or the faint tang of disinfectant. A kind of smell that clung to a place where life and work blurred together too often.

Faint light from the streetlamps outside spilled in, casting distinct, angular shadows across the furniture. I had studied the layout beforehand, memorizing the flow of the house through property records and stolen glances from the street. With Lynda at book club and you doing what you thought you did best, I had the house—and my purpose to myself.

My pulse was steady, a slow rhythm that matched my footfalls. Moving with precision, I avoided any wasteful motions or reckless gambles, gliding through the hall, attuned to every creak and shift of the house. The distant hum of the heater; the faint rustle of branches against the windowpane—all of it became part of the house's breathing, and I moved in sync with it.

The living room greeted me with one of the most extravagant Christmas trees I'd ever seen. It stood tall in the corner, decked out in whites and golds. An elegant, soulless thing. The scent of pine filled the air, artificial yet mildly convincing, masking the darker scent I carried with me. As much as I wanted to admire the tree, I had to find a place to hide. Lynda would be home soon, and I needed to disappear before then. I scanned the room, searching for the perfect spot. The hall closet was too obvious—Lynda might rummage through it for something. There was no basement, and even if there were, I couldn't risk losing track of her movements.

The stairs seemed to beckon. Decorated with garland and festive lights for Christmas, they cast a warm, inviting glow, that pointed me upward like an airport runway. Each step upward creaked, but the rest of the house remained silent, oblivious to my intrusion within its walls.

I stalked my way up, committing every detail to memory. There were three bedrooms and a bathroom on the second floor. I noted the layout, mentally mapping my route should I need to make a quick exit. The largest bedroom was clearly the primary—the room you shared with Lynda . . . assuming you still shared it.

The wooden post bed towered in the center of the room, its frame sturdy enough to survive a medieval siege. The bedding was a masterclass in perfection, tucked so neatly it could make a drill sergeant weep. But the floral pattern? Bright and cheerful, like it had wandered in from an entirely different season—springtime in December, because apparently, consistency is overrated.

An en suite bathroom gleamed through the open door; its fixtures polished to perfection. A walk-in closet stood slightly ajar, revealing neatly hung clothes and organized shelves. The room was a study in precision and care. Lynda's touch, no doubt.

Another framed photo on the nightstand snagged my attention—a picture of you and Lynda, the poster children for marital bliss. Honestly, the variation between the joy frozen in that frame and the current tension thick enough to cut with a butter knife was almost comedic. It was like the photo was trying a little too hard to sell the idea that happiness lived here. Nice try, picture, but I wasn't buying it.

There was a narrow gap beneath the bed, covered by a decorative baby pink sheet that hung off the box spring. From the door, it would be impossible to see anyone hiding there. It was tight, but I could fit.

I slipped my bag off my shoulder, pulling my pistol free and shoving the knife into my pocket. Operating with rapid, calculated efficiency, I had no time for hesitation. This would have to do, and I would work with it. I crouched low, scanning the space beneath the bed for anything that might betray my presence. Satisfied, I shoved my empty bag toward the wall, out of sight, and slid underneath.

The cool hardwood floor pressed against my back, an un-expected luxury given the situation—like the universe's way of saying, "At least you're comfy while trespassing." With my weapons in place and my breathing almost annoyingly even, I willed my pulse to behave. It had other plans, thumping away like a drummer at their first rock concert.

The anticipation buzzed through me, sharp and zippy, like I'd just licked a battery on a dare. Every groan of the house was exaggerated, each distant creak a potential doom-laden alarm. My ears strained so hard to pick up vibrations, I half-expected to develop echolocation any second now.

Then, the front door creaked open, the sound carrying up the stairs like a carrier pigeon. I froze, my entire body as still as Evan, Lile, and Ben rotting in my yard. It had been twenty minutes since I'd wedged myself into this hiding spot, and now she was finally here.

Lynda.

How did I know it was her? Let's just say your house may be big, but old homes have a way of snitching on their occupants. The faint shuffle of her shoes, the distinctive metallic jingle of keys hitting the dish near the door—it was like the house was tattling just for me.

Her footsteps echoed faintly, conscious and unhurried, like she was auditioning for a role in a slow-burn thriller. I tightened my grip on the pistol, the cold metal nudging me like an overly serious friend saying, "Focus, buddy—this isn't a dress rehearsal."

But then her steps faltered, pausing just long enough to send a ripple of unease through me. Did she sense me? Did she know? My heart pounded harder, the tension winding up tight, like a rubber band about to snap.

I adjusted my grip, and every muscle poised for anything. Upstairs in this oversized house, I felt like the world's least comfortable ghost, waiting for the living to arrive.

Chapter 38

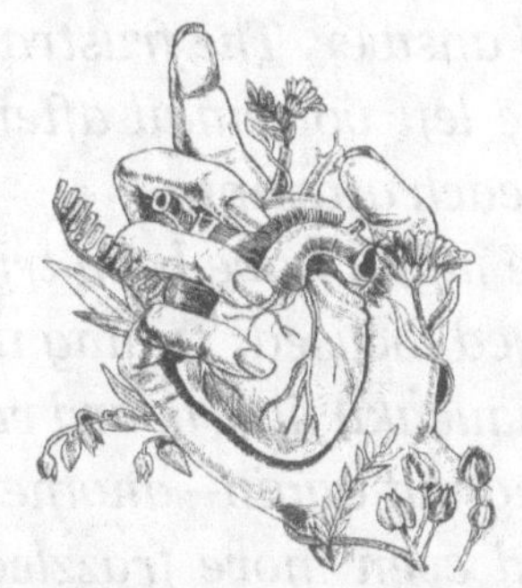

Lying under the bed, I couldn't hear much beyond my own breathing and the muffled chaos downstairs. It was like the house was hosting a secret party, and I wasn't invited. I strained to pick up anything that might clue me in on Lynda's whereabouts. The occasional creak of floorboards and distant murmurs were all I had to work with—hardly the soundtrack of a master plan.

I mentally ran through my next steps, each one rehearsed as if prepping for a heist movie. The knife tucked into my belt pressed against my side, reminded me that it was on my team. Anticipation was maddening, like a game of musical chairs where there's only one more chair and the stakes are way too high.

From downstairs, Lynda's voice floated up, soft but distinct. She was talking to someone—or maybe just herself, who knows? The words were garbled, leaving my imagination to fill in the blanks. Was she calling for backup? Had she spotted something out of place? I shoved doubt aside; there was no room for second-guessing, I was already hiding under the fucking bed.

Her voice grew louder, tinged with worry. Then came the unmistakable sound of her phone dialing, followed by the relentless ringing. No answer. The frustration in her voice was almost comical as she left voicemail after voicemail, her tone climbing higher with each attempt.

The bed above me might have been trying to crush me into submission, but I stayed focused. Timing was everything, and I wasn't about to let a squeaky floorboard ruin my moment.

Lynda's voice rang out again—another call, another round of rings. She sounded even more frazzled now, like someone trying to order pizza during a blackout. It went to voicemail again, and I could hear her starting to leave a message, only to cut herself off with a sharp gasp.

Her footsteps finally approached the stairs, each one sending a jolt through me like I was wired to the house itself. She was getting closer, blissfully unaware of the danger lurking just a few feet away.

My grip tightened around the knife handle; my muscles ready to spring like a cat stalking its prey.

The rest of the house faded into irrelevance as I zeroed in on the moment. This was the culmination of all my planning and preparation. No room for hesitation now.

As Lynda reached the top of the stairs, I steadied my breathing, every nerve on high alert. The plan was clear; the execution was imminent. All that was left was to see if reality would cooperate with my carefully crafted script.

Lynda wandered into the room to the other side of the bed, placing something that sounded suspiciously like glass on the table—probably the world's most fragile alibi—before pivoting and heading into the bathroom. The door clicked shut, and a few minutes later, the shower sputtered to life.

I blinked under the bed, trying to process this unexpected plot twist. Showering? Now? After that frantic voicemail spree downstairs? Was this her version of battle prep? Scrubbing the stress away before plunging headlong into whatever chaos awaited her? Honestly, I half-expected her to emerge in full war paint, ready to face the apocalypse she'd evidently been predicting into everyone's voicemail inbox.

The water cascading down filled the room, a soothing backdrop that almost masked the absurdity of the situation. If this was her plan, I could only hope it involved a squeaky-clean conscience to match.

Lynda showered for about ten minutes, and within that time, dark thoughts swirled in my mind. Maybe I could go in there and stab her. You know, pull a Norman in the shower like in the movie Psycho. The image played out vividly in my head, but I knew I needed to do something less drastic. I had to be strategic and calculated. I was either going to wait for her to fall asleep or jump scare her.

Either way, I couldn't stay under this bed forever, and I had to stick to that 24-hour schedule before you came home and found me. I'll admit, the thought of you walking in and catching me sent a shiver down my spine—not because of the confrontation, mind you, but because I was on your side of the bed. Your sacred side. The hallowed ground of your nightly kingdom. I could already picture the horror in your eyes, the melodramatic gasp as you exclaimed, "Of all the places, you had to invade my side?" Honestly, the fallout from that alone might kill me faster than the plan going sideways.

At this point, I'd only been under the bed for a little over an hour, but it felt like I'd aged a decade. The darkness was doing double duty as both my hiding spot and my personal purgatory, shielding me from view while slowly driving me to the brink of madness.

The shower finally stopped, and I heard Lynda moving around in the bathroom. My heart pounded like it was auditioning for a drumline, each beat echoing in the cramped space. I knew I couldn't linger much longer—every second increased the odds of her discovering me and frankly, I wasn't ready to explain why I was lying under her bed like a dust bunny.

The bathroom door creaked open, and Lynda tiptoed softly across the floor. She moved with the kind of relaxed confidence that only comes from being blissfully unaware of the weirdo lurking just a few feet away. Apparently, whatever paranoia had gripped her earlier had been rinsed away along with shampoo suds.

I took slow, steady breaths, trying to wrangle my thoughts into submission. The plan was clear, but the execution required finesse. Timing was everything, and I couldn't afford to blow it now.

Lynda settled onto the bed, and I felt a surge of determination. This was the moment I'd been waiting for. The shadows of her heels peeked into view, dangling just above the floor like tiny, oblivious lookouts.

She sighed, frustration dripping from her voice as she left another voicemail. "James, it's me," she said, her tone shaky. "I noticed the fan fell out of the window, but no one was in the house. I'm not sure what happened. Please call me back as soon as you get this."

She ended the call pausing as if to gather her thoughts. Then, another call. More ringing. Still no answer. "Hey, sweetie, it's Mom," she began, her voice softening. "I just wanted to check in and see how you're doing. I miss you so much, and—"

But then, I budged, because if there's one thing I've learned, it's that nothing kills the mood like eavesdropping on a heartfelt voicemail to someone's kid. Even I have my limits.

Oh well.

Before she could finish her message, I sprang from

underneath the bed with the kind of speed and grace that would've impressed even the most seasoned action hero. Lynda barely had time to react as I launched myself onto the bed, knife gleaming like it had been waiting for its moment in the spotlight. The phone slipped from her grasp, still connected, as my blade found its mark with unsettling precision.

Her eyes widened in shock, her voice catching in her throat as she tried to scream. Blood poured from her neck, staining the bed in dramatic crimson pools that turned the daisies to roses and would've made a crime scene photographer weep with appreciation. The phone's screen dimmed as I ended the call, careful not to leave any incriminating noises—because, you know, priorities.

The festive lights and candles radiated an almost obnoxious cheeriness, as if they were throwing a party for the carnage I'd just caused. It felt like the room itself was winking at me, saying, "Nice work, buddy! Really brightened the place up—well, except for the blood." I stood there, chest heaving, staring down at her fading form.

Satisfaction coursed through me, but it was tinged with something darker—like the universe whispering, "Congrats, you've peaked in the worst way possible."

I rounded the bed, grabbed my bag, and pulled out the vial. With hands that were only slightly shaky (thank you, adrenaline), I pressed it against her neck to collect the blood I needed. The liquid flowed steadily, filling the vial as my mind raced with conflicting thoughts.

Triumph? **Check.**

Unease? **Double check.**

A fleeting moment of "What am I doing with my life?" **Absolutely.**

As I waited for the vial to fill, my gaze landed on a broken picture frame on the floor that must have fallen with the scuffle. The glass shards sparkled like they were auditioning for a HSN jewelry ad, and I realized it was that wedding photo of you and your now deceased wife. Your happiness really did feel like a cruel joke now, a Hallmark moment gone horribly wrong. But still, I snatched the photo, folded it up, and slipped it into my pocket.

Inspiration, *I told myself.* Or maybe just a souvenir for my questionable life choices. *Not that I wanted a memento of your ugly, hairless mug.*

I left Lynda sprawled gruesomely over the bed and did one last sweep of the room. I didn't come loaded down—just the basics: a pistol, a knife now christened with your wife's DNA, and, naturally, my ever-reliable, slightly skewed moral compass.

With my bag packed and my nerves fraying, I bolted downstairs to the only place left to go: the fuck out of here.

At the bottom step, something caught my attention—a whiff of coffee.

I froze, my gaze snapping into the kitchen. The pot sat on the burner, half-full, its red power light glowing faintly like a tiny, judgmental eye. Lynda must've brewed it earlier, maybe as part of her nightly routine. Or maybe she'd made it for you. Either way, it felt weirdly significant, like the ghost of her last normal moment.

A mug sat on the kitchen island, half-full, as if she'd planned to come back to it. I realized it was the faded mug from your office. Perhaps that's how she realized the fan had fallen.

For a split second, I pictured her standing there earlier, scrolling through her phone, sipping her coffee like life was just another mundane Tuesday. Oblivious. Blissfully unaware of the storm barreling toward her. If she'd known, would she have lingered? Would she have savored that last sip, turned off the coffee pot, maybe even taken a moment to breathe in the quiet before everything shattered?

But the thought didn't linger long. I wasn't here to mourn her rituals or her ignorance. Lynda was collateral damage, a pawn in a game she didn't even know she was playing.

Truthfully, I didn't fucking care. Not about her coffee, her routines, or her life.

*What I cared about—what burned in my chest like a wildfire—was you, James. A man who deserved every ounce of pain I could conjure. A man who had to feel it, deep in his bones, the way I'd felt it. Lynda's blood was a prelude to a symphony of suffering I had planned for you. I wanted you to hurt. Not just physically, but in every way a person could. I wanted you to drown in the weight of your guilt, to choke on the realization of what you'd lost. I wanted you to see her lifeless body and know, without a shadow of a doubt, that it was **your fault.***

And when you did realize, and when the grief and the horror consumed you, I'd be there.

In your mind, your memories.

Ready to deliver the final blow.

Because this wasn't just revenge—it was justice, I was the one holding the scales.

Banishing those thoughts until later, I tightened my grip on my bag, moving toward the back door. The cold air hit me like a slap, but I barely registered it. The night stretched out before me, silent and indifferent, the world blissfully unaware of the fresh mess I'd left behind.

My hands, still sticky with blood, twitched at my sides. The vials in my bag pressed against my hip, warm and oddly comforting.

The streetlights hummed; their halos were too bright. The night air tasted metallic, thick on my tongue like pennies. Houses warped and pulsed in my vision, their windows flickering with shapes that seemed to watch me. The Christmas lights smeared together in a neon haze, forming patterns that almost made sense.

"Good. You're listening," *something whispered.*

I let out a shaky laugh, though I wasn't sure why. The world felt thinner, like I could reach out and tear through it. There was a buzzing deep in my skull—persistent, electric. It wasn't fear. It was something worse.

Excitement.

I clenched my jaw.

Focus. There was work to do.

The painting.

I imagined the brush gliding through Lynda's blood, the deep red soaking into the canvas. A message in every stroke, just like the others. The picture would be perfect—although the person depicted was better off dead.

Chapter 39

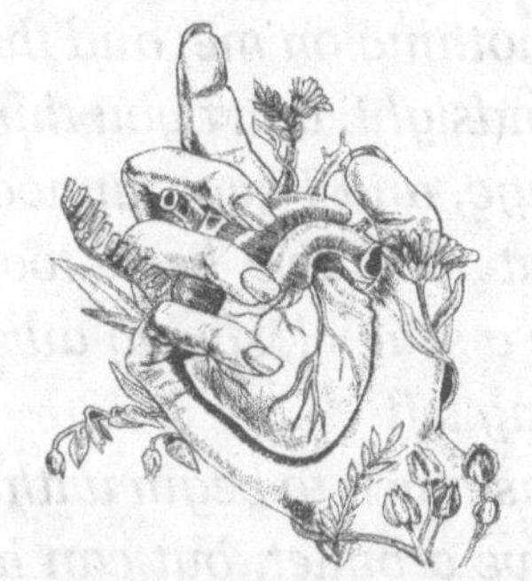

Cassandra's Letter to
Detective James Hall Continued

Slipping back onto Chippen's Hill, the night swallowed me whole, utterly indifferent to the chaos I'd just unleashed on your wife. Poor, poor Lynda.

The cool breeze brushed against my flushed skin, but inside, I burned with something close to euphoria. Seven kills in, and still—nothing.

No remorse.

No hesitation.

The first time, I'd been unsure, maybe even a little nauseous. But now? Now it felt like second nature. Rejuvenating, even. Just a serene rush that greeted me like an old friend after a job well done.

I inhaled deeply, savoring the metallic perfume of blood clinging to my clothes. It smelled like justice—or maybe just bad decisions. Either way, I wasn't complaining.

They'd come for me soon, the police. They'd barge in, throw me around like a rag doll, just like the first time I was arrested a year ago. But this time? I'd go willingly. I wanted to see their faces—the ones who'd humiliated me, accused me of crimes I hadn't committed. Sure, I'd been dating Qualley, but that wasn't illegal. And the pistol? Purchased and carried legally. I'd jumped through their hoops, passed their tests, answered their questions. They had nothing on me, and they let me go.

Big mistake in hindsight, don't you think?

I promised revenge, and I kept my word. Not by going after you directly—that would've been too easy. No, I carved through your life like a scalpel, slicing away every piece of you until there was nothing left.

Not that there was much to begin with.

A man can survive a bullet, but can he survive the knowledge that his loved ones suffered because of him? Can he live knowing he was powerless to stop it?

That's the real punishment.

And soon, James, you'd know exactly what it felt like to be hunted.

I stepped into my studio, kicking the door shut behind me. My sweatshirt peeled off like a second skin, landing on the floor with a wet slap. My jeans clung to my thighs, sticky with Lynda's blood. My face, my hair, my hands—all painted in varying shades of red. The dried viscera cracked against my skin like old leather, but I didn't care.

There'd be time for a shower later.

I had work to do.

I grabbed the blank canvas I'd set aside earlier, its pristine surface practically begging for what I was about to give it. Setting it on the easel, I reached for the vial I'd packed before leaving. The sacrifice I'd taken.

Unscrewing the lid, I tilted it, watching as Lynda's blood slithered into the tray of paint. The two merged seamlessly, creating something richer, thicker—more personal.

I mixed it slow and steady, until it was a perfect consistency.

My fingers twitched—not with nerves, but with anticipation. This was art. And I was an artist.

I pulled the photograph of you and Lynda from my pocket, studying it for a moment.

You, the man who started all this.

You, so sure of yourself, so full of self-preservation.

I believed you'd crack soon, spilling regrets onto the pavement like blood I'd taken from your acquaintances.

I set the picture on the easel's ridge just beneath the canvas as a reference. My gaze traced your features—not exactly charming, not particularly memorable.

You thought yourself invincible, didn't you? A god in your own little world, protected by the badge and the system that always favored men like you.

But you were wrong.

Sometimes, someone like me comes along.

A smirk tugged at my lips. It wouldn't be long now. You'd unravel, spiraling into your own personal coffin, as inevitable as the tide turning. And when you did, I'd finally be free.

*I glanced at my phone. 11:11 PM. Perfect. I closed my eyes and made a wish: **James Hall would shatter, piece by piece, and I'd savor every fracture.***

My thumb hovered over my music app as I scrolled, searching for the perfect soundtrack. Something poetic. Something that resonated with the art I'd created these past few months. My eyes drifted to my trophies—the delicate organs suspended in jars, their crimson hue catching the studio lights. They appeared to pulse, almost alive, whispering their suggestions.

And then it hit me.

***"Killer Queen"** by Queen. Because, really, what else could it be?*

A grin tugged at my lips as I hit play, the familiar melody unfurling in the studio like lazy smoke from an all-too-casual fire. The rhythm slithered against the walls, alive and insistent, whispering into every corner and crevice, coaxing my inspira-

tion to the surface.

"Extraordinarily nice . . ."

I eased onto my rolling stool, the leather creaking beneath me in a way that felt almost conspiratorial. I dragged the tray closer, its wheels groaning faintly against the concrete floor, as if protesting its involvement in my little act of genius.

The air felt thick, heavy with mingling scents of oil paints and that unmistakable coppery tang—Lynda's blood persistent as an uninvited guest. My fingers brushed the cool metal edge of the tray, and a ripple of excitement shivered through me. My tools lay before me—brushes, palettes, and that gorgeously grotesque crimson concoction—all waiting with bated breath for their cue.

"She's a Killer Queen . . ."

The faint smile on my lips widened as I reached for a brush, its bristles pristine, unsuspecting of the work ahead. The room was practically humming, charged with the promise of transformation—the alchemy of vengeance into art.

I picked my best brush. Only the expensive ones would do for what I had planned. It dove into the blood-paint mixture, bristles greedily soaking up every drop of crimson as if they couldn't get enough.

The first stroke slid across the canvas—then another, and another.

"Dynamite with a laser beam . . ."

My hand moved fluidly, each motion instinctive, as if my fingers had already memorized the painting before it existed. The song buzzed in the background, coaxing the lines of your face into sharp relief. Each stroke carried every detail, whispering something wicked.

"Fastidious and precise . . ."

I couldn't help but sing along, my voice low, tinged with the same giddy satisfaction that droned in my chest. Bit by bit, your face took shape on the canvas. You were oblivious to the *portrait being etched in blood—blissfully ignorant of the justice waiting to meet you.*

"She's out to get you . . ."

This wasn't for me.

This was a gift.

"You wanna try?"

And trust me—I always make sure my gifts are unforgettable. Enjoy your Cassandra Kessler originals, Jamsey. I'm sure they'll make great additions to your home décor!

Happy Holidays, James!

**Sincerely yours,
The Queen of Hearts<3**

Chapter 40

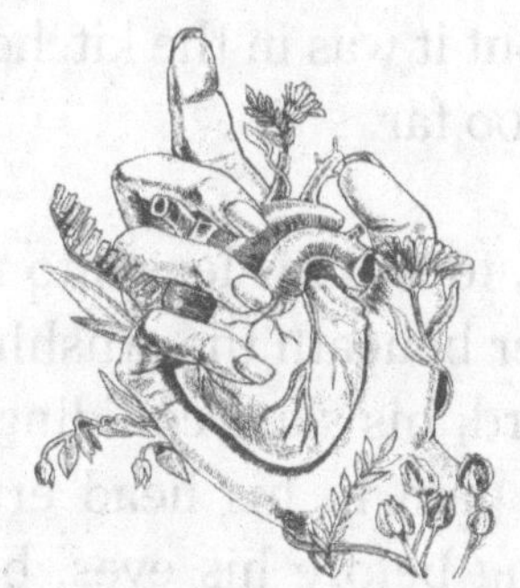

Detective James Hall

James dropped the letter, the load of its dreadful words crushing down on him like an anvil. Trembling hands betrayed an unraveling storm within. He stumbled backward, collapsing onto the cold, unyielding floor, his knees buckling with a dull thud that echoed through the empty house. The canvas, overturned in his frantic movement, toppled to reveal the sinister secret taped to its back.

From his prone position, his vision swam, then sharpened on the missing wedding photo. The faces of what once was. His own face had been cruelly slashed away with Cassandra's violent precision, leaving an emptiness where his happiness had once been imprinted. The sight tore through him like a lightning strike, paralyzing him as the pain in his chest exploded into an unforgiving crescendo.

A guttural groan escaped his lips, raw and animalistic, as his hand clawed at his chest, fingernails scraping against the cotton of his shirt in a futile attempt to wrench away the agony. The realization hit him, sharp and searing: *this was no ordinary pain.* His heart was betraying him, succumbing under the weight of stress, panic, and despair. Every tick of the clock felt amplified, mocking him as time slipped through his fingers like sand in a decaying hourglass.

His mind screamed at him to act—to get help. He needed his phone. Desperately. But it was in the kitchen.

The kitchen was too far.

Too far.

Struggling to rise, to will his legs into motion, they betrayed him, folding like paper beneath the crushing weight of his body. He crumpled backward, his skull colliding with the unforgiving hardwood floor. The pain in his head erupted into stars, tiny bursts of light dancing before his eyes, but he didn't stop. He couldn't.

Dragging himself forward inch by inch, evading hopelessness was his only fuel. Sweat slicked his skin and pooled in the hollow of his back as he clawed at the floor, leaving behind a grim trail of vomit and exertion. Each breath was a ragged gasp, each movement a slow crawl through the tightening vise that was crushing his lungs.

The world spun wildly around him—a kaleidoscope of shadows, light, and very few memories. He collapsed yet again, his cheek pressed against the cold floor, his breath rattling like wind through a broken window. The edges of his vision darkened, his surroundings blurred into indistinct shapes as the creeping numbness threatened to drag him into unconsciousness.

This cannot be it.

She cannot win.

Thoughts cut through the fog in his mind like a flare, reigniting a flicker of determination. But his resolve wavered as unbidden images flooded in—the faces of his children. Their laughter. Their innocence. Their joy. Each hit him harder than any physical blow could, an unrelenting reminder of everything he stood to lose, all he had not received because of his absence in their lives. The weight of his failures bore down upon him like a crushing tidal wave.

They would hate him.

They would curse his name.

But midst regret and sorrow, a fragile glimmer of hope dared to emerge. Perhaps one day, they could forgive him.

The burning pain in his chest began to ebb, giving way to a terrible, all-encompassing numbness that spread through his limbs, slow and unrelenting. He could barely feel his fingertips anymore, his arms heavy and useless. His breaths grew shallower, weaker, as his heart's relentless rhythm slowed to a mournful dirge. The cold seeped into his bones, stealing what little strength remained. Inch by inch, it claimed him, rendering him less a man and more a fading shadow.

With his last of his strength, he choked out the words that had haunted him for so long, his voice a broken whisper lost in the void.

"Forgive . . . me . . ."

His final breath escaped his lips, shuddering and broken, a haunting exhale that carried with it a lifetime's worth of regrets and unspoken apologies.

The world fell silent as time itself seemed to pause, holding its breath as James Hall slipped into purgatory, leaving behind nothing but echoes of the man he once was.

A single tear slid down his cheek, carving a solitary path through the sweat and grime on his face. It was a testament to everything he'd been—his love, his failures, and the unbearable weight of what could never be undone.

And then there was nothing.

James Hall was no more.

Just a name.

Just a man who fought, who stumbled, who shattered under the bulk of his sins.

The house, once filled with life, now stood empty, a hollow shell that bore witness to his final moments. Somewhere, in the depths of it all, a clock ticked onward, indifferent to the tragedy it overlooked.

Outside, the world remained unchanged, its indifference a cruel memento that life goes on, even when one man's story ends.

It would move on without James Hall.

Epilogue

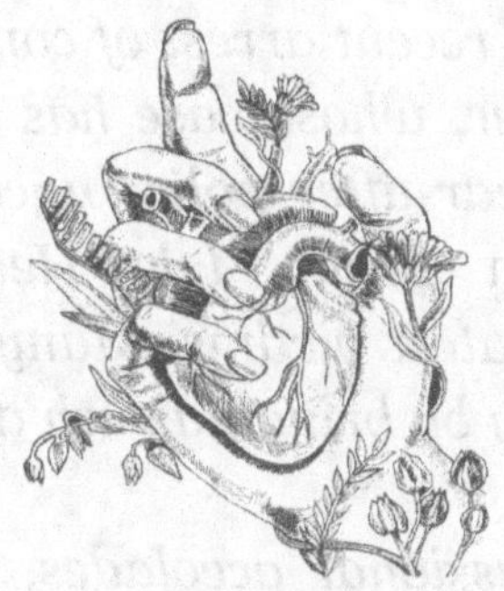

Shadows form around her face as a soft beam of light diffuses through a small, slit window within the six by nine-foot cell. It highlights snarled, auburn spirals of her hair. She's still, posture unnerving, composed.

A newspaper clipping rests within her fingertips; the page crinkled from months of handling. Her fingers curl loosely around the edge of it, nails meticulously clean, contrasting the grime of the cell.

She draws her hand across the picture on the page. Her eyes gleam, pupils dilating sharply as she focuses on the photograph; the detective's face stares back at her. Her expression shifts—at first a flicker of amusement, then something deeper, darker. She reads the article that goes along with the photo for what might be the hundredth time:

Detective James Hall, Dies Unexpectedly at 64: A Legacy of Justice and Sacrifice

By: Elizabeth Fuller

Detective James Hall (64), 30-year veteran of the City of Bristol's police force, passed away Thursday due to complications from a heart condition. Known for his relentless pursuit of justice, Hall built a reputation as one of the department's most dedicated and effective investigators. His death comes as a shock to colleagues and loved ones alike.

Hall was instrumental in solving several high-profile cases, including his most recent arrest of convicted spree murderess, Cassandra Kessler, whose case has made national headlines over the past year after police uncovered three missing Bristol officers: Ben Prout, Lile Henderson, and Evan Matthews to be her latest victims. Many credit Hall with ensuring the city's safety by bringing such dangerous individuals to justice.

Despite his professional accolades, Halls's personal life was recently marked by misfortune. His wife, Lynda, was tragically murdered only three weeks ago and whose circumstances are still under investigation. He leaves behind three children and three grandchildren. Sources close to the family suggest that Halls's grief weighed heavily on him in his final days.

"James was a man who gave up everything for his work," said Chief of Police, Bill Douglas. "His loss is a blow to the force and everyone who knew him."

The department plans to honor Detective Hall with a memorial service later this week. Details to come. Friends, family, and colleagues are encouraged to attend and celebrate the life of a man who dedicated himself to the betterment of his community.

At the bottom of the clipping, an advertisement for funeral services is barely legible, but highlighted in jagged red ink is one word from the obituary: "Legacy"—her way of mocking the facade Detective James Hall left behind. She saw through the narrative of a righteous, untouchable figure. *The red ink was her anger, her obsession; the blood she was willing to spill to achieve her goal. It wasn't just an act of defiance, but of personal promise:*

Your legacy ends with me.

"You thought you'd won," she mumbles, voice muted as though speaking to the photograph itself. "But look where you are now."

Her lips curl into a sneer, revealing just the edge of her teeth, as if savoring a private joke. It widens as she reclines back against the cold concrete wall, holding the photo up towards the light.

She traces a finger again over the image, lingering on the detective's eyes, then trailing down to the stern set of his jaw.

The detective's face illuminates as she twists the clipping left, then right. She remains half-shrouded in shadow, her expression unreadable save for her gleaming eyes, and the mocking twist of her crimson lips.

Folding the photo carefully, she tucks it beneath her thin mattress. The article wasn't just a keepsake to her—it was a talisman, a fixation that fuels her dark thoughts. A replacement for her discarded hearts.

The cell feels colder as she sits, motionless, legs pressed against her chest. She fixes her attention onto the far wall; mind undoubtedly unraveling new schemes, new games, inspired by the face of the one who tried—and failed—to truly stop her.

She locks her vacant stare, unblinking, as if she notices someone watching her. The silence within the space feels ominous, the stillness electric with unspoken threat. She doesn't speak, but her smirk deepens as she turns her head slowly towards the bars of her cell, sensing a presence.

There is a distant clatter of keys and the murmurs of guards, but in her cell, there's an eerie stillness. A tall figure stands a few feet from the entrance of the cell. It watches her. She doesn't take her eyes off of it. She is not afraid—hasn't been for a long time. Her heart beats faster, but her expression remains composed. A flicker of curiosity brakes through her usual cold demeanor.

And then, she recognizes him.

Qualley.

He looks exactly as she remembers; his honeyed eyes burning with intensity, his lips curving in that familiar smile that always sent a thrill through her. But, she realizes something is off about him, she can't place it. His skin seems paler, almost translucent, his edges blur slightly like smoke taking form.

"Cassandra."

Qualley stands just beyond the bars of her cell, leaning casually against the steel frame, his hand tucks into the pockets of his leather jacket.

Her breath catches in her throat at the sound of his voice: low, suave, familiar.

For a moment, she couldn't move. Her mind wrestles with the impossibility of what she sees, but her heart doesn't care. The bed creaks as she eases her way to stand up onto her feet, cautiously tiptoeing over to the bars, and placing her hand where Qualley had placed his.

"Qualley," she breaths, voice trembling, disbelieving with longing.

"Miss me?" he says, smirk widening.

She rests her head on the bars, closing her eyes. "You're . . . here."

She opens her eyes, ensuring she wasn't seeing things. Her fingers brush against the steel, reaching for him. "Of course I'm here," he replies smoothly. "Did you think I'd leave you all alone in a place like this?

A tear slips down her cheek. She doesn't wipe it away. "I—I miss you so much."

He steps closer, the faint glow around him softening the harsh lines of the cell. "I'm always with you, Cassie. I never left."

She swallows hard, her voice thick with emotion. "I did it all for you, you know. Every step, every plan, every . . . life I took. It was all for you."

He studies her for a long moment, then nods. "I know."

A small, genuine smile tugs at her lips—the first in a long time. "I'd do it all over again if it meant keeping you close."

He chuckles lightly, reaching through the bars to brush a strand of hair from her face. The touch is faint, almost imperceptible, like a feather against skin, but it feels real enough to send a shiver down her spine.

"My Cassandra, you don't have to prove anything anymore," he says, a gentle softness within his voice. "You've already shown the world who you are. Now it's time to let go of the anger."

She looks up at him, eyes searching his. "I can't let go. You're all I had left. They took you from me."

"You'll always have me," he says, his voice a low promise. "Right here." He places a hand over his chest. She notices Qualley's expression changing.

His smirk remains, but his gaze grows almost unnerving. Without a word, he reaches up and unzips his jacket, baring his chest.

"What are you doing?" she asks, confused.

He doesn't answer, placing his hand again over his chest directly above his heart. His fingers press down, sinking into his skin as though it were clay.

She breaths, her hands flying to her mouth. She takes a step back.

Qualley didn't flinch. His expression remains calm; his eyes lock on hers as he pulls his hand back. When he withdraws it, he holds his own heart still beating in his palm. It glows, pulsing with dim crimson light, filling the cell with an unnatural warmth.

"This," he says, "is yours. It always has been."

She stumbles back, her hands clutching the edges of the cot for support, before falling to her behind on the floor.

"No . . . no, no, no!" she stammers, shaking her head violently, shrieking.

Her breaths come in sharp, ragged gasps as she stares at the heart, its glow reflecting in her wide, tear-filled eyes. She wants to reach out, to touch him, to take what he offers—but terror roots her in place as his person shifts, morphing.

"No!" she screams again, sinking deeper into the floor.

Qualley's sharp jawline continues to relax; his mischievous smirk flattens into a scornful leer. His amber eyes lighten into icy blue and within seconds, the beautiful face of Qualley is gone, replaced by the unmistakable visage of Detective James Hall.

"No!" she screams, voice cracking with terror as she stumbles back into the wall. "Not you! Not . . . you!"

James stands there, still holding Qualley's heart, his face blank and expressionless. "You wanted justice, didn't you?" he asks, his voice cold. "Well? Here it is."

Her screams echo through the cell block, raw, unrelenting. She claws at her hair, shaking her head as if trying to wake from a nightmare.

"Get out! Get out!"

The sound of boots pound on the concrete floor, growing louder. Keys clang closer and closer. Two officers rush to the cell, their faces a mixture of alarm and confusion as they unlock the door, bursting in.

"Kessler!" one of them shouts, grabbing her by the shoulders. "Breathe. Do you hear me? Breathe!"

She thrashes against their grip, her eyes wide and wild, still fixed on the figure that only she could see.

"He's here!" she cries, her voice breaking. "He's here. He won't leave!"

The officers try to restrain her as she fights against them.

The glowing heart and image of James fades like smoke from a fire. It leaves nothing but the cold reality of the cell. She collapses to her knees, breathless, her shrieks tapering into frantic sobs. Her hands tremble as she clutches at empty air where the heart had been, where *he* had been. Qualley.

The officers exchange uneasy glances, maintaining their grip on her, firm but hesitant.

"It was him," she whispers hoarsely, barely audible. "He came for me . . ."

A doctor comes in with a stretcher; a needle is stuck into her arm, subduing her almost immediately. She feels the pinch—it brings her back to the real world, enough to be aware the officers hauling her onto the stretcher. Her gaze remains fixed on the empty space in front of her, lips trembling as she whispers again and again:

"Your legacy ends with me . . ."

She drifts completely into darkness.

Acknowledgments

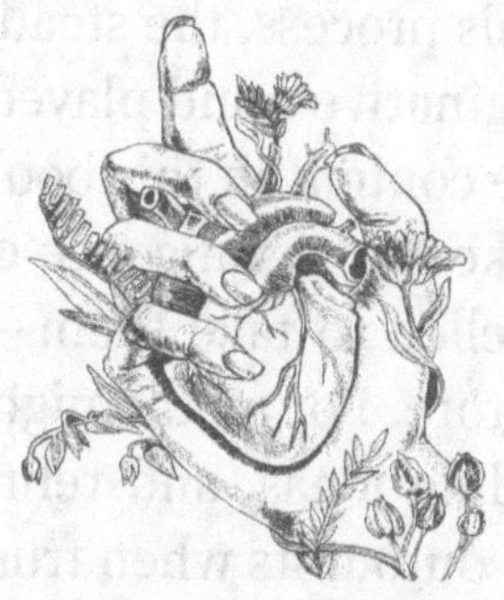

To think that this project began as nothing more than a school assignment and grew into something so profound is utterly surreal to me. First and foremost, I must extend my heartfelt thanks to my instructor for that pivotal course, Abigail Rose-Marie. Her insightful guidance, paired with her ability to balance constructive criticism with unwavering encouragement, served as a beacon throughout this journey. Her belief in my potential, reflected in her positive feedback, gave me the confidence to push forward when self-doubt loomed. It was her thoughtful critiques and affirmations that fueled my determination to see this project through to completion. For that, I am deeply grateful.

I've never been the type to complete massive undertakings like this. More often than not, I'd get frustrated halfway through, set the project aside, and move on, never to return. But this story—*this story*—was different. I believed in it so fiercely, so completely, that there was no path forward other than to see it through to the very end. From the first draft to editing, proofing, formatting, uploading, and finally publishing, this has been a journey of determination, passion, and growth. For those of you who stumbled upon this acknowledgment before diving into the story itself, I hope that what lies ahead will meet, or perhaps even exceed, your expectations.

Of course, I did not walk this path alone. It is impossible to speak of this journey without paying tribute to my incredible husband, Travis. Without him, I sincerely doubt I would have completed that very first draft. Travis, you have been my anchor throughout this process, the steadying force when I felt unmoored. Your imaginative mind played a vital role in brainstorming much of the content in this book. Together, we crafted intricate details like the significance of the hearts and why Cassandra felt compelled to take them—threads that became the lifeblood of this story. For all the nights we spent locked in deep discussion, trading ideas, and refining this tale; for enduring my emotional outbursts when frustration threatened to consume me; for your unwavering belief in me even when my own resolve faltered; for the financial generosity that allowed me to bring my vision to life; and most importantly, for the boundless love you offer me every single day—I am forever grateful. Thank you, my love, for standing by my side through it all.

My gratitude extends far beyond just one person. My family and friends have been a wellspring of encouragement and kindness, their support a steady flame that kept me going when doubt crept in. To every friend who listened, to every family member who cheered me on—your belief in me and in *Crimson Keepsakes* has meant the world. You reminded me that art, even when created in solitude, flourishes in the presence of community. This book exists because of the collective love, patience, and inspiration that surrounded me. For that, I am eternally thankful.

And, of course—you—dear reader. Thank you. Truly, thank you. Not just for picking up this book, but for sharing your time, your imagination, and your heart with the characters within these pages. Each story is a conversation—a dance between the writer and the reader—and you bring life to this work in ways I can only dream of. Your willingness to journey through the highs and lows, the light and the shadows, has given these words a purpose beyond their ink. Whether you laughed, cried, paused for reflection (or to throw up), know that you've honored the emotions woven into every chapter.

As a writer, I pour pieces of myself into every sentence, but it's your engagement, your interpretation, that transforms this into something greater. You've made this story more than I ever could alone, and for that, I am deeply grateful. You hold in your hands not just a book, but a shared experience—and I hope it has left you with resonance that linger long after the final page.

Much Love,
M. A.

About the Author

Monique Skallberg is a storyteller and aspiring novelist, currently pursuing a Bachelor of Arts in Creative Writing and English with a concentration in Fiction at Southern New Hampshire University. Set to graduate, November 2025, she is a proud member of Sigma Tau Delta, Alpha Sigma Lambda, and the National Society for Leadership and Success honor societies. As a United States Air Force veteran, Monique served seven commendable years as a Traffic Management Supervisor. Before embarking on her military journey, she earned a certificate in International Baking and Pastry from Lincoln Culinary Institute. When she's not writing, Monique enjoys reading, indulging in nostalgic episodes of *Gilmore Girls,* and cherishing moments with her husband and son.

Crimson Keepsakes is her debut novel.